WOLFEBORN

A Medieval Romance

By Kathryn Le Veque

Part of the de Wolfe Pack Generations Series

De Wolfe Motto: *Fortis in arduis*

Strength in times of trouble

Patrick de Wolfe's (Nighthawk) youngest son, Titus, is front and center in this rip-roaring Medieval Romance that will have you on the edge of your seat!

When a de Wolfe mates, he mates for life. And when he falls for a woman, he falls harder than most. But when a scorned woman is involved, anything can happen...

And usually does.

Titus de Wolfe is the youngest of four talented and accomplished sons of the Earl of Berwick. On a visit to London on behalf of his father, Titus meets the woman who will change the course of his future.

Katiana de Edington is that woman.

Daughter of a very rich merchant, she's not of the nobility. But she's smart, educated, and vivacious, and undeniably beautiful. Titus is smitten. So smitten, in fact, that he marries Katiana without permission.

That's when the trouble begins.

A local ally of de Wolfe has been planning on a marriage between his daughter and Titus. When news of Titus' unexpected marriage is made known, the knives come out. Titus and Katiana should be enjoying their newly married life, but all of Berwick is now on the alert against the storm of politics gripping the country and enemies who were once allies. When the House of de Wolfe is sucked into the conflict between Edward II and Thomas of Lancaster, someone close to Katiana decides to use her to his advantage. With his wife in trouble, Titus calls forth the de Wolfe Pack to save her... and seek revenge.

Wolves mate for life, and Titus will risk his to seek justice for the woman he loves.

It's an all-out battle in the north as the de Wolfe Pack prepares for war.

Author's Note

Here we are again—the de Wolfe Pack continues on!

Wow, this is a big story. Many locations, many characters. I've blended them altogether, so I hope you'll enjoy the humor, the fast pace, and the complexity of it. Here we go!

I have adored writing stories about William and Jordan de Wolfe's (The Wolfe) offspring and grand-offspring. So many fantastic stories to be told. The one thing I've kept out of them, for the most part, is the politics of England during the spread that their stories take place. Not entirely, of course, because it is much discussed, and we even see a king or two, but they're not like other families—for example, the de Lohr Dynasty or the Executioner Knights. Those are all politics, all the time. Even the de Russe Legacy is very much wound around the politics of England. But not the de Wolfe Pack.

The sons of Patrick and Bridey de Wolfe (Nighthawk) seem to the exception to the not-too-many-politics rule. Every brother had some brush with kingly politics—especially Magnus, who was captain of the king's guard (WolfeAx). But in this book, we're getting into a time in England's history where Edward II was having a horrific time with his warlords, much like his great-grandfather, John, did. Not that the warlords didn't have a reason, but with Edward II, they seemed to have some very specific reasons—mainly, the favorites he seemed to keep in Hugh Despenser (The Elder and The Younger) and, most infamously of all, Piers Gaveston.

The research about Piers is really fascinating. Some of the stories I read about are things that even Hollywood couldn't come up with. As they say, sometimes truth is stranger than fiction. Piers met his ending at the hands of some anti-king warlords who were really acting of their own accord (Thomas of Lancaster, who had five earldoms to his name and was the largest landowner in England after the king), but instead of the execution of Piers furthering their cause, it had the opposite effect—it swung noncommittal warlords back to the king's side because of the way it was done. In order to get to Piers, they had to essentially sacrifice the Earl of Pembroke because Piers was in his custody—and he had pledged to protect the man—and then Lancaster comes along and kidnapped him from Pembroke. This made Pembroke look like a dishonorable lord, and given that Pembroke was well liked, that didn't go over well with some of the other warlords. In this case, de Wolfe included.

I'm telling you this, as the reader, so you understand where Titus' story starts. There is a big ol' mess going on with de Wolfe getting sucked into it, so ready or not, here comes Titus' tale. One thing I do want to mention here—because I've given it a lot of thought—is that the Battle of Bannockburn came in 1314, two years after this book is set. It was a disastrous English defeat, as history tells us, but I want to make it clear that the House of de Wolfe was not involved. They did not participate in Bannockburn, primarily because the House of de Wolfe is deeply intertwined with the Scots—not only did William de Wolfe marry a Scot, but so did a few of his sons, so they had a large contingent of kin in Scotland, which kept them from supporting the English against Robert the Bruce. Plainly put— they just stayed out of it, but I can only imagine how that must have enraged the English king.

Now, keep in mind that 1312 A.D. was a very busy year for our de Wolfe cubs because two books are set in this year— WolfeShield (Ronan's story) and now Titus' story, but they take place in different times of the year. Ronan's comes first, in early May, while Titus' story runs concurrently at the start with the action taking place in the summer. Simply put, 1312 A.D. was a VERY busy year in the annals of English history, so there's a good deal going on. I've had to do quite a bit of delicate dancing to make sure these stories mesh and characters aren't in two places at once.

Titus spent the first few chapters of Ronan's story at a tournament in Middlesborough before the tourney ended and everyone split up, but as we find out, he was at the tourney for a reason. The Executioner Knights have found their way into the de Wolfe Pack in the fourteenth century, which makes this take an awesome crossover. I love taking families and, in this case, a guild like the Executioner Knights and expanding it, giving it new life in new centuries. Keep in mind that when the Executioner Knights were first formed, it was at the tail end of the twelfth century with William Marshal and Christopher de Lohr and men like Maxton of Loxbeare, Alexander de Sherrington, and the like. The de Wolfe series begins about thirty years after de Lohr, so with de Wolfe, we take up most of the thirteenth century and are heading into the fourteenth century. The only house that can't really be part of this is Gaston de Russe and his crew. Remember that Gaston's story takes place about two hundred years after Christopher de Lohr. That time difference is between our modern time and, essentially, the Regency! That's a long spread!

The usual pronunciation guide:

- Katiana—Cot-TEE-ah-nuh (Katia is pronounced COT-tee-uh) Basically, Katiana is "Tatiana" with a "K" instead of a "T." Interestingly, it's not her real name—she explains in the book how she got it.

And with that, I won't delay you any further. This one moves quickly—and it's complex—but there are some truly funny and poignant moments in it, so I hope you enjoy it. Titus isn't like some of the other knights I write about—he's got an irreverent side that's hilarious at times. He's a keeper!

Hugs and Happy Reading!

DE WOLFE PACK GENERATIONS

The grandsons of William de Wolfe are referred to as "the de Wolfe Cubs." There are more than forty of them, both biological and adopted, and each young man is sworn to his powerful and rich legacy. When each grandson comes of age and is knighted, he tattoos the de Wolfe standard onto some part of his body. It is a rite of passage, and it is that mark that links these young men together more than blood.

More than brotherhood.

It is the de Wolfe birthright.

The de Wolfe Pack standard is meant to be worn with honor, with pride, and with resilience, for there is no more recognizable standard in Medieval England. To shame the Pack is to have the tattoo removed, never to be regained.

This is their world.

Welcome to the Cub Generation.

Legend of Knights/Characters and Their Origins/Locales

(Because sometimes you need a scorecard to keep track of the players!)

At Callerton Castle:

- Paulus de Edington

At Thornton Tower:

- Edmund de Allery
- Zora de Allery
- Ansel de Edington

At Edenthorpe Castle:

- Cassius de Wolfe
- Damian de Lohr

At Berwick Castle:

- Peter Summerlin
- Krister Grimsson
- Rian de Llion
- Esper de Tracy
- Bowen de Shera
- Magnus de Wolfe
- Markus de Wolfe
- Scott de Wolfe
- Troy de Wolfe
- Patrick de Wolfe

- Blayth de Wolfe
- Thomas de Wolfe

At Westminster Palace:

- Denys de Winter

At Lonsdale House/Lioncross Abbey Castle:

- Morgen de Lohr

PROLOGUE

Year of Our Lord 1292
Roxburgh Castle
Scottish Borders

HE'D HEARD HIM being nasty to his sister before.

They all had. Roxburgh Castle might have been a large and strategic bastion sitting upon the border between Scotland and England like a lion preparing to pounce, but it was also full of gossip, social standings, and politics. It was part of the de Wolfe empire in the north, but it was also a royal garrison, making it a target for every spoiled lord who wanted his equally spoiled children to foster within its thick stone walls of royal glory.

That's where the de Edington children came in.

Their father was a royalist at all costs. Loyal to the Crown and the prestige more than to the man who sat upon the throne. He worshipped at the altar of the institution of the monarchy, so the fact that Roxburgh was garrisoned by the de Wolfe family, but owned by the Crown, made it a paradox in Paulus de Edington's book. He didn't really view the enormous and powerful House of de Wolfe as part of the equation when it came to Roxburgh. It was all royal, no matter who commanded it.

That meant it was imperative his children foster there.

And so, they came.

Ansel de Edington was the eldest. Arrogant, snot-nosed, mean-spirited, but very bright, he had the same attitude his father had when it came to the House of de Wolfe versus the royal troops that were stationed at Roxburgh. He'd do anything for those royal soldiers, but when a de Wolfe knight gave him a command, it was with misgivings that he would follow it. That had resulted in several beatings, something that never broke his arrogant spirit but at least made him more willing to do as he was told, and more quickly than he would usually do it. Ansel, in the six years he'd been at Roxburgh, had been a boil on the butt of almost everyone there, the garrison commander included.

Blayth de Wolfe was fourth son of one of England's greatest knights, William de Wolfe, and command of Roxburgh belonged to him. Blayth was part politician but all soldier, and he'd had many dealings with many entitled fathers and sons over the years, so he knew how to deal with them, but Ansel had proven a particular challenge. The young man simply didn't understand when things went against his wishes or when someone else might have more privilege than he had because they'd earned it. Roxburgh ran very much on a merit system when it came to wards, pages, and squires because Blayth believed that men should work for what they wanted and be rewarded for it. Not simply because they were born into it.

But Ansel didn't agree with that at all.

That's where the sister came into play. Her name was Katiana de Edington, and she was the sweetest, prettiest, most angelic non-de Wolfe child in all of England. At least, Blayth's wife thought so. Lady Asmara de Wolfe was in charge of the female wards, young ladies who came to Roxburgh to be educated. Asmara herself had come from a Welsh warring family, and, truthfully, she was more comfortable with a sword than with a needle and thread, but she had ladies around her that were some of the finest women in England.

One such lady was a former beguine, a widow who had lived in a nunnery after her husband died, but she came to Roxburgh to help train young ladies as a way of earning a living and imparting her knowledge, which was extensive. They called her *Ma dame Lesparré*, or Madam Lesparré, and she was an excellent tutor. She had taken Katiana under her wing, an eager but very young child, yet even the intimidating Madam Lesparré couldn't save little Katiana from her brother's spoiled rages whenever the situation didn't go his way.

And that's exactly what was going on now.

Titus de Wolfe was a nephew of Blayth and Asmara, the youngest son of Patrick de Wolfe, Earl of Berwick, who was one of Blayth's older brothers. He happened to be fostering at Roxburgh, away from his home of Berwick Castle, because his father wanted him to have a perspective from a different border castle. God only knew how many times Berwick had been threatened, but usually it was from the same clans. Roxburgh was also quite volatile, from different clans with different reasons, different tactics. That was something Titus needed to learn.

But what he'd been educated on, aside from the Scots, was the nature of man. In this case, it was the nature of a young lad who was simply a bad seed. Titus had heard the knights muttering about Ansel, and that was what they called him—*a bad seed.* Innately given tendencies for bad and immoral behavior. No self-control. Selfish and demanding. All of these things covered Ansel de Edington, who took out his rages on his younger sister when he could get away with it.

But not today.

Titus wasn't going to let him.

Titus was in the stables to prepare his grandfather's horse, a man who happened to be visiting Roxburgh this day, when he heard the beating. He had no idea what was happening until he heard the voice of Ansel and the pleas for mercy from his five-year-old sister. Titus had a rope in his hand for the horse, but the sounds drew him. He followed them, his footfalls muffled by the dirt and straw floor, until he came to the last stall in the stable.

There, he saw it.

The sister, Katiana, was on her side, curled up in a ball, as Ansel used something in his right hand to whip her. Titus couldn't tell what it was because it was moving too quickly as Ansel brought it down on his sister, again and again. Whatever it was seemed to be painful, because she was crying out, begging him to stop. Having two younger sisters of his own, sisters he loved, Titus began to see red. He didn't like Ansel Edington as it was, but this… this sealed his opinion of the boy.

He had to act.

Thinking fast, he dropped the rope and grabbed Ansel by the hair. Yanking hard, he pulled the boy backward, toward him, and in the same motion grabbed whatever he was using to beat his sister with. It happened to be a branch of some kind, green and soft, which meant it hurt a great deal upon tender skin. With the branch in his hand, he threw Ansel onto the ground and began beating on him, whipping him, and then kicking him when he tried to get up.

"See how you like it," Titus said as he struck him about the head. "How does it feel, you bastard? Do you like it? *Do you?*"

"Titus!"

Titus stopped mid-strike, looking up to see his Uncle Blayth and his grandfather standing in the mouth of the stable, looking at him in shock. Startled, and realizing he was probably in a good deal of trouble, he stepped away from Ansel.

But the switch was still raised.

"I… I was punishing him," he said, stammering. "He was… I found him…"

"Save me, my lords!" Ansel screamed, struggling to his feet, his hand over the right side of his head where his ear was bleeding badly from the whipping. "Titus attacked me! He means to kill me!"

Titus looked at Ansel in shock and outrage. "If I could, I would!" he fired back angrily. "Tell them what happened, de Edington. Tell them that I caught you beating your sister again and I came to her defense. *Tell them!*"

Ansel's eyes widened as the tables turned on him. "He is lying," Ansel said. "Look at me! He was beating my sister, and when I tried to stop him, he turned on me! You must save me!"

"It was Ansel, my lord. Do not believe what he tells you."

Katiana was on her feet, the entire right side of her body bloodied from the beating she'd taken with the soft switch. The four of them turned to her as she stood at the edge of the stall, her left hand over her right arm, which was marred with injury.

A tiny little girl who had clearly been damaged.

That was what William de Wolfe saw. As the father of eight children and, at this point in his life, nearly forty grandchildren, he knew a little something about children in general. He knew about their behaviors, their loves, their dreams. Being a man of solid moral character and a decent nature, what he saw before him hurt his heart. All he could see was a little girl who had been badly treated, and he would stake his life on the fact that Titus hadn't done it. He knew his grandson—he was a kind, generous lad. A little passionate about things, and, at times, he could be silly and a bit wild, but he didn't have a bad bone in his body.

William hadn't, however, heard the same for Ansel de Edington.

Pushing between the boys, he went to the little girl.

"Your name, my lady?" he asked kindly.

The little girl had the hiccups from weeping. Tears and dirt and blood were streaked all over her face. "Ka-Katiana de Edington," she said, eyeing William with enormous eyes that were the color of bronze. "Ansel is my brother."

William was a very tall man, and quite big, so he crouched down in front of her to be a little less intimidating. "I see," he said. "And he did this to you?"

Katiana nodded, now looking at her brother and breaking down into tears again. William, taking pity, put a big hand on her head to comfort her.

"He will not do it again," he said. "You are safe, I promise. Why do you weep?"

She wiped at her eyes with a shaking hand. "Because… because I am afraid of him," she whispered.

William's jaw twitched faintly. "I assume he has done this before?"

She nodded, once, and tried to stop crying. William sighed, disgusted with the entire situation, and patted her gently on the cheek.

"Where does Titus come into this?" he asked. "Did he hurt you, too?"

The little girl shook her head fervently. "Nay, my lord," she said. "Titus pulled Ansel away and punished him. He stopped him from hurting me."

That was all William needed to hear. Standing to his full and imposing height, he looked at Ansel.

"How long have you been at Roxburgh, de Edington?" he asked in a decidedly unfriendly tone.

Ansel was terrified. "Six years, my lord."

"How old are you now?"

"I have seen fifteen years, my lord."

"And in the six years you have fostered here, you have not been taught that we do not beat women?" William asked. "That we protect them and respect them, and make sure they are safe and happy in all things, but no matter how angry they may make us, we do not lay a hand on them? Have you not learned this?"

Ansel was at a loss. He was cornered and he knew it. Trembling, he moved his gaze to his sister as he struggled to come up with an answer.

"My... my father gave me permission to discipline my sister," he said, sounding both weak and arrogant. "I will tell my father that..."

"Tell your father what?" William said, his eye narrowing. He was particularly frightening to children with his one patched eye and growling voice. "Tell him that his son is a foolish and pathetic child who beats on his tiny little sister to make him feel more like a man? By all means, tell him. You will have the opportunity, too, because I am sending you home. You can face him personally. You are not worthy of fostering at Roxburgh Castle, nor any of the de Wolfe properties, and I shall make sure that your father knows that. Go back to your chamber and stay there. Do not leave for any reason or you shall feel my wrath."

Petrified with fear, Ansel took off running. William and Blayth watched him go before looking at each other, eyebrows lifted at the behavior of such a child. Blayth, an enormous man with a scarred head beneath graying blond hair, finally shook his head in disgust.

"It needed to be done," he said in the quiet, deliberate speech that was his normal pattern because of a head injury years ago. "Young Ansel has been a troublemaker the entire time he has been here. That was bound to happen at some point."

William was still angry at the nasty young man. "Why did you not send him home before now?"

Blayth cocked an eyebrow. "Because he was under the close watch of my knights, and we were trying to give the lad a chance to grow up," he said. "But truthfully, we cannot help him. He does not want to be helped. Like his father, he is full of ambition and doesn't care whom he slanders or hurts along the way, so the fact that you have dismissed him personally will have far more weight than if I did it. Let's face it, Papa—you're a bigger man than I."

He was grinning by the time he finished, and William, though still angry, cracked a smile. "I am older, in any case," he said. But his smile faded as he looked at Titus, who was still standing there with the switch in his hand. "And you—you are not one driven to violence that I am aware of, so clearly, Ansel's actions pushed you beyond your endurance. Though I do not condone fighting like that between men who should be allies, I understand why you did it. It was noble of you."

Titus thought he was going to be in real trouble until that moment. With a sigh of relief, he dropped the switch.

"He's done it before," he said. "I've seen him. We all have. If he becomes angry, he knows he cannot beat any of us, so he beats his sister instead."

William shook his head, thinking of a young man who would target his own sister in his rage. He looked at Blayth.

"And you knew about this?" he asked.

"I did," Blayth replied. "We have been keeping him far from his sister, so he must have gone out of his way to find her this night."

"What was he upset about?"

"I was informed earlier that he received a tongue lashing from one of the knights for neglecting his studies," Blayth said, his gaze drifting to the girl. "I should have known he'd go to great lengths to get to her."

William looked at the young girl also. "How did your brother find you, my lady?"

She looked up at him. "I was helping in the kitchens tonight," she said, still sniffling. "When I came out to collect some eggs, he was in the kitchen yard."

"And he captured you?"

"How did he know you were in the kitchens?"

Katiana shrugged. "I do not know, my lord," she said. "But all of the girls have duties, and mine have been in the kitchens for a short while."

William could only guess how Ansel knew. He was probably stalking her and knew that if she had kitchen duties, it would only be a matter of time before she showed herself in the kitchen yard. He put his hand on her blonde head gently.

"He is going home," he said. "You will remain here, and from this day forward, Titus shall be your champion. If you need help or if you are afraid, I want you to go to Titus right away. He will protect you and find you the help you need. Do you understand?"

Katiana nodded, her big eyes turning on Titus, who was both proud and fearful of such a responsibility at his age. He was the same age as Ansel, on the cusp of manhood. But he was ready for it.

He hoped.

"Titus?" William said. "Lady Katiana will be your responsibility from now on. She is very young and fragile. You will make sure she is protected."

Titus squared his shoulders and went over to Katiana, holding out a hand to her. "Come with me," he said. "I will make sure your wounds are tended. Are you hungry?"

Hesitantly, Katiana reached out to take his hand, and, with surprising gentleness, Titus led her from the stable, asking her what kind of food she wanted to eat and promising her that she could have anything she wanted. It was a surprising show of compassion for such a young man. William followed the pair at a distance until they were out of the stables, heading toward the kitchens.

"Titus will take care of her," he said, turning to Blayth. "But you know that sending Ansel home will not be met with quiet resignation by his father."

Blayth nodded slowly. "Paulus is a big man with a big mouth," he said. "He has raised his son in the same fashion."

"He has," William agreed. "I will send him home with a Questing knight so he understands that this was my decision. Hopefully that will keep Roxburgh away from his rage."

Blayth made his way over to him, pondering the situation. "May I suggest that you summon de Edington to Questing to retrieve his son?" he said. "Bring the man to you. He'll be less in control if you deal with him at Questing rather than sending someone to Callerton Castle. Edington created this mess—he should see the results of his labor as Questing demands he fetch his son home."

A gleam came to William's eye. "He will be quite humiliated."

Blayth had no sympathy. "For any man who would tell his own son that he had permission to lay hands on his sister, he deserves no less."

William nodded. "Agreed," he said, his gaze moving to the vast upper bailey of Roxburgh, bustling with people going about their business. "But something tells me that it will not be the end of it. Men like Paulus de Edington simply do not go away."

Blayth looked at his father, his expression suggesting agreement, but there was nothing to be done about it. A lad like Ansel, amongst lads that were being taught right from wrong, would be like a cancer. He'd try to turn them to his way of thinking if he could. Both Blayth and William had seen it before.

Something tells me this will not be the end of it.

Little did they know when, exactly, that statement would come back to haunt them.

And just how much it would cost them.

CHAPTER ONE

Year of our Lord 1312
Month of May
Callerton Castle, Northumberland

THE RATTLE HAD come.

That wet, horrific rattle when the lungs are failing and the end of one's life can be told in weeks, if not days. It had come for Paulus de Edington as much as he'd been trying to ignore it. As much as the physic had been attempting to stave it off. But death was coming, and there was nothing either one of them could do about it.

The time had come.

It was early in the evening of a warm spring day, a faint band of light sitting on the horizon as the sun set in the west. The night itself was shades of blue, all of it fading into black as the stars emerged high above. In the keep of Callerton Castle, a vigil was taking place as an older man lay upon his messy, smelly bed, his body covered with a rash and a fever ravaging his body.

Beside him stood another man, small and somewhat meek,

bearing the robes of a priest. He'd come from a local priory, a poor establishment, but they were a healing order. He'd come to serve, but it had turned out to be an assignment that would have tested the patience of Job. He watched the ill-tempered man on the bed suffer, sweating and ill, knowing his prayers would do no good. At this point, nothing would do any good, short of a miracle. He was waiting for the man to awaken so he could try to make him more comfortable in his final hours.

It had been a long, hard journey of watching a man die.

"Samson?"

The man on the bed suddenly awoke, his eyes popping open. He'd spoken the name of the man in the robes, who nearly jumped out of his skin at the piercing sharpness of the man's voice. Samson was a ridiculous name considering his diminutive size, but it had been foisted upon him by a spiteful superior, and he'd been too weak to refuse it.

Samson the Weak, they teased.

Weak, indeed.

"I am here, Lord de Edington," Samson said, leaning over so the man could see him. "You were asleep most of the day. How do you feel?"

Paulus de Edington's eyes moved slowly in the direction of the priest. He didn't move his head or even the rest of his body. Only his eyes. Once he found the old priest who had been nursing him for the past couple of weeks, he seemed to relax.

"Good," he mumbled thickly. "You are here. I dreamt that you had left."

"Nay, my lord," Samson said. "I am here. I have been praying."

"God is not listening."

Samson shook his head. "Nay, he is not," he said hesitantly.

"I… I am afraid that the time has come for us to come to terms with this, my lord. For two weeks, you have refused to allow me to notify your family of your illness, but the time has come. They must know before it is too late."

Paulus sighed heavily, closing his eyes. "What do they care?" he muttered. "The truth is that they do not. My son only wants what I have, and my daughter… I mean nothing to her, and that is of my doing. I am certain she does not care if I live or die."

Samson went to a bowl next to the bed, one that contained a dirty rag, and wrung it out. He put it across Paulus' forehead.

"Whether or not your children care is not at issue," he said. "They must be notified. Would you not like to see them before you go?"

Paulus' eyes opened. "I would not like to see my son," he said. "You do not know Ansel. He has too much of his mother in him—careless and arrogant."

"I am sure it is not as bad as that."

"Why do you think he is not here?" Paulus said. "He is trouble. He has always been trouble. When he was here, he contested every command I gave, stole my money, tried to turn my men against me, so I sent him away to serve at Thornton Tower. 'Twas a cold trick to play on my old friend, Lord de Allery, but it could not be helped. Better Ansel at Thornton Tower than here. You may send him word after I am gone."

"And your daughter?"

"She lives with my father's sister in London," he said. "Kati-ana… she has all of my mother's kindness, but I've not been a good father to her. Mayhap… mayhap I should like to see her before I go. She lives at the home of Lady Ethyl de Edington on Coleman Street."

"I will send word right away, my lord."

Paulus sighed faintly, thinking of his lovely daughter, whom he'd never given much of a chance in life. There had been reasons for that, of course, reasons that didn't seem to matter anymore.

"I sent her to London because it seemed best for her," he mumbled, turning his head slightly in search of the window and the fresh air. "It was not safe for her to remain here."

"Why not?"

"Her brother," Paulus said. "He was never kind to her, you know. He would beat her and blame it on me. Or he would push her down the stairs and say it was an accident. For some reason, he liked to hurt her. I like to think I raised a son who knew right from wrong, but he did not. Ansel was an evil boy, and he grew into an evil man."

Samson took the cloth from his head and dipped it in the water again. "Then I shall pray for him, my lord," he said. "You have never spoken of him, so I did not know."

Paulus fell silent for a few minutes, gazing at the sky beyond the window. "Will you do something for me, Samson?"

"Whatever you wish, my lord."

"In my solar, there is a chest," Paulus said. "It is in a cabinet, at the very bottom. You will find it and you will give it to my daughter."

"What is it?"

"Everything I do not want my son to have," Paulus rumbled. "I cannot keep him from this castle or my property. He will even inherit the title of Lord Callerton, which has been in my family for generations. But the money… I want it to go to my daughter. I have always told her that I had no money to give her, but that was not true. I had it. But now I realize that I do not want my son to have it. Will you do this for me?"

Samson nodded hesitantly. "But your son… he will expect it, will he not?" he said. "What if he comes to me and demands it?"

Paulus sighed heavily, restlessly. "He will not know," he said. "If he asks what you know, lie to him. Samson, it is not a sin to lie to an evil man."

Samson wasn't so sure. He was a priest, and priests didn't lie. At least, the pious ones didn't. Pious ones didn't steal, either.

But that's exactly what he did.

As Paulus de Edington breathed his last, Samson wrote two missives—one to Ansel de Edington at Thornton Tower in Northumberland and one to Lady Katiana de Edington, courtesy of Lady Ethyl de Edington in London.

Come home now. Your father is dying.

As Paulus took his last breath, Samson left with the chest of de Edington coin and never looked back.

CHAPTER TWO

Year of our Lord 1312
Month of June
Lonsdale House, London seat of the House of de Lohr

MORGEN DE LOHR, Earl of Hereford and Worcester, had to sit down.

What he'd just heard had taken the breath out of him.

"God's Bones," he finally muttered. "Tell me again, Titus. And leave nothing out."

Titus de Wolfe could see that the news had shaken him. News like that would shake anyone, and, in truth, it was probably shaking warlords all over England once they received it. Titus didn't like being the bearer of bad tidings, but in this case, it was his duty.

As an Executioner Knight.

"Then we shall start from the beginning, my lord," he said. "My orders, from you, were to go to the tournament in Middlesbrough so I could be in the north and hear news of the movement of the king and his enemies. We knew that the Earl of Lancaster and his allies were after the king and Piers

Gaveston. We knew that the pair were traveling together, and we knew that they were in the north."

"And what happened?"

Titus lifted his eyebrows for emphasis. "Lancaster has rallied his allies, and they are preparing for battle," he said. "As of March, Gaveston was reinforcing his property of Scarborough Castle because of this. But sometime between March and May, Lancaster and Henry Percy, aided by Robert Clifford, convened a war council and divided up the country. Who should attack whom and so forth. We assumed they did this to be more efficient and end the conflict once and for all."

Morgen sighed heavily. "They had hoped it would," he said. "But, much like de Wolfe, de Lohr has remained as neutral as possible, mostly because I do not like Lancaster and do not want to lend the man my power—because the truth is that Lancaster and his closest allies have been a rebel faction within that rebel faction, often acting independently from the group, and that is where the trouble lies. What else do you know?"

"I know that the king and Gaveston were in Newcastle in early May, about the time I was at the tournament in Middlesbrough," Titus said. "They split up, with the king going to York and Gaveston fleeing back to Scarborough."

Morgen grunted unhappily. "I am sure that Edward went to York in order to separate himself from the man who has split England in half better than any enemy invasion ever could have," he said. "But now we come to the meat of the situation— did Gaveston finally surrender to Lancaster, then?"

Titus shook his head. "Nay, my lord," he said. "This is where the situation becomes... difficult. When the pair split, Lancaster supposedly continued after Edward, leaving Pembroke and Surrey to deal with Gaveston. He did indeed surrender to Pembroke, but on their way home to Pembroke Castle with Gaveston as Pembroke's prisoner, the party stopped in the village of Deddington. What Pembroke didn't realize was that Lancaster's ally, the Earl of Warwick, had been tailing him."

Morgen closed his eyes against the information he knew was coming. "And this is where the blow comes," he muttered. "Tell me again what happened at that point."

"Warwick abducted Gaveston from Pembroke's custody," Titus said, watching Morgen's reaction. "They have taken him to Warwick Castle. I'm told they are convening a court to judge the man for crimes against England."

That was the worst news of all, as far as Morgen was concerned. As the man in command of a covert and elite group of spies, warriors, and assassins, a group started by William Marshal a hundred years earlier and known as the Executioner Knights, he was more intrenched and involved in the political dealings of England than any man alive. This particular report was a devastating jolt to the stability of England, something the Executioner Knights worked toward but something that was increasingly difficult to orchestrate.

Sometimes Morgen felt as if he was losing control of the country he loved, now with Thomas of Lancaster, an inarguably greedy and immoral warlord, kidnapping another allied warlord's prisoner. Had they been enemies, that would have been expected, but they were not. They were friends.

At least, they were up until this travesty.

Morgen knew what a high-profile prisoner abduction meant.

"And now, it comes," he muttered. "This will not be a court of justice. It will be a court of condemnation. The original agreement was to hold Gaveston as a prisoner to use him as leverage against Edward. But Lancaster does not see it that way."

"My lord?"

"My suspicion is that Gaveston will be executed and Lancaster will have irreparably damaged our cause."

"I do not understand, my lord."

Morgen looked at Titus. "Because Lancaster had no right to take Gaveston from Pembroke's custody," he said, frustrated. "Pembroke swore an oath to the man's safety, and he was one of the men we trusted not to do anything foolish. He would keep him safe while we negotiated with Edward. But Lancaster could not wait for that—the man is stupid and irresponsible, and now he intends to judge Gaveston on his own. No one will trust him after that, and families like de Wolfe, men like your father and his brothers, who have thus far remained tepid when it came to siding against the king, will have every reason to be driven back to Edward's side. I cannot imagine your mighty father siding with Lancaster's desire to turn England into his own personal demesne."

Titus, who had been around the politics of England all his life, understood what Morgen was saying. "That is true, my lord," he said. "I suspect they would all rather side with Edward than a corrupt warlord like Lancaster."

"So goes de Wolfe, so goes the rest of the country," Morgen said with regret. "If your father and his brothers support the king after this, Lancaster will have no one but himself to blame, but that will put de Wolfe and their allies at odds with Lancaster and Warwick. Christ, if ever a man was attempting to tear this country apart, it would be Thomas of Lancaster."

"Then what do we do, my lord?" Titus asked. "What would

you have me do?”

Morgen wasn't sure how to answer that. This was the report he'd been dreading. For months, the warlords against Edward had been planning and maneuvering for the moment they would capture Gaveston, and, frankly, Morgen felt foolish that he hadn't seen this coming. He wasn't at all surprised that Lancaster and Warwick had abducted Gaveston to suit their own agenda. With that realization, he headed over to a table against the wall, an elaborate piece of furniture with the de Lohr lions carved on each corner, and poured himself a large measure of wine.

“Baxter de Velt is deep in the house of Warwick,” Morgen said. “I've not received any news from him since this entire situation took hold, but that does not concern me. He is in the confidence of Warwick and cannot do anything to jeopardize that position. Warwick has no idea that Bax is spying on him.”

Titus knew that. Bax was a good friend of his, as they'd practically grown up together, since both of their fathers were northern warlords. Their families had been allied for generations.

“I was planning to return to my post at Pembroke Castle, but I can go to Warwick instead,” Titus said. “Would you have me go there to see what I can discover about their plans for Gaveston?”

“How?” Morgen said. “According to what you've told me, Pembroke and Warwick might be mortal enemies by now. Warwick would not let a Pembroke knight into his domain and into his confidence. You'd be walking into a dangerous situation.”

Titus cocked an eyebrow. “Not if I visited as a de Wolfe knight and not a Pembroke one,” he said. “I can tell Warwick that I've come to see the situation for myself on behalf of the de Wolfe empire. He would not dare deny me entry and risk the wrath of my father and uncles. Once there, I can get Bax alone and he can give me a full report, which I will send back to you."

Morgen took a long swallow from his cup. "I suppose that might work," he said reluctantly. "But we have agents stationed with Lancaster, Arundel, and Gloucester. You, so far, are the only one I've had a report from about this situation, so if you can get a report from Bax, we can see what we're dealing with. Whatever it is, I can promise you it is not good."

Titus could only nod, eyeing the wine longingly because he'd not been offered any. "The last I heard, Edward and Isabella were in York," he said. "Surely the king must know what is happening to his favorite."

Morgen nodded. "We have more knights with Edward who will observe and report back to me, but the silence is frustrating."

"It is because everything is happening quickly and, as you said, the situation is dangerous."

"Agreed. No one wishes to make a wrong move that could cost him."

That was quite true. The Executioner Knights were heavily into the spy aspect of their duty at this point in time, mostly because England was about to tear itself apart once again due to warlords being against a king. Morgen had many well-trained spies and assassins at his disposal, from some of the best families in England. Each one of his core agents, like Titus, was a legacy knight, from a family that had long served king and country. They were all the best of the best, including several that were trained at the Blackchurch Guild, the most elite training school for knights in all of England and probably the world. Every man worth his weight in gold, all of them centrally commanded by Morgen de Lohr, who had fallen into that position when his cousin passed it down to him.

But Morgen was more than up to the task.

"Then plan to proceed to Warwick Castle," he said. "But first, I want you to go to Westminster Palace and see Denys de Winter. He's the head of the king's guard, and he'll know what is happening with Edward right now. I want to know what Edward knows."

Titus gave up longing for the wine. If Morgen wasn't going to offer it to him, he was going to take it. He went over to the table with the pitcher and poured himself a cup.

"Isn't Denys in the north with the king?" he asked.

Morgen shook his head. "Nay," he said. "I prefer he remain at Westminster, so he feigned illness so Edward would not insist he accompany him north. Denys should be able to tell you something, but you, of course, must tell him what you told me. He will need to know."

"Aye, my lord," Titus said. "Is there anything else?"

Morgen didn't care that Titus was drinking up all of his good wine. After what the man had been through over the past few months, he'd earned it.

"Aye," he said.

"What is it?"

"Did you win the tournament?"

Titus smiled weakly. "Of course I did," he said. "I have long been a tournament champion before I was ever involved with you and your network of spies. I have longer arms and a longer reach, something most men lack. These gangly arms serve me well."

Morgen cracked a smile, watching Titus hold out his arms.

They were quite big, as was the rest of him. The de Wolfe men were all quite large, but Titus more so because his father was a giant. Patrick de Wolfe was the tallest man Morgen had ever seen.

"And the purse was pleasing?" Morgen asked.

Titus nodded. "Very pleasing," he said. "I've long earned enough money to be richer than my brothers. As the youngest of four sons, I must earn my way, and I've done well at it. Well enough to purchase my own property someday."

"What does your father say about it?"

Titus shrugged. "He wishes for me to remain at Berwick," he said. "As you know, my eldest brother, Markus, will inherit the earldom of Berwick and Berwick Castle is the seat, but Markus already has two very wealthy properties. Cassius, the next eldest, is the Duke of Doncaster, so he does not need or want Berwick. That leaves Magnus, who is captain of the royal knights, and finally me. My father worries about Magnus and me. He wants us both to marry heiresses."

A smile played on Morgen's lips. "And what do you want?"

Titus grinned, a very easy smile that was frequent. He wasn't the brooding sort, or the serious sort, but the sort that could be quite lively. He was the center of attention in any given situation simply because he was so amiable. It was something all of the horrors of war or the dirty dealings of the Executioner Knights couldn't beat or push or bleed out of him. Even now, delivering such terrible news to Morgen, Titus' warmth wasn't far from the surface. It was always there, waiting to be unleashed.

"I want a beautiful wife with big, soft breasts, plenty of money, and the sense to let me do as I please," he said, though he wasn't entirely serious. "I want a big castle with hordes of sheep and cattle, one that is self-sufficient and prosperous, and I want to be left in peace. Do you happen to know an heiress with those qualifications?"

Morgen snorted, shaking his head as he went back for more wine. "I do not," he said. "If I did, I would not tell you. I have my own sons to find brides for."

Titus held out his cup as Morgen poured the wine. "Christie and Kurtis are already married," he pointed out. "Blake and Bing are already two of the most sought-after knights in England, and Myles and Tevin are too young to be pledged still."

Morgen cocked an eyebrow. "They are twenty-four and twenty-two years of age, respectively," he said. "They are not too young."

"They are," Titus insisted. "They do not wish to be tied down at such a young age. Let them live a little before they are bound by the harness of matrimony."

Morgen was trying hard not to laugh, because Titus was quite animated about it. "You do not know what you are talking about," he said, pouring the man some more of his fine wine. "You have no children of your own, so you do not know the struggle. In fact, you are far too old to not have been married already."

Titus gulped the wine. "That is what my mother says."

"What does your father say?"

"He tells her that I am too young."

Morgen couldn't help but laugh as he turned away from the wine table and headed back to his chair. "You are going to be an old maid, Titus," he said. "And before you get any ideas, my daughters are already spoken for."

The grin on Titus' face broadened. "Abbie and I have been

in love for years," he said, speaking of Morgen's eldest daughter. "We wish to marry desperately."

"Shut your lips. She hates the sight of you."

"Andrina does not," Titus teased. "She worships me."

"She would burn you at the stake if she could."

"What about Camberley?"

"I will let her go into a convent before I would agree to a marriage."

"Jennet?"

"She is only thirteen years of age, you swine!"

Titus burst out laughing. It was always great fun to tease Morgen when the mood was right, like it was now. Morgen was facing something unimaginably difficult, and Titus had been around him long enough to know that when the mood was as heady as the one they'd just tasted, when the entire world was turning asunder, a little humor helped Morgen. Some men were annoyed by it, but Morgen wasn't. He was a good man, with a good heart and the weight of a country upon his shoulders. Cup in hand, Titus went to sit in front of Morgen on a stool, looking up at the man as Morgen tried not to make eye contact and grin. But he eventually gave up the fight.

"Get out of my sight and go to Westminster," he told him, a smile playing on his lips. "See your brother and tell him everything. When you are finished, report back to me, and then you shall go north to Warwick. I think you are right when you suggested going as a de Wolfe envoy and not a Pembroke knight. It would get you in to see Bax, at the very least, and you simply need a few minutes with him. You can leave as soon as he tells you what he can, and then I want you to make it back to Lioncross Abbey with all due haste."

Titus cocked his head curiously. "Lioncross, my lord?" he

said. "Are you going home?"

Morgen nodded wearily. "I am," he said. "Warwick is close to Lioncross, as is Gloucester, and if we are to head into civil war, then I must be at my seat. And we must prepare. However, I am not leaving for at least a week, time enough for you to speak to Magnus and return to me one last time before heading north."

Titus understood. He downed the last of the wine in his cup and set it down on the table before collecting his helm from the chair he'd set it in.

"Where are Christie and Kurtis, my lord?" he asked. "I've not seen either of them in quite some time."

Morgen thought on his eldest sons. Christopher, or Christie as he was known to the family, was the future Earl of Hereford and Worcester and utterly worthy of the title. Kurtis, however, was the beast—a brutal, raw, deadly knight who had been part of the Executioner Knights for the past three years. He was more of a follower than a leader, a man who would carry out orders and kill anyone who stood in his way. Truthfully, Morgen worried about him sometimes because he seemed to lack a soul, but he was never unfair, never immoral. Simply a killing machine.

As if they all hadn't been reduced to that these days.

"Christie is at Lioncross," Morgen said. "Kurtis was at Trelystan Castle the last I heard because the House of de Lara was having trouble with a local lord, and Christie sent his brother up there to scare them into submission. That is what Kurtis is good for."

Titus smiled faintly, picturing the monstrous de Lohr and the last time he saw the man. The House of de Lohr was known for its big, blond, fully capable and rather dignified warriors, but Kurtis the Barbarian was something of an anomaly.

"I think that Kurtis is secretly a de Velt," Titus said. "Are you sure he was not born to the family and you stole him away?"

Morgen chuckled as Titus referred to perhaps the most frightening, intimidating house in all of England. The de Velt family was born from blood and conquest and still, to this day, provoked fear in the hearts of men all through England with a mere mention of the name. But Morgen eventually shook his head.

"I do not think so," he said. "Kurt looks like me too much, but he did foster with de Velt."

"It shows."

"Thankfully for us, it does. No one will dare tangle with Kurtis."

"True," Titus said as he donned his helm. "If there is nothing else, my lord, I am off for Westminster."

Morgen stood up from the chair he'd been seated in, moving in Titus' direction. "Nothing more," he said. "You have your orders. I will see you in a day or two."

"Aye, my lord."

With that, Titus quit the solar, a rich and lavish chamber, and headed into the vast entry of Lonsdale, where there was usually a small boy or two waiting to jump out of the shadows and rob him. More knights had been robbed at Lonsdale, victims of de Lohr children, than perhaps any location in England. But the de Lohr boys were men now, and their children, what there were of them, were too young to rob anyone these days. For now.

Titus considered himself fortunate.

The major-domo, a friendly man named Raimond, was

there to open the entry door for him, an elaborately constructed panel, and Titus went on into the bailey of the enormous manse in search of his horse.

He had a man to see.

CHAPTER THREE

I T HAD STARTED out like any other normal day.

The sun was shining in the great expanse of blue sky overhead and the gulls were riding the drafts overhead, having flown in from the sea. Puffy white clouds darted across the sky, pushed around by the breeze that often settled in over the river and blew the boats around. Even the temperature was moderate on this fine spring day, which meant that she could wear her new surcoat, the one that had been made for her by the finest seamstress in London. It was quite a feather in her cap to wear a garment made by the skilled hands of Madam Claret, a Parisian dressmaker who had a booming business catering to the vain women of London.

Her plan today was to see and be seen as she made her way to the spice merchant over on the street of the merchants. The merchant in question had all manner of ingredients, spices and otherwise, from all over the known world. It was always such a treat to visit him because he would have edibles for his customers so they could taste the quality of his product. She looked forward to a slice of dried apple with a turmeric and cardamom coating, or a piece of apricot that had been sprinkled with cinnamon and nutmeg. He even had the rarest of the rare, a seasoning that was white like salt but was quite sweet. In fact, they called it sweet salt, and he sprinkled that on pieces of lemon or quince for his customers. The spice merchant was a smart man and allowed his clientele to taste his wares because he had more business than he could handle.

She wanted to make it over there before he closed.

In truth, Katiana de Edington had wanted to go to the spice merchant early in the morning before all the rest of the customers rushed the place, but her aunt moved slowly in the morning, slowly enough that Katiana had been dressed and waiting for four hours before her aunt decided she wasn't going to accompany her after all. She encouraged Katiana to go alone and select the spices herself, good training for a young woman who had yet to find a husband. With Aunt Ethyl, the subject of the day—and every day—was trying to attract a husband for her beautiful niece. Why Ethyl should think herself a good teacher when she'd been a spinster her entire life was a mystery, but she didn't wish for her niece to suffer the same fate, and at Katiana's age, she was considered beyond a desirable marriageable age.

Still, Ethyl was determined to see her married.

Katiana suspected that was also why her aunt agreed to pay for Madam Claret's expensive new garment, so that she would appear wealthy and properly dressed to any unmarried man who might see her out and about in London today. Not that she minded, because the silk surcoat was absolutely stunning. It was the color of a topaz, which brought out the bronze color of her eyes, and embroidered with golden bees all around the neckline and edges. With her dark blonde hair braided and arranged, she made quite a sight on the street outside of her aunt's London townhome on Coleman Street on the north side of London, just inside the city walls.

For her journey to the street of the merchants, she'd chosen a small brown palfrey from her aunt's stable to complement the color of her surcoat. It was an older animal, a little lively because it hadn't been ridden in a while, but Katiana considered herself a fine horsewoman and didn't see an issue with the fact.

But therein lay her mistake.

The little palfrey was excited. The grooms saddled it up and put tassels on the reins, dressing up the little beast as was often done when ladies traveled. They presented him to Katiana, who was delighted with the ribbons and tassels, and she mounted the horse with ease. But the moment she gave the horse a small kick to get him moving, the beast caught sight of the ribbons and tassels blowing in the breeze, and became startled.

After that, everything passed in a blur.

Katiana held on for dear life as the horse bolted from the courtyard behind the manse, darting through the gates, which happened to be open to the street. As she tried to rein the animal in, it continued to be frightened by the tassels in its line of sight and sprinted down the street, out of control.

And took Katiana right along with it.

Katiana was trying desperately to stop the animal, who was running and bucking, knocking into people and smacking into wagons that were in the way. Women were screaming and men were ducking aside as she struggled with the horse, who was running at top speed to get away from the ribbons and tassels that haunted it. The beast ran down Coleman Street, where her aunt's home was located, and then headed west on Catte Street. Katiana knew there was a city gate at the end of Catte, and she hoped to get the horse out onto the open road, where it could simply wear itself out, but the horse seemed to have other ideas.

Down the alleyways they went.

The animal wanted to head into the heart of London, it seemed, but Katiana pulled on the reins with all her might, directing it west, toward Ludgate. That would take them out of the city walls and on the road toward Westminster, but it couldn't be helped. It was better than letting the horse head into crowded London and possibly kill someone, herself included. She had no desire to meet her maker on the back of a frightened steed. She was finally able to direct the horse through Ludgate, blowing past the gate guards and shouting her apologies.

On they went.

The horse didn't seem to be losing any energy. Katiana finally stopped pulling at him because they were on a road that wasn't heavily traveled, between the city gates of London and Westminster Palace, so she let him have his head. Oddly, it seemed to calm him down a little, and his pace slowed, but not enough. Once they neared the more heavily populated area of Westminster, she began tugging on the reins again, and that seemed to panic him. There were people up ahead, and she screamed at them to get out of her way, including a knight on a warhorse. He was off to her left, but suddenly, he turned his horse around so it was facing the direction her steed was running in, and as she charged past, he spurred his horse alongside her and grabbed the reins.

The knight did the trick. With his strength and control, he managed to bring her palfrey to a stop across the street from Westminster Abbey. The towering spires and enormous rosette set above the northern door framed the head of the knight as she pushed her hair from her face and gazed up at him.

"Thank you, my lord," she said, breathless. "Had you not stopped him, we would be in Cornwall by now. I do not know what came over him. He has never been like this."

The knight didn't say anything. He dismounted his own steed, holding on to both horses firmly but standing next to Katiana's palfrey. He was so tall that he was eye level with her as she sat there, trying to regain her composure.

"I know you," he suddenly rumbled from behind the lowered faceplate. Then he quickly flipped up the plate. "Forgive me, my lady. That was quite inappropriate for me to say. But... I think I know you."

Katiana found herself peering at the man. She could only see his eyes and part of his nose. When her brow furrowed in concentration as she tried to recollect where she'd seen those golden eyes, he abruptly removed the helm, and she found herself looking into features that were vaguely familiar.

"I feel as if I have seen you before, also," she said. "What is your name?"

"Titus de Wolfe, my lady."

Katiana's eyes widened dramatically. "Titus!" she gasped. "It *is* you! I can hardly believe my eyes. But you are so... so *tall!*"

He grinned because she was clearly excited about seeing him again. "You have me at a disadvantage, my lady," he said. "A thousand apologies, but I must ask your name. I fear that my memory has failed me."

Katiana could see that he didn't recognize her, at least not to the point where he could recall her name. Not that she'd known his name, either, so she wasn't innocent in this situation, but she hadn't seen Titus de Wolfe in twenty years. Ever since her brother had been sent home from Roxburgh Castle for offending William de Wolfe, and, shortly thereafter, Katiana's father recalled her home as well.

And that was the last she'd seen of her young knight in shining armor.

Until now.

God's Bones, but he'd grown tall. His father was a giant, and Titus had been tall even as a boy, but nothing like he was now. The man had to be six and a half feet tall. He was broadly built across the shoulders, big in the arms and chest, and he had big, muscular legs as well. But the face... She'd never forget that face, not if she lived to be a thousand years old. Titus was quite handsome with his square jaw, full lips, and golden eyes. They leaned more on the side of green, but they were a spectacular shade of gold in certain light. She'd never seen such a beautiful man in her entire life.

God, it was good to see him again.

"I am not surprised that you cannot recall my name," she said quietly. "You saved me, once, from my bully of a brother. At Roxburgh Castle, many years ago. Your grandfather made you my protector after that. Now do you remember me?"

It was Titus' turn to become wide-eyed. "De Edington's sister?" he said, putting a hand out to indicate the height of a small girl. "Katia?"

She laughed softly. "Katiana," he said. "But you may call me Katia if you wish. My brother did, though no one seems to any longer. A childhood nickname that is lost to time."

Titus was gobsmacked. "Great Bleeding Christ," he exclaimed softly. "Little Katia. What in the world are you doing here, in London? On a horse that was trying to kill you, no less?"

She chuckled. "I have been living with my aunt, who lives on Coleman Street," she said. "I have lived with her for a few years."

Titus couldn't take his eyes off her. "And I've not seen you, not once," he said. "I cannot believe that I have not."

"Do you spend a lot of time here, then?"

He nodded. "Enough," he said. "My older brother, Magnus, used to be the captain of the king's knights, so I've come here many times on business. These days, I spend time either at Pembroke Castle or at Berwick, but I do come to London on occasion. Certainly enough over the past year that I find it odd I've not seen you when I have visited."

"London is a busy city, with many people," she said. "But we've seen each other now, haven't we? I would say that is a good day."

He nodded before she even got the words out of her mouth. "Indeed, my lady, it is," he said. But then he started looking around, back up the road she had come from. "Are you alone on this intrepid beast? Where is your escort?"

Katiana turned to look up the road because he was. "Probably out searching for me frantically," she said, finally sliding off the palfrey because her buttocks were sore from the ride. Gingerly, she began to pull off her dainty leather gloves. "I was in the courtyard of my aunt's home when this silly horse took me on a chaotic ride. I think my hands are ruined."

She was blistered underneath the gloves. Titus took one of her hands before he'd even asked permission to look at her palm, red and blistered in one spot. He inspected the damage closely before releasing her.

"Nothing that some salve will not cure," he said. "Shall I take you back to your aunt's home?"

Katiana didn't want to go. She wanted to stay and talk to Titus for the rest of the day, but she knew the man had other things to do, unfortunately for her. On her feet next to her palfrey, she could see just how tall he really was. She wasn't too short, but average in height, and she found herself looking into his sternum. She had to crane her neck back to look him in the eye.

"There is no need," she said. "I can find my way back home. Surely you have more important things to attend to."

He shook his head. "I have nothing more important to attend to at this moment," he said. "I would not dream of letting you return to the city without an escort."

"I do not want to be any trouble, my lord, truly. It would—"

"What is this 'my lord' nonsense?" he demanded, cutting her off. "Since when do you not call me by my name?"

She fought off a grin because he was overly irate, an act if ever there was one. "Since I was five years of age," she said. "I must address you formally, and you know it."

"Not if I give you permission to call me by my name," he said. "I am deeply wounded that you should not call me Titus."

"Very well. If you're going to cry about it."

His eyebrows flew up as if she'd just horribly insulted him, but he couldn't manage to hold the expression. He broke down into soft laughter.

"Now I remember now why I liked you," he said. "You are witty. You were a witty child, too."

She rolled her eyes. "I was a frightened, timid little thing afraid of my own shadow," she said. "I cannot remember being witty at that age."

"You were," he assured her. "Promise you will call me Titus or I *will* cry. Then you'll be sorry."

She shook her head solemnly. "I do not want to be sorry," she said. "Titus it is. You must call me Katia, though I've not heard that since I was a child. No one calls me that any longer."

"Not even your brother?"

Her smile faded. "Nay," she said. "He is in the north these days. I've not seen him in years, thankfully."

His smile faded also. "Still the same Ansel?"

"Still the same."

Titus grunted. "Then he can stay in the north," he said. "I apologize if I am about to say something offensive, but I never liked him."

"Nor I."

"Good. Then you are not offended."

Katiana shook her head. "Nay," she said. "He has the same traits you remember of him as a boy, only now he is a man. He serves at Thornton Tower, in fact. It is close to Berwick. I'm surprised you've not seen him."

Titus shook his head. "I haven't," he said. "But we are not close allies of Thornton. That's Edmund de Allery's property."

"It is."

"Why is he not at Callerton Castle with your father?"

Katiana lifted her slender shoulders. "A castle can only have one king," she said. "My father and Ansel are so much alike that they were close to killing each other while they were both at Callerton, so my father sent him to de Allery simply to be rid of him. I cannot even imagine the havoc he is wreaking there."

"And you came to live with your aunt?"

She nodded. "My grandfather's youngest sister," he said. "She lives in our family's townhome in London, and she always has. She hates my father, and he hates her. The arrangement has been agreeable for the both of them."

"Living with her is pleasant for you?"

"My aunt is not a difficult lady to live with," she said. "We get on well, so I am not displeased."

His eyes glimmered at her, and a smile was on his lips. "Good," he said. "May I return you to your aunt, then?"

"If you are certain it is not too much trouble."

"It is no trouble at all."

She nodded, struggling not to smile openly about it because she was thrilled. She'd always liked Titus, even as a young girl. He had been kind and thoughtful, at least as much as a young man could be. But that young man had grown up.

… God's Bones, *how* he'd grown up.

"Then I accept," she said. "Mayhap you will tell me what you have been doing these past several years. How long has it been, anyway?"

Titus cocked his head in thought. "It was the year your brother left Roxburgh to return home," he said, gathering the reins of both horses. "Twenty years ago, at least. As I recall, you left Roxburgh shortly thereafter."

Katiana thought back to that time in her life. "It seems so long ago," she said. "I was so young that I hardly remember it. But I do remember when your grandfather appointed you my personal protector."

Titus grinned as he put his helm back on. "That was my first official assignment," he said. "I was fifteen years of age and thought I could conquer the world and rescue every damsel in distress in the meantime."

"Have you rescued many damsels, then?"

He shook his head. "Not too many," he said. "None as pretty and fragile as Katiana de Edington. But let's not talk about me—let's talk about you on the ride back to your aunt's home. Would you like to ride with me on my horse? I think it might be safer than putting you back on your frothing beast."

Katiana glanced at the horses. "Would you mind if we

walked?" she said hesitantly. "My hands are raw, and, quite honestly, there is a part of my backside that is rather sore from that wild ride."

Titus looked up at the angle of the sun. "It is about midday," he said. "Where did you say your aunt's home was?"

"Coleman Street," she said. "But if you'd rather ride because it will be faster, I will certainly comply. I do not want you to waste most of your day because of me."

He seemed to eye her strangely, as if there was something on his mind that he was hesitant to speak of. But Titus was a forthright man, in any case, so he simply spoke up.

"It is not a waste of my time, nor do I want to return you faster," he said. "The truth is that I would very much like to hear what you have been doing for the past twenty years, but the reality is this—if I were your husband and you had disappeared on a wild horse, only to return an hour or two later in the company of an unfamiliar knight, I might have to cut off something of his that he considered very vital. I do not wish to offend your husband if he is out looking for you."

"I am not married."

"Your betrothed, then."

"I am not betrothed."

He scowled at her. "That's madness."

"Why is it madness?"

He looked her up and down, incredulous. "Katia, I am not entirely sure you are aware of this, but somewhere in the past twenty years, you have grown up to become a goddess among women," he said. "You are absolutely beautiful. And you are not married?"

She grinned, flushing at the compliment. "Nay."

"Madness!"

Katiana started laughing. "Then it is madness," she said. "But I am not married, nor am I betrothed. However, the same can be said for you. I should not like to offend your wife by taking a leisurely walk back to London in your company. If I was your wife and found you in the company of a strange woman, I might have to rip all of her hair out."

He beamed, a big grin with big teeth and slightly prominent canines, as most of the de Wolfe men had. "Is that so?" he said. "You flatter me, my lady."

"You have not told me if you are married, Titus," she said sternly. "Tell me now, or I'll not take another step with you."

He shook his head. "Much like you, I am not married, nor am I betrothed," he said, his eyes glittering at her. "Therefore, we may walk back to London without fear of enraged husbands or furious wives. Shall we go?"

That seemed to settle the subject, and he swept his arm out toward the road, indicating that they start their journey back. With a smile on her lips, Katiana nodded.

"We shall," she said. "But if you become weary and want to ride, you will let me know."

He chuckled. "I will, I promise," he said. "But if *you* become weary, please tell me."

"I will."

With the questions and concerns out of the way, they began to walk back in the direction Katiana had come, a long stretch of road that would take them to Ludgate, and after that, it would be another significant walk to Coleman Street. Katiana wasn't entirely sure she could walk that distance in the delicate slippers she was wearing, but she wasn't going to say anything.

She was rather looking forward to this.

Titus had both horses plodding along behind him rather

calmly. She turned to look at her palfrey, who was understandably exhausted.

"Look at him," she said. "A few minutes ago, I thought he would never stop. Now he looks as if he is going to fall over dead."

Titus turned to look at the horse, noticing a few remaining ribbons and tassels on the reins. "I would wager to say that the décor on his bridle spooked him," he said. "Horses do not like flashy dress where they can see it."

Katiana paused, picking all of the ribbons and tassels off the horse. "Then I will keep these safe," she said as they resumed walking. "I did not put them on. The grooms did."

"They were trying to make him look lovely to match his rider."

She smiled at more of his flattery. "Titus, you are going to give me a swelled head if you keep saying things like that," she said. "Then I shall become unbearable, and you will be to blame."

He laughed softly. "If anyone deserves to have a swollen head, it is you," he said. "I seem to remember your brother being quite arrogant, and for no good reason."

Her smile faded. "He and my father share that trait," she said. "That is why they cannot live in the same home."

"Understandable," Titus said. "Since I've not seen you in twenty years, what happened when he returned home? And why did your father send for you shortly thereafter?"

Katiana picked up her skirts a little so they wouldn't become overly dirty. She was wearing her new clothing and didn't wish to soil it on her very first outing.

"That was a bit of an odyssey," she said. "I do not know what was said or what happened when Ansel was initially sent home, but my father sent for me because he had been horribly insulted by the House of de Wolfe and did not want me to spend another moment in their custody. That is why I left. I am sorry I did not have the opportunity to bid you farewell."

Titus glanced at her. "I woke up one morning and was told you had gone home," he said. "I hesitate to say this because I do not wish to bring up painful memories, but I hope your father was not cruel to you when you went home, since you were the catalyst that sent Ansel away."

Katiana shook her head. "I did not go home," she said. "I was taken directly to Warwick Castle, where I remained until just a few years ago. Ansel was sent to Beeston Castle. I heard rumor that my father tried to send him to Kenilworth, where all the great knights train, but your grandfather must have informed the master knights of Kenilworth of Ansel's behavior. They would not take him."

Warwick Castle. That set off a warning bell in Titus' mind, but he didn't comment on it. After the conversation he'd had with Morgen earlier that day, he thought it quite a coincidence to meet an old friend who had fostered there. Of course, questions began to flood his mind—was it possible that Katiana shared Warwick's stance against the king? He wondered. But the fact that she fostered there was of interest to him. He would keep the knowledge tucked in his memory in case he needed it.

He continued to focus on her brother's trajectory as a knight.

"God's Bones," he said with some irony. "I cannot imagine rejection by Kenilworth pleased your father much."

"I do not know," Katiana said honestly. "My father and I rarely speak. And I've not seen my brother in years, which is perfectly to my liking. I do not mind saying that he was a terrible brother. I'm sure he's grown into a terrible man."

Titus shrugged. "Some men grow up," he said. "They are not always terrible."

"Ansel was born terrible."

Titus couldn't argue with that, remembering the boy that the knights at Roxburgh used to call a bad seed. "Then you spend your time with your aunt these days," he said. "What do you do for entertainment?"

Katiana shrugged. "We play card games, I suppose," she said. "I read aloud because my aunt has terrible eyesight. I also play the harpsichord and sing."

"You do?" He looked at her, pleased and surprised. "I should like to hear you sometime. Will you play for me?"

"If you wish, of course."

"Are you good at it?"

She gave him a wry twist of the lips. "Now you ask?" she said. "I have just agreed to play for you. If I tell you I am terrible, will you tell me you do not wish to hear at all?"

He fought off a grin. "Absolutely," he said, pretending to be quite serious. "I will not sit through a dreadful song. I'd rather hear cats fighting."

"I think you would sit through it, no matter how appalling, and still tell me that you liked it."

"I would not. I would demand you stop."

She looked at him, a gleam to her eye. "We shall see."

A dark eyebrow lifted. "Does that mean you are going to put me to the test?"

"You will never know until it is too late."

He couldn't help it; he started chuckling with that bright laughter that Katiana remembered from so long ago. The Titus she remembered was well liked, a congenial lad with a ready smile. She was glad to see that hadn't changed, and somehow, it did her heart good. Not everything was the dull existence she had been leading all these years, without family she loved or friends to keep her company. There were days, long ago, when she knew a lad like Titus de Wolfe who could light up an entire room with his congeniality, and she did so long for that kind of joy again.

"I will take my chances," he said, breaking into her train of thought. "But you are clearly accomplished."

"All noble-bred young women must be."

He nodded, but it was clear he wanted to say something more. He was looking at the street up ahead, at the few people around them, going one way or the other, but his mind seemed to be working. Katiana kept glancing at him as they continued along the road because the lull in the conversation seemed odd.

"Are we finished speaking on me?" she finally said. "If we are, I am glad. I would like to know about your life since we last saw one another. Surely you have had some fantastic adventures. Have you traveled many places?"

He turned to look at her, which, with his height, made it seem like he was looking down at the top of her head. But he was looking at her seriously, an expression that didn't seem natural to his face.

"I am not done speaking on you yet," he said. "May I be honest with you?"

"Of course."

"You will not be offended?"

"I cannot answer that until I hear your honesty."

She had a point. Titus took a deep breath before speaking.

"It is the madness I spoke of," he said.

She looked at him curiously. "What madness?"

"That you are not yet married."

Realizing they were back on that uncomfortable subject, she shrugged her shoulders as she looked at the ground passing beneath her feet.

"It is no great mystery," she said. "The truth is that men are looking for younger women of wealth, and the reality is that I am not young and I have no wealth. My father has not given me a dowry and never will."

Titus scowled. "Why in the hell not?"

"Do you always use strong language when addressing a lady?"

He was properly contrite. "My apologies," he said. "But why not? That makes no sense."

She shook her head. "You would have to ask him," she said. "I am not married, nor am I betrothed, but that does not mean there has not been any interest. There has been, in fact—a baron's son last year, and before that, I had three in one year, all of them approaching my father with the intention of courting me, but my father told them that there was no money. I would have nothing more than my clothing and what jewels were left to me by my mother."

Titus was appalled. "I've never heard anything so shocking in my life," he said. "I've never heard of a father not providing his daughter with a dowry."

"Now you have."

"But who bought you that dress?"

Katiana fingered the beautiful garment. "My aunt," she said. "She has a clothing allowance and some wealth of her own, left to her by her mother, my grandmother. But the rest of the de Edington wealth belongs to my father. And before you ask, my aunt does not have enough money to give me a dowry. Not if she wants to live comfortably until she dies."

Titus shook his head in disbelief. "Absolutely incredible," he said. "So she dresses you well in the hopes that a man will overlook your lack of fortune and take you on your beauty and accomplishments alone?"

"That sums it up as well as anything."

Titus didn't know what to say to that. He found himself shaking his head at a father who would not provide for his own daughter, especially one as magnificent as Katiana.

"Astonishing," he muttered. "Positively astonishing."

Katiana looked at him. "Why?" she said. "Would *you* marry a woman without a dowry? Of course not. What sane man would?"

"And you are so calm about this?"

Katiana came to a halt and faced him. "Do you expect me to be hysterical?" she said. "Titus, I have seen twenty years and six. I may as well have seen fifty years, because in the eyes of any prospective husband, I am a spinster. I am ancient. My aunt dresses me in lovely clothing in the hope that some man will fall madly in love with me and forget about my lack of dowry, but that has not happened yet. It will never happen, I am certain, so I have resigned myself to that. It is nothing to become distraught about, and certainly not in front of you. We have only just met again after not seeing one another for many years, and I am not going to weep on your shoulder about this. I do not know what you expect from me."

She was growing incensed, and he could see that he'd offended her. "Forgive me," he said softly, sincerely. "I did not mean it the way it sounded. It seems that you think I am criticizing you when I only meant to express my incredulity. You are beautiful and accomplished, and I... I was clumsy,

Katia. Please forgive me."

She took a deep breath to calm her annoyance. "There is nothing to forgive," she said as she resumed walking. "But I do not wish to speak on my marital state any longer. Agreed?"

"Agreed, my lady."

"And stop telling me how beautiful and accomplished I am."

"I'm so very sorry. I never meant it to sound patronizing."

"Then let us not discuss it any longer, shall we?" she said, setting a line he was not to cross. "Now, let us speak of you. How long did you remain at Roxburgh after I left?"

Titus felt as bad as he possibly could. From the moment he saw her horse charging in his direction until this very second, he'd mostly behaved like a silly fool. He'd always been a bit of a chatterbox, and sometimes, he simply lacked tact. But the truth was that his pleasant surprise at realizing who the woman on the runaway horse was had turned into excitement, and he'd managed to insult her with his inept attempts to hold a conversation with her. Nay—*more* than a conversation.

He wanted to know about her.

When he realized who she was, someone could have knocked him over with a feather. He had been that astonished. The pretty little lass with the big, bronze-colored eyes had indeed grown into a goddess. He'd never in his life seen a more beautiful woman, and that had triggered his inelegant behavior. Rather than be smooth and composed, he'd been thoughtless and reckless. When he was supposed to be speaking to Denys de Winter at Westminster, he found himself escorting this glorious creature back to her aunt's home.

And he wasn't sorry about it at all.

But at the moment, he needed to amend his behavior and

hope she didn't hold a grudge.

"I wasn't at Roxburgh too much longer after you departed," he said in answer to her question. "About a year later, I went to Rule Water Castle, which is the largest outpost in the de Wolfe empire. Men call it Wolfe's Lair, and it is quite active. I saw a good deal of action at the castle."

"How long did you stay there?"

"Five years," he said. "Until I was knighted by my father and sent to another de Wolfe outpost of Wark Castle, where I had been stationed once before. I've been at nearly every outpost that our family controls, but I have also spent time on the Welsh marches and in London. I've been quite busy."

She glanced up at him, her features warm and relaxed again now that they'd moved away from the subject of her spinster-hood.

"Then I hope you return to London often and visit me, should time allow," she said. "It does my heart good to see an old friend such as you, one I associate with fond memories. I did so enjoy my time at Roxburgh, in spite of the way it ended. You were always very kind to me, and I appreciated that."

Titus smiled. "I would like to visit you when I am in London," he said. "I think your horse running wild was quite fortuitous, don't you think? He reintroduced us."

She laughed softly. "He did," she said. "I was supposed to go to the spice merchant today, but I think the day ended better than I'd hoped."

"It is not over," Titus said, seeing that they were coming up to the junction in the road that would lead them to Ludgate and the city of London beyond. "But I will say again that if you grow weary of walking, we can ride together on my horse. It is a long way back."

Katiana had to admit that her slippers were becoming loose. More walking and they would fall off completely. They simply weren't made for long walks. With a sigh, she surrendered.

"Very well," she said. "I fear that my shoes will not withstand the extended walk into London."

Titus came to a halt. "No trouble at all, my lady," he said. "It will be my pleasure."

After fastening the reins of her horse to the rear of his saddle, he turned to her and put his enormous hands on her waist, lifting her up without effort onto the back of his saddle. Deftly, he mounted in front of her, no mean feat with a man his size. As he settled in and adjusted the reins, he reached around behind him, took one of her arms, and pulled it around his waist.

"You'd better hold on," he said. "I would hate to lose you."

Katiana was hesitant to put both arms around his waist, but the truth was that she was more comfortable that way. He had a very big warhorse who seemed to want to shuffle around, and, fearful she was going to lose her balance, she held tight to Titus.

Of course, it felt very good to do so.

"Ready," she told him.

She felt him pat her left hand. "Hold tight," he said. "I'll get you home safely, I promise. But do you want to stop at the spice merchant first?"

"I think not," she said. "Everyone is probably out looking for me, so it would be best to simply go home."

"As you wish."

"But the next time you visit, mayhap we can go," she said, wondering if she sounded too forward. "The merchant has bits of food set out so you can taste his spices. They can be quite delicious."

"I would like that," he said without hesitation. "I will come tomorrow."

"Tomorrow?" she said, leaning sideways so she could see his profile. "You do not need to come so soon. Surely you will be occupied."

He couldn't really turn his head with his helm on, but he could see her in his periphery. "I do have business here, that is true," he said. "But it will not take all day. Unless you are occupied tomorrow, in which case, I will simply come at your convenience."

Katiana was slowly coming to realize that he wanted to see her again. And soon. It was sweet and flattering, but she struggled not to become too excited about it. *He's only being kind,* she told herself. *Don't get your hopes up, lass. He's a de Wolfe.*

There was no possible way that she was worthy of a de Wolfe.

But it was fun to dream while it lasted.

"Tomorrow is agreeable," she said. "The morning is usually the better time to shop, but you can come at your convenience."

"I will come at sunrise."

"Why so early?"

"Will you not be awake?"

"Of course I will."

"May... may I tell you something at the risk of offending you again?"

"Proceed at your own risk."

He snorted at her empty threat. "I'm happy that we met again, Katia," he said. "I've not had much happiness in my life as of late, but this has been an unexpected pleasure. I want to thank you for that."

Katiana was in danger of blushing furiously. "It has been a happy circumstance for me, also," she said. "It has been good to talk to you again. I am glad it will not be for the last time."

He didn't reply, though she couldn't have known it was because he didn't want to incriminate himself. Or perhaps even sound too leading. She couldn't even see the rather silly smile he had on his lips, all the way to Ludgate.

But somehow, she could feel it.

CHAPTER FOUR

Thornton Tower
Northumberland

"HAD WE NOT had the help of Berwick, I am not entirely sure we could have fended them off, my lord." A man with dark hair and a bushy white beard spoke with both exhaustion and gratitude. "Your assistance was more welcome than you know."

The appreciation was aimed at the Earl of Berwick himself. Patrick de Wolfe, a massive knight with pale green eyes and dark hair that had great streaks of white in it, was watching his men help secure the rather large castle known as Thornton Tower.

The Scots had done a good job of beating on it.

But it had ended favorably when men from Berwick had routed Scots who had slipped over the River Tweed at one of the smaller crossings, past Northwood Castle, which was a massive bastion that covered a good deal of territory, and headed deep into Northumberland only to attack Thornton Tower. No one was quite sure why, but speculation was that they were looking for an easy target. Northwood, Berwick, and Castle Questing were far too large for a group of raiding Scots. Thornton wasn't exactly easy, but it certainly wasn't built up like some of the bigger castles were.

The Scots took a chance that ended badly for them.

Fortunately, it hadn't been the case for Thornton Tower. It was sunset on a day that had hinted to the promise of a warm summer, with a crystal sky and gentle breezes as the English armies buttoned up the castle for the night and began to settle down to rest. It was a beautiful evening as the torches were lit, illuminating the sky against the coming night.

The smell of roasting meat was in the air.

For the moment, all was well.

"I feel as if we chased them to your doorstep," Patrick said, trying not to sound as exhausted as he felt. "Or at least I did until I realized the Scots we were chasing were reinforcements for the group that was trying to breach your gatehouse. You've got a pile of dead Scots to deal with now, de Allery."

Edmund de Allery, Lord of Thornton Tower, knew that. He'd been through hell. He looked like hell and smelled like hell. He wasn't a warrior by choice, but rather, in this case, by necessity.

And he was damn sick of it.

"I'll push them all into the moat and let them rot," he said, running a hand through his dirty, dark hair. "But please—let us not speak of the foolish Scots any longer. Come inside and let me show you and your men some hospitality. It has been a very long time since we last saw one another, my lord. I fear I've not been a good neighbor."

Patrick didn't want to be rude to the man, but he also didn't want to spend an over-amount of time with him. It wasn't that de Allery was just a bad neighbor—he was a selfish one. Whenever the call for assistance went out across the border, de Allery bottled himself up in his castle and refused to help. Patrick thought about leaving him to fend for himself when the reivers who had harassed some nearby farmers had led him to the gates of Thornton Tower, but then he started to think that if de Allery was indebted to him somehow, it would make him more apt to be a responsive ally. But there were other reasons he didn't want to spend an over-amount of time at Thornton. It didn't take him long to remember that one of them was heading in his direction as he entered the keep.

Lady Zora de Allery, Edmund's only daughter, was not someone that Patrick had a fond memory of. Truth be told, he'd completely forgotten about her until the moment he saw her. She was tall, with dark, bushy hair like her father, pale skin, and a look about her that suggested she'd just crawled out of the grave. There was something cold and intense about her, as he'd seen when she had fostered at Berwick years ago. She'd spent a few years at Berwick before Patrick's wife, Brighton, had enough of her and sent her off to Alnwick Castle without her father's permission.

Patrick wondered if that incident was going to come up again tonight.

But he'd try to avoid that conversation for the sake of peace. He'd done enough fighting today and didn't want to include de Allery in that activity. The man's daughter was directing the servants into the great hall, located inside the keep of Thornton, when she caught sight of Patrick entering with her father.

A man as tall as Patrick was rather hard to miss.

"Lord Berwick," she said, dipping into a practiced curtsy. "You honor our house, my lord. Welcome."

All Patrick could remember about Zora was her knack for causing trouble. Even at a young age, she gossiped and schemed and tried to manipulate those around her. Patrick had really only heard about it from his wife, which was why Zora had been sent on her way. But he did remember that Zora had sworn her undying love to his son, Magnus, for a time until he left Berwick, and then she'd fixated on Titus. Titus had been young, and he'd only been at Berwick a short while before moving on to Wark Castle, but Patrick remembered the trouble Zora stirred up with his sons, declaring to all who would listen that she would marry one of them.

Troublemaker, indeed.

"My lady," he greeted her with polite reserve. "It is agreeable to see you again."

Zora smiled, showing off big teeth. "I am flattered that you would remember me," she said. "You have so many young pages and wards at Berwick. I'm honored that you would know me at all."

"I never forget a face, my lady."

That seemed to please Zora. She indicated a table that was already set up with a good deal of food. "Please sit," she said. "My father sent word that you were coming, so we have prepared a feast in your honor. We have wine from Spain and a cook that trained in Lisbon. We have the finest food on the border, and I'm sure you will enjoy it."

Patrick nodded, sitting down to a fleet of servants falling over themselves to make sure he had enough wine and food. As he leaned back while servants made sure his trencher was full, more knights came in from the bailey, including the ones he'd brought with him from Berwick. Rian de Llion and Espen de Tracy were two of his warriors, young men who had taken the place of older knights who had retired or moved to other, easier, posts. They were followed by a knight who wasn't actually a knight in the literal sense, though he was a warrior. He was a cousin of Patrick's wife, a distant cousin from the land of the Northmen, sent by her father, who happened to be king of the Northmen.

His name was Krister Grimsson, and he couldn't have looked more like a Northman if he tried. He was tall and big, with a cascade of white-blond hair that tumbled down his back. His father was a cousin of the king of the Northmen, a man known as Magnus the Law Mender, and Magnus, feeling that Krister was the finest warrior in all the land, had gifted him to Patrick. Some men gave their relatives cattle, some gave horses or money, but Magnus gave men.

Patrick couldn't send him back.

Not that he wanted to, because he and Krister got along famously, but the man was essentially a slave. Or a spy. Patrick couldn't figure out which, even a few years after Krister had arrived. But the man was hell in battle, especially against the Scots, whom he detested, and Patrick was grateful for him. As Rian and Espen took a seat across from Patrick and Krister joined them, the only de Allery knight came in through the entry.

Patrick didn't know anything about Ansel de Edington beyond the name and the fact that the man's father was a warlord in the north. He seemed to remember that he had fostered at one of the de Wolfe properties, but no more than that. Ansel wasn't particularly big, but he was broad, with pockmarked skin and shaggy brown hair. He swung a sword like a madman and had personally cut down several Scots. Patrick was just sampling his wine when Ansel plopped down at the table and bellowed for food in a tone that shook the entire table.

"We've started the funeral pyres, my lord," Ansel said to de Ellery. "We'll have nothing but ashes come the dawn, enough of a deterrent to keep the Scots away."

Patrick's eyes flicked over to him. "You're burning them?"

Ansel fixed on him. "Aye, my lord."

Patrick pondered that news, but it was clear he wasn't happy with it. "Do you know the clan?"

Ansel shrugged. "One clan is like another," he said, grabbing the cup of wine that a servant set in front of him. "They're all savages and deserve to be burned like dogs."

That didn't sit well with Patrick. Both his mother and wife were Scots. "If you have been on the border any length of time, you know that is not a true statement," he said. Then he turned to Edmund. "I suggest that you not burn the bodies and discover which clan they're from. If they're Gordon or Elliot, you may have real trouble on your hands if you do not return their dead. They will not appreciate the bodies being burned."

Edmund's brow furrowed. "This is the first trouble we've had in some time," he said. "I think we should burn the bodies and throw the remains into the moat as a message of what we will do to anyone who attacks us again."

Patrick collected his wine. "You know that living on the border is a balance," he said. "If you show their dead such blatant disregard, they'll not take kindly to it. They will perceive it as a slight, and you will have more trouble than you can handle."

"Then what should we do?"

Patrick took a big drink of wine, smacking his lips before answering. "Pile them in a field to the north and let them come for them," he said. "That will show them you have some mercy. It may do more for you than burning the corpses."

"But they're animals that deserve to be treated accordingly," Ansel cut into the conversation, unwilling to be left out of the decision making. "You cannot show Scots any mercy at all. They'll think you weak."

Patrick turned to the man. "How long have you served on the border?"

"Six years, my lord."

"And how many Scots raids have you been involved in?"

"Four, my lord."

"I've been here my entire life and have been involved in dozens of raids and innumerable battles," Patrick said. "I think my experience in such matters is worth more than yours."

Ansel stiffened, insulted, but before he could reply, Edmund stepped in. "Young Ansel is an excellent knight," he said quickly. "His father and I are friends. That is how he came to serve me. He has been instrumental in helping me manage Thornton Tower. We are grateful for his service."

Patrick was weary and snappish, an unusual state for him. "That may be, but when it comes to the Scots, you'd better take your advice from someone who knows them," he said. "Pile their corpses in the field to the north and let the Scots claim them."

The Earl of Berwick had spoken. Feeling humiliated, Ansel simply got up and left the table, leaving de Allery embarrassed. The truth was that Ansel was used to running Thornton Tower because Edmund was usually too timid to stand up to him. Ansel had come from a father who didn't want him around, foisting his son onto an old friend who found himself stuck with a knight who gave commands and ran circles around de

Allery. It was a nightmare situation, to be honest.

He knew he'd get an earful from Ansel once Berwick had departed.

As Edmund tried to think of an apology for Ansel's behavior that didn't sound too much as if he was making excuses, Zora returned with more servants and more food.

"I've had the cook prepare dishes with fish, Lord Berwick," she said to Patrick as several steaming piles of food were set upon the table. "There are eels with onions and raisins, fish pie with ginger, and fish balls that are fried in fat. I am sure they will be to your liking."

Patrick eyed the dishes on the table. He didn't have the heart to tell her that he hated fish. Berwick was on the coast, with a large fishing population, but he couldn't stand anything that came out of that briny, smelly water. As Zora took a seat across from him, where Ansel had been seated, he smiled weakly.

"You have gone to great lengths to show good hospitality, my lady," he said. "Thank you for your efforts."

Zora smiled, pleased with herself. "May I fill your trencher, my lord?"

He let her. Although his memories of her were not particularly good ones, she had gone out of her way to present him with good food. She was trying to be a good hostess.

But he really hated fish.

The trencher before him was full of many different things. He could see the fish balls, the eels, the fish pie, but it was surrounded by other things he did like to eat. Directly across the table from him, Rian and Krister and Espen were already well into their food, knowing how Patrick felt about fish and trying not to laugh. He thought Rian might have been grinning as he shoved food into his mouth, but he couldn't be sure. Picking up the large knife on the table, Patrick stabbed a piece of sauced mutton and took a bite.

It was old.

Very old.

Slowly, and with great reluctance, he chewed.

"It has been a long time since we have seen a de Wolfe at Thornton Tower, my lord," Zora said, watching him eat with eagerness in her expression. "In fact, it has been a long time since I have seen anyone from Berwick. I trust Lady Berwick is well?"

Patrick suspected she really didn't care about the woman who had sent her away, but she was asking to be polite.

Or start a fight.

"She is," he said, chewing. "My wife is quite well."

"And your sons?" Zora asked. "I did not know Markus and Cassius well, but I was well acquainted with Magnus and Titus. I hope they are well, also?"

Patrick choked down the mutton and looked for something else on the trencher to eat that wasn't so old and overly sauced. "Magnus married two years ago," he said. "He lives at my outpost at Raechester Castle with his wife and baby son."

Zora seemed to force a smile at the idea of Magnus, once a man she greatly desired, married. "Congratulations to Magnus," she said. "How wonderful. Please give him my best wishes for a long and healthy life."

"I will," Patrick said, daring to put his knife into something that looked as if it had bones, but he couldn't tell what it was. "Titus is well, also. He splits his time between Berwick and Pembroke."

"Pembroke?" de Allery repeated. "He serves Aymer de Valence?"

Patrick shrugged. "In part," he said. "Titus is an excellent liaison between de Wolfe and our allies. He is politically astute, that one. If there is intrigue and mystery and the threat of warfare, Titus is usually involved in it. He seems to have a bit of a diplomat in him, like my grandfather. Everyone loves and respects Titus."

De Allery seemed both curious and concerned. "Whom does de Wolfe side with?" he asked. "It would seem that if Titus serves at Pembroke, he is part of the rebellion."

Patrick wasn't sure which way de Allery leaned when it came to the king and the warlords banded against him, so he didn't want to get into any heavy political discussion. In fact, between Zora's time at Berwick, Titus and Magnus, and the burning of the Scots, the entire conversation was turning out to be a balancing act. Any one of those subjects had the potential to be incendiary.

"Nay, he is not part of any rebellion," he said. "Titus is simply the eyes and ears of the de Wolfe empire. We have thus far remained neutral, but it is prudent to stay abreast of what is happening with Pembroke and his allies, don't you think?"

De Allery pondered that. "I do," he said. "He is your youngest son, is he not?"

Patrick nodded. "Aye."

"He must not be married if he spends so much time between Pembroke and Berwick," de Allery said. "No wife would tolerate that."

Patrick smiled weakly. "I am sure a wife would not," he said. "Nay, Titus is not married, much to the chagrin of my wife."

De Allery nodded confidently. "And she *should* be concerned," he said. "What your son needs is a wife to settle him.

Keep him close to Berwick and his family. Mayhap there is a maiden in the north who can settle him down and give him great contentment and satisfaction."

Patrick had a piece of unknown meat on his knife, putting it in his mouth but still having no idea what it was. "Mayhap someday," he said, chewing the tough meat. "He does not seem interested in marriage, so I've not hunted for a bride for him yet."

"You do not need to hunt," de Allery said. "There is one sitting right in front of you. I shall give her to you, happily."

He meant Zora. Patrick stopped chewing, finding himself looking straight into Zora's hopeful face. It took him a moment to realize he'd been set up. Like a fool, he'd walked right into that trap, not realizing de Allery was deftly steering him in that direction. Unaware, he had followed.

God, did he feel stupid.

Now, it was starting to make some sense. The lavish meal after the fight, Zora acting the perfect chatelaine, keeping the conversation pleasant, and expensive wine that flowed freely. When she told Patrick that her father had sent word that Berwick was part of the skirmish against the reivers, that should have been his first clue. A message had been sent and, clearly, a plan had been laid.

And Patrick had walked right into it.

"And I am certain your daughter would make a pleasing bride," he said after a moment, struggling to swallow what was in his mouth. "But, as I said, Titus is not ready for marriage. He is far too busy."

De Allery poured him more wine, personally. "But he will be ready someday," he said. "Think of it, my lord—Zora is my only child. If Titus marries her, he inherits Thornton Tower.

That would keep him close to Berwick, and you would have yet another jewel in the de Wolfe crown. Thornton is a rich property, which is why the Scots wanted it, I am sure. Truly, it is a perfect solution."

Patrick had to take a drink of wine, washing down the meat that he very nearly choked on. "That is tempting," he said, struggling not to cough. "But I cannot speak on anything so serious at this time. I would need to speak with Titus before I could conduct any business on his behalf, and this is not the time nor the place. I am sure you understand."

De Allery was like a dog with a bone. He wasn't about to let the subject go. "But you *will* speak with him?"

Patrick didn't want to agree. He wanted off the subject. But he also didn't want to insult a man he was trying to court as a more congenial ally.

Damn, if de Allery hadn't played him well.

"Mayhap," he said. "But I cannot say when or where or how, so we must leave it at that. I make no promises of anything other than I will bring the subject up if the time and situation seems right."

"That is all I ask, my lord."

Patrick was fairly certain that wasn't all he would ask. He'd already asked a great deal. Patrick had to wonder if this was a trap they set for any father of an unmarried son or if it was simply formulated for him. In any case, he simply nodded his head and downed the rest of his wine. After that, he wasn't feeling particularly social, and across the table, his knights knew it.

Rian, Espen, and Krister were watching him carefully. They, too, had seen how de Allery had deftly manipulated Berwick, and how Zora had seemed quite eager for the conversation to go in that direction. But Patrick had been caught off guard and was trying not to commit himself to anything. He needed help.

It was Krister who took the cue.

"Titus would make a terrible husband," he said in his thick accent. "He is married to England. What woman would want to be married to a man who puts country above everything else?"

"That is true," Rian said, pouring himself more wine because he, too, thought the food was terrible, and he wanted to wash the taste out of his mouth. "He is never in one place long enough to grow roots. When was the last time he was in Berwick?"

"Some time ago," Krister said.

"Months," Espen piped up, overlapping him.

"I would forget about Titus, my lord," Krister said to de Allery. "He would make your daughter miserable. Surely she has better prospects if it is a husband you seek."

De Allery wasn't particularly thrilled with the direction the conversation had taken, and his brow rippled as he looked at the big Northman.

"She has many," he said. "But like Lord Berwick, I must be selective. She has a great dowry and a great inheritance. A marriage into the House of de Wolfe would be most attractive because Thornton Tower could become part of the de Wolfe lands. They have so many in the north, but that would mean it was staffed with de Wolfe men. It would be protected, and my daughter would be well regarded. It would be an honor."

He stressed the last five words, making sure Patrick knew where he stood on the matter, but Patrick was still in the midst of wanting desperately to be off the subject.

"We should return home soon," he said, avoiding answering de Allery altogether. "It is less than an hour's ride home, and the moon is full tonight. We can make excellent time."

"You will not stay?" de Allery said, suddenly anxious. "But… but you must let us show our gratitude for your assistance, Lord Berwick. We would be greatly shamed should you flee so quickly."

Patrick could hear desperation in the man's voice. He'd been inclined to try and make the man more of a compliable ally, but he didn't like how de Allery had steered the conversation right into marriage with his daughter. Patrick knew for a fact that his wife would go to war against de Allery personally before she'd allow Zora to marry one of her sons, so it was really out of the question.

But he wasn't quite sure how to tell de Allery that.

He was walking a fine line.

"When we left this morning to chase Scots, I told my wife that I would return shortly," he said. "If I do not return soon, she will think something has happened and will come to find me herself. I do not wish to worry her, and I am certain you can understand that."

De Allery nodded meekly, unhappy that he would not have Patrick as his guest. "Nay, we would not want Lady Berwick to be frightened," he said. "But… but will you return, as my guest? And bring your lady wife? As I said, I fear I've been a terrible ally, and I should like to make amends. Will you come?"

Come back so you can bully me more about a marriage? Patrick thought grimly. But he forced a smile as he set his wine down.

"We shall," he said. "My wife would be quite agreeable to do so. I am certain she will enjoy the visit."

"I hope so," Zora answered before her father could. "Lady Berwick taught me nearly everything I know. I would like to show her how well I learned her lessons."

Patrick eyed the woman. Either she'd completely forgotten about Brighton sending her away or she was lying through her teeth. He suspected the latter. In any case, he stood up and indicated for his men to do so as well. They began moving away from the table, toward the door, as Patrick faced de Allery.

"If you do as I tell you and put the Scots in a pile to the north, I do not think you will have further trouble," he said. "At least for a while. But you should find out who attacked you and why. Though I suspect you were a target of convenience, it would be prudent to know if some clan has suddenly decided you are their enemy."

He moved away from the table as de Allery followed. "I will do what I can," he said, still clearly distressed that his guests were leaving. "We live a peaceful existence here, and I've never had a great need for spies or scouts, so if you hear of anything, I would be grateful for the information."

Patrick nodded. "I will do what I can," he said. "But I would be careful for the next few days. Keep your gates secured. Do not go outside of the castle unnecessarily."

"We will not, my lord," de Allery said. "You have my thanks."

They were at the entry door. The bailey of Thornton Tower was in front of them, lit up with enough torches to harness the light of the sun. Rian, Espen, and Krister were already shouting to the Berwick men, who had settled down for a meal and were now on their feet again. Horses were being brought forth. Patrick put his helm on and headed out into the bailey just as his horse was brought out from the stable yard. The big, dappled beast had been his trusted companion for years. Mounting up, Patrick waited impatiently for his men to mount their horses also.

He was fully aware that they were leaving in a hurry. A *great* hurry. He knew it looked as if they were running from de Allery, but he honestly didn't care. Hopefully the man would figure out that it was because he'd tried to trap him into committing his youngest son to a marriage, a tactic that was, in the end, unseemly and asinine. Perhaps it was because de Allery didn't have a lot of visitors and lived like a hermit, so he wasn't polished on his social skills. Or perhaps it was because he didn't care if he tried to bully the Earl of Berwick to get what he wanted.

Dumping his daughter on a de Wolfe son.

Not as long as Patrick had breath in his body was that going to happen.

The gates of Thornton Tower opened wide, and Patrick led his contingent of about eighty men out into the night. But almost immediately after coming through the gates, they began to smell smoke. Not just any smoke, but sickly-sweet, acrid smoke. As they headed northeast, they could see the reason for the stench—off to the southeast, near the eastern wall of Thornton Tower, they could see what looked like a bonfire. Only wood wasn't the fuel. Patrick, and the others, knew that they were looking at a funeral pyre. And he suspected who had given the order to start it.

Ansel de Edington, evidently, would have the last laugh.

But Patrick knew that only meant trouble.

CHAPTER FIVE

Westminster Palace
London

"I'VE HEARD."

"About Gaveston?"

"Aye. Word came a few days ago."

"Does Edward know?"

Sir Denys de Winter drew in a long, slow breath. He and Titus were standing in the middle of the vast northern courtyard of Westminster Palace, out in the open but far enough away from anyone else in the bailey that they couldn't be overheard. They could also be sure that no one was eavesdropping, so this was how they normally conducted their clandestine conversations.

Hiding out in the open.

Since Titus was Magnus' brother and Magnus had been the king's captain, it was all quite normal. De Wolfe and de Winter were close friends and allies. Denys was from the great military family of de Winter, an astonishingly capable commander, and Magnus' best friend. He was positively enormous, tall and muscular, with a crown of fair hair and big, dark eyes. He had a ready laugh and a booming voice, enough to scare the wits from most sane men. When Magnus had resigned his post two years ago as captain of the king's knights, Denys was the natural replacement.

He also happened to be an agent for the Executioner Knights.

"My suspicion is that Edward knows," Denys said after a moment. "My last report was that he was in York with Isabella and that Lancaster was pursuing him."

Titus' eyebrows lifted. "Then all you've heard is that Pembroke has taken him hostage?"

"Aye," Denys said. "Why do you ask?"

"Because if you knew the latest, then you would know that Lancaster and Warwick have abducted Gaveston from Pembroke's custody," Titus said. "He's been taken to Warwick Castle, where Lancaster and Warwick plan to try the man for treason."

It was Denys' turn to look surprised. "Christ, are you serious?"

"I wish I wasn't."

"I had not heard *that*."

Titus nodded ominously. "Now you have," he said. "That happened almost eight days ago. It has taken me that long to ride to London and inform de Lohr. He told me to tell you, but he wants me to go to Warwick and keep an eye on the situation."

Denys frowned. "Is that wise?" he said. "Warwick knows that you are a Pembroke knight. Won't he think you've come to retrieve Gaveston?"

Titus shook his head. "I will go to Warwick Castle as a de

Wolfe knight," he said. "Warwick and Lancaster know that de Wolfe has remained somewhat neutral in this situation. All I have to tell them is that I am the eyes and ears of the Earl of Warenton, the Earl of Berwick, and the Earl of Northumbria, among others. I've got one father and five powerful uncles who command nearly the entire stretch of the Scottish border and significant portions of Northumberland. Do you think, for one moment, that Warwick is going to deny me entry?"

"Of course not," Denys grunted. "He'll put you right in front of the action in the hopes of gaining de Wolfe support."

Titus nodded knowingly. "Exactly," he said. "Trust me when I tell you that I will be perfectly safe. But de Winter, on the other hand…"

Denys knew what he meant. The House of de Winter was an enormous warring house, related to the Earl of Surrey and the Earl of Norfolk, and they always, without fail, supported the Crown. They had never been against the Crown in the history of the family, so Denys served the king whether he wanted to or not. Secretly, he sided with the rebellion, but as Morgen had told him, he was more valuable to them on the inside of Edward's circle. But something like this—with the king's closest companion and advisor a prisoner of the rebel warlords—he, more than anyone, knew how badly this could go.

"I must send word to my father," he said with regret. "He will want to know what has happened. He has troops with the king as we speak, men who have been protecting him from Lancaster and his allies. But I fear we've been alone in much of our endeavors, Titus. So many warlords side with Lancaster. Edward has done everything he can to make sure England's warlords are insulted and devalued. It's his own damnable fault."

"You know that is why my father and uncles have remained neutral," Titus said, lowering his voice. "De Winter has long been an ally. They do not want to go to battle against de Winter's army. De Lohr, too. That is why we have all stayed out of this, but I suspect the tides will be turning now that Gaveston is Warwick's prisoner."

"Why would you say that?"

"Because Pembroke gave his word that Gaveston would be treated fairly," Titus said seriously. "Lancaster and Warwick turned against him by abducting Gaveston. Now Pembroke looks like a fool, and Lancaster intends to hold his own court to judge Gaveston. He is doing this without the support of his allies, save Warwick and a few others. He acted on his own and took Pembroke's prisoner. Don't you see where this will lead?"

Denys did. "No man wants to live under Lancaster's rule," he said. "He has overstepped himself."

"Exactly."

"And that means that men like your father will be driven to support Edward."

"They will have no choice unless they want Lancaster to rule all of them unjustly," Titus said. "By abducting Gaveston, he proved that he cannot be trusted."

Denys could see the bigger picture. "Then I must send word to my father right away," he said. "He must know what has happened. Lancaster is just looking for an excuse to get rid of Gaveston."

"He will execute him, and when he does that, he has sealed his fate."

"Only he does not realize it yet."

The impact of those words hung in the air as Titus and Denys looked at one another, each man knowing what was coming. It wasn't so much that the rebel warlords of England would swear fealty to Edward again. It was the mere fact that the Earl of Lancaster, the richest and most powerful warlord among them, was taking justice into his own hands and usurping the king's power in all things. And he wanted it badly enough to betray an ally in Pembroke.

No one needed a demigod ruling England.

"I'll send word to my father at some point, but not now," Denys said. "Men have seen us talking, and they know you. The only saving grace is that you are Magnus' brother and de Wolfe is neutral, though I know some of them might know you've been at Pembroke's side. In any case, if they see us meet and then I immediately send a missive to Norwich Castle, it will look suspicious."

Titus nodded. "Agreed," he said. "But do not wait too long. If I could ride to see Davyss de Winter myself, I would. How is your father, anyway?"

Denys smiled faintly at the mention of his beloved father. "Old," he said. "Old and refusing to stand down. He still commands Norwich, even at his age, and even though my brother, Devon, has virtually taken everything over for him. But Papa is healthy, and for that, we are grateful."

Titus smiled. "He is much admired by all of us," he said. "My father has always been fond of him."

"And my father is very fond of Atty."

Atty was a family nickname for Patrick de Wolfe, something that close friends and allies called him as well. When Patrick had been a very small boy, a mild speech impediment had prevented him from properly pronouncing his name. "Patrick" came out as "Atty," and it stuck. To call such an enormous, powerful warrior by a childhood nickname seemed foolish, but for Patrick, it was natural. Even his grandchildren called him Atty.

It was something timeless and endearing.

Titus knew that. He had known Denys his entire life, and the man was like family, but he refrained from what came naturally to him and kept his hands to himself. Normally, he would have clapped Denys on the shoulder or otherwise shown his affection now that the conversation had turned to something more pleasant. But Denys was right—men were watching them.

He had to stay neutral.

"Right," he said, looking about casually. "And with that, it seems that there is nothing more I can do here, so I will be in London for another day or two before heading to Warwick Castle. Other than send word to your father, what do you plan to do? Will you try to get a message to Edward?"

Denys shrugged. "I cannot get a message to him now, not if he is running from the warlords intent on capturing him," he said. "My only duty now is to keep Westminster from falling to an enemy army."

"Do you think it will?"

"Angry warlords have marched on London before."

"True," Titus said. "Let us hope it does not come to that."

Denys couldn't disagree. "I only have about a thousand men here," he said. "We can hold it if we need to, but not much more than that. I cannot protect the city."

"What about the Tower of London? How many men are there?"

"Five hundred at the most. It will hold even if London falls."

Titus grew serious. "I do not have to say this, but I am going to," he said. "If it looks as if Westminster is going to fall, get out of here. Get on a boat and go across the river. Go back to Lonsdale or return to Norwich, but do not stay here. Edward isn't worth dying for, Denys. Please."

Denys' dark eyes twinkled dully. "What *is* worth dying for, Titus?"

"Not a man who has never been kind to you and who threatened to take your father's lands if he did not properly serve him."

The humor in Denys' features faded. "You forget to whom you are speaking," he said softly. "I can get closer to Edward than anyone. I can end this conflict once and for all with only my bare hands. Edward may not be worth dying for, but England is. And for a better England, I am not beyond doing what needs to be done. Even to a king."

Titus understood. Denys was the king's captain, but he could also be the king's assassin. Sometimes an Executioner Knight had to do what needed to be done, regardless of the politics of it.

Even regicide.

Denys was in a prime position for it.

"Let us hope it does not come to that," Titus muttered. "Now, I must take my leave. I've been here long enough."

"It was good to see you, Titus."

"And you, Denys."

"I wish you good fortune in your endeavor with Warwick. I think you are going to need it."

Titus gave him a lopsided smile as he began to back away. "Much like you, I will do what needs to be done."

Denys took a step or two after him, following him as he turned away. "Titus?"

Titus glanced at him. "Aye?"

Denys was hesitant. "Be… cautious," he finally said. "Gaveston is not worth dying for."

Titus knew that. He appreciated Denys' concern. Flashing the man a cheeky smile and giving him a bold wink, he headed for the western gatehouse of Westminster.

Denys watched him go, praying it wouldn't be the last time he saw him alive. With the way things were going with the winds of war in England, anything could happen.

And anything probably would.

CHAPTER SIX

TITUS' PLANS HAD deviated just the slightest. He was supposed to return to Morgen after speaking with Denys, but he didn't. Morgen could wait a day or two.

Katiana couldn't.

Even after his discussion with Denys, Titus' mind wasn't where it should have been. He should have been thinking about Morgen and Warwick and the mess going on in Warwickshire, but instead, he was thinking about a tiny little girl he used to know many years ago.

He couldn't get her off his mind.

Titus may have been irreverent at times, even foolish in a good-natured sort of way, but he had a deeply introspective side to him as well. He wasn't afraid to speak his mind and tended to have little tact when he was being direct, but that introspective and rational side of him was something that kept him grounded. He suspected that aspect of his personality would take over some day and temper the Titus that everyone knew and loved, but he hoped it wasn't too soon, because another unfortunate aspect of his personality was that he was impulsive. That wasn't a particularly good trait in a man who wielded a sword for a living, but that impulsiveness could also be viewed as bravery few men had.

In this case, his impulsiveness, or bravery, was starting to take hold.

He didn't want to go to Warwickshire, not just yet.

He wanted to stay in London.

So, he took a room at the most notorious tavern in town, known as The Pox, and spent the night listening to the laughter and brawls in the common room below. Once he fell asleep, however, he slept through it, a talent he'd always had. As his mother had so kindly put it, Titus could sleep through the invasion of the Normans and never stir a muscle.

He'd left word with the tavern keep to wake him well before dawn, and somewhere in the darkness of his snoring and dreaming, there were several sharp raps at his door. Instantly awake, which was a conditioned trait of a knight, he was up, washing his face in cold water and dressing for the day. He'd told Katiana that he'd be outside her aunt's home at sunrise, and he intended to keep that promise. Once he'd finished dressing, he'd quickly packed his saddlebags and headed down to the livery to collect his horse.

The clip-clop of the animal's hooves on London's empty streets rattled the predawn silence. Some people were up, and he could see lights in the windows as he headed up Walbrook Street and into the Jewish part of London. It was a quiet area, not hugely traveled by anyone other than the Jews, but it was a shortcut to Coleman Street. A few people were out at this time of the morning, looking at him strangely because a Christian knight in the Jewish sector wasn't a frequent sight, but he was focused on Catte Street up ahead. That signified the end of the Jewish section of London, and beyond that was Coleman Street.

This area of London was significantly richer than the others. The manses were large and well kept, and servants were out at this time of the morning, going about their duties. The homes on this street, though wealthy, were also in many shapes and sizes and manner of upkeep. Some looked positively distressed, leaning out over the narrow street, while others were well kept and the walls whitewashed. A few even had flowers in window boxes above street level, an unusual sight because most people didn't take the time to plant flowers around their home. Still, some did, and it was a bright spot in an otherwise dingy city. Titus happened to be looking up at one of the flower boxes over his head when he caught something in his periphery. A small, cloaked lady standing in front of Katiana's aunt's home, which he was just coming to.

A smile tugged at Titus' lips when he realized who it was.

"So you think you were awake and dressed before me, do you?" he said as he came close. "I will tell you, quite plainly, that you are wrong. *I* was awake well before you were."

Katiana gazed up at him, trying not to openly grin at the sight of him. "I am going to tell your mother that your attitude is most unkind," she said. "It does not matter if you were awake before me. It would be the polite thing to tell me that you were slower than I."

Titus broke out in a cheeky smile. "Please do not tell my mother," he said. "She will be quite angry with me if she thinks I have been unkind to a lady. I haven't really been, have I?"

"Do you acknowledge that I was ready and waiting before you?"

He sighed dramatically. "Very well," he said. "I surrender."

"Then I shall not tell your mother."

Because he was smiling so openly, she smiled in return.

Titus dismounted his horse, his eyes riveted to her. Katiana was wearing a dark blue cloak with a hood pulled over her head, her nose and cheeks pinched pink from the cold air.

She was the most beautiful sight he'd ever seen.

"I thought that yesterday might have been a dream," he said. "I am glad to see that it was not. I am glad I did not imagine any of it."

"You did not," she said. "I, too, am glad to see that it was not a dream caused when I hit my head from falling off my wild horse."

He laughed softly. "You have suffered no ill effects from yesterday?"

She shook her head. "Nay," she said. "Though my hands are still blistered, they will heal. Mayhap we can go to the apothecary after the spice merchant. The cook put butter on my hands to soothe them, but I cannot go around with butter on my hands until they heal. The apothecary should have something less smelly."

"And slippery."

"Exactly," she said, snorting. "Shall we go?"

Titus nodded, but he was looking around. "Aren't we to have an escort?" he said. "Surely your aunt would not leave you alone with a strange knight."

Katiana looked up at the manse behind her, the dark windows, the darkened doorway. She began to walk away, motioning Titus to follow her, which he hesitantly did. They were at least two houses down the block before she spoke.

"I did not tell her that I was going with you," she said. "In truth, I did not tell her anything at all. Some of the servants saw you when you returned me yesterday, but they did not speak of it, and she did not ask. She didn't even know something had gone wrong with the horse. I am sorry to say that my aunt does not pay an over-amount of attention to me. I can come and go as I please."

He looked at her, rather shocked. "Is that so?" he said. "That is curious. I would think a maiden aunt would watch you like a hawk."

Katiana shook her head. "Only when it comes to suitors," she said. "She only takes interest when she is matchmaking. Otherwise, she prefers her dogs, her sleep, her sweets, and her wine."

He eyed her as they walked down the street. "What makes you think I am not a suitor?" he said. "You do not know what my intentions are."

She looked at him without concern. "What are they?"

He turned his nose up at her and looked away. "I am not going to tell you now," he said. "I'm offended that you would not think I am a suitor or a predator of women. What do I look like? Some bleary-eyed fool with no interest in a beautiful woman?"

Katiana giggled at him because he was being overly dramatic. "*Are* you interested in women?"

"Of course I am."

"Should I go back and tell my aunt that I need an escort?"

She paused as if to turn around, but he grasped her by the elbow and pulled her along. "Nay," he said flatly. "No escort could prevent me from doing what I wanted to do, if I wanted to do it, so let them be. It is safer for them if they do not come."

Katiana eyed him, a smile on her lips. "Very well," she said. "But if you make one unsavory move against me, I'll run back to my aunt. Are we clear?"

"We are, my lady." He paused a moment as if thinking on

her words before scowling. "Unsavory move? What does that mean?"

Katiana chuckled at him. "Leave it alone, Titus," she said. "I was only jesting. Let's think ahead, shall we? Have you broken your fast yet?"

He shook his head. "Nay," he said. "Have you?"

"Nay," she replied. "I am a little hungry. Shall we find something to eat?"

He looked at her, smiling. It seemed to be a perpetual gesture when he looked at her. "Are you brave?"

"Not when it comes to breaking my fast," she said warily. "Why do you ask?"

He laughed. "Because there is a tavern near the Thames that serves excellent food," he said. "My friends and I go there frequently. In fact, I slept there last night. I'd be happy to pay for your meal if you would like to go there."

She nodded. "Very well," she said. "But why did you ask if I was brave?"

"Because sometimes they have odd dishes."

"Are they tasty?"

"I think so."

She shrugged. "Then let us break our fast there," she said. "Though I have lived in London these past two years, my aunt does not leave her home. I've not been to the taverns or inns."

"And for good reason," Titus said. "You do not want to go in without a man with a sword to most of them."

"Is this one of those?"

He cocked his head. "This one more than any other."

That sounded a little ominous, but off they went.

And Katiana couldn't have been happier.

C3

KATIANA'S FIRST CLUE that the tavern Titus took her to wasn't exactly safe was when they approached the entry door and a man came spilling out, sprawling on the boardwalk in front of them, and three or four men came piling out after him, throwing punches.

Her introduction to the most notorious tavern in London had begun.

As she cringed in surprise and a little fear, Titus didn't see anything wrong with it. He laughed at the group of brawlers as he took her by the arm and led her inside. The common room of the tavern wasn't particularly busy at this time in the morning, and he pulled her over to a table by a window where they could watch the river ambling by. It was private and surprisingly quiet even with the men fighting out front, which had turned into an entanglement of drunk men trying to both fight and hug one another. That's when Katiana realized why Titus hadn't seemed concerned with it.

"What *is* this place?" she asked.

Titus pulled her chair over so she was sitting closer to him, within arm's length should he need to get to her quickly. But also because he rather wanted to.

"It is called The Pox, and it has been here for over a hundred years," he said, looking around. "It's a tavern, but it's also a place that gamblers frequent. Here, a man can bet on anything and everything. In the evening, it can become quite… lively."

Truthfully, Katiana was a little excited to be at a tavern. She'd never been to one in her life. "Do you gamble?" she asked.

He obviously refused to look at her as he answered. "I cannot tell you," he said. "You threatened to tell my mother once before. I cannot risk that you would follow through."

Katiana giggled. "I promise I will not repeat anything you say to me," she said. "I would not betray your confidence."

"Swear it?"

"I said so, didn't I?"

He grinned a naughty grin. "I have gambled once or twice," he said. "Have you?"

"Never!"

He snorted. "Well and good that you haven't," he said. "It is a nasty thing to do."

Katiana was prevented from answering when a busty young serving wench appeared. She didn't even look at Katiana, but her face lit up when she saw Titus.

"So you're back, are you?" she said with delight. "I was hoping you would return. It has been a long time since I last saw you, and you went straight to your chamber last night, so I didn't have a chance to speak with you. Where have you been keeping yourself, young lord?"

Katiana was greatly amused, as Titus was clearly uncomfortable. "I've been busy," he said, indicating Katiana. "My friend and I have come for some food. What's ready this morning?"

The wench looked at Katiana as if only just now seeing her. "Good morn to you, m'lady," she said, still quite friendly. "You don't look like the other friends he brings in here."

Katiana began to laugh as Titus, mortified, hastened to explain. "I do not bring anyone in here," he said quickly. "No one but colleagues or brothers."

The wench could see the humor in it, and she appreciated Katiana's laughter. "He's right," she said to Katiana. "I just meant you didn't look like the usual assortment of knights that he congregates with. You're much prettier."

Titus closed his eyes and hung his head in relief as Katiana dipped her head in gratitude. "My thanks to you," she said. "We've not seen each other in years. We were childhood friends."

"Is that so?" The wench seemed genuinely interested. "Then you don't know what this one has been up to since you last saw him? Give me a pence and I'll tell you everything."

She laughed uproariously, as did Katiana, while Titus lifted his hands and made strangling gestures at the wench, who slapped him on the shoulder.

"I was only jesting, m'lord," she said. "Your secrets are safe with me. For a gold crown."

More laughter from the women. Titus looked as if he wanted to crawl into a hole.

"I suppose I deserve that," he said, trying to be a good sport. "But can you stop insulting me long enough to bring us some food? The lady is famished, and we'd like to eat before we both grow old and die."

Still laughing, the wench winked at Katiana before heading off toward the kitchen. Titus put his elbow on the table, his chin in his hand, smiling thinly as Katiana continued to snort.

"She seems to know you well," she said. "I think you spend more time in here than you let on."

"Are you going to tell my mother now?"

"I told you that I would not betray your confidence. I meant it."

His smile turned real. "You are kind," he said. "And in my defense, a great many knights spend time here. It is not just me."

"You need not defend yourself, Titus. You are not answerable to me."

His smile faded. "I know," he said. "But I've not seen you in many years, and I do not want you to think I am some foolish man with loose morals. I was rather hoping…"

He faded off and shrugged, pretending to focus on putting his saddlebags on the chair next to him. As he fussed with the leather satchels, Katiana was watching him carefully. The mood between them had abruptly changed, and she wondered why.

"You were rather hoping *what*?" she asked.

He shook his head, unwilling to look at her. "It does not matter."

"Since when can you not be truthful with me?"

He looked up at her then. "I was not being untruthful," he said. "We've only just reintroduced ourselves after many years. Our conversation since yesterday has been light and witty. I've enjoyed it greatly. Katia, I do not know you well enough, nor do I have any right, to speak more boldly than I already have."

"What does that mean?"

"It means our conversation should always be light and witty and no more significant than that."

He wasn't making much sense to her, but he seemed strangely uncomfortable. That wasn't like him, at least from what she had remembered.

The man clearly had something on his mind.

"Titus," she said quietly. "Look at me."

He did, taking a deep breath and squaring his shoulders as he did so. "What is it?"

"Tell me what you were hoping for. Please."

His gaze fixed on her, and she could see that he was considering her question. As she watched, his expression grew more and more tense until he finally shrugged and looked away.

"I was going to say something very stupid," he said.

"I will be the judge of that," she said. "What is it?"

He sighed sharply. "You will not laugh?"

"Not unless you mean that it should be humorous."

"I don't."

"Then I will not laugh."

"I was going to say… I was going to say that I was rather hoping to make a good impression on you."

She smiled because it was a sweet thing to say. "Is that all?" she said. "I think it is delightful that you should hope that. But I must tell you that you've never made anything *but* a good impression on me."

He looked at her, guarded. "Do you mean that?"

"I do."

He smiled timidly. "I am glad to hear that," he said. "When we were children, it was much different than the way it is now. You have grown up, and so have I. I feel as if we are just meeting for the first time."

Katiana nodded. "In a sense, we are," she said. "But please know that you could never do anything to change my opinion of you, Titus. Not ever. You will always be my champion."

He smiled broadly, and Katiana swore she saw a blush to his cheeks. "That is good to know," he said. "At least someone considers me her champion."

Katiana shook her head with irony. "God's Bones, Titus," she said. "Do you not know what you look like? You're enormous and handsome. You're everything a man should be. Either you're being incredibly modest or incredibly unobservant not to realize there must be scores of women who would want you for their champion."

He was becoming embarrassed with her flattery. "Mayhap

there are a few."

Katiana laughed softly. "Of course there are," she said. "And I am certain there will be many in the future, so you may be my champion until you find the woman you wish to marry. I doubt a de Wolfe wife would want to share you with me."

His smile faded. In fact, he frowned as he sat back in his chair, studying her. "That would be none of her affair," he said with some anger. "And who's to say that I will not marry *you*? You have no husband and I have no wife. Who's to say that it would only be a natural progression from those years ago when my grandfather made me your protector? Maybe we were meant to be together even back then."

His words stabbed at her heart more than they should have. Looking at Titus, so tall and handsome and proud, Katiana was shocked to realize that she would have given anything in the world for him to be her permanent champion. *Her husband.* She had briefly entertained romantic thoughts for him yesterday, but she'd quickly chased them away because she knew that she was no match for a de Wolfe.

Unfortunately, the feelings were back and stronger than ever, because his words gave her something very dangerous—

They gave her hope.

It was her turn to avert her gaze.

"Now you are spouting madness," she said, trying to make light of words that were steadily carving into her. "We are no more meant to be together than a cat is to be meant for a dog."

"Why not?"

She looked at him, exasperated. "Stop being so foolish," she said. "You are a de Wolfe. You must have a fine wife from a fine family with an enormous dowry that will make you quite rich. I do not have any of those attributes."

He didn't like her answer. "Now *you're* spouting madness," he said. "I do not need a fine wife from a fine family."

"Aye, you do."

"I do not," he fired back. "Markus had to marry well because he is my father's heir. Cassius married so well that he is now a titled lord. Magnus married a member of the de Lohr family, while I… I want to marry someone I can't live without."

Katiana laughed, but it was uncomfortable. "You can surely live without me," she said. "You've been doing it for fifteen years."

"I did not realize what I was missing."

Katiana had no idea what to say to that. They were into a conversation that had her bewildered and edgy. Thankfully, they were precluded from further conversation when the serving wench arrived bearing great trenchers of steaming food. Behind her, another woman brought a small iron pot, also steaming, and set it on the table. There was a fish and fruit pie, stuffed eggs that had been battered and fried, copious amounts of roasted pork, and plenty of bread and butter.

Katiana dug into it with gusto, trying to keep the mood light with a subject that could have, and should have, sent her running. She didn't think he was doing it to upset her or hurt her, but if he kept it up, that was certainly where it was going to end up.

And Katiana didn't want it to.

"This looks delicious," she said, deliberately changing the subject. "How fortunate you must be to come here often and eat food like this."

Titus was spooning out some of the pork, which had come in the pot. "It is very good," he said, eyeing her as if knowing exactly what she was doing. "But I cannot tell my mother that it is sometimes better than the food she serves at Berwick."

Katiana chuckled. "Do you spend much time at Berwick these days?"

He shook his head as he ripped up the loaf of bread, handing her the soft middle. "Not as much as I would like," he said. "Though I was in the north earlier in the month."

"Oh?" she said curiously, taking the bread. "To visit?"

"To compete."

"Compete at what?"

"A tourney," he said, dipping his bread into the pork gravy and taking a big bite. "There was a big tournament at Middlesbrough."

"Did you win?"

He stopped chewing and looked at her as if she'd just said something shocking. "Of course I did," he said. "Did you think I would not?"

"I think you would succeed in anything you attempted."

He resumed chewing, now with a grin. "You would be correct," he said. "But the truth is that with three older brothers, I must succeed at everything I do because my brothers are great men, men that I admire and look up to. I do not want them to be ashamed of me."

Katiana was listening seriously. "I'm sure they would never be ashamed of you," she said. "But what, exactly, are you doing these days? You mentioned that you spend your time between Pembroke and Berwick. Do you not serve your father?"

Titus had a ready answer for the question. He always did because he certainly couldn't tell her the truth—*I'm a spy and an agent for the Executioner Knights.* He couldn't tell her that he played a dangerous game, pretending to be a simple, noble knight when what he really did was covert and sometimes sly.

He couldn't tell her that he was about to involve himself in a situation that was probably the most dangerous he'd ever faced.

Nay, he couldn't tell her any of that.

But he had an answer.

"I do serve my father," he said. "But I have also been the eyes and ears of the de Wolfe empire when it comes to the warlords who are opposed to the king. I've been with de Valence at Pembroke Castle most recently. There is a good deal going on in this country, and my family must be abreast of it."

She was listening with interest. "That is important work," she said. "Where will you go from here?"

"Back to Pembroke," he said, mouth full as he shoved more food into it.

"To stay?"

"For the time being."

Katiana picked up a piece of bread and scooped up some butter with her knife. "Do you enjoy being in Wales?" she said. "I hear that it can be a violent place."

"You've never been there?"

She shook her head. "I've never been anywhere," she said with regret. "My aunt was hoping to visit Paris in the fall, but we will probably not go. She tends to speak of things and never do them, so I suppose I shall be stuck here."

"Would you like to go to Paris?"

"Someday, I would."

"Anywhere else?"

She finished buttering her bread. "Mayhap," she said. "But I would not know where to go."

He swallowed his food and took a big swig of wine. "There are many places to go," he said. "Paris, Avignon, Madrid, Barcelona… many wonderful places in this world."

"And you have been to there?"

He nodded. "My father thinks that all young man must see important cities at least once in their lifetime," he said. "After we finished fostering, he sent us on a journey that took us to several great places. But my mother's father lived in Bergen, a city of Northmen. My brothers and I visited there when we were younger."

"Did you like it?"

Titus shrugged. "It was very cold," he said. "And we took a great longship across the sea, which was rough. I was sick for months, it seemed."

She smiled as she chewed her buttered bread. "But you survived."

"I did."

"I envy you, having traveled out of England."

"Don't," he said, before taking a big swallow of wine. "I was very happy to be home."

"And you intend to do great things here, is that it?"

Titus' gaze lingered on her before he went in for another bite. "It is," he said. "Given my birth order, I must make my own way. I want to serve well and earn the attention of men who can reward me for a job well done."

She cocked her head. "That has a mercenary sound to it."

He shook his head. "I did not mean it that way," he said. "I simply meant that I intend to be rewarded."

"Or you must marry well," Katiana said before she could stop herself. Realizing her mistake in bringing up marriage again, like a fool, she poured him more wine from the pitcher and quickly changed the subject. "I think you'll do very well. As you have said, you succeed at everything you try. But surely your father has an outpost that you can take command of. I've heard the de Wolfe empire has dozens of castles. There must be one lonely tower, somewhere, crying out for a competent commander."

He nodded his thanks as she filled his cup, his hands full of bread and pork. "There are a few, that is true," he said. "I was at Wark Castle for a time, a smaller castle right on the border, and every day was a day that we were on alert. That kind of command becomes exhausting because you can never relax. I'm not sure I want to be that vigilant for the rest of my life."

She was cutting up her eggs, relieved he hadn't focused on the marriage comment. "Then what *do* you want to do?"

He paused, thinking. "I want to inspire men," he said. "My grandfather was a great leader of men, and I should want to do what he did. I want to train them and teach them. I want them to understand their responsibilities to king and country, but also to themselves and their people. In battle, I am one sword, and a formidable one at that. But as a commander and a trainer of men, I am a thousand swords on the field of battle. I can do more and accomplish more in that way than I ever could alone. The nature of men is not a good one, but with help, they can understand their purpose. They can do good in the world."

Katiana had stopped eating, listening to him as he spoke. "Some men might say that you sound as if you want to be an emperor and control those around you," she said. "But I see altruism. You want to accomplish good things, and you want to share that belief."

He nodded. "Exactly," he said, pointing his knife at her. "You understand that."

She resumed eating her egg. "I do," she said. "I think it is a generous attitude. But how can you accomplish such things if you are one of many in the de Wolfe empire? I do not mean to diminish you, of course, but surely you would have a plan?"

His eyes twinkled as he looked at her. "I always have a plan," he said. "But if I tell you, you must not tell anyone."

"I told you that I would never betray your confidence."

"I have had two offers of a position within guilds of excellent reputation," he said. "I am considering both of them."

"Oh?" she said, interested. "What guilds are these?"

He was in the process of piling pork and gravy on top of his bread and butter. "Kenilworth Castle is one," he said. "The master knights of Kenilworth are the best trainers of knights in the world. Kenilworth has vacillated between a Crown property and a baronial property, going back and forth with owners, but through it all, the master knights have remained. They are a core unto themselves, and they continue to train men. That is where I trained in my youth for two years, right before I was knighted. I was offered a position to train men there, and it remains an open invitation."

Katiana was duly impressed. "What a great and noble calling," she said. "Will you accept?"

Titus shrugged. "My father does not think it is good enough for me," he said. "I am a de Wolfe, after all. He feels my calling is something more."

"What more?"

Titus shook his head slowly. "I am not certain," he said. "But something greater than a trainer, clearly."

"What is your second offer?"

He smirked. "If my father looks down upon the Kenilworth offer, then you can imagine that he would absolutely shun an offer from the Blackchurch Guild."

Her brow furrowed. "Blackchurch," she muttered thoughtfully. "I think I have heard the name. What is it?"

"Only the most elite training ground for warriors and assassins in the entire world," Titus said proudly. "Kenilworth trains noble knights to do noble deeds. But Blackchurch… they train a man to do anything and everything. The education is without limit. I've heard they even have pirates teaching men to think like a pirate. Men who pass the training there become the greatest warriors in the world, mercenaries, or knights for kings and lords, spies and assassins—anything at all. Men who pass the test are the most sought after in the world."

"How fascinating," she said. "But how do they know about you? How did you receive the offer?"

That brought Titus' conversation to a halt. They knew about him because of the Executioner Knights, something he wasn't even supposed to know anything about, much less speak about. He had been giving Katiana a pretty, noble speech about the good he wanted to do when the truth was much different. He liked serving under Morgen de Lohr as a spymaster, but in his case, his intentions really were altruistic. He felt he could do more good that way—good for the country, for his family— than simply being a knight or a garrison commander in the de Wolfe empire. The truth was that Titus had ambition that ran outside of the norm. But he couldn't tell Katiana that, for obvious reasons.

Let her think he was a humane, simple knight with normal knightly ambitions.

He was afraid of what she would think if she knew otherwise.

Odd how two days and two substantial conversations with the woman were coming to mean something to him. When he'd first seen her yesterday, he'd been thrilled. As he'd told her, the conversation had been warm and witty, something that wasn't usual in his world. And this morning… this morning, he was coming to see a woman of grace and beauty and warmth, with a sharp mind, and that was something he liked very much. Of all times in his life to find a woman he was interested in, this was probably the most inconvenient.

Even with all of his friends and brothers and family, Titus had always felt rather solitary, especially in the spy business. It *was* a lonely profession. But in two days, and two conversations, he'd caught a glimpse of something that didn't make him feel so solitary anymore.

And he liked it.

"When one has been a knight for as long as I have been, your reputation precedes you," he said vaguely. "I am a de Wolfe. My family is well known. Any reputable training guild is going to seek men like me. Offers are expected."

Katiana smiled. "I can imagine they would be," she said. "You are my champion, after all. They know you are the best, and so do I."

Titus stabbed a piece of pork and dropped it in his mouth. "Indeed, I am, my lady," he said. "Which reminds me—you told me that you were the best with a harpsichord."

She shrugged. "Mayhap not the best, but I am very practiced."

"You also said that you would play your harpsichord for me sometime."

Katiana was finished with her eggs and now sipping on the warmed, watered wine. "Of course I will," she said. "There is one at my aunt's home. Mayhap she will permit me to invite you to feast one evening, and I shall play for you."

"I do not want to wait that long."

She lifted her eyebrows in surprise. "I am afraid there is

nothing more I can do."

He grinned at her and dropped his knife, reaching across the table to take her hand. "I can."

He winked at her as he stood up, gently pulling on her so she would do the same. Puzzled, Katiana let him pull her through the common room and back into the guts of the tavern, where there were many rooms and people sprinkled through-out. It smelled of old ale and rubbish. He took her into a dingy back room in particular and proudly pointed to what looked like a wooden box with legs in the corner.

"There," he said. "I believe that is the instrument you need."

Bewildered, Katiana went over to the cabinet and opened the lid to see the customary ivory and dark keys. But it was a very small box, not at all like the instrument she was used to playing on, though it was beautifully painted and well made.

She ran her hands all over it.

"I've never seen one like this," she said with delight. "Who does it belong to?"

"The tavern keeper," Titus said, coming to stand next to her. "I told you that this is a gambling place. Men can bet on anything, and they can bet anything. One night, a man had no more coinage and bet this instrument, which he was taking home to his wife. As you can see, it never made it. I saw it when I was here once before, just sitting here and being very lonely. Play something for me."

Katiana put her fingers on the keys, and the familiar sound filled the air. It wasn't quite in tune, but good enough. She ran her hand along the top of it, noting the fine painting.

"This is exquisite," she said. "I've simply never seen one that looked like this. It's very different."

"Sit down," Titus said, pulling out the cushioned stool for

her. "Play whatever you wish."

Katiana sat down, marveling over the small, compact instrument. She thought it might be something called a clavichord, which was making a name for itself in Paris. It hadn't quite come to England yet, or so she thought, but she'd heard women speaking of it in the marketplace.

Carefully, she put her fingers on the keys, playing a chord that was surprisingly rich and full, if not slightly out of tune with some of the notes. But she didn't care. Delighted, she began to play a tune she'd learned a few years ago, a sweet love song, something most maidens had in their repertoire if they played any instruments. All women ever sang about was love and romance. As she began to play the notes in an expert fashion, her pure, high voice filled the air of the stale chamber.

Come roam with me, my love,
Come roam far with me,
Away from this hard world,
And love only me.

They said that you loved me,
They said that you cared.
They said that your strong heart,
Wasn't mine to be shared.

When she was finished, the chamber was perfectly silent. Katiana looked over her shoulder to see Titus standing there with an expression of shock upon his face. But behind him, at the chamber's wide door, stood three or four people who began demanding more when she came to a halt. Hesitant, and the least bit embarrassed, she looked at Titus for help.

But he had none to give.

"My God," he breathed. "You lied to me."

She looked at him, startled. "When did I do such a disgraceful thing?"

He came to stand beside her, his shocked expression now full of warmth. "You lied when you said you knew how to play this instrument," he said. "You did not play it. You created beauty such as I have never heard before. You touched the keys and perfection came forth. And you sing like an angel."

Realizing he'd meant it all as a compliment, Katiana blushed furiously. "I do not have many talents, but this is one of the few," she said. "I learned my lessons in music well."

He snorted at the understatement. "I would say that you did," he said. "You are astonishing in your talent. Play something else for me. Please."

Feeling flattered and the least bit giddy that he was so appreciative, she turned back to the keyboard, pondered her next song, and then began to play a haunting, delicate melody. After the first few bars, she lifted her voice.

O lovely one... my lovely one...
The years will come... the years will go...
But still you'll be... my own true love...
Until the day... we'll meet again...

O lovely one... my lovely one...
My love for you... will never die...
My heart is yours... till the end of time...
When you will be... my own true love...

When she was finished, she turned to look at him again,

only to see that he was looking at her with a smile on his lips, his eyes glittering. But the crowd in the doorway was about ten or twelve people now, and they all began cheering her, shouting out requests. Mortified, Katiana looked to Titus, who took the hint. He turned to the doorway crowded with people and waved his hands at them.

"Be gone," he barked. "The lady is playing for me and me alone. Go away or you'll not like my reaction."

Everyone scattered except for one man, and Titus recognized him. He was the tavern keep, the man who owned The Pox. His name was Griswold, but Titus didn't know anything beyond that. He pointed to the instrument.

"I hope you are agreeable that she may play it," he said. "Mayhap I should have asked permission, but I did not think of it."

Griswold was a middle-aged man with stringy, curly hair, a big gut, and fists the size of a man's head.

"It has not been played in some time," he said. "I thought I was hearing things."

"May she continue to play it?"

Griswold nodded firmly. "As long as she likes," he said. "She plays very well."

"Aye, she does."

"And she sings well."

"You've never heard better."

The corner of Griswold's mouth tugged with a smile. "Is she your lady?"

Titus turned to look at Katiana, who was inspecting the keys of the instrument. After a moment, he returned his focus to Griswold.

"She is," he said. "Why do you ask?"

Griswold pointed in her direction. "Because I was thinking…" he said, trailing off. But he picked up again quickly. "I was thinking she might teach some of my girls to play it. I would pay her well, of course, but the instrument just sits there. Imagine what my customers would think if a couple of my girls could play it. We would have music here every night."

Titus cocked an eyebrow. "My lady is from a fine family," he said. "It would not do for her to come to this place on a regular basis. I am sure you understand."

Griswold waved him off. "Of course I do," he said. "But if I made the girls bathe and dress properly, mayhap they could go to her? Does she have an instrument in your home?"

Titus rather liked the feeling of Griswold assuming he and Katiana were married and lived together. In fact, he liked it quite a bit. It gave him a feeling he'd never had before—one of belonging and pride. For the first time in his life, he felt proud of himself and of someone else. It was a strange feeling, but wholly marvelous.

"There is one," he said after a moment. "I must speak with my lady before I can agree. I will let you know what we decide."

Griswold nodded, his gaze still on Katiana as she stood up and looked inside the cabinet, fussing with something.

"You're one of the de Wolfe knights, aren't you?" he asked.

Titus nodded. "My father is the Earl of Berwick."

That made Griswold take a second look at him. "I see," he said, looking Titus up and down. "You know that you should not bring your lady in here. It's not fitting for someone of her breeding. But I'm glad you did. It was good to hear music again."

With that, he walked away. Titus watched him go before making his way back to Katiana, who was picking at the internal workings.

"Is something wrong with it?" Titus asked, peering over her shoulder.

She stepped back and brushed off her hands. "It is out of tune," she said. "I have little instruments at home for my aunt's harpsichord, but these strings are different. I'm not sure they will work."

"You know how to tune it?"

She grinned. "Fine young ladies are taught to do many things," she said. "I can even make paints if I need to."

He smiled in return. "Fascinating," he said. "And speaking of fascination, did you see me speaking with a man just now?"

She shook her head. "Nay," she said. "Why? Who was it?"

"The tavern keep," Titus said. "He was so impressed with what he heard that he wondered if you would be willing to give his wenches lessons. He said he would pay you well."

Her eyes widened. "Me?"

"You."

She appeared a bit bewildered. "I… I do not know," she said. "I suppose I could, but I do not think I would want to come back here alone to do it. How does he propose I teach them?"

"You have an instrument at your aunt's home, do you not?"

"I do."

"Then teach them there."

Katiana was clearly entertaining the suggestion. After a moment or two, a smile spread across her lips, and Titus smiled in return. She had the most beautiful smile. He nodded, and she nodded, and he held out his hand to her.

"Good," he said, clearly commenting on her reaction to the tavern keep's offer. "It would be a good way for you to make your own money. That is never a bad thing. Now, let us finish our meal. We've a spice merchant to see."

Katiana put her hand in his, and he helped her up from the stool, still holding her hand as he took her from the chamber and back into the vast common room that was starting to fill up at this time of the morning. He took her over to their table, helping her to sit and still holding her hand. When he sat down, still grasping her, Katiana began to chuckle.

"Titus?" she said.

"Aye?"

"I need my hand if I am to finish my meal."

"You have another hand. Use that one."

Her laughter grew. "Aren't you *ever* going to release my hand?"

"Probably not."

She sighed dramatically, reaching over the arm he was holding fast to collect her knife. "That may be quite inconvenient in the years to come," she said. "I do need it for some things, you know."

"You do not need it right now."

He was determined to hold her hand, and she thought it was both sweet and hilarious. He collected his cup, draining it, and then went for the pitcher. She was watching him closely, thinking this might have something to do with the marriage comments he'd made earlier. It was obvious that something was happening with him, and she wanted to know what. Whatever it was, it couldn't go any further. She knew that even if he didn't.

Or refused to.

"Titus," she finally said, her tone serious. "Why are you holding my hand?"

He had just poured himself more wine. "Because I want to."

"Why?"

"Because I like you."

"I thought we were friends."

He looked at her. "We are."

She lifted her hand, the one he was holding, to make a point. "Do you always hold your friends' hands so tightly?"

He didn't say anything for a moment. He was busy with his wine, with a last piece of buttered bread that hadn't been eaten.

"I must ask you a question," he finally said.

"What is it?"

He looked at her, full-on. "I must go away for a time," he said. "I have duties to attend to, but when I come back, I should like to see you again."

"Of course you may see me. You know where I live. You may see me anytime."

He shook his head. "That is not what I meant," he said. "You do not have to give me an answer now, but I want you to think on it."

"Think on what?"

"Whether or not you would allow me to court you."

Katiana yanked her hand away, looking at him with some horror. "You cannot ask me that, Titus," she said. "You and I… It is out of the question."

"Why?"

She was gearing up for a strong defense, because it was. For a conversation that had thus far remained pleasant and even sweet at times, the mood suddenly plummeted as she faced off against him.

"You know I am not of your social standing," she said deliberately. "You know I have nothing. No dowry, no family to speak of. We have discussed this. You must have a fine wife, an heiress, if you are to gain anything through marriage. You said yourself you have to earn it. Marriage is the best way to do that. Must I really explain this to you?"

He sat back, his manner serious. In fact, Katiana had never seen this side of him before. He wasn't looking anything like the Titus she'd seen over the past couple of days.

"I am not a man who will rely on his wife for his fortune," he said in a low voice. "I thought I made that clear. I will make my fortune on my own, through deeds and service. I would be a weak man indeed if I relied on my wife for property and money."

"It is the way things are done."

"It is the way weak men are made rich."

Katiana shook her head in exasperation. "Have it your own way," she said. "But courting me… marrying me… I cannot give you anything, Titus, and I refuse to allow myself to hope that we could have a successful marriage."

"If the past two days are any indication, we could have what most men only dream of."

Katiana sighed and averted her gaze. "You cannot base your life on two days of glory," she said softly. "We've not had to deal with anything that is real—families or money or anything else. It has only been the two of us, seeing each other again for the first time in many years. We are happy to see one another, that is true, and the past two days have been wonderful. I will not deny it. But you cannot base the rest of your life on so short an experience."

Titus knew that. He knew it all too well. But he also knew that she made him feel a way he'd never felt before. The logical part of him knew that she was right in everything she'd said, but the impulsive part—the part that sometimes ruled him—was keen to ignore it. He only knew how he felt when he was with her.

He didn't want to think about anything else.

"Let's get through the day, then," he finally said. "Let us experience more of this glory together, and then we shall discuss it again. But know that I am serious, Katia. When I return from the north, I want to court you. And I want you to let me."

Katiana could see that he was serious. She'd never seen him so serious. But she had a heart and hope to protect, and she wouldn't let either be destroyed because of Titus' refusal to face facts. But there was a large part of her that very much wanted to agree with him, damn the cost and consequences.

"Let us get through the day," she said, repeating what he'd said. "I am anxious to get to the spice merchant and show you all of his wonderful things."

Titus smiled faintly, but it was without much humor. "Then let us finish here and be gone," he said. "I'm not entirely sure where the street…"

He suddenly trailed off, catching sight of something outside the window. He was tracking something, or someone, and Katiana turned to see a big, fair-haired knight pass the front window and come in through the entry door. He was heavily armed, bearing the tunic of the royal house.

Titus was on his feet.

"Denys?" he said, calling to the man over the heads of the patrons between him and the entry door. "Over here."

Denys' head snapped in Titus' direction, and he pushed between the tables until he came to him. He didn't even look at Katiana seated at the table. He was solely focused on Titus.

"I thought I might find you here," he said, his voice low. "De Lohr sent word. He wants to see you immediately."

Titus' brow rippled with concern. "What's happened?"

Denys glanced around, finally noticing Katiana sitting at the table and looking at him curiously. His gaze lingered on her for a moment before he returned his focus to Titus.

"Not here," he muttered. "Get to Lonsdale without delay."

Titus didn't have to be told twice. He picked up his saddle-bags, digging in his purse and throwing a few coins onto the tabletop.

"I must take the lady home first," he said. "I will make all haste to Lonsdale when I am done."

"Nay," Denys said shortly. "I will take her home. You are needed now."

Titus didn't like the urgency in Denys' tone, but he didn't argue. He turned to Katiana, who was on her feet by now, and forced a smile.

"This is Sir Denys de Winter," he said. "He is the captain of the king's knights. He will see you home safely, my lady."

Katiana nodded, sensing the same apprehensive urgency that Titus was. But she didn't ask questions, nor did she argue. Titus was an important man, far too important for her. She simply nodded her head.

"Thank you," she said, addressing Denys before turning to Titus. "Be safe in your travels, Titus. And thank you for a lovely meal."

Titus nodded firmly. Then he took her hand and kissed it. Their eyes locked for a moment, and then he released her hand and quickly bolted from the table and out the front door. Katiana watched him go, not realizing there was a hand in her face until Denys cleared his throat softly.

"My lady?" he said. "May I escort you home now?"

She smiled wanly at him and headed for the door as he politely took her elbow. "I live on Coleman Street," she said. "If it is too far, I can make it home myself. I do not wish to be any trouble."

Denys grunted. "If Titus found out I allowed you to return home on your own, I would be the one in trouble," he said. "Clearly, you do not know that side of Titus. When he makes a request, it is as good as a command and is not meant to be disobeyed."

Katiana glanced at him as they passed through the entry door. "I knew Titus when he was a young man," she said. "I fostered at Roxburgh, and he was my personal protector."

"Is that so?"

"It is," she said. "His grandfather appointed him to my side."

That brought a genuine smile from Denys. "Ah," he said. "The great William de Wolfe. Another man whose requests were not meant to be disobeyed. That means you must be very important."

Katiana grinned. "Not really," she said. "But Titus seems to think so."

Denys' smile faded as he looked at her. "That," he said, "was obvious."

Katiana wasn't quite sure what he meant, but she could guess. She'd seen that look in Titus' eyes as he'd looked at her.

And so had Denys.

CHAPTER SEVEN

"**H**E'S DEAD."

Titus thought he wasn't hearing correctly. "He's *what?*" he gasped. "Who's dead?"

"Gaveston."

Titus had barely entered Morgen's cluttered solar when the news was flying out at him, fast and furious. He felt as if the words had been delivered as body blows. He came to a halt, stunned, and may have actually staggered.

His jaw dropped.

"Who told you this?" he demanded incredulously.

Morgen looked weary. Old and weary. He was sitting behind his table, the one that overlooked the River Thames, and he lifted an open missive on the tabletop, extending it to Titus.

Titus took it and read it.

"My God," he muttered when he'd read it twice. "Lancaster actually did it. He executed Gaveston."

Morgen was looking out over the river as it meandered past the manse built by his forefathers. The news had reached him earlier that morning by way of one of Pembroke's men, who had received the missive addressed to him and not to de Lohr.

Spies sometimes addressed missives to men not in a position of power, soldiers or even servants, simply to get the message through. Simple men would be overlooked if they received a missive or two.

This message was most definitely meant for de Lohr.

"I've been sitting here, thinking," he said after a moment. "What we are dealing with is nothing compared to what my great-grandfather had to deal with. What William Marshal had to deal with during the reign of Richard and subsequently John. I remember hearing stories from my grandfather about the lengths John would go to in order to steal a kingdom from his brother. Christopher de Lohr and William Marshal had to contend with two warring brothers, but once again, we are dealing with a king so hated by his warlords that they would do anything to punish him and bring him to his knees. Even killing his favorite. But in this case, it will not work in their favor, not as they had hoped."

Titus knew that. He'd been playing this game long enough to know what all of this meant.

"And it begins," he muttered ominously. "The tides will shift in Edward's direction. In truth, Lancaster and Warwick have done Edward a great favor. Gaveston was the sacrifice, though I'm not sure Edward will see it that way, at least not at first. But when he sees the warlords lining up to support him against the ambitious Lancaster, he will realize this was for the best."

Morgen shrugged weakly. "This is a crushing blow to the rebellion," he said. "I intend to send Lancaster a strongly worded missive declaring that, precisely. Lancaster could not have done more damage to the resistance had he deliberately tried. I intend to declare my support of Edward, so Lancaster will know he has lost the southern marches. I am not entirely sure what Warwick and Gloucester will do, but I suspect Warwick will side with Lancaster, since he was part of Gaveston's execution. And Gloucester…"

"You may have war on your doorstep, my lord."

Morgen knew that. "That is true, but I have powerful allies, everywhere, that will support me," he said. "Not that I need their support, however, because I have one of the largest standing armies in England. But it is good to know I have support from all corners of England, which brings me to my next point. You must ride to Berwick and tell your father. Tell him that Northumberland must be secured from Lancaster and his allies, at all costs."

Titus nodded. "I will leave today," he said. "But after I deliver the message, where would you have me go? Shall I go to Warwick, as we planned?"

Morgen shook his head. "Not now," he said with some irony. "Lancaster has already lowered the ax, so to speak, so there is no longer any reason for you to go there. Return to your father and remain under his command for now. If I need you, I will send for you."

Titus nodded. "As you wish," he said. He started to turn for the door but came to an unsteady halt. "You know my father will want to know if you wish to have him send men to Lioncross Abbey. Berwick is far removed from the turmoil that will engulf the Welsh marches if you lend your support for the king because your close neighbors Warwick and Gloucester might have something to say about it. He will want to send you help."

Morgen looked over his shoulder at him. "I will gladly take any men he wishes to send me."

That had Titus coming away from the door and back toward Morgen. There was something in the man's manner that concerned him beyond normal concern. "You are worried, aren't you?" he said, almost accusingly. "You are worried that Warwick and Lancaster might do something drastic."

Morgen shrugged. "I would be a foolish man if I did not prepare for my unhappy neighbors," he said. "Pembroke and I will create a very large, united front, something Lancaster and his allies cannot break. De Lara holds the mid-marches, and he will side with me. Further north sees an alliance with your family, the hereditary kings of Anglesey, so I do not see any of us falling to Lancaster and his scorched-earth campaign when he realizes we are no longer with him. But there will be trouble, have no doubt. Tell your father to send me only what he can spare, because I suspect, at some point, Lancaster will try to move into Northumberland."

Titus waved him off. "Between my uncles and my father, we have tens of thousands of men protecting our properties," he said. "Northumberland belongs to de Wolfe, and Lancaster would be foolish to move against us."

"True. But we also thought he would be foolish to execute Gaveston."

He had a point. Titus conceded that with a nod of his head. "Right," he said, turning for the door once more. "In that case, I shall leave for Berwick today. I must gather my things first, but I will be out of the city before the sun sets."

"Ride swiftly, Titus."

Titus paused at the door. "Even if I ride swiftly, it will take twelve or more days for me to reach Berwick," he said. "I will move as quickly as I can, but it will take time."

Morgen knew that. "You can only do your best," he said.

"But Titus… if it comes down to war, remain with your father. Remain at Berwick. You will not come into the heat of the fighting under any circumstances."

Titus looked at him strangely. "Why not?"

Morgen fixed him in the eye. "Because I may lose several agents in this war," he said ominously. "If I do, then I must have experienced agents to rely on once the fighting is over. I will need men like you."

Titus understood. He didn't like it, but he understood. Men like Bax de Velt would be in the middle of it, forced into the war by the very men they were assigned to spy on. There were others on the front line, so Titus well understood Morgen's request. He needed some of his agents to stay alive.

Titus hoped he was able to comply.

Something told him that it was going to be a challenge.

CHAPTER EIGHT

"I T CAME EARLY this morning, darling, while you were out to the spice merchant."

Standing in the entry hall of the enormous manse on Coleman Street that had belonged to generations of de Edingtons, Katiana found herself looking at a broken seal and an open envelope. Having just returned from her morning adventure with Titus, she was at a loss that her nosey aunt had already read the contents.

"And you read it?" she said, perturbed. "It is addressed to me."

Ethyl de Edington didn't seem concerned. An old woman with a crown of gray hair, round and pretty, she had lived her life as a spinster in a fine home and was queen of her domain. That meant she read any missive that came into the house, whether or not it was addressed to her.

"I know," she said evenly. "I'm sorry to say that my brother is not doing well. You are requested to return to Callerton Castle with all due haste."

Puzzled, but still quite annoyed, Katiana read the contents. It was very simple, actually. Just a few words that were not in her father's writing. She'd seen his hand before, and this wasn't it.

Puzzlement won out.

"He's dying?" she said. "But who wrote this?"

Ethyl went to her and plucked it right out of her hand. She peered at the careful writing. "A scribe," she said as if it was some great mystery. "A priest? Someone who is learned. The writing is quite fine. That suggests education."

Katiana looked at the woman, finding her behavior odd. "This speaks of your brother," she said. "Are you not concerned?"

Ethyl shrugged, handing the missive back to her. "As concerned as he would be for me should I be dying," she said as she turned for the hall. "Come with me, darling. Let us discuss your return to Callerton Castle."

As concerned as he would be for her, meaning not at all. Ethyl had no love for her nephew and had never made any secret of it. She took her grandniece into the hall of the de Edington manse, a house with no name when most usually did simply to identify the structure and the family. But not de Edington. The locals mostly called it Lady Ethyl's house.

And it was.

"I wish the missive said more," Katiana said as she followed Ethyl into the chamber. She stopped to look at it once again. "It says absolutely nothing. How long has he been ill? What is his illness?"

"Does it matter?" Ethyl said, tinkling a silver bell on the table to summon the servants. "He is dying, and that is all you need know. I will send you back to Callerton with a pair of stable servants. They will ride with you as your escort."

Katiana was still looking at the missive, even as she took a seat at the table as several servants rushed forth with wine and trays of the sweets her aunt had a fondness of. It was close to the nooning hour, after Titus had returned her very quickly before they could even make it to the spice merchant. He'd given her an excuse that he had been summoned for something important, and she didn't push him. His business was no concern of hers. In truth, she was simply grateful he'd spent any time with her at all.

It had already been an eventful morning.

Titus had left her with a promise of calling on her again, very soon, as he apologized that their morning did not go as planned. He'd had Denys return her home, but Katiana well remembered her last vision of Titus as he departed the tavern and disappeared from view.

From view perhaps, but not from her mind.

In fact, she couldn't stop thinking of him, even in the wake of the missive that she had received. She was going to return to Northumberland, to Callerton Castle, and all she could think of was to tell Titus that she was leaving. He never said when he'd return to call on her, and she didn't want him to come to the manse only to discover she wasn't there. She would have to make sure one of the servants told him where she had gone, because she surely didn't want Aunt Ethyl to do it. If the old lady sank her claws in to him, thinking he was a good marriage prospect for her grandniece, he'd never get away.

And marriage wasn't something that was possible between them.

Sadly enough.

"I suppose that is well enough," she belatedly replied to her aunt's offer of an escort. "As I recall, we go north through Nottingham and Leeds. Callerton is near Ripon."

"I know where it is, dear girl," the old woman said, delving into the platter of delectables in front of her. "The servants will know the way. They will make sure you arrive safely."

Katiana set the missive on the tabletop, moodily slouching in her chair. "I must leave right away."

Ethyl shoved a sweet into her mouth, made from chopped chestnuts soaked in wine, cinnamon, honey, and coated with a honeyed shell. "Everything can be ready on the morrow," she said, chewing. "In fact, I'll send my major-domo to make all of the arrangements. Would you like to take my cart, dearest? The one-horse cart that is gaily bedecked with blue and red paint? I cannot drive it any longer, as it is too taxing on my hands and arms, but you can use it if you wish. It might be more comfortable to travel in than on the back of a horse."

Katiana smiled weakly. "That is very gracious, Auntie," she said. "It will carry my baggage easily."

"It will," Ethyl agreed. "Put it on the back. It has a little place for it. Ah, I used to drive that carriage around when I was a young woman. It was quite sporting, truly. I made quite a sight on the streets of London with my white horse pulling that lovely carriage. I must make sure the wheels are still steady. It has been sitting for some time."

With that, she rang for her major-domo, a rather handsome younger man she simply liked to keep around. He was not particularly bright, but he was eager. When he appeared, Ethyl told him what was happening and what was needed, and the man went off to ensure that everything was prepared. Feeling gloomy, as preparations for her trip home were in the works, Katiana reached out and plucked one of the sweets off the tray in front of her, the same wine-soaked chestnuts, and popped it in her mouth. It really was quite delicious, but it wasn't enough to take her mind off the change in her immediate future.

Her father was dying.

She was much like her aunt in that she was somewhat ambivalent to it, but she didn't hate her father like Ethyl did. Katiana didn't have any profoundly happy memories of him, either. He was simply her father, who had sent her away at a very young age and didn't seem to want her around very much. The only thing he'd really made an effort at was keeping her separated from her brother, and that had only been after the disastrous time in her life when they'd both been fostering at Roxburgh Castle. Ansel had made it his mission in life to beat on his younger sister, for whatever reason, and even an apathetic father like Paulus had been aware of that. That was why Katiana hadn't seen her brother in almost fifteen years. But if she had received a missive regarding her father's health, then surely Ansel had received one, too.

That meant she would more than likely see him at some point.

Already, she was nervous.

The nooning meal came at some point after that, but Katiana didn't feel much like eating. She'd already eaten four of the wine-soaked treats, but it wasn't that. It was the simple fact that now Ansel was on her mind when he hadn't been for years. Excusing herself from the hall with the ploy that she needed to start packing, she left the chamber and hurried up to her room, an enormous bower that overlooked the street. She loved to watch people, and did so, frequently, from the bench seat built into the window. But today, there would be no people-watching.

She had bags to pack.

Pulling out a trunk and two smaller capcases, she began to

pull forth items from her wardrobe. She had a talent for organization, so in little time, she had neat piles of clothing—shifts, dresses, surcoats, stockings, and the like. Though she was working as if she was focused on her task, the truth was that her mind was wandering.

Thinking.

Apprehensive.

Thoughts of Ansel wouldn't leave her. Undoubtedly, the same person who sent her the message had also sent Ansel one. There was no doubt in her mind. The last she heard, he was at Thornton Tower serving an old friend of her father's. Katiana knew the de Allery family, the family that inhabited Thornton Tower, because they had a daughter her age. Zora de Allery had fostered at one of the de Wolfe properties and been at every party Katiana had attended when they were younger. She had been at every de Wolfe feast, and every gathering—anything that involved the de Wolfe family. Katiana and Zora had not exactly been friends, but they hadn't been enemies, either. Zora seemed to want friends who were from more powerful families, and Katiana simply didn't fall into that category.

Katiana was certain that, these days, Zora was married. Surely she had married into a fine family and was rich beyond measure. Ansel was serving her father because that was what Paulus wanted, though she wondered if that situation had ruined the alliance between Thornton Tower and Callerton Castle. Ansel had always been a wicked soul, and she couldn't imagine he had outgrown that. She remembered hearing the knights at Roxburgh speak of her brother being a bad seed, something she didn't really understand because she was so young, but something she came to understand very well as she grew older.

The fact was that she didn't disagree.

Ansel *was* evil.

She could only imagine that he'd grown more wicked as the years went by. She could only imagine what kind of man he was now, and how surely that must have been damaging to the de Allery household. But her father, who had always shown apathy toward his children, probably considered his own son another man's problem. Living in London as she had over the past few years, Katiana had been removed from all of that. Now, unfortunately, she was going to have to face it again.

She was going to have to face Ansel again.

The more she thought about it, the more apprehensive she became.

So she tried to focus on packing, or at least pretend she was focused on packing, trying to keep the fingers of fear from clutching at her. They grabbed at her even now as she began placing her neat stacks of clothing into her trunk, because she realized that she was packing to return home again. To face her brother again. To face their life that she had been happy to leave behind.

Soon, she would no longer be able to avoid it.

"My lady?"

A soft rap on the door distracted her, and she turned to see one of her aunt's maids enter. The woman's name was Anne, and she probably spent more time with Katiana than she did with Ethyl, who had many maids. Anne was older, and Ethyl liked to surround herself with younger folk because it made her feel younger to be the center of a younger crowd, so Anne was often sent away to attend to Katiana or to more mundane things in the house. Katiana smiled weakly when she saw the woman.

"I'm sure you have heard the news," she said. "I must return to Callerton Castle with all due haste. Aunt Ethyl says that I shall leave tomorrow."

Anne nodded, but she stood by the door, seemingly nervous. "I've not come about that, my lady," she said. "There's someone… There is a knight here to see you."

Katiana looked up sharply from her trunk. "A knight?" she repeated. "What knight?"

Anne put her fingers to her lips to quiet her. "Your aunt does not know, my lady," she said, whispering loudly. "The knight asked that we not alert her. He has only come to see you, and he is in the yard, at the kitchen door."

Katiana's brow furrowed. "Who in the world is it?"

"He gave his name as Titus de Wolfe, my lady."

Katiana fled her bedchamber and down the corridor before she even realized she had moved. Suddenly, she was racing to where Titus was, down in the kitchen. She had no idea why he was here, but she suspected that it could not be good. He said he would return to call upon her, but he'd never said when. Surely, he could not have meant in a few hours.

She would soon find out.

Truthfully, she wasn't running because she was concerned. She was running because she wanted to see him again. She didn't even know why she'd asked Anne who the caller was, because it could be no one else but Titus. It wasn't as if she knew a herd of knights who came around the back door, asking to speak with her.

It could have only been one.

By the time she hit the kitchen, she was flushed from running down all those stairs. The kitchen was steamy at this time of day as things were boiled or cooked or heated. She pushed through the servants, several of whom seemed to congregate near the kitchen door, and Katiana could hardly blame them. Her gaze fell on tall, dark, and handsome Titus lingering by the back door, his hair catching the light of the sun, and she had to pull the cook's assistant away from the door in order to get to him.

"Titus?" she said almost incredulously. "What are you doing here?"

He turned to her quickly when he heard the sound of her voice, his features lighting up at the sight of her.

"I'm very sorry to intrude," he said. "I want to be as inconspicuous as possible, but I seem to have drawn a crowd."

Katiana turned to see about a dozen maids and kitchen servants standing behind her, very nearly all of them fawning over Titus. Not that there wasn't a good deal to fawn over, but it struck her as being particularly hilarious. Biting off a grin, she moved through the door and shut it behind her, shutting out all of those longing expressions.

"You will have to forgive them," she said. "It is not often that they see such a handsome young man. But I fear our time is limited before rumors of your beauty reach my aunt, who has a penchant for fine young lads. You'd better state your business in a hurry before she comes."

He scowled. "A penchant?" he said. "What does she do? Eat them?"

Katiana broke down into laughter. "Nay," she said. "But she fancies them. She never married, but that does not mean she does not appreciate a handsome man."

He cocked an eyebrow, almost fearfully. "You never told me that."

"You never asked."

That was true. Titus was trying not to chuckle as he reached out and took her hand, pulling her with him as he walked away from the kitchens with its doors and windows where nosey servants could eavesdrop.

"Then let me indulge in the last few moments of privacy with you," he said. "But the truth is that I cannot stay even if your aunt demands it. I've been summoned home. I am leaving London tonight."

Katiana's features fell. "Leaving?" she said. "Oh, Titus… I hope it is not terrible news?"

He shook his head. "Nay," he said. "My father has summoned me home, but as you know, there is a good deal of turmoil in England right now, and I suspect he simply wants me out of London. But I could not leave without telling you. Without saying what a marvelous two days I have had with you. I'd forgotten what it was like to be happy in a way that a man can be when he's smitten with a beautiful woman. It has meant a great deal to me."

Katiana's smile returned because it was a sweet thing to say. "I echo the sentiment," she said. "You brought joy into my world, Titus. It is time with my champion that I shall always treasure."

He smiled because she was, but it was clear he wanted to say more. "I do not know when I will return," he said hesitantly. "But I do not… When I do come back, I hope you will let me call on you again."

"Anytime you wish," she said. "I will be here. Well, I suppose I will. You see, you are not the only one who has been summoned home. I received word this morning, whilst I was out with you, that my father is dying. I will be leaving for Callerton Castle on the morrow."

He grew very serious. "I'm very sorry to hear that, Katia," he said. "I did not know your father, but I know he has long been a de Wolfe ally."

Katiana nodded. "He was always proud of that."

"Has an escort been sent for you?"

She shook her head. "My aunt is sending me north with a couple of stable servants," she said. "She is letting me use her small carriage so the ride will be more comfortable."

Titus stared at her. Then a look of bewilderment rippled across his face. "Servants to escort you?" he said, aghast. "To protect you? What madness is this?"

She shrugged. "Not madness, I assure you," she said. "Auntie does not employ soldiers, but she has an army of servants to do her bidding. She can spare a couple."

"That's the most foolish thing I've ever heard of."

"Foolish or not, that is all she can offer."

"Does your aunt even realize what lurks on the road between London and Northumberland?"

"I do not know, but she must. Surely she must."

He looked at her as if she had lost her mind, and before Katiana realized what was happening, he'd grabbed her by the hand and was pulling her back toward the kitchen door.

"Titus?" she said, concerned. "What is the matter? Where are you going?"

He came to the door and threw it open, startling a half-dozen servants that were still standing there.

"Announce me," he said simply.

Now it was Katiana's turn to look at him as if he'd been robbed of his senses. "Announce you to whom?" she asked.

He charged on into the kitchen. "Your aunt," he said patiently. "Take me into your hall and summon your aunt. I wish to speak with her."

Katiana's eyebrows lifted in surprise. "You want to—"

He cut her off, though not harshly. "Is the hall through there?"

He was pointing to a doorway that led to a servants' hall and then the main living area beyond. Katiana nodded unsteadily, and he continued on, pulling her behind him all the way. Once they reached the main entry area, with wooden-paneled walls painted with birds and, strangely, swords and maces, he let go of her hand and gestured for her to call for her aunt. When a nice-looking young man appeared from another chamber, Katiana sent him in search of Ethyl.

They didn't have long to wait.

As suspected, word of a handsome knight seeking Katiana had gotten back to Ethyl with lightning speed. She was already on the move when her major-domo found her and, in a flurry of silk and heavily rose-scented perfume that smelled more like tallow than the flowery smell, she appeared down the stairwell, her gaze immediately finding Titus as he stood in the middle of the entry.

"Katia!" she gasped. "I heard you had a suitor call upon you. Will you not introduce me to this handsome young knight?"

Katiana could already see her aunt lusting after Titus. That was clear the moment she laid eyes on him.

"This is Sir Titus de Wolfe, Auntie," she said. "His father is the Earl of Berwick. I fostered at Roxburgh Castle when I was a young lass, and he fostered there, too. We are old and good friends."

"De Wolfe!" Ethyl lit up. "Your family owns the north!"

Titus could see, in those few words, that Ethyl de Edington was more than likely a bold, foolish old woman who was influenced by money and politics. He already didn't like her. The only saving grace was the fact that Katiana said they got on well, so for her sake, he would be polite.

But already, he knew it was going to be a struggle.

"My lady," he greeted Ethyl evenly. "My family is indeed from the north. I was born in Berwick."

"How delightful," Ethyl said, going to him and standing a bit too close with her tallow-rose scent. "We are honored with your visit. Will you come into the hall and allow us to show you our hospitality?"

Titus shook his head. "With regret, I cannot stay," he said. "I had come to tell Lady Katiana that I was heading home to Berwick immediately, but she has told me of her intention to head north as well."

Ethyl wasn't happy that she wouldn't have a man in her hall, one she could ply with wine and perhaps even steal a kiss from. "Aye," she said. "That is true."

"She said you were sending her north with two servants as escort."

Ethyl looked at Katiana, now trying to figure out where the conversation was going. "That is all I can spare," she said. "She will be quite safe, I am sure."

Titus shook his head. "Forgive me, my lady, but I am equally sure she will not be," he said. "I would, therefore, ask permission to ride escort for Lady Katiana. She and I will travel the same road, and it would be no trouble at all to see her safely to Callerton Castle."

Katiana's eyes widened. She truly had no idea of Titus' motives when he'd asked to be introduced to her aunt, but quickly, she looked at Ethyl, who seemed positively delighted at the request.

"Sir Titus, the honor is ours," the old woman said, looking to Katiana gleefully. "Did you hear that? He wishes to be your escort!"

Katiana nodded to her aunt's obvious question. "Of course I heard him, Auntie," she said. But then she looked at Titus hesitantly. "Are you certain, Titus? I would not wish to be a burden."

His eyes took on a warm glow as he looked at her. "You could never be that," he said. "And I can sleep at night knowing I am your protection and not two weary servants. It is settled, then?"

He was looking at Ethyl at this point, who nodded fervently. "Settled, indeed," she said. "How thrilling! Come, we must celebrate!"

She grasped him by the arm and tried to pull him into her lavish hall, but he politely resisted.

"Again, my apologies," he said, nicely but firmly. "I simply do not have the time. I have a few things to attend to, but I will be here before dawn. Make sure Lady Katiana is prepared to travel lightly. We must move swiftly."

"Lightly?" Katiana found her tongue. "But I shall be driving my aunt's small conveyance. It will carry my trunk and other things."

Titus shook his head. "No trunk," he said. "A satchel is all you can bring, because you will be riding with me. It will be safer and swifter."

"No trunk for a lady?" Ethyl said, outraged. "That is unheard of, my lord. A lady must have her things."

Titus smiled politely at her but returned his attention to Katiana. "A small satchel only, please," he said. "I will see you upon the morrow."

He started to turn for the door, but Katiana came up behind him. "Wait," she said. "I thought you said you were leaving tonight?"

Titus paused. "I can wait until tomorrow morning," he said. "I should not like to take you out of the city after dark, so I will wait."

Katiana was still rather overwhelmed with his offer. She glanced at her aunt, who was several feet away and looking rather puzzled, before returning her attention to Titus.

"Are you sure?" she said softly. "You do not have to do this, Titus."

He gave her a half-grin. "I am your champion," he said. "Do you truly think I would let you travel north without a proper escort? It is my duty, Katia."

"But…!"

"My grandfather made you my duty long ago, and I am not one to shirk duties, so be ready at dawn," he said before she could protest. "And tell your aunt there is no need for servants. I will travel better without them."

Katiana sighed. "You know better than to suggest two un-married people travel alone," she pointed out. "The servants must come, for propriety's sake."

He made a face suggesting that he knew she was right but was unhappy with it just the same. "Very well," he snapped softly. "But they had better be upon swift mounts. I will not wait for them if they move slowly."

"Aye, commander."

"That's lord commander to you."

She burst out laughing, soft giggles that buoyed the mood between them. He was about to take her hand and kiss it, but thought better of it with Lady Ethyl watching every move he made. He suspected she might not be so inclined to allow Katiana to travel with him if he was openly kissing her hand, or anything else, on her person. He had the woman's permission and wanted to keep it. With a wink to Katiana, he fled the manse.

At dawn the next day, she was waiting along with a male and female servant while Aunt Ethyl remained inside and sulked. If Titus wasn't going to flirt with her, or show respect for her home or her position, then she had no use for him.

But Katiana did.

For her, the journey north had begun.

CHAPTER NINE

Callerton Castle

I T STILL LOOKED the same.

It also smelled and felt the same. It smelled like his father and felt like generations of his family's failures. Although Ansel hadn't been home to Callerton Castle in years, it hadn't changed. Nothing had changed.

It was still the same dingy place he hated.

He'd received a strange, oddly worded summons about two weeks prior, one telling him that his father was dying and he was to come home. He hadn't recognized the writing, and nor had Lord de Allery, so Ansel wasn't entirely certain that it wasn't some sort of trick. Perhaps there was an ambush waiting for him. He waited two weeks before making any attempt to come home, and only then with the use of about fifty de Allery soldiers. Lord de Allery wasn't exactly agreeable to letting Ansel take them, but Ansel had taken them regardless of his liege's opinion, because that's what he did—Lord de Allery denied him and he did what he wanted anyway.

And here he was.

Ansel had been admitted through the gatehouse of Callerton Castle only because he was recognized by one of the older sergeants, but he was told to keep the de Allery men outside. Ansel agreed until the gates opened, and then he ordered the de Allery men to charge inside. A brief fight had broken out, and a couple of de Edington men were wounded as the de Allery men took over the gatehouse and shut out the de Edington army. It was vastly confusing for them when they were called off from retaking their gatehouse by Ansel, their lord's son, so they backed away.

It was a very strange standoff in the bailey as Ansel made his way inside Callerton's round keep.

Inside, it smelled the way it always did—of dust and mold, of dogs and urine. The keep had always had a stink to it. There was no one to meet him, so he took the stairs two at a time, up to his father's chamber. He didn't even knock—he simply shoved the door open, removing his gauntlets as he did so. His gaze fell on the only occupant in the chamber, his father, as the man looked startled to see him.

"Ansel!" he rasped. "You… you are here!"

Ansel tossed his gloves onto a worn table against the wall. He was several feet away from his father, appraising the man as one would appraise something disdainful. There was no affection there, only duty, and sometimes not even that.

"I thought you would be dead by now," he finally said. "The missive made it sound as if you were on death's door."

Paulus could hear the disappointment in his son's voice. Disappointment that he wasn't dead yet, and that told him everything he needed to know.

It was still the same Ansel.

"I will be gone soon enough," he said. "Now that you are

here to make sure of it, it could be sooner than expected."

Ansel stared at him for a moment before breaking into a grin. "I would not think to hasten your death," he said. "Not when there are so many things to discuss. Isn't that what I'm supposed to say? That it is time for us to make amends for years of a desolate relationship?"

Paulus coughed, a low and slow heave that shook his entire body. It took him a moment to catch his breath. "Say it all you like, but it is not true," he said. "You and I are too much alike, Ansel. There is no sentiment involved. Only ambition. Only greed."

Ansel nodded in agreement. "True," he said. "Everything I learned, I learned from you."

"And you learned well."

"Then you know why I have come."

"Of course I do."

Ansel took a long, deep breath before sitting down in the nearest chair. He faced his father expectantly.

"Well?" he said. "Then tell me. Where is the money?"

Paulus coughed again before answering. "There is none."

The smug look faded from Ansel's face. "What do you mean by that?"

"What do you think I mean?" Paulus said, finding a surge of strength against his greedy son. "I mean that there is none. What money there was vanished long ago. It is all gone. You will inherit a big castle, an army, six villages that have been taxed into the ground, and no money. They only way you can get money is to sell it. That is what I have left you, Ansel."

Ansel couldn't believe his ears. He stared at his father as if the man had gone mad before finally shaking his head in disbelief. "Nay," he said. "That is not true. Callerton always had a fortune."

"Not any longer."

"Handed down from father to son."

"Listen to me, boy. There *is* no money."

Ansel was coming to realize that his father wasn't joking. At least, he was trying to convince Ansel that the family was destitute.

His eyes narrowed.

"You're lying," he growled. "Where is the money, Father?"

"Gone. It has long been gone."

Ansel bolted to his feet. "That is not true," he snarled. "Stop lying to me, or this will not go well for you."

"Is that a threat?" Paulus said, mildly amused. "Then, by all means, threaten me. Kill me. But if you do that, then you will never know if I am truly lying to you or not. But if you are smart, you will believe what I am telling you and listen to what I have to say. For once in your life, shut your mouth and listen to me. Will you do this?"

Ansel began to pace around like an enraged bull. "Damn you," he said. "Damn you for doing this. What did you do with the money? How did you lose it?"

Paulus watched his son twitch. "That does not matter, because it was mine to do with as I pleased," he said. "It was never yours, Ansel, but if you listen to me, I will tell you how to gain a treasure worthy of a prince."

Ansel snorted at whatever scheme his father was preparing to spout forth because whatever it was, he already didn't like it. But he had little choice.

"Go on, then," he snapped.

Paulus was studying him carefully. "Your sister has been summoned home as well," he said. "You've not seen her in years, but trust me when I tell you that she grew into a fair beauty. I sent her to London to live with Ethyl in the hope that the old cow could find her a husband."

Ansel rolled his eyes before plopping down in the chair once more. "Why are you telling me this?" he demanded. "When you die, Katia becomes my problem. How old is she now? And still not married? No man will want an old maid for a bride."

"Untrue," Paulus said. "A woman of your sister's beauty is highly prized. You just have to find the right… buyer."

Ansel was about to roll his eyes again, but his father's tone had him looking at the man. "Buyer?" he repeated. "What do you mean by that?"

Paulus snorted, a horrible, wet sound. "Think like a man with a head for business, Ansel," he said. "Think like the greedy bastard that you are. Your sister is old for a bride, but she is beautiful. She would not be too old for a rich widower who was looking for a woman to bear him more sons, or for a Spanish mercenary who would pay handsomely for an English beauty. You are looking at your sister as a burden when she could bring you your fortune if you find the right buyer. *Now* do you understand?"

Ansel did. He sat back, kicking his feet out as he leaned against the wall, not nearly as agitated as he had been only moments earlier.

"Sell her to the highest bidder," he finally said.

Paulus nodded. "Mayhap there is a Northman who wants a woman to cook and clean for him and bear his children somewhere," he said. "The point is that you can use her to gain your fortune. That way, she is no longer your burden, and you have the money you want. See how simple it is?"

"Mayhap."

Paulus waved him off. "You will see," he said. "But the one thing you must do with her is keep her safe. Do not hit her or strike her. Do not mar her in any way. No man will want to buy damaged goods. You must take the best care possible of her if you are to get the highest price. Do you understand this?"

Ansel pondered that, thinking that it was perhaps a good idea, while Paulus watched his features ripple with his thoughts. Furrowed brow, a hint of a smile… Ansel had never been very good at concealing his thoughts.

But Paulus was.

In truth, it horrified him to make such a suggestion, but he had no choice. Right after he'd told the priest to take his coffer and give it to Katiana, he'd discovered that the same priest had run off with his money. What he told Ansel was the truth— there *was* no money. His suggestion to sell Katiana for a high price was to both satisfy Ansel's greed and to send Katiana far away from her brother with a man who had paid a good price for her. Men did not usually abuse or mistreat things they paid a great deal for, so it was the only way Paulus could think of to save his daughter, tragic as it was.

Now, if Ansel only fell for it. His son was intelligent, but he wasn't particularly sharp at times. His thoughts were very basic, but strong. He strongly loved money and power. He strongly loved battle and could fight with the best of them. But he had always been cruel to his sister, so if he thought he could get money out of her, then he would do so. Ansel's greed would be Katiana's salvation. Otherwise, Paulus was fearful of her future under her brother's care after he was gone.

"Well?" Paulus said after a few moments. "Do you agree to my plan for your sister?"

Ansel had been mulling over the entire situation. When his father spoke, he looked at the man before rising from his chair again and approaching the bed.

"I do," he said. "There are even brothels in London who will pay a high price for a virgin. If she *is* a virgin."

That suggestion made Paulus' blood run cold, but he didn't show it. "See if you can find her a husband first," he said. "You may get more money for her that way, and, truthfully, you do not want to condemn her to life in a brothel. Your mother would not like that."

Ansel shrugged. "That does not concern me, since the bitch never did anything much for me."

"She gave you life."

Ansel didn't have anything to say to that. He stood at the edge of the bed, looking toward the lancet windows and seemingly lost in thought. But after several moments, he finally scratched his chin and returned his attention to his father.

"I will do what I must in order to gain the best price," he said. "You said that she is on her way here?"

Paulus nodded. "She should be," he said. "Word was sent to her the same time it was sent to you."

Ansel cocked his head thoughtfully. "But London is far away," he said. "It will take her time to get here. And how is dear Aunt Ethyl?"

"Still an old hag."

That made Ansel grin. "And hopefully close to death," he said. "When she dies, her manse becomes mine."

"That is true."

"And when you die, Callerton and everything else becomes mine."

"That is also true."

"Time to die, old man."

With that, he yanked the pillow out from underneath Paulus' head and came down on the man with his full body weight, the pillow slammed down over his face. Paulus began yelling and coughing as Ansel held the pillow down tightly, smothering the life from his father. Weak as he was, it still took several long minutes for Paulus to lose consciousness, and after that, Ansel kept the pillow over his face until his father's chest stopped heaving and the man lay still. Then, and only then, did he remove the pillow, put it back under his head, and quit the chamber.

At the bottom of the stairs, Ansel ran into a servant. He told the man that Paulus had requested he not be disturbed for the rest of the night, not even for sup, so the servant spread the word to the kitchen. Ansel dined on boiled mutton later than night as his father lay dead in the chamber above him, but no one knew that until the next morning when a servant discovered Paulus cold and stiff in his bed. Word spread quickly to Ansel, who played the grieving son for about an hour. That was all he could muster. Callerton Castle, officially, was his.

And so was a sister who would soon make her way back home and into his care.

Ansel had plans for Katiana.

CHAPTER TEN

*L*UTON*... *HARTWELL... LUTTERWORTH...*

Those were the names of the villages they'd passed through so far. Even with the servants tagging along, they'd moved swiftly because the roads had been good. At this time of year, there was usually a good deal of rain, but it had been an unusually dry season. That meant the roads were passable, and the small towns they passed through weren't seas of mud, human waste, and filth.

But it also meant they would reach their destination sooner rather than later.

Katiana didn't like that prospect at all.

Because of the servants tagging along, Titus hadn't engaged in the usual banter with her. When it was just the two of them, he spoke freely and frequently, but with the servants, Katiana was coming to sense that he didn't want an audience. In fact, he seemed insulted that the servants had to come along at all and that he didn't have Katiana to himself.

That's where Ethyl had been cunning.

She sent a female servant to sleep with Katiana so a certain knight couldn't circumvent the rules of propriety. It was clear to

Katiana that the servant had been told to stay with her at all times. It was hilarious, but it was also frustrating, because Katiana had been hoping the trip north would have seen her and Titus having hours of lovely conversation, building a friendship between them. Or perhaps even more. But the "even more" was the problem—Katiana knew there couldn't be "even more," so perhaps the female servant was for the best.

As much as she didn't like it.

Still, she was able to be close to him. She rode on the back of his warhorse, an enormous animal who went by the highly unlikely name of Jesus. It was a blasphemous name, and the first time Katiana heard Titus shout at the horse because he had been behaving in a naughty fashion, she thought that he had been cursing. But the first night when they'd stopped for food and shelter and she heard him say that he needed to "feed Jesus," she was forced to clarify who, exactly, Jesus was.

Jesus was a big, beautiful gray warhorse.

But Jesus had a mischievous streak. He would nip, jump, and snort. He didn't particularly like having two people ride him, so he kept swinging his big head, trying to snap at Titus. Titus would slap the big neck, or smack the nose, and every so often he'd mutter "ridiculous Jesus" or "ridiculous beast." The horse would behave for a time, but the second night when Titus lifted Katiana from the horse and set her on her feet, Jesus swung his big tail and caught her across the face. Titus had shouted at him.

Damnation, Jesus!

The days had been long and the nights had been lonely. Titus pushed their little group hard during the day, and they'd been able to cover thirty to thirty-five miles at a stretch. He would find an inn at nightfall and always made sure that

Katiana had a hot meal, which she would try to pay for, but he wouldn't allow it. He made sure she had a warm bed and a meal in the morning before they departed and, so far, had paid for everything. That made Katiana uncomfortable, as Ethyl had sent her with money to cover the trip, but Titus didn't seem concerned by it.

But he did seem distant.

On their fifth day of travel, she discovered why.

They'd stopped on the outskirts of Leicester about two hours before sunset. Up until that day, Titus had been intent on traveling until dark. He didn't waste any daylight. But on this day, they stopped early, and he found a tavern called Christ the King, which seemed particularly fitting given the name of Titus' horse. Jesus was taken across the road to stay in, appropriately, a stable with a manger, while Titus escorted Katiana into the tavern, with the servants bringing the baggage behind them.

Titus left the three of them standing just inside the door while he went to find the tavern keep and make the arrangements for rooms for the evening. Though Katiana and the female servant had slept in the same chamber, Titus refused to have the male servant in the same room with him, so the man was relegated to sleeping in the common room. Katiana stood with the servants, watching Titus as he struck a deal with the tavern keep. When he seemed satisfied, he came back over to the door where his small party was waiting.

"You two," he said, pointing to the servants. "Take the baggage and follow the tavern keep. He will show you where we are sleeping. You are to stay to those rooms and not leave them for any reason."

The servants looked confused by the order, looking at one another, before the male spoke.

"We are to… to sleep in the chambers, my lord?" he asked. "*I* am to sleep in the chambers?"

Given that he'd spent the last several nights in an open room, Titus understood the confusion, but he was oddly impatient. "Aye," he said shortly. "You will stay in one chamber and the woman will go to the other chamber. Go there and stay there."

The female servant's gaze moved to Katiana. "But the lady, my lord?" she said hesitantly. "Will she come, too?"

Titus simply pointed a finger at the tavern keep standing several feet away, a silent command that the servants should go to him. The male started to move, but the female was slower. She had her orders from Lady Ethyl, after all.

She wasn't to leave the young lady alone, even for a moment.

"But… the lady," she said, gesturing to Katiana. "She should come with me."

Titus was extremely intimidating when he wanted to be. With his size and natural commanding presence, there were few who would challenge him. His eyes narrowed as he bent over, fixing the woman in the eye.

"*Move,*" he growled.

That was enough for her. She took off, scurrying after the male servant, and the two of them followed the tavern keep into a corridor off the common room. That left Katiana and Titus alone.

She looked at him curiously.

"What was all that about?" she said. "Why are we even here? There is still daylight to travel by."

He grinned, that cheeky grin that had been the downfall of many a maiden. "Because I have suffered all I can," he said. "I have spent five days with those two boiled-brained fools following us about, spying for your aunt. I will not tolerate them any longer, so whilst they stay to the rooms for fear of my wrath, I am taking you somewhere for a good time."

Katiana's eyes glittered. "Is *that* what happened to you?" she said. "I thought I'd offended you somehow, Titus. You have hardly spoken to me since we left London."

He took her hand in his big, gloved mitt. "It was because of those spies your aunt sent with us," he said. "I did not want to say anything that would be reported back to your aunt, so I have spent five days trying to figure out how to be rid of them. Yesterday, it finally came to me."

"What did?"

"How to be rid of them."

"How?"

Titus gave her a tug and pulled her out of the tavern and into the street. It was still fairly well traveled at this hour, and he pointed up the road.

"There is a festival in town," he said. "I saw the bills for it when we were in Lutterworth. Some kind of celebration for some saint, I'm sure. There are always celebrations for saints, and almost every village I know has a patron saint of something. I thought we might join the festivities and leave the escort behind."

Katiana nodded eagerly. "We should."

"Good," he said as he started to walk in the direction he had pointed. "The tavern keep said it was up the road, near the church."

"How far?"

He shrugged. "I do not know," he said. "Not too far, I think."

Katiana was in traveling clothing, the same dress she'd worn for five straight days. It was dark green, woolen, and plain, but it had a high neck, long sleeves, several skirts, and a cloak sewn onto the back of it. It was actually quite nice and fit her figure quite well, something that hadn't escaped Titus' notice. On her feet were leather boots, up to her knees, designed to protect her feet and lower legs from rocks kicked up from the road. They were a lot better than the protection she had on her feet the last time she and Titus had to walk.

"Have you noticed that since the day we were reintroduced, we seem to have done quite a bit of walking?" she said.

Titus came to a halt, grinning. "That is true," he conceded. "Would you prefer to ride? I do not know how far it is. It could be a mile or two."

She shook her head. "I have the proper shoes to walk," she said, sticking out her foot so he could see the boot. "But you are bedecked in armor and protection. Isn't it cumbersome?"

He looked down at himself. His helm had been in the baggage the servants had carried, but he was indeed wearing everything else as if preparing to go to war. That's what he wore when traveling, so it wasn't anything unusual in his world.

"Compared to what?" he said. "Wearing a simple tunic and breeches? Compared to that, it is cumbersome, but this is the attire of a knight, and I am a knight. It is no trouble."

Katiana didn't press him. She simply smiled and nodded. "Then let us keep walking," she said. "After riding all day, it feels good to stretch my legs."

"Then let's stretch."

They did. Titus tucked her hand into the crook of his elbow as they headed up the road, flanked by residences, until they reached an intersection. It was busier here, with people all along the street, and they could see off to the east that something was going on. There were more homes, and merchant stalls, and a square of sorts, and beyond that was a large churchyard and the stone spire of a church over the rooftops.

They could hear the music in the distance.

Thrilled that they had found what they were looking for, they walked in the direction of the crowds, passing through the square that was full of people and entertainers. There was a man with trained dogs, and another man with a pig who was picking objects for people to bet on. The men who ran the games or the entertainment had people working for them who would walk among the crowd and pull men and even women toward the games, encouraging them to throw coins or bet on any number of things.

As they watched the goings-on with interest, a small parade of happy people came from the churchyard. There was a man on stilts, about twice as tall as a normal man, and he wore long robes upon which pieces of fruit had been sewn. The children screamed in delight as he walked amongst them, pulling the fruit off the robe and nearly pulling the man down in the process. But he recovered nicely, walking quickly as the children ran after him. That left Titus and Katiana in stitches, laughing at the frantic children and the man trying to escape them.

"What do you think so far?" Titus asked her. "Should we go and watch the dogs dance?"

Katiana nodded eagerly. "I do love dogs," she said. "I have always wanted one, but my aunt says they give her an itch. I have to settle for the cats in the stable yard."

"Don't you like cats?"

"I do, very much," she said. "But a dog... that is different.

Cats do not depend on you. Dogs do. I suppose I would like something to have for my very own."

Titus' smile faded. "You've never had that, have you?"

She shook her head, watching something in the distance. "It has always, and only ever been, just me," she said. "Not even a pet. That is a lonely way to live. Oh, look—a pony that jumps through hoops. See him over there?"

She was pointing, and Titus turned to see a gray pony that was, indeed, jumping through a wooden hoop. They headed in that direction, their arms looped together, but as they moved, they happened to pass by a puppet show. It was a small wagon that had been converted in such a way that the puppets were on a stage for the children to see, and there was a horde of children and mothers watching them. But the puppets began to beat on each other, and suddenly, a king appeared and all of the beating stopped. The children cheered, and boiled sweets came flying out at the audience.

The scramble began.

Katiana had been closer to the children and the puppets, and she was bumped by a couple of children as they rushed to pick up sweets. More were flying through the air, one of them hitting Titus in the head. He stopped, frowned, and picked it up off the ground, eyeing it. He blew at it, brushed it off, and put it in his mouth as Katiana chuckled. She wasn't entirely sure it was a good idea to eat something off the ground, but he didn't seem to care. His face soon lit up with delight.

"Delicious," he said, looking around. "Quickly—get me more of those sweets. See that child over there? Punch him in the face and steal his candy. He has a good deal of it, and I want it."

Katiana's laughter grew. "I am *not* going to strike a child and steal his treats," she said. "Neither are you. Look around; mayhap there are more on the ground."

Titus frowned that she wouldn't fight a child for his sweets, but he indeed looked around and managed to come up with three more slightly dirty treats. He shared one with Katiana, who agreed that the honey-cinnamon sweet was delightful. Titus found two more of the candies that the children hadn't picked up, and they continued on toward the dancing pony.

It was a delight to watch the trained pony, but more than that, it was a delight to watch Katiana as she enjoyed the show. At least, that's what Titus thought. He'd brought her to the faire because he wanted to spend time with her, and, as he'd told her, he simply couldn't do that with Ethyl's spies as their constant companions. He'd spent five days traveling with her perched behind him, feeling her warm body against his, thinking that it was about the most wonderful sensation in the world.

It was something he didn't want to be without.

He'd never genuinely thought about marrying someone in his entire life. He'd always thought that being tied down to the same person for the remainder of his days was tedious. The same face, the same voice. He didn't like anyone well enough to consider that. Of course, he'd seen his brothers in their marriages, and they were all quite happy. His parents were quite happy. But Titus was coming to realize that their happiness didn't happen overnight. It took time. It had to be with the right person at the right time, among other things, and perhaps he'd been too immature to realize that. Immaturity at his age sounded rather ridiculous, but it was the truth. Or perhaps he'd simply been too obstinate or ignorant to really give a relationship with a woman much thought. He was too busy being an Executioner Knight to think about marriage and family.

... Wasn't he?

The truth was that once he left Katiana at Callerton Castle, the situation would change. She would be back under the control of her father, if the man was still alive, and if not, then she'd be under the control of her brother. The mere thought of her being at the mercy of Ansel made his blood run cold. He didn't know why he hadn't thought of that until this very moment, but the thought of Katiana being left to the whims of Ansel de Edington was a horrifying thought. Titus knew, as he lived and breathed, that he'd never be able to sleep if he left her in that situation and went about his business.

There was another problem.

He *had* business. He had a good deal of it that required his focus, and a woman—a woman he was thinking romantically about, no less—wasn't part of that equation. Watching Katiana clap happily for the dancing pony made him think about leaving that sweet, witty woman with her beast of a brother, and there was no telling what would happen. Did that mean he loved her? That he wanted to marry her? Titus had to think hard about that. All he knew was that he was greatly reluctant to leave her alone at Callerton with Ansel on the prowl.

"Titus?"

It took him a moment to realize that she was talking to him. "Aye?" he said.

She smiled. "You were a million miles away," she said. "I asked you where we are to go from here. Should we find some food?"

He nodded before she was even finished speaking, reaching out to take her hand again. "Aye," he said. "Those sweets have made me hungry."

Katiana let him hold her hand, as bold as it was, because it was starting to feel completely natural. He'd done it so many times that she was coming to crave it.

"I can smell the food from here," she said, pointing over toward the church. "I saw people in that direction eating something."

"Quickly, now. We must get over there before it is all gone."

He picked up the pace, and Katiana did, too. Giggling, she practically skipped beside him as they hurried over to the vast yard in front of the church. It was filled with musicians, people dancing, and tables of food near the entry to the church. Titus went right up to one of the tables and began grabbing things in spite of an old woman trying to moderate him. He took a loaf of bread in the shape of a cross, cheese, a basket that had honey buns in it, and other things. All of it was put into the basket, and as the woman followed him around, begging him to be sparing, he reached into his purse and dug out a few coins. He put them right in her hand, paying for the fact that he'd taken more than his share.

"Come along," he told Katiana. "Let us find a place to eat."

They did. There were a few old yew trees near the north side of the church, and he had her sit beneath the branches of one of them, putting the basket down before stripping off some of the most restrictive pieces of protection so he could sit down. There was a small pile next to him by the time he sat on the grass, stretching out his legs and demanding he be fed. With a grin, Katiana doled out the food, and he took everything from her, shoving it into his mouth but making sure she also had enough to eat. Around them, the sounds of the festival floated upon the air, and in the sky above, shades of sunset were forming.

It was perfect.

"I cannot recall the last time I attended a festival like this," he said, mouth full of bread. "It seems like ages ago."

"You said you were at a tournament last month," Katiana said. "Wasn't that something of a respite? With food and music?"

He shrugged, leaning back on one elbow. "I was not there to eat and dance," he said. "I was there to compete. To win."

"Did your brothers compete, too?"

He shook his head. "Nay," he said. "But my cousin, Ronan, did. I had several friends there. We lost one of them, unfortunately. It was a sad business."

Katiana looked at him with concern. "Lost him?" she said. "How?"

"He died."

"What happened?"

Titus cocked an eyebrow, lending a clue to the fact that he thought the situation had been terrible, indeed. "He was speared by a joust pole," he said. "Only it turned out that the pole had an illegal spear tip. It went straight through him. He died in the arms of his pregnant wife."

Katiana stopped eating, closing her eyes to the horror of it. "God's Bones," she muttered. "I am so sorry to hear that. What a tragic thing."

"It really was," Titus said. "Tournaments are dangerous enough without unscrupulous knights playing dirty tricks to win."

Katiana resumed eating, though she still wasn't over the terrible death of Titus' friend. "But you like to compete?"

"I do," he said. "I'm good at it. I've been trained for it. And it has made me rich, so I will continue competing until I am so old that I can no longer hold a joust pole."

He sounded rather firm about it. Katiana reached into the

basket again to pull out some cheese, break it in half, and hand him the larger portion.

"I've never even been to a tournament," she said. "Honestly, I live in a hole compared to the life you lead, Titus. I'm rather embarrassed."

"Why?"

"Because I cannot tell you glorious tales of my great adventures."

He smiled. "It will not be like that forever," he said. "You will find a husband who will take you to great places, and then you will have many stories to tell."

Katiana rolled her eyes. "Are we on that subject again?"

"What subject?"

"Of my not being married," she said. "Now you speak as if it will be a certainty."

"It will be."

"You know I do not want to talk about it."

He rolled over onto his stomach, looking at her. "I don't know why you are so irritated by the subject," he said. "Remember that I asked you to think about it."

She frowned. "Think about what?"

"If you will allow me to court you."

Her irritation was growing. "And I told you that it was impossible."

She was digging around in the basket again, and he reached out, grasping the hand that was fishing. Katiana looked at him, wary, as he brought it to his lips for a gentle kiss.

"It is not only possible, it is probable," he said quietly, his eyes glimmering at her. "I do not know why you resist. You told me yourself that you have no suitors."

"And I told you why."

"And I told *you* that I do not need a wife with wealth," he said. "I want someone I like. Someone I can talk to. A beautiful, practical lass who will fall at my feet in worship."

"I will *not* fall at your feet."

"Then I will fall at yours."

He wasn't kidding. Katiana could tell by the expression on his face that he was quite serious. But that only made it hurt more.

"Titus," she said sadly, squeezing his fingers as they held her hand. "Your family will expect a great marriage from you. I am not a great marriage."

"My parents will love you."

She held up a hand to stop him. "Wait," she said. "Before you go any further and we end up in an argument, I want you to stop this line of thinking. Please. You are fine and handsome and a joy to my heart, but I am not of your social station. A de Wolfe must have a properly placed wife, and that simply isn't me."

"Then you are not opposed to it because you do not think of me in that way?"

"In what way?"

"As a lover and a husband."

She snorted ironically. "I could only be so fortunate," she said. "Nay, Titus, if all things were equal and there was a chance at happiness, I would put my arms around you and never let you go. Marrying you would be the fulfillment of everything good I thought I would never have in my life, so nay, you are not lacking in any way. But I am."

He pushed himself up so he was sitting on the grass, looking at her very carefully. "You are not lacking," he said quietly. "Katia, I've never wanted to marry anyone in my life. Not that there hasn't been ample opportunity, but I have always been too busy for it. Too focused on my own wants and goals to have to worry about a wife and children. But I am serious when I say that I want to court you. I have never wanted anything more."

Katiana knew that. She could see it in everything about him. Their conversation had moved beyond a gentle flirt to something serious, and she didn't like it. It made her heart race. Would that she could have had a chance with him, there was nothing she would want more. There was nothing she wouldn't do for the opportunity. But she was being far more pragmatic than he was.

He was being reckless.

"Titus—"

He cut her off. "Please, Katia."

"Titus, you are hurting me. This talk is excruciating."

He backed off, sensing this was a situation he wasn't winning. "I do not wish to do that," he said. "I would never deliberately hurt you. But your argument is unsound. You are from a good family in the north. Our marriage would be considered a reasonable one. How can I make you understand that?"

She looked at him. "And you can see yourself married to me?" she said, incredulous. "Put aside the fact that I am unsuitable. You already know you want to marry me? We have only known each other for a few days."

"I've known you since you were small."

"You know *of* me, and we were acquainted, but you do not know *me*."

"But I want to. Very much."

"Why?"

It was an honest question that deserved an honest answer.

"I'm not sure," he said truthfully. "All I know is that the past few days have meant more to me than I could have imagined. You're beautiful and sweet and witty. You have talent and grace. I look at you and you make me feel very strong and very weak."

"Weak? How?"

He shrugged. "Giddy, I suppose," he said. Then he cracked a grin. "Does that sound strange coming from a man my size?"

She fought off a smile. "Strange but endearing."

"Do… do I make you feel giddy?"

Her smile broke through. "You've never made me feel anything else."

He had an expression on his face that suggested he was feeling giddy at that very moment. Standing up, he brushed his breeches off before extending his hand to her.

"Come with me," he said softly.

Katiana put her hand in his. "Where are we going?"

He pulled her to her feet. "Over there," he said, pointing to a group of dancers in the area near the musicians. "I feel like dancing."

There was that impulsiveness again. Titus was actually a terrible dancer, but he saw an opportunity to interact with Katiana in something other than a conversation or on horseback. He didn't seem to be gaining much headway with his marriage talk, and he was trying to figure out if he was pushing it because she was resistant and he wasn't accustomed to having his wishes denied, or because he truly was serious about her. He believed that he was very serious, but this was new territory for him, and her resistance was something he wasn't used to. He was used to women, and men, obeying orders and wishes. But not Katiana—she was trying very hard to convince him that marriage between then was not feasible. Perhaps if they had a few moments to dance with one another, that closeness could accomplish something that conversation couldn't.

He wanted to find out.

The villagers were having an ecstatic time dancing to the musicians that had evidently been playing all day, because they seemed positively exhausted. The citole player had bloodied fingers from plucking strings for hours, but they weren't to be given any respite in the next few minutes. As Titus and Katiana walked to the edge of the crowd, dancing a simple carole dance, the musicians ended their song, and Titus boomed at them to continue playing. This coming from a man who was well over six and a half feet tall sent the musicians into a frenzy as they picked up the pace with the next song.

Grinning at Katiana, Titus pulled her into the pack of revelers.

Fortunately, Katiana knew how to dance. She could do it very well. Titus was too big and, simply put, uncoordinated when it came to moving his feet in any regular pattern, and Katiana could see that. He'd already kicked one couple who had strayed too close and ended up stepping on some woman's foot. She was still off howling about it. Therefore, to spare Titus any further embarrassment, she had him stand in one spot while she simply danced around him.

Titus was good at keeping up with her. He held her hand when he was supposed to and let her spin in a circle around him gracefully. He knew she was doing it to save his pride, and he thought that was rather sweet of her. No one he'd ever known had tried to spare him in such a way, but Katiana did. She was an elegant dancer and moved around him gracefully. But the more he watched her, the more enchanted he became.

The more she touched him, and the more he touched her, the more he wanted.

They came to the part in the dance when the men lifted the women up, over their heads if they could get them that high. It was no feat at all for Titus, who lifted Katiana up, straight up so she was over his head and her hands were braced on his shoulders. It was an incredibly intimate position as her body draped against his, and at that moment, something changed between them. The flirting, the witty banter, and the conversation that had gone on since they'd been reintroduced suddenly changed into something warmer and deeper and far more serious.

The mood changed.

When the men in the dance were to lower the women back to their feet, Titus simply lowered Katiana enough that she was face to face with him. They were a mere few inches from each other, with Katiana's body against his as she hung off the ground. Her hands were still on his shoulders, but she was looking at him with a mixture of curiosity, doubt, and perhaps even a little excitement. She seemed to be breathing unnaturally fast.

"You're supposed to put me down," she whispered.

The smile never left his face. "In a moment," he said. "I do not know if I've ever been this close to you."

"Of course you have," she said. "We've been riding on the same horse for days."

"Jesus hates that we are," he said. "But, then again, Jesus does not approve of most things. He's hell in battle, but he's a very peculiar horse."

"You will make sure that Jesus knows it was not my idea to ride on him."

"He already knows. Jesus knows everything."

He started to laugh, as he did when speaking of a horse named Jesus. It really was quite naughty of him to have named his horse that. Because he was laughing, Katiana began to laugh simply because he was being so dastardly about his horse's name. But just as he opened his mouth to say something, a couple bashed into him from behind because Titus was simply standing there in the middle of a crowded dance. Titus stumbled, grabbing hold of Katiana so she wouldn't fall. He ended up clutching her against his chest as her arms went around his neck for support.

The fact that he'd been jostled and nearly dropped Katiana infuriated him. Titus set her to her feet and whirled on the pair that had smacked into him. An enormous hand shot out and grabbed the man around the throat as the woman in his arms shrieked. Titus cocked a fist and was preparing to slam it into the man's face when he heard a voice beside him.

"Titus," Katiana snapped quietly but firmly. "You will not hit him. It was an accident."

Titus froze, looking over his shoulder to see Katiana standing beside him, frowning. When their eyes met, she lifted her eyebrows.

"Do as I say, please," she said calmly. "Release him. He has done nothing wrong."

Titus looked at the man, who was gazing back at him in pure terror, before releasing his grip and unclenching his fist. He even went so far as to smooth out the wrinkles he'd caused to the man's tunic. Then he turned to Katiana.

"Should I put him to bed now, too?" he said sarcastically. "I'll take him by the hand and lead him home to ensure he returns safely."

Katiana eyed him. "I do not think that will be necessary," she said. "But if you feel that you must, then go right ahead."

His eyes narrowed. "You seem so concerned for him, so I thought I'd ask. What is your pleasure, my lady?"

Katiana was trying very hard not to smile at Titus as he verged on a tantrum. "My pleasure is that we should continue dancing without any unnecessary fighting."

He was grossly unhappy that she'd stopped his fury, but there wasn't any force behind it. He was being petulant for show, mostly. The tantrum was his version of surrendering kicking and screaming. Moreover, if he'd really wanted to strike the man, he would have done so. But Katiana's soft, firm voice had been like throwing water on a fire. Other than his mother and grandmother, Titus had never let another woman tell him what to do in his entire life.

Until now.

And it seemed like the most natural of things.

"I do not feel like it any longer," he said, turning his nose up at her as people danced around them. "I want to find some ale or wine."

Katiana started to walk away, but he just stood there. When she looked at him, puzzled, he cleared his throat loudly and looked down at his arm. He kept looking at her and then at his arm, again and again, until she figured out what he wanted. Now, she couldn't help but grin as she went to him and put her hand in the crook of his elbow.

Then he started to move.

"God's Bones, Titus," she muttered. "You are impossible."

"That is not true," he said. "I am very possible. But my feelings are easily hurt."

"Because I asked you not to strike that man?"

He simply looked away, and Katiana sensed the game afoot. Somehow, she'd injured his pride. It was probably only the fact that she'd asked him to behave in front of witnesses and nothing more, but she took the hint.

"Then I am sorry," she said, somewhat exaggerated. "I simply didn't want our lovely visit to the faire to be ruined by a fight. I did not mean to hurt your feelings."

He grunted and shrugged. "It is of no matter."

He sounded hurt, and he even wiped at his eyes to show that he'd been growing teary over it. It was all such an overt act for sympathy that Katiana couldn't help but laugh at him. Silently, of course. He was carrying on, and she thought it was hilarious.

And endearing.

Somehow, the massive knight feigning the teary eyes was so incredibly charming. But it was more than charming—it was Titus as he had always been, the loud, humorous, thoughtful, and caring boy who had grown into a knight with the same qualities, only greater. *He* was greater. The man had been speaking of a marriage since nearly the moment of their reassociation, but she'd resisted strongly. Yet now… now, she was wondering if she could really go through the rest of her life without his joy and intensity. He lived his life passionately, and that was something she lacked. Her life was predictable. Sad, even. Seeing life through Titus' eyes had given her a taste of what it was like to actually be happy.

He made her happy.

For the first time, her resistance against his desire to court her was beginning to waver.

"It is of great matter to me," she said as they headed toward the tables that held the drink. "What can I do to prove it to you?

What more can I say?"

"Say?" he repeated, cocking his head in thought. "There is nothing more you can say. My injured feelings require a great gesture."

"What should I do?"

"Can you not think of something?"

"If I could, I would not ask you."

He came to a halt and faced her, fists on his hips. "I've never asked for a kiss from a woman, and I'm not about to start now," he said. "I have brought you to a fine festival, I have procured food, I have danced with you, and now I must tell you what more you can do to ensure the insult you dealt me will not stay with me forever? There is only one thing that will soothe me at the moment."

God's Bones, but the man could be petulant when he wanted to be. But it was all the more charming to her, truthfully. He was like a little boy with the playful edge to his personality that most men lacked. He wasn't afraid to show it, and she found that incredibly refreshing in a world full of serious, dedicated, and sometimes humorless men. She wished she had the ability to be as unbridled as Titus could be.

"May I remind you that it would not be proper for me to kiss you, out here for all to see?" she said. "It is bad enough that we have come here without an escort, just the two of us. Now you want me to kiss you? You must think poorly of me, Titus, that you should expect me to kiss you in the open like this."

He eyed her a moment before turning for the tables of drink just a few feet away. He didn't say anything, simply poured himself a cup of wine and downed it, followed by a second cup in short order. He kept his back to her, and Katiana could feel the humor draining from the situation. Her smile faded as she watched him drink, and she was starting to think that the man was at his end with her. Not that she blamed him. He'd been kind and thoughtful, and she'd been resistant and reticent. He spoke of marriage; she spoke of unsuitability. He told her she was beautiful and accomplished, and she told him not to say it anymore.

Suddenly, Katiana was getting a good picture of just how she had behaved with him.

It was a wonder the man was still speaking to her.

Still, she couldn't give in to his demand for kisses. She was afraid what more he would demand, and she didn't want to open the door for greater physical interaction. If he expected kisses, what more would he expect tomorrow night or in two nights? The problem was that the way she was feeling, she wasn't sure she could put up much more of a fight. Big, strong, and handsome Titus had her maiden's heart fluttering. But she suspected all he was really doing was teasing her.

Could they really wed? Did he truly believe they could wed?

Or was he simply behaving on the spur of the moment?

Sighing faintly, she turned away from him and started walking. Back through the crowd, skirting the dancers, and heading out to the section where the entertainment and trades were. She was just entering the area when someone suddenly grabbed her by the arm.

"Stop," Titus said, greatly concerned. "Where are you going?"

He had her by the arm, but she pulled herself free. "Back to the tavern," she said, having no idea why she was bordering on tears. "I want to go to sleep."

She started to walk, but he grabbed her again. "Wait," he said, sounding as if he was trying not to beg. "Why?"

She pulled her arm from his grip a second time. "Because… because I do," she said, moving away from him so he couldn't grab her again. "We have a long day ahead of us tomorrow, and a longer week still. We do not have time for faires."

He was walking behind her as she headed away from the festivities, back the way they had come. "Katia?" he said. "What has happened? You were joyful just a few moments ago. What did I do? Was it the kiss?"

At least he was willing to acknowledge that he'd had a part in her change of mood. She supposed the least she could do was give him an answer. Anything at all. With a heavy sigh, she came to a halt and turned to him.

"I think it is everything," she said truthfully. "You seem to not to want to listen to me. You seem to want to tell me how things should be and what you want, but have you ever asked me what I want?"

"What do you want?"

"I do not want to kiss you in public and then be punished because I do not comply."

He was properly contrite. "I am sorry," he said. "I did not mean… I did not mean to make you unhappy."

Katiana wondered if he even understood what she meant. "You did not," she said. "I'm simply tired. I want to go to sleep."

"I was hoping you would sit up with me tonight," he said softly. "We could… talk. We have not had much chance of that throughout this journey."

She looked at him a moment before finally shaking her head. "Talk?" she said. "So you can tell me you want to court me and then badger me when I resist? I am tired of that, too, Titus. I think you have met a woman who isn't willing to agree to everything you want, so the more I resist, the more you persist. I think it is becoming a game with you to see how much you can bully me until I surrender. That shows an incredible lack of respect for me, or have you not realized that?"

He was looking at her as if she had wounded him. Or as if she had pointed out something he hadn't realized, something significant enough that made him reconsider his stance. After a moment, he shook his head and averted his gaze.

"I did not mean to bully you," he said. "But you're right—when I want something, I do not relent until I get it."

"How on earth can you want me?" she said. "Up until a few days ago, you probably never even gave me a second thought. And now you want to court me? Your father would never permit you to court the daughter of a lesser baron with nothing to her name. I'm simply not suitable, and you know it."

He looked at her then. "That is not true," he said. "Katia, I'm about to tell you something that you can never repeat. Once I tell you, it must stay with you forever. Will you swear this to me?"

Katiana wasn't sure what was coming, but she was both curious and wary. "I would never repeat anything you told me in confidence," she said. "But I wish you would not."

"It's important," he said. "It's important you understand something. I do not think you are giving my father the credit he deserves. He is not the narrow-minded man you seem to think he is. Of course, any parent wants a great marriage for their child, but I have three brothers, and two of them married women that weren't perfect. My eldest brother, Markus, married a woman with four children who was several years older than he was, and I have never seen two people happier. Katiana came into the marriage with virtually nothing, and that didn't matter to my father. Of course, she has Aragon nobility in her blood, and she had some advantages, but she was well beyond what is considered reasonable marriageable age, especially for the heir to Berwick."

Katiana hadn't known that. "I see," she said. "Then I am glad your brother found happiness."

Titus held up a hand to ask for patience. "That's not all," he said. "This is what you must not repeat. My brother, Magnus, married a courtesan. I'm sure you know what that is, so I will not repeat it for your delicate ears. But Violet—she goes by Violet—was forced into the situation. She was taken at a young age by an immoral man who groomed her as his whore. Sorry… I should not have said that word, but it is the truth. Violet is a fine, sweet woman who quite literally had nothing when she married Magnus. But he did not care because he married for love. My father wanted him to be happy, so he has accepted Violet, and so has my mother. They love her dearly. All this to say that my parents want me to be happy, so they will approve of whomever I choose. Katia… I choose you. But not if you do not think of me as a viable marriage prospect. If you only want to think of me as a friend, then in all seriousness, I will never bring up marriage again. You have my word."

Katiana stood there in stunned silence. That wasn't something she had expected to hear from him, and her resistance, her confusion, began to fade. As if someone had pulled the cork from a barrel, everything was draining out of her.

It was strange what a difference one impassioned plea could make.

"I truthfully never thought I would marry," she finally said. "I'm so much older than what is desired for a bride. You do understand that, don't you?"

Titus nodded. "I do," he said. "But you're ageless. You're

young and beautiful and ageless. And you're still younger than I am, so it is of no matter to me. I told you before that I do not want a girl, Katia. I want a woman, and you are a woman."

"But why me?"

He grinned. "Why not?" he said. "I do not know if I can explain this to you, but I've never had a woman make me feel as you do. I do not want to leave you off at Callerton never to see you again. I want to know you are mine and that you will be waiting for me, always. No matter where I go or what I do, I want to know that you belong to me and I belong to you. I've never felt like that in my life."

Katiana could see that. She could see the raw truth in his face, and she believed him implicitly. Perhaps he hadn't been making a game out of wanting to court her. Perhaps he'd been serious the entire time and she'd simply been to blind to realize it.

Perhaps it was time for some truth of her own.

"The moment you took me out of that stable those years ago, after Ansel had pummeled me, was the moment I became yours," she said softly. "You were my champion then, and you are now. Mayhap I've not married yet because God knew I could belong to no one else but you. Mayhap He made my horse run wild so that you could save me yet again. It seems to me that it was something that was preordained a long time ago, Titus. But the dream of you… it always seemed out of my reach."

Titus realized that she was finally coming around to his proposal. She was finally starting to agree, and he couldn't contain the smile on his face.

"And mayhap I haven't married yet because I always knew, deep down, that you were the one all along," he said. "I will admit I've not thought much of you over the years, but I think that is natural. You went your way and I went mine. But seeing you again those few days ago… I knew then, Katia. I knew that I was meant to be yours."

"And you are *certain* about this, Titus?"

"You are the easiest decision I have ever made."

Katiana's features seemed to take on a glow all their own. "Then if you are truly certain…" she said.

"I am."

"And this is not something you will regret tomorrow."

"Never."

"Then I am agreeable if you would still like to court me."

The smile on his lips nearly split his face in two. "I want to do more than court you, Katia," he said. "I want to marry you. Tomorrow if I could."

She giggled. "I'm not entirely sure that would be a good idea," she said. "But I share your sentiment. I am looking forward to the rest of the journey back to Callerton. I think you can speak in front of the servants because I do not care if they report back to Aunt Ethyl."

He snorted. "Nor do I, now," he said. Then he closed the distance between them and reached out, taking her hand and kissing it sweetly. "I know I asked for a kiss from you, but mayhap you'll let me do the honors until you're comfortable returning the gesture."

She looked at him rather coyly. "That might be sooner than you think, but not for all to see."

He was greatly encouraged by that. Taking her hand, he placed it into the crook of his elbow, but his eyes never left her face.

"Then mayhap we should share a meal at the tavern and

speak more about that very thing," he said, jesting with her and watching her blush. "Or would you rather go back to the faire?"

"I would rather go back to the tavern."

He smiled at her as he began to walk her back toward the tavern. "Mayhap they'll have a harpsichord and you can play for me," he said. "If they do not, then mayhap you can simply sing."

"If that would make you happy."

"*You* make me happy, Katia. I can hardly believe I'm saying it, but you do."

She glanced up at him. "I think we make each other happy, Titus."

"I hope we do. I truly do."

"Would you mind if we do not summon the servants to join us for the meal?"

He patted her hand. "I was hoping you would say that," he said. "That whole escort business is becoming tiresome."

She chuckled. "As long as you promise to behave yourself and not demand kisses in public, I do not think we need them."

"Can we leave them behind, then?"

She laughed. "How cruel," she said. "You would leave them to fend for themselves?"

"If it means I can spend a few minutes alone with you, I'd do anything."

Smiling, and blushing, Katiana didn't reply. She didn't have to. One coy look from her said everything he needed to know.

And he was absolutely thrilled.

CHAPTER ELEVEN

Nottingham… Barlborough… Doncaster…

In the days following Katiana's agreement to Titus' proposal, there was some kind of magic in the air. As the servants rode their small palfreys and watched the goings-on from behind, Katiana and Titus chattered up a storm. Katiana held on to him from behind, her arms wrapped around his trim torso, but other times, she would put a hand up and gently touch his face. Whatever flesh was exposed from the helm, she would touch it tenderly, and, if he was able, he would kiss those fingers.

The servants watched in shock.

Nottingham and Barlborough passed normally enough. At least, after a day of flirting and finger kisses, Katiana would retreat to her chamber with the female servant and Titus would retreat to his chamber, alone. They never made any attempt to remove the female servant or get together once they'd gone to bed. But when they reached Doncaster, the situation changed.

Titus' second-eldest brother, Cassius, was the Duke of Doncaster, and Titus wanted to deliver the same information to him that he was going to deliver to his father. He also wanted

Katiana to meet his brother, so they proceeded to Edenthorpe Castle, seat of the Dukes of Doncaster, and surprised his brother most joyfully. Cassius de Wolfe was the beauty of the family, so it was said, and Titus presented him to Katiana with just that introduction. Cassius, embarrassed, rolled his eyes but greeted Katiana kindly. And with that, they were whisked into Edenthorpe, guests of the Duke and Duchess of Doncaster.

The fortress itself was impressive to behold. It had an enormous curtain wall made from gray stone and a gatehouse that was three stories tall, busy with excitement because Titus' arrival caused quite a commotion. Servants and solders were running toward them as the horses came to a halt in the bailey, and from the keep, a woman in fine silks, with her dark hair pinned to the back of her head and a baby on her hip, came hurrying in their direction.

So did three rambunctious little boys.

Erik, Dacian, and Vincent de Wolfe had their father's looks in every way. Erik was the eldest at seven years of age, with his father's size and curly hair, while Dacian and Vincent were two and three years younger, respectively. They were all dark-haired, hazel-eyed copies of their father, while the baby, a boy nearly one year of age, looked much more like his mother, with green eyes and fair skin. Little Bennett, or Ben as the family called him, was already a terror, which meant he fit in well with his brothers, who were all terrors themselves.

"Astonishing, Cass," Titus said as he looked over the brood. "Four sons. It is like looking at us all over again—Markus, you, Magnus, and me. Congratulations, old man. I'm thrilled for you."

Cassius was proud of his growing family. "They act like us, too," he said. "Given that I grew up with three brothers, I have some experience in handling young boys. You've not met the baby yet, but you've met the other three. They remember you. Don't you, lads?"

The older boys were eyeing Titus curiously. Vincent shoved a finger up his nose, promptly removed by his mother, who moved through the crowd of children to embrace her husband's younger brother.

"Welcome, Titus," Dacia, Duchess of Doncaster, said warmly. "What a wonderful surprise to see you here. Will you stay with us long?"

Titus shook his head. "I am traveling north, to Berwick," he said. "We will only be here for the night. Allow me to introduce Lady Katiana de Edington. Lady Katiana is a very old friend. We fostered at Roxburgh together many years ago, and I am escorting her home before I continue on to Berwick."

Dacia was a beautiful woman, refined and elegant, with a heavy dusting of freckles across her nose and cheeks. She turned to Katiana, a smile on her face.

"Welcome, my lady," she said. "It is an honor to meet you."

Given Dacia's superior social position, Katiana curtsied politely. "The honor is mine, Lady Doncaster," she said. "I was admiring your children. They look a great deal like their father."

Dacia grinned as she looked at her boys. "They act like him, too," she said. Then her focus moved to Titus. "And they act like *you*, though I do not even know how that is possible. It must be something in the de Wolfe bloodlines that causes us to have these wild animals to continue the de Wolfe legacy."

Titus grinned at her but was distracted when Erik and Dacian crowded around him, curious about his weapons. The truth was that he hadn't seen the boys in nearly two years, so he wasn't certain they remembered him in spite of what his brother had said. As he unsheathed his broadsword to show the boys the wolf's-head hilt, Dacia moved closer to Katiana.

"You must be weary from travel," she said. "I have a lovely chamber where you can rest. Would you like to come with me?"

Katiana looked to Titus, who had heard his sister-in-law's offer. He nodded faintly, and that gave Katiana the confidence to accept.

"Thank you, my lady," she said. "I would be very grateful."

Dacia began waving at the servants who were standing around. "Take her satchel," she said, pointing to the sacks that had been set on the ground when Jesus and the other horses were taken to the stables. "Take Titus', too. I will put him in the keep with us. And the servants can go to the kitchens. The cook will find them a bed."

Everyone was moving with her steady commands, including her husband and brother-in-law, who moved aside as Dacia pulled Katiana with her. The boys were still milling around their father, but Dacia called to them, and they trotted after her in a little herd, all of them heading toward the substantial keep of Edenthorpe. Titus and Cassius watched them go.

"You married a woman who can move mountains," Titus said. "I've seen battle commanders with only half her ability."

Cassius grinned. "Why do you think I married her?"

"You are a fortunate man."

"Agreed." Cassius glanced at his brother. "Now that she is gone, you can tell me what is so urgent at Berwick that you cannot stay more than one night."

Titus had his hand up, shielding his eyes from the late-afternoon sun as he watched Katiana take the steps to the keep. He dropped his hand as he looked at Cassius.

"Trouble," he said quietly. "I've come with news, Cass."

"What news?"

"Last month, Pembroke captured Piers Gaveston," Titus said. "I know you've been trying to remain neutral in the war between Lancaster and his allies and Edward, but did you hear this?"

Cassius nodded. "I did," he said. "I have my own emissaries who keep me informed. Certainly nothing like the information that you and de Lohr receive from your web of spies, but I know enough. I am in constant touch with Uncle Scott and Papa, too, so we are all aware of what is happening. Why? What's it all about?"

Titus shook his head, feeling the same disgust he'd felt the first time he heard the news. "I was hoping to have the opportunity to tell you what I have been sent to tell Papa," he said. "Doncaster is slightly out of my way, but it is important that you know. The gist is this—Pembroke captured Gaveston and swore an oath to protect him until he could be tried by the rebel warlords. Before that could happen, Lancaster and Warwick stole Gaveston from Pembroke and, after a trial which I'm sure was a mockery, executed him."

Cassius stared at him a moment before closing his eyes, briefly and tightly, as if to ward off what he'd just been told.

"God's Bones," he muttered. "They actually did it?"

"They did."

"Then that is the end of Lancaster and his allies."

Titus nodded. "Exactly," he said. "Papa and Uncle Scott and the rest of them were content to stay neutral, though we both know they were in heavy contact with Pembroke."

"They have also been in heavy contact with de Winter."

"I know," Titus said. "They've been talking to both sides but not committing support to either, but after this... after this,

Papa will not support Lancaster or Warwick. Rather than let the allies hold Gaveston against Edward, they executed the man simply to be rid of him. They took the matter, a matter that should have been decided by every warlord opposing Edward, and made their own decision about it. Morgen is beside himself. He is leaning toward supporting Edward, and given that he's on the marches, that means he's in close proximity to Warwick and Gloucester."

"Is Gloucester in on this, too?"

Titus shrugged. "He's close to Warwick, as you know," he said. "Who is to say if he'll support what Warwick and Lancaster have done? Meanwhile, we have some very big warlords on the Welsh marches who could very well go to war against one another."

Cassius could see what chaos was on their doorstep. "Papa will send his army to Lioncross," he said. "None of our uncles will let Morgen face Warwick and Lancaster alone, which means we will be part of an enormous battle if it comes to that."

Titus nodded slowly. "As I said," he muttered, "it is a mess."

"I thought you were exaggerating, but I see that you were not."

"Nay, I was not."

"What would you have me do? Can I help?"

Titus scratched his bristly chin. "You can send word to your allies," he said. "De Royans, for one. There's another de Lohr at Shadowmoor Castle that should know of this situation. Bowes Castle, Richmond, Beverly… they all must know. And they must be prepared."

"I will send out missives in the morning," Cassius said. "And you… you are in the middle of it. Were you with Pembroke when Gaveston was captured?"

Titus shook his head. "I was in Middlesbrough, following the news of the armies as Lancaster chased Edward and Pembroke went after Gaveston," he said. "I was told to keep my ears open and report back."

"And what news there is."

"That, dear brother, is an understatement."

Cassius smiled weakly, clapping his brother on the shoulder. He didn't want to diminish what was going on, and he feared for Titus' role as an Executioner Knight, but that wasn't something he chose to focus on. They were knights, and they had their duties. Sometimes, those duties were dangerous.

Like now.

He hesitated to let his mind wander to where this could all end up.

"At least I get you for the evening," he said after a moment. "Come into the hall with me. I've got some fine wine from Spain I want you to try."

Titus grinned. No matter what the situation, or the peril of it, his smile wasn't far from the surface. In this case, he did it to alleviate any fear Cassius might have been feeling. They both knew the stakes.

But they weren't going to dwell on them.

"I'm always happy to drink up all of your wine and eat your food," he said. "You know I live for that."

Cassius laughed softly, patting his brother on the head. "That is the brother I know and love," he said. "Come along, Titus. I only have you for the night, so we'd better get started."

Titus was more than happy to comply.

ଔ

THE KEEP WAS astonishing.

In noble homes, many times the family's wealth was displayed by the furnishings they had—rugs, tapestries, furniture, even plates of silver, pewter, or gold on the mantels. Sometimes, it was an overt display, but sometimes, it was spartan.

In the case of Edenthorpe, it was overt.

There were hides on the floor of the entry. There were rows and rows of massive antlers mounted on the walls from deer that had been killed over the years. Everywhere Katiana looked, there was something refined or expensive on a wall or on the floor, and the little boys running around her and their mother weren't impressed with any of it.

But Katiana was.

Dacia kept up a running conversation as they headed through the entry and up the mural stairs that led to the upper floors. Katiana responded appropriately, but her attention was affixed to her surroundings to the point of her being dumbfounded. Even the stairs were covered with hide that had been nailed down so no one would trip, and once they reached the floor in which the guests were usually housed, she noticed that there were exquisite tables against the walls that contained expensive items upon them, like pitchers and trays and candlesticks made of pewter. Some even had precious stones sunk into them.

Everything she saw was astonishing.

Unfortunately, she didn't have time to stop and look at everything because her hostess had a destination in mind. Katiana followed Dacia down a corridor whose only light came from lancet windows built into the thick stone wall. At the very end was an enormous door of oak and iron that looked as if it was built to keep out monsters of myth. In fact, it was a little frightening, but Dacia opened it as if it were nothing at all, revealing the exquisite chamber beyond.

"Many years ago, this room belonged to me," Dacia said, shifting the baby to her other hip. "When Cass and I married, we moved into the chamber my grandfather used to occupy, but I still consider this my favorite chamber. I hope you are comfortable here."

Katiana looked at her surroundings with awe. "I am certain I will be, my lady," she said. "You are very kind to show me such hospitality."

"It is my pleasure," Dacia said.

Off to her left, her older boys were fussing with something over by the hearth, and she went over to grab Erik, instructing him to take his brothers out of the chamber and wait for her in the corridor. Erik might have been wild, but he was obedient. As the boys trotted out, Dacia once again returned her attention to Katiana.

"Would you prefer to rest alone, or would you like some company?" she asked. "I will admit that it is not often we have lady visitors, so please speak up if you would like to be alone. Otherwise, I might remain indefinitely."

She meant it as a little joke, smiling, but Katiana was frankly surprised that so fine a lady should want to keep her company. "I am not particularly weary," she said. "Truthfully, it is not often that I have a chance to converse with someone new. If you are not too busy, I would welcome the opportunity."

Dacia smiled brightly. "Give me a moment, please."

With that, she left the chamber, and Katiana could hear her speaking to the little boys outside. At least two were protesting, and someone started to cry, but their voices faded away. Katiana stuck her head into the corridor only to see that it was empty. The little family had evidently wandered off. With a shrug, she closed the door.

She was wearing her traveling clothing today, as she usually did, with the addition of another cloak because the morning had been misty when they departed Barlborough. There was a big wardrobe near the hearth, and she went to it, opening it up to find the pegs upon the doors. Removing her cloak, she hung it up just as someone knocked at the door. Katiana bade them enter, and a pair of servants came forth, bearing a basin and water and a few other things. As they came into the chamber, another servant came in after them bearing Katiana's satchel. More servants brought forth a pitcher and cups and plates of fruit. All of it ended up on the large, exquisitely carved table in the chamber.

Intrigued by the booty, Katiana went over to the table to inspect it after the servants departed. The basin was empty, but the pitcher next to it was full of water that had rose petals floating in it. Delighted, she stopped her inspection and went to her satchel, pulling forth a cake of precious soap that smelled of lavender. It was heavenly to wash her hands and face in the cool, fresh water, and by the time she was finished, there was a knock at the door again.

"May I come in, my lady?" Dacia asked as she stuck her head in.

Katiana nodded. "Please," she said. "Thank you so much for the water. It's so lovely to be able to wash the dirt of the road from my face."

Dacia smiled as she came to the table. "I had the servants bring up some food and drink," she said, peering in the nearest pitcher. "This is boiled juice from apples and pears, with honey and cinnamon. My little lads cannot get enough of it, so drink it while you can, because if they smell a hint of it, they will fight you for it."

Katiana laughed softly. "I will give them a battle, I warn you," she said, accepting the cup that Dacia had poured for her. "How delightful that you have four children. They must keep you very busy."

Dacia rolled her eyes as she poured herself another cup. "Busy is not the word for it," she said. "Chaotic is more like it. They rule this castle, and Cass could not be prouder. Erik is seven years of age and already he tries to command the army."

"Do the soldiers do as he commands?"

"Of course they do!"

The women giggled at the idea of a seven-year-old commanding an army, who went willingly. Katiana sipped at her drink and discovered that it was delicious.

"No wonder your sons love this," she said. "It is quite tasty."

Dacia nodded as she pointed to the nearest chair. "Sit," she said. "You must be weary. I want to hear about your interesting name. I've never heard it before. Are you named for someone?"

Katiana nodded. "I am," she said. "My mother named me for her grandmothers—Katherine and Anna. That was my name when I was born—Katherine Anna—but my mother called me Katie Anna, and somehow that became Katiana. I've gone by it ever since."

"How lovely," Dacia said. "I like it."

"Thank you."

"Where did you start your journey today?"

"Barlborough," Katiana said. "I believe it is near Sheffield. Do you travel much?"

Dacia shook her head. "Not with four children," she said. "Cass does, of course, but he mostly goes north to visit his family. His parents come here from time to time. They've been here for the birth of every grandchild. I do love them so. Do you know them?"

Katiana shook her head. "Nay," she said. "As Titus mentioned, I fostered at Roxburgh. That was the demesne of Lord Blayth and his wife, Lady Asmara. I was very young, but I remember them as lovely people."

"They are," Dacia agreed. "The entire de Wolfe family is full of lovely people, including Titus. How did you manage to convince him to escort you home?"

Katiana cocked her head thoughtfully. "It was a fortuitous coincidence," she said. "I had just received word that my father was dying, and Titus happened to be heading home to Berwick. Since we were traveling in the same direction, he offered to escort me, and I accepted."

Dacia's features fell. "Then this is not a pleasant journey for you," she said. "I'm very sorry about your father. I did not mean to sound callous with my questions."

Katiana shook her head. "You did not," she assured her. "My father and I do not have much of an association, to be perfectly honest, so this journey is simply a duty. I am going to Callerton Castle because I have been asked to go and for no other reason than that."

"Callerton Castle is your home?"

"Callerton Castle is where I was born," Katiana said. "My home is in London with my father's aunt."

"And that's where you found Titus?"

"Aye," Katiana said. Then she chuckled. "In truth, he found me. My horse spooked, and had it not been for Titus, I would have ended up in the Thames. He saved me."

Dacia smiled broadly. "How gallant," she said. "Though being gallant is not usually something Titus is known for."

"What do you mean?"

Dacia giggled. "It is simply that he's the youngest of four enormous and powerful brothers," she said. "Titus has spent his entire life trying to live up to the deeds of Markus and Cassius and Magnus. He's a wild lad, Titus is. He's quick to anger, the first man to throw a punch in a fight, and on the tournament field, he cannot be bested. Surely you know these things about him."

Katiana smiled weakly. "To be honest, I've not seen Titus in many years until just recently," she said. "When we last met, I was a very small girl of five years of age, and he was ten years older than I was. My brother, who is Titus' age, had a penchant for beating me. One night, Titus heard him and intervened. He was my champion. My experience with him was one of great honor and compassion, so the Titus you speak of… I've seen glimpses of him, but I've not had much experience."

Dacia appeared slightly contrite. "Then I have said too much," she said. "I did not mean to give you a bad impression of Titus. He's the lifeblood of his family. There is nothing he wouldn't do for those he loves. He's very loyal and thoughtful."

"I can well believe it," Katiana said. "But between you and me, I saw evidence of the wild boy you speak of only a few days ago."

"Is that so?"

Katiana tried not to burst out laughing. "We were at a faire outside of Leicester, and as we passed a puppet show, the puppets started throwing sweets to the children watching the performance," she said. "Titus liked the sweets and wanted me to fight a young boy who had collected many of them. He wanted the boy's hoard of delights."

Dacia snorted. "*That* is the Titus we know and love," she

said. "Some things never change, but I am delighted to hear it. And I am delighted he brought you to Edenthorpe. I'm only sorry that you cannot stay longer."

Katiana was touched. Already, she liked Dacia, a woman who was showing her genuine warmth and kindness. "Thank you, my lady," she said. "I am sorry I cannot stay longer, too. I do not have many friends, so this is an unexpected treat."

"Then you shall have to come back and stay with us," Dacia said. "Will you come?"

"I would be honored."

"Good," Dacia said, happy. "We can visit and go into town and spend money at the merchants' stalls. There is a man with the most marvelous perfumes. If you like that sort of thing, that is."

"I love it."

"Can you read?"

"I can, very well."

"Excellent!" Dacia was clearly thrilled. "My grandfather accumulated a vast number of books during his lifetime. Mayhap you would like to read some of his books, and then we can discuss them. You may as well know I have a love of reading."

"That suits me perfectly," Katiana said. "Did your grandfather collect anything on music? Books or compositions?"

"I'm not sure," Dacia said. "Why? Are you a musician?"

Katiana nodded. "I am," she said. "I can play the harpsichord and sing. I've also written songs from time to time."

Dacia was fascinated. "How very clever of you," she said. "You must come back very soon, and we'll go through everything my grandfather has to see if there is anything about music. I do not have a harpsichord, but our church has a *ponere.* It is a small organ with pipes and bellows. The sound is beautiful."

Katiana nodded. "Westminster Abbey has one as well," she said. "I've heard it many times. I would love to see the one in your church sometime."

"How exciting," Dacia said. "I'm so happy Titus brought you here. I think we shall get on splendidly."

Katiana grinned. "I agree," she said. "I am looking forward to returning at a time of your convenience."

"We shall make plans before you leave," Dacia said. "I realize that will be tomorrow morning, but we can speak on it now and then correspond once you return to Callerton. Do you expect to stay long?"

Katiana shrugged. "I do not know," she said. "I would hope not. I prefer to return to London as quickly as I can."

"Then I shall send word to you in London," Dacia said. "Where do you live?"

"At the home of Lady Ethyl de Edington on Coleman Street."

"I shall remember. In fact, I shall—"

A knock on the door interrupted her, and both women turned to see a servant standing in the doorway.

"What is it, Abie?" Dacia said.

The male servant stood respectfully out in the corridor. "His lordship asks you to join him in the hall, my lady," he said.

Dacia looked at Katiana and lifted her shoulders. "The men have summoned us," she said. "I can tell them that you are resting, if you like. You do not need to go down until you are ready."

Katiana stood up, but as she did so, she noticed the very dusty traveling dress she was wearing. "I would like to change my garment," she said. "Poor Titus has had to look at me in this dusty mess for days. It would be nice to wear something that wasn't covered in dirt."

Dacia was on her feet. "Of course, my lady," she said. "May I help you?"

"Surely you should not trouble yourself."

Dacia flashed a grin at her and moved to the bed where her satchel was sitting. "What do you have?" she said. "Open up your bag and let us look through your things."

Katiana chuckled. "You will be sorely disappointed," she said. "Titus would only let me bring one bag, so I do not have anything pretty with me. I wish it were not so. I would so like to look… presentable."

She almost didn't finish the sentence, perhaps thinking she sounded too silly, but Dacia caught on. She could see that Katiana wanted to look pretty, and she suspected why.

She'd seen the way Titus had looked at Katiana when they were first introduced.

"I think I have something that would fit you," she said, looking her over. "I'm a little shorter than you are, but I'm sure I have something. It would be nice to look lovely for an evening, wouldn't it? I am sure you haven't had much opportunity, traveling as you have. Wait here and I will return."

Katiana watched her rush off. Perhaps the least bit excited that she might have something lovely to wear for Titus, she quickly went about washing and grooming for the evening. She didn't want to put her dirty, sweaty, travel-weary body into Lady Doncaster's beautiful dress, so she went back to the basin of water and the lavender soap. Using the cloths that had come with the food to cover it, she washed every part of her body that she could reach whilst still wearing her shift. The traveling dress had come off, and the kirtle beneath, leaving her in the fine linen shift, which was then pushed around as she washed arms, legs, underarms, and other areas that needed it.

Once that was finished, she hurried back to her satchel to collect her combs and pins. Katiana's hair was long and straight, but there was texture to it. The dark blonde color was bronze in certain light, nearly the same color as her eyes. She had a small traveling mirror, a little thing made out of polished bronze, and she inspected herself as she combed her hair furiously, finally pulling the hair around her face back and braiding it. Then she pinned it up, like a bun against the back of her head, with the pins she brought. She was very nearly finished when the chamber door opened again, and Dacia appeared with a garment that was dark red and silky.

One look at Dacia's face and Katiana knew she was going to love it.

Hopefully, Titus would, too.

CHAPTER TWELVE

"**A**ND THAT'S WHEN I took his damnable head off and took great pleasure in unseating him. The purse I won was enormous!"

Titus was boasting. He was also tipsy, which meant the boasting was coming more naturally than usual. He was facing his brother and Damian de Lohr, who had come in from the gatehouse to listen to a wild story of a tournament in Middlesbrough that included fights, too much food and drink, and the death of a knight. Titus was having a grand time telling the story, for there was no better storyteller in the entire de Wolfe family than Titus himself.

"Well done," Cassius said, slamming his cup against the tabletop. "But what about the bastard that killed de Brito? What happened to him?"

Titus was sitting on the table, one foot propped on his chair and the other on the floor. He sobered at the question.

"He was a de la Londe knight," he muttered. "You know the house. Brutal, unethical scum, and anyone who serves them has the same character. We beat the man to a bloody pulp and then some. We let him linger for a day or two before he finally succumbed to his injuries. All the while, his men tried to take him from us. The lord who sponsored the tournament tried to buy him away from us. But we would not let him go. We let him die a long, lingering, painful death."

Cassius nodded in approval. "Excellent," he said quietly. "Has de la Londe protested the treatment?"

"He cannot protest the death of a man who killed unjustly. Vengeance was ours."

"And Ronan?"

Titus lifted his eyebrows. "That is something of a story in and of itself," he said. "He promised de Brito as the man lay dying that he would take care of his pregnant widow. I do not know what has happened since, but Ronan wasn't too keen on it."

Cassius frowned. "Take care of a pregnant widow?" he said, aghast. "And do what? I'm certain Ronan's wife has something to say about that."

"I'm sure she does, even if she is a worthless bitch."

Cassius was a little more tactful that Titus, but he couldn't disagree. Their cousin, Ronan de Wolfe, had been married to a woman who didn't seem to think marriage should keep her from having lovers. It was one of those family secrets no one really talked about but everyone knew. Titus reached over to grab the pitcher and pour himself more wine.

"All tragedy aside, it was an excellent tourney," he said. "I went to London immediately thereafter, and I've been there ever since. And now, I am heading back to Berwick."

Cassius took another swig of his wine. "And Lady Katiana?" he said. "Where is she bound for?"

"Callerton Castle," Titus said. "She received word that her father is dying, and since I was going to Berwick, I offered to escort her."

Cassius regarded him. "That is not something you would usually do."

"What do you mean?"

"You know exactly what I mean," Cassius said. "Since when do you take the time for anything other than your own needs or wants? You're not usually so chivalrous, Titus."

Titus frowned. "I am the very model of chivalry."

Cassius guffawed. "Would you be so chivalrous if she was not beautiful? I doubt it."

Titus was unhappy with his brother's teasing. "Let me tell you something, you smug dog," he said. "Lady Katiana and I knew each other long ago. I told you that we fostered together, but only for a short time. I met her again quite by accident in London recently, and we have formed a friendship. Nay… more than that. I am going to marry the woman, Cass, so you may as well know it. I am taking her home so that I may ask her father's permission to marry her."

Cassius didn't believe he was serious for a moment because Titus had never shown any real interest in marriage. He was too wrapped up with the Executioner Knights for such a thing.

"You said her father was dying," Cassius pointed out.

Titus conceded the point. "If he is dead by the time we arrive, then I will have a problem, because I am assuming her brother will be at Callerton."

"She has a brother?"

"She does," Titus said. "Ansel de Edington and I have never gotten on. The man is a brutal, nasty bastard who used to take pleasure in beating his sister. The last time I saw him, we fought. I am not entirely sure he will be pleased to see me, nor am I entirely sure he will give me permission to marry his sister."

"What do you intend to do?"

Titus shrugged. "I am not certain," he said. "But I will tell you this—I am not leaving her at Callerton. She's not seen her brother in many years because the man liked to beat on her, so there is no possibility that I will leave her there and continue on to Berwick."

"You will take her with you to Berwick?"

Titus may have been tipsy, but the conversation was sobering him up. "I will not leave her behind, Cass."

Cassius could sense that the conversation had turned serious. He glanced over at Damian, who had been sitting silently throughout the entire exchange, and the knight took the hint. This was a conversation meant for the brothers only, given the subject, so Damian got up from the table and headed out, making some excuse about checking posts for the evening.

But Cassius was glad to have him away.

"Titus," he said when Damian had disappeared from the hall. "Are you serious about all of this? I've never heard you speak this way before. You've never once mentioned your desire to marry."

Titus was looking at his cup of wine. "And you never once mentioned your desire to marry before you met Dacia," he said, finally looking at his brother. "Things change. Men meet the right women and things change."

"Even so, you must do this the right way," Cassius said. "Let's hope the father isn't dead, but if he is and Lady Katiana is the ward of her brother, then you must, unfortunately, deal with him. Mayhap the man has changed over the years."

"I doubt it," Titus said. Then he started to look around the hall. "Where are the women, anyway? Why are they not here, with us?"

Cassius looked over his shoulder and spied one of his most trusted servants. He called the man over, muttered a few words to him, and sent the servant off at a swift pace.

"I'll summon them," he said. "Does Lady Katiana know how you feel about the situation?"

Titus nodded. "Of course she does," he said. "She's a brilliant woman, Cass. She can sing and play an instrument. She writes her own music. She's witty and kind and elegant. She's everything a woman should be but seldom is."

"And you want to marry her."

"Very much."

Cassius still wasn't sure if he believed him, but Titus seemed convinced. "I'm not entirely sure you should go to Callerton Castle alone," he said. "Mayhap I should go with you. Me and about four hundred men. Why not let me negotiate for your bride? If the lady's brother has the final word, it might go better for you if I do."

Titus looked at him as if surprised by the offer. "I do not like the sense of not fighting my own battles," he said. "But… but I want this badly, Cass. I would not ask you to intervene on my behalf, but if you're offering, I shall accept."

That was a little shocking to Cassius, who had been certain Titus would refuse. But that was the moment Cassius began to think that Titus truly was serious about all of this. If he was asking for Cassius' help, because Titus asked for no man's help, then he must want it badly, as he'd said.

That told him his that his brother's intentions were real.

"Very well," Cassius said. "I'll go with you. Where is this Callerton Castle, anyway?"

"On the northern edge of the Pennines, south of Newcastle," Titus said. "At least, it's in that area. I planned to stop and ask for directions in Darlington or Auckland."

"Does the lady know?"

"I've not asked her."

Cassius put his cup to his lips. "You would think she would know where her home is," he said. "Ask her."

Titus shrugged and went back to his wine, thinking on Katiana and feeling strongly, more than ever, that he wasn't going to leave her at Callerton. He could tell by the way Cassius was looking at him that he believed him to be mad, or worse, that this was some kind of whim, but Titus had never felt more whim-less in his entire life.

He was determined.

Since the hour of the evening meal was rapidly approaching, soldiers began to wander in from the bailey and take their seats at one of several tables in the great hall. Damian even came back in, but he stayed away from the dais where Cassius and Titus were sitting. Titus was still seated on the table, now into his third cup of fine Spanish wine, but his back was to the door. He didn't see when Dacia and Katiana entered the great hall until Cassius thumped him on the leg.

"Titus," he muttered. "Get off the table and sit in your seat like a well-bred man, unless you want Lady Katiana to see how ill-mannered you are."

Jolted from his train of thought, Titus was already off the table, turning to see Dacia and Katiana approaching the dais. Truth be told, it was difficult for him to keep his astonishment off his face.

He'd never seen anything so beautiful.

Katiana was wearing a gown of dark red silk, something that looked stunning with her coloring. Dacia had her by the hand, leading her up to the table, and Titus couldn't take his eyes off her. He came off the dais as the women drew near.

"Good eve to you, my lady," he said, having eyes only for Katiana. "Did you bring that dress with you?"

Katiana was close to flushing because of the way Titus was looking at her. "Lady Doncaster was nice enough to loan it to me," she said. "I did not bring anything suitably nice for a feast in a duke's hall, so I am grateful for her generosity."

Titus turned to Dacia, who was smiling openly at Katiana. "Thank you, my dearest girl," he said, grabbing Dacia by the upper arms and kissing her rather forcefully on the cheek. "Thank you so very much. She looks beautiful."

Dacia chuckled, wiping the wine-smelling wet spot on her cheek and looking to her husband, who simply shook his head at his brother's behavior. Titus was demonstrative, more so when he was drunk, so Dacia giggled as she headed over to the dais where her husband was sitting. That left Katiana alone with Titus, who was riveted to her like a moth to flame.

He couldn't look at anything else.

"Do you like the dress, then?" Katiana said, holding out the skirt to show him. "Lady Doncaster was so very kind to loan it to me."

Titus' eyes glimmered at her. "I like it," he said. "You are magnificent in it. And it has made me realize something."

"What?"

"That I have missed you in the short time we have been separated."

Katiana smiled coyly. "It has been a very short amount of time."

"Are you saying that you did not miss me?"

She laughed softly. "Of course I missed you," she said.

"How can I not miss you?"

Titus took her hand and turned her for the hall entry. "Will you walk with me?" he said. "Once we sit at the table, I must share you with Dacia and Cass, and I do not want to share you at the moment."

She didn't particularly want to share him, either. Katiana smiled up at him, looping her arm through his as he led her from the hall, out into the evening that was surprisingly mild. Overhead, an occasional nightbird sang and the moon hung low in the sky. Titus and Katiana were so engrossed in looking at one another that Katiana very nearly stepped in a puddle of unknown origin. She gasped and froze, and Titus took quick action by swinging her into his arms and carrying her to safety several feet away.

"That was very gallant of you," she said as he put her on her feet. "You helped me avert a disaster."

Titus took her hand as he faced her beneath the starry sky. "It would not do to have that lovely dress ruined," he said. "In truth, I wanted to get you away from Cassius and Dacia for a reason."

Her eyes twinkled. "I thought you did not wish to share me."

"I don't," he said. "But I have another reason. I wanted to tell you that Cass has agreed to negotiate for our marriage."

Katiana looked at him curiously. "What do you mean?"

Titus lifted his eyebrows. "I mean that if your father has passed by the time we reach Callerton, it is a probability that I will have to negotiate with your brother," he said. "The last time I saw Ansel was when I pounded him for striking you. Something tells me that he has not forgotten that."

Katiana's smile faded. "I think that is a fair statement."

"That will put me at a disadvantage."

Katiana sighed heavily, all of the joy gone from her face as she thought on her father, and her brother, and how men she hadn't seen in years should suddenly be responsible for her future happiness. Everything she wanted and hoped for would come down to them.

Everything.

"It does not seem fair that two men who have disregarded me my entire life should still be in control of it," she said after a moment. "My father was apathetic at best, and Ansel… Titus, all he has ever done is torment and hurt me. And he hates you. I know he does. He will never give you permission to marry me, so we must pray that my father is still alive. At least there will be a chance."

Titus was thinking the very same thing, though he hadn't wanted to voice it. It distressed him to know that Katiana had the same mindset he did.

"That is why Cass is coming with us," he said. "He is an excellent negotiator. Ansel does not know him and should therefore have no prejudice against him. Honestly, Katia, I am not without means to buy myself a bride, though I'm loath to put it in those terms. I will offer them a goodly sum of money for you if that is what it takes."

Katiana shook her head, becoming increasingly despond-ent. "Let us speak of this in truthful terms, Titus," she said. "All we've ever spoken of is a desire to court and to wed. We've not spoken of the reality of the situation except briefly. The reality is that my father will more than likely agree to a betrothal simply to be rid of me. No man wants a spinster for a daughter. But if my father is dead and Ansel is the new Lord Callerton, he will deny us out of spite. Worse still, he might even try to find another husband for me simply to punish you for beating him down those years ago. He was a nasty, vindictive lad back then, and I do not think he has changed. I cannot imagine that he has."

"Mayhap," Titus said. "But you do not know that for certain. We can hope for the best."

Katiana gazed up at him, pain in her expression. "If he had changed, my father would not have sent him to serve at Thornton Tower," she said quietly. "My father sent Ansel away because he could not tolerate him. That does not speak of a changed man to me."

She had a point. Titus sighed faintly. "That is very possible, but I do not see where I have a choice," he said. "I must ask permission, from your father or your brother. That is why Cass is coming—to ensure success."

Katiana simply looked at him a moment before hanging her head. "I do not know why I did not think of this sooner," she said. "What we were to ultimately face, that is. I suppose I was simply caught up in happiness I've never known before. But now that we are speaking of it, the truth is that this marriage may not happen at all. I've been given a taste of happiness I never thought I would experience, but mayhap that is all it will ever be—a taste."

"You do not know that, Katia. I will not give up. You must believe that."

She pulled her hand from his. "Even if my father is still alive, if Ansel has his ear, I am sure my brother will poison my father against you," she said. "He will have something to say about this, and it will not be good."

Titus could see that she was working herself into a bit of a state. "You must have faith that Cass will ensure our marriage," he said. "My brother is very persuasive. I have complete confidence in him."

Katiana was still looking at the ground. "May I ask you a question?"

"Of course, love."

She suddenly looked up at him. Her smile, for a brief moment, was back. "Love," she murmured. "You called me 'love.'"

He grinned, his teeth reflecting the weak moonlight. "Did I offend you?"

"Nay."

"Then what is your question?"

"How badly do you want to marry me, Titus?"

"I should think that is fairly obvious."

"Tell me."

"So badly that I will do anything to gain your hand. Even if it means giving my entire fortune to your father in exchange."

She pondered that before looking to her feet again. It was clear that she was mulling something over. When she finally spoke, he barely heard her.

"There is one way to force him into an agreement."

Titus frowned. "How could I do that?"

"If I am… compromised," she said softly. "No man will want another man's leavings. That will practically ensure his agreement, and if we take it to the church, they will insist on a marriage no matter what my father or brother say."

Titus stared at her. He hadn't expected to hear that coming out of her mouth. After a moment, he sighed heavily and scratched his chin, turning away from her as he pondered her suggestion. He found himself looking up at the sky, mulling it all over, the advantages and disadvantages. So much hinged on whether Paulus de Edington was still alive. If he was, there was a chance. But if he wasn't…

The question remained if Titus was willing to take that risk.

"I think compromising you would be a desperate move," he finally said. "I may be the dandy lad of the family, foolish in some ways, reckless in others, but I'm not stupid. When the situation is serious, I understand the greater implications better than anyone. If I compromised you… there would be no turning back."

Katiana suddenly turned away from him, skirts gathered, running for the keep. Startled, Titus took off after her, his long strides catching her easily. He grasped her before she could reach the stairs leading into the keep, but she fought him. She smacked his hands and tried to pull away.

"Let me go," she demanded. "Release me, Titus."

"I will not," he said, trying not to hurt her as he attempted to maintain his grip. "Not until you tell me why you ran. What did I say?"

She was starting to weep. "It *would* be a desperate move," she said tightly. "I am so ashamed to have suggested it. I should not have even said it. But… but I am terrified that this joy we've found in one another is only temporary. It would be easier to walk away from it now than go through the tribulation of being denied permission to marry. It would destroy me, Titus. To feed my hopes and dreams only to see them dashed? It would be easier to part ways and forget we ever spoke of such things."

He scowled. Grasping her by both arms, he gave her a gentle shake. "Look at me," he commanded softly. "Katia, look at me now. Do it."

She wouldn't do it. She kept her head down, moving it from side to side when he tried to force her to look at him. Unable to stand it any longer, Titus began kissing the cheek that was facing him. He pulled her against him, his muscular body against her soft one, and tenderly kissed her cheek and forehead, feeling her resistance fade.

She was beginning to tremble.

"You must think me shallow and fickle if you think I would walk away from you simply because your father may or may not agree to a marriage," he murmured. "Or because Ansel thinks he could prevent such a thing. When I told you I wanted to marry you, I meant it. I did not mean only if it was easy. I meant no matter what comes. But if you do not think I am worth the effort, then you must tell me now so we may part as friends. If you are not brave enough for the task, you must tell me."

She looked at him sharply, her eyes wide. "I *am* brave enough," she insisted softly. "But I am also fearful. Fearful that what we both want will not happen if we do not do something about it. We are trusting our future to men who do not care if we are miserable or not!"

"So you think we should take our happiness into our own hands?"

"*Shouldn't* we?"

It was a very good question, because he understood what she was suggesting. It wasn't that she didn't have courage—it was that she was unwilling to trust men who had disregarded her for her entire life with her happiness. She wanted to take control of it, and, truthfully, he wasn't opposed in the least. He was only going to her father or, possibly, her brother because it was the proper way to do things. He was trying to do what was right by her. But maybe doing right by her was to make their decision for them and not trust it to men who might possibly deny him purely out of spite. At least, one of them would.

It was a situation that threatened to destroy everything.

But then a thought occurred to him.

"When my father met my mother, she was a postulate," he said quietly. "She was meant for the church, but my father fell in love with her and married her without anyone's permission. He simply married her and faced the consequences because he knew, once they were married, that neither the church nor man could tear them apart. My parents took their happiness into their own hands. They acted first and sought permission later. Mayhap it is my destiny to do the very same thing."

Katiana looked at him, surprised. "Did they truly marry without permission?" she said, incredulous. "Was your father punished for such a thing?"

Titus shook his head. "Not really," he said. "His father was very upset with him, from what I was told, but there was no punishment. Until my mother's father showed up in Berwick, not realizing she was married, and brought a husband for her. My father had to fight a giant Northman to keep my mother. It's quite a story, truly."

Katiana smiled faintly. "It sounds like it," she said. "I do not care if my father or brother are angry, but I do care if your father is. I've already told you that I do not feel adequate for a de Wolfe son, so his anger is a… concern. He might think I have coerced you into it."

Titus snorted. "My father knows that no one short of God can coerce me into anything," he said. "And he cannot become angry at me for doing the same thing he did. But the question remains—are you brave enough to do this?"

This time, Katiana grasped his hands and held them tightly. She'd never done that before. "Oh, Titus," she breathed. "For the chance to be with you, I will be as brave as you want me to be."

With a glimmer in his eyes, Titus put his arms around her and pulled her to him, slanting his lips over hers in the first true kiss they'd ever experienced together. It was sweet and warm, sending fire through his veins in a manner he'd never experienced before. The woman set him on fire in so many ways that it was difficult for him to think clearly. But the taste of her, the sweet smell of her, filled him like strong drink. Even if he hadn't been slightly tipsy, he was positively drunk with her. He knew then that he would never, ever let her go. He'd kill anyone who tried.

Even her brother.

It was incredible to him that less than two weeks ago, he was focused on his duty for the Executioner Knights and the turmoil that was erupting as a result of Lancaster and Warwick's movements. Now, his focus was on a woman that consumed his entire being. That impulsiveness that marred his character was verging on causing a good deal of trouble, but on the other hand, nothing had ever felt so right. As he tasted Katiana and inhaled her scent, it seemed to him that there was nothing more important than what was happening right here, right now. When he heard Katiana gasp for air because he'd been feasting on her, he realized that he should probably loosen his grip before he smothered her.

But God... things were heated and sultry between them.

"We will go tonight and rouse the priests in the village," he said, his voice heavy with passion. "We shall be married and we will ride to Callerton and announce it. After that... let them rage, but they cannot separate us."

Katiana was breathing heavily, struggling to catch her breath. "This seems like a dream."

"It is no dream, I promise."

She took a couple of deep breaths before lifting her hand and running her fingers through his hair. All the while, she simply studied him.

"You knew this was right from the beginning," she murmured. "You spoke of courting, and I resisted. But you knew, even before I did, that this was meant to be."

"Are you sure of it now, too?"

She nodded, a smile tugging at her lips. "Let us begin our forever tonight," she said. "Let my forever begin with you."

Titus grinned, kissing her hands, her face, and finally her lips. "I already know that I cannot live without you," he said, his lips against her flesh. "I would kill for you and I would die for you. If that is not love, I do not know what is."

Katiana laughed softly. "That sounds quite romantic," she said. "What lady would not wish for her knight to speak of love and killing in the same breath?"

Titus was so giddy that he joined in her laughter. "I can do better than that," he said. "I can speak of kisses and rotting bodies that will heat your blood until you beg for more."

Katiana continued to laugh, putting her hand over his mouth to stop him. "I will settle for love and death," she said. But quickly, she sobered as she gazed into his eyes. "When will we go to the church?"

Titus' attention turned in the direction of the stable where he knew Jesus was bedded down for the night. But the village was about a half-mile from the castle, and he didn't want to walk that stretch with her in the darkness. This evening's plans called for swiftness and safety, and that was what he intended to do.

From this point forward, there was no turning back.

"Now," he said, releasing her from his embrace and taking her hand. "Come with me, my lady. We've something to do."

Katiana followed without hesitation.

CHAPTER THIRTEEN

"THE GATEHOUSE GUARDS said that Titus and the lady went through the gates and headed toward the village about an hour ago," Damian said. "No one stopped him, Cass. No one would dare stop Titus de Wolfe unless they wanted to come away missing teeth."

They were in the great hall of Edenthorpe and the hour was growing late. More than an hour earlier, Titus had taken Katiana from the hall and disappeared.

Vanished.

Cassius had no idea where his brother had gone, and the fact that Titus had left the castle, at night, no less, was incredibly puzzling. Therefore, he listened to Damian's report and tried not to let his confusion show. He simply nodded his head as if it really didn't matter what Titus was doing.

"Mayhap he took her for a moonlight ride," he said, unconcerned. "He'll be back. It's not as if he can keep her out all night."

Damian was as confused as Cassius was, but he had no restraint about showing it. The expression on Dacia's face only seemed to exacerbate it. But Cassius refused to display any concern whatsoever, so Damian simply turned around and headed out of the hall. That left Cassius and Dacia sitting alone on the dais. The boys never joined them in the hall for meals because Dacia didn't like her children around a bunch of unruly soldiers. More than that, she looked forward to the time alone with Cassius.

But this evening, she'd been excited to sup with Katiana and was greatly disappointed that Titus had taken the lady away. She hadn't been concerned at first, but twenty minutes later, and then thirty, she grew curious. She sent a servant out to find them only to be told that they were nowhere to be found. That brought her husband's attention, and soon, soldiers were looking all over the castle for Titus and the lady he'd brought with him. When they came to the gatehouse, however, they were told by a pair of sentries that Titus and the woman had left the gates.

Yet no one seemed to know why.

In truth, Dacia thought she might know why but she was afraid to voice her thoughts. As Damian headed off, she spoke with great hesitation.

"He's fond of her, you know," she said quietly. "Titus, I mean. He's fond of Lady Katiana and she is fond of him."

Cassius didn't react other than to take a swallow of wine from his cup. "He's simply taken her on a moonlight ride," he said, glancing at his wife. "I can remember doing that with you on occasion."

Dacia gave him a lopsided grin. "Every time you did, we had a child."

"I've taken you out more than four times."

"Possibly. But it's the four times I remember more than the others."

Cassius cracked a smile, reaching out to take her hand. "I'm sure there will be more moonlight rides in the future and more children," he said. "But I do not need moonlight in order to bed my wife. I can do that without any inspiration at all. You set my blood boiling with a mere look."

Dacia shushed him. "Quiet," she admonished him. "Someone may hear you."

"Who?" Cassius demanded, looking around. "In case you've not yet realized it, we've been abandoned."

"They'll return."

He paused a moment before glancing at her. "Where do *you* think they've gone?" he asked. "Did Lady Katiana give you a clue?"

Dacia shook her head. "Nay," she said. "She didn't say anything to me. Is it possible that Titus knows someone nearby and has gone for a visit?"

"Mayhap the lady knows someone nearby. Mayhap he took her there."

Dacia sighed faintly, thinking on the lovely Lady Katiana and how sweet she was. Dacia had truly enjoyed their conversation. The lass didn't seem particularly strong-willed or even manipulative, but she knew that Titus could be when he put his mind to it. Perhaps their vanishing had been his idea. Dacia knew that Titus wasn't a danger to the lady by any means, but she seriously wondered why they'd disappeared. Cassius didn't seem too concerned, but Dacia suspected that was all an act. Cassius wasn't the nonchalant type. She caught the attention of a servant and called the woman over with the intention of having their meal brought to the table, which they'd been holding off on, when the very man in question suddenly appeared in the great hall entry.

And he was holding Lady Katiana by the hand.

"There they are," Dacia said with relief. "See, my darling?"

Cassius did. He sat up in his chair, watching Titus and the lady cross the floor in their direction. Dacia quickly ordered the meal for the entire table as the vanishing couple drew near.

"My apologies for delaying your meal," Titus said. "Where's the food? We are hungry."

"It was ready over an hour ago," Cassius said, frowning. "Where did you go?"

Titus didn't answer right away. He pulled out a chair for Katiana to sit before taking the chair next to her. Servants were swarming around them, bringing cups of wine and putting bread on the table. Titus took a big, long drink before replying to his brother.

"Into the village," he said, smacking his lips. His tipsy condition had worn off long ago, and he took another drink as if looking to quickly reclaim it. "We went to the church."

"Oh?" Dacia said, looking between Titus and Katiana. "My lady, if you wished to pray, I would have been very happy to summon the priest to Edenthorpe. You did not need to go out into the night."

Katiana smiled wanly as Titus answered for her. "We did not go to pray," he said. "We went to be married."

Dacia's eyes widened as Cassius slammed his cup on the table and nearly toppled it. "What?" he said. "You went to... *Married*? Titus, what did you do?"

Titus was quite calm. "I just told you," he said. "I found a priest and we were married, not a half-hour ago."

Cassius looked as if his eyeballs were going to pop from his skull. His focus moved between Titus and Katiana before he finally looked at Dacia to see what her reaction was.

Her features mirrored his own.

Shock.

"I think you'd better start from the beginning, Titus," Dacia said. "I did not even know the two of you were courting. I suppose I suspected, but did you truly go into town and find a priest?"

"We just spoke of this, Titus!" Cassius blurted. "Not an hour ago, we spoke of my going to Callerton Castle and negotiating a betrothal on your behalf. Was that not good enough? You could not wait for me to do it?"

Titus held up a hand to calm his nearly irate brother. "Cass, listen to me," he said with surprising calm. "What we discussed was all well and good an hour ago, but afterwards, the lady and I spoke of the situation. We spoke of how her brother positively hates me, and, chances are, her father is already dead and Ansel is now responsible for her. The man would deny my request to marry her purely out of spite, and then where would we be? I would fight him, and possibly kill him, or he would have me ousted from Callerton, whereupon I would have to ride to Berwick and beg Papa for his army. You know it would be a mess, all of it, because I would not give up. I've got too much depending on me right now for something like this to drain my focus, so the lady and I decided to take control of our future and our happiness. We do not want to chance what could potentially happen. I am sorry if you do not like it, but that is what we've done. If you'd prefer I leave tonight, then we can do that. I can find lodgings somewhere else."

By the time he was finished, Cassius was less irate and Dacia was positively sympathetic. Cassius finally shook his head, sighing heavily as he sat back in his chair.

"Don't be daft," he mumbled, rubbing his forehead to stave

off the headache that threatened. "You're not going anywhere tonight. I suppose I'm surprised more than anything. You *truly* married her?"

Titus nodded, looking at Katiana, who was smiling timidly. He took her hand and brought it to his lips for a tender kiss.

"I did," he said. "I do not regret it, nor will I ever. When something is right, you know it. You feel it in your heart and in your soul. All I know is that I cannot be without this woman, Cass. I think you know something about that. When a man wants a woman to be his wife… nothing else matters."

Cassius didn't have an argument for that. He looked at Dacia, who was smiling knowingly at him. Of course Cassius knew how Titus felt, but the fact remained that he'd done something wrong.

Quite wrong.

He'd gone about it the wrong way.

"Titus," Cassius muttered, shaking his head. "I wish you'd told me what you planned to do."

"Why?" Titus said. "So you could talk me out of it? No offense, Cass, but this marriage is not between you and me and the lady. It's only between me and the lady, and we will make the decisions that are best for us."

Cassius' jaw twitched. "So you've made it," he said. "What now? Are you going to ride to Callerton and tell them that you've married her without permission and dare them to challenge the marriage? Dare them to try to punish you? They will have a serious grievance against you, Titus. I do not know who their magistrate is, but they can take you before the magistrate and charge you with any number of things, thievery among them."

Given that Cassius, as a duke, was the itinerant justice for his domain, he knew a little something about the laws of the land. Titus knew his brother wasn't trying to be cruel, only a realist, but he was starting to feel defensive.

"I'll pay them a goodly sum for the marriage," he said steadily. "I will compensate them for it."

"But what if her father already has someone selected?" Cassius said. "Have you considered that? What if her father or brother already have a husband in mind for her? What then? Because if they have someone already in mind for her and a deal has been struck, he can charge you with thievery as well. This is serious, Titus. Do you not understand that?"

Titus remained cool. "You are not my father, Cassius," he said. "Rage at me all you like, but it has been done. As I said, we can find lodgings elsewhere if you prefer we leave tonight."

Before Cassius could reply, Dacia stood up and held out a hand to Katiana. "Come with me, my lady," she said briskly. "You and I will eat in your borrowed chamber whilst you wait for Titus to join you. Come along, now."

She took the hand of Katiana, who looked at Titus with concern, but Titus touched her cheek and nodded. He appreciated what Dacia was doing, removing Katiana from what was becoming an increasingly distressing conversation. Cassius was not finished with him, so it was best to remove Katiana before she became too upset and the evening was ruined.

But Katiana wasn't ready to leave yet.

She had something to say to Cassius.

"My lord," she said, holding up a hand to gently put a halt to Dacia's tugging. "I realize you do not agree with what we have done, but allow me to explain something to you that will mayhap help in that regard. You see, both Titus and I are concerned with my brother's response to Titus' request to marry me, concerned enough that in order to assure our happiness, we were compelled to take matters into our own hands. You do not know my brother, but let me assure you that our concern is well warranted. I can further assure you that neither my father nor my brother has any future husband selected for me. My father shirked his duties long ago by sending me to live with his aunt in the hopes that she would find me a husband, and my brother has nothing for me but contempt. Not every family loves one another as the House of de Wolfe does. We do not all enjoy such familial affection and security. Sometimes, great danger is involved. In this case, that is what we are facing."

She was well-spoken and concise. Cassius didn't want to engage in any manner of argument with her, and he appreciated the fact that she was trying to take the heat off Titus, but the fact remained that Titus had done something he should not have done. Cassius tried to be polite in his response.

"I understand that, my lady," he said. "But my brother has—"

"Forgive me, my lord, but you do not know the situation at all," Katiana said, interrupting him. "You do not know what we are facing. When I was a small child, as far back as I can recall, I feared my brother. He was a nasty bully of a lad, and when he became upset, he would find me and he would beat me. I do not mean a slap. I mean he would take his fists to me and punch me in the face and body until I bled. One time, he dragged me from the castle, took me into the forest, and tied my hair to a rope and strung it up in a branch. I remained there for a day and a night until my father's men found me. When I was brought back to the castle, half-dead from exposure, all my father could do was look at me without comment and walk away. He did not discipline my brother. He simply let him do whatever he pleased. I could go on and on with the horrible things he did to me, like shoving cloth up my nose and gagging me in the hopes that I would suffocate, but there are too many stories like that to tell. This is the man we are to face."

By the time she was finished, Cassius was looking at her with great concern. He sighed softly, shaking his head to the horrors she described, and tried desperately to maintain his logical perspective.

"I am sorry for you, my lady, truly," he said. "But the fact remains that—"

Emotional, Katiana slapped the tabletop with both hands in an uncharacteristic display, cutting him off for the last time. "If my father is dead, and I have every reason to believe he is by now, then we will be facing my brother when we return to Callerton," she said through clenched teeth. "Titus wanted to do the proper thing and ask his permission, but I will tell you now that my brother will not allow it. He will send Titus away and treat me like an animal, or worse, so believe me when I tell you that it would do no good to seek permission from my brother for a marriage. I am as good as dead if I am left in his charge, but if you truly feel that it would be the right and proper thing to do, then Titus and I will not consummate this marriage. We will return to Callerton and you can try to negotiate a betrothal with my brother. But I will tell you now that it will be to no avail. He hates de Wolfe and everything your family stands for. He'll kill me before he allows Titus to marry me. Now, you can choose my fate and I will abide by your decision no matter what Titus says. The choice is yours."

Cassius was watching her, his expression full of sorrow and disgust. Behind Katiana, Dacia had tears streaming down her cheeks, and Cassius could see that. He could see how upset his wife was, and he was infuriated by it. Not because Katiana had been so brutally truthful with him, but because she had made him the final judge of the situation. She'd put the burden on him. Cassius was a fair and just magistrate and knew the law. He knew what was right. But he also knew that if even half of what the lady said was true, it would forever damage his relationship with Titus were he to go against his brother's wishes.

And condemn an intelligent, lovely young lady to a terrible fate.

"Dacia," he finally muttered, looking away. "Take the lady out of here. I want to talk to Titus."

Sniffling, Dacia took Katiana by the hand and led her from the hall, leaving Cassius unable to look at his brother. Titus was riveted to him, however, trying to get a sense of what Cassius was thinking.

He didn't have long to wait.

"Damn you for putting me in this position," Cassius said after a moment. "Now you've put me in the middle of it."

Titus blinked slowly. "Nothing she said was untrue," he said. "Cass, if you do not intend to help me, then I only ask that you do not get in my way. I must do as I must."

Cassius looked at him. "You are my brother, Titus," he said. "I suppose if the situation were reversed, you would not abandon me. I know you wouldn't. I will not abandon you, either, but this is… difficult."

"Then let me make it simple for you," Titus said, leaning forward with his elbows on the table. "I am going to put this into perspective, so listen to me. You heard everything that Katia told you. Everything is true. She is in great danger from her brother. Now… imagine it's not Katia in danger, but Dacia. What would you do if Dacia was in that position, with a brother positioned to abuse her? Even kill her?"

Cassius rolled his eyes. "But she's not in that position."

"But what if she was?"

"Then I would kill the bastard. Is that what you want to hear?"

"Now you know how I feel."

Cassius knew that. He knew it very well. "Tell me something, Titus," he said. "This wasn't something impulsive, was it? It's not because you simply want to bed the woman and you feel that you need to marry her because of it?"

Titus snorted. "I've bedded many women that I've not felt the need to marry," he said. "And so have you. What made Dacia different? I'm sure you can't tell me, other than to say it was just a feeling you had, a feeling in your heart that told you she was the woman you wanted to marry. I have that same feeling for Katia, Cass. She's worthy to be my wife, and the joy is in discovering just how deeply I am destined to love her. Can you understand that?"

Cassius gave up. He poured himself more wine and took a long drink. "I understand it," he said. "If you feel that this is meant to be, then I'll not argue the point with you any longer. I just wanted to make sure this wasn't a whim, or worse—that she had coerced you into it. But I do not get that sense."

"You do not get that sense because neither is true."

"Are you still leaving for Callerton on the morrow?"

Titus nodded. "I am," he said. "Though I have been thinking about going straight to Berwick and having Papa announce the marriage to de Edington. There is no possibility that the man will strike back against the mighty Earl of Berwick."

Cassius frowned. "Do not tell me that you would hide behind Papa."

Titus shook his head. "Not hide," he said. "But given how much her brother hates me, it might make it easier for our family, all the way around. De Edington cannot turn it into a personal vendetta, and, more importantly, it keeps Katia safe behind a de Wolfe wall."

Cassius understood. "So you'll take her back to Berwick and let Papa smooth the situation," he said. "If de Edington is as bad as you say he is, then I cannot disagree. But when then? You still have a duty to de Lohr. Are you simply going to leave her at Berwick and continue your life as a spy?"

Titus shrugged. "I do not know," he said honestly. "I've not thought about it. Of course, I would like to continue serving de Lohr. It is what I am trained for. But I do not want to go away for months at a time and leave my wife behind. It sounds so strange to say that—*my wife*. I have a wife."

Cassius looked at him, a glimmer of mirth in his eyes. "You certainly do," he said. "I can tell you from personal experience that they are quite agreeable to have."

"Only agreeable?"

"They are wonderful."

The brothers shared a chuckle, a rare event given the tension of the conversation. But in the end, they were brothers, and close ones at that, and Cassius would support anything Titus did.

Foolish or not.

This was their moment of truth.

"Thank you for your counsel, Cass," Titus said softly. "Thank you for not throwing us bodily from Edenthorpe. I'm sure that crossed your mind."

Cassius grinned. "Not particularly," he said. "But you did surprise me."

Titus chuckled. "Why?" he said. "Papa did the same thing when he married Mama. Marrying without permission is a de Wolfe tradition, I think."

Cassius snorted. "A tradition that can get one into a good deal of trouble," he said. "But you are right—Papa married Mama without permission. Poppy did, too, or so I recall, though his situation was much more of a mess than this one. He married a woman meant for his liege."

"I suppose marriage is never straightforward, no matter how much we would like it to be."

"I would agree with that," Cassius said. "Now, retire for the evening and make sure this union can never be broken, by anyone. And send my wife back down here to me. You do not need an audience for what you are about to do."

Titus flashed a smile. "Katiana likes Dacia a great deal."

"I think the feeling is mutual."

Titus stood up, reaching out to put his hand on his brother's shoulder from across the table. "Good sleep to you, Cass," he said. "I will see you on the morrow."

Cassius nodded. "Indeed, you will," he said. "And Titus?"

"What?"

"Congratulations."

Titus simply grinned and left the dais, making his way from the hall as Cassius watched him go. He pondered the situation his brother found himself in, and now that he was calmer about it, he was coming to understand why Titus did what he did. When emotion was involved, and certainly something as strong as love or a budding love, a man would do anything for a future with a woman who made him feel something he'd never felt before. Cassius understood that all too well.

But something told him that Titus was in for trouble.

It was just a hunch he had.

❧

"I only have a sleeping shift," Katiana said as she pulled her linen shift from her satchel. "I do not have anything grand to sleep in."

Dacia was inspecting the fine linen shift. "Did you not bring a robe?"

Katiana shook her head. "It would not fit in the satchel," she said. "I have a beautiful one back in London, made from silk with rabbit fur cuffs. It is perfect for cold nights."

"It shouldn't be too cold tonight," Dacia said, letting go of the linen. "Moreover, you'll be sleeping with your husband, and I imagine he'll be quite warm. If he's anything like Cass, you will not have to worry about freezing to death."

Katiana grinned, lowering her gaze as her cheeks flushed. "I've slept alone my entire life," she said. "This will be a new adventure for me."

Dacia knew there was a good deal of truth in that statement, in more ways than one. Katiana was a new bride, after all, and presumably a virgin, so Dacia felt some responsibility about the situation. More often than not, brides had no idea what they were in for until it was all over. Dacia debated about whether or not to say anything, but her concern won out.

She had been a virgin bride herself once, after all.

"Forgive me for being so bold," she said. "If you do not wish to speak of this, then you just need to tell me and I'll not bring it up again, but... but you do know what is about to happen, don't you?"

Katiana knew exactly what she meant, and it was a struggle not to become embarrassed about it. "I've been told," she said. "I've never experienced it myself, of course, but it has been explained to me what is to happen."

"Good," Dacia said. But she put her hand on Katiana's arm and squeezed gently. "I, too, had things explained to me and thought I knew everything, but that wasn't the case. It was much different than what I was told."

"How so?"

"It is great fun once you have some practice," she said, smiling. "But the first time… my advice to you is to simply relax and let Titus do the work. Men usually know what they are doing."

Katiana looked at her, cocking her head curiously. "And how is that?" she said. "How do they know what to do and we do not?"

Dacia chuckled. "Because one of you must know what to do or it will all end in a disaster."

Katiana started to giggle. "That never made any sense to me," she said. "Women must remain chaste, but a man is encouraged to do… *that*. I am not entirely sure I like the idea of my husband touching another woman before me. In the same manner he will be touching me."

Dacia's eyes twinkled. "Jealous?"

Katiana burst out laughing. "Possibly," she said. "I've never even considered such a thing before, but it's bloody well outrageous that he's touched another woman before me."

Dacia was glad that Katiana was finding some humor in the situation, and they shared a hearty laugh. "Do not let it bother you," she finally said. "Look at Cass; he's beautiful. He's the most beautiful man I've ever seen. It used to drive me mad thinking of the women he'd been with before, but he told me that before he married me, he'd only been with shadows. I was the only light he'd ever known."

"That's very sweet," Katiana said. Then her humor faded. "I… I did not mean to shout at him tonight. I hope you were not offended."

Dacia shook her head. "Of course not," she said. "I'm only sorry you've had to endure so much in your life from a brother. A man who should always protect you. That's simply not right, Katiana."

"I know," Katiana said. "It's not right, but it took me years to understand that. I went through my childhood thinking that was my role in life. It was only when I grew older that I realized how wrong it was. And I cannot let a man like that have dominion over my life and happiness. For once, I must take that control. I've never done it before, but when it comes to my entire life's happiness, I must."

Dacia reached out and grasped her hand. "I do not blame you," she said. "I am on your side, I promise."

Katiana appreciated that. "Then I hope Lord Doncaster is not too upset about it," she said. "I hope he understands our reasons, even if he does not approve."

"He understands."

The reply didn't come from Dacia. It came from a decidedly male voice. They both turned to see Titus standing in the doorway, smiling his easy smile when he saw that he had their attention.

"Sorry," he said. "The door was open and I heard what you said. Cass understands and he supports us, so please do not worry. We've decided that it would be best to continue on to Berwick tomorrow and let my father announce the marriage, but I realize that will defeat the purpose of your being summoned home to see to your father. If you would still like to continue to Callerton for your father's sake, I will understand."

Katiana thought on that seriously. "I told you that I am only going home out of duty," she said. "I received a missive about my father and duty is sending me home, but nothing more. There is no affection or sentiment. Whether I am there or not, my father's fate will be the same. I cannot stop him from dying. Either he will or he won't."

"Do you still want me to take you there?"

"Nay, she does not," Dacia said. She'd been standing silently throughout the conversation, but she had something to say about it. "Why would you take her to a place where she has only known heartache? Where there is a brother waiting to harm her? Titus, if you take her back, you can never let her out of your sight for a moment. She will be in danger ever second of every day. You should go to Berwick and have Papa send her father a missive, announcing the marriage. If he is still alive, he shall answer, and you can make plans to visit at that time. But if her brother answers, then you know she is never to go home again. Not ever."

Katiana was looking at Dacia with gratitude. She'd never had another woman stand up for her or even really show her much more than cursory concern, so Dacia's defense of her was truly endearing. She hardly knew the woman, but already, she felt a bond with her. She reached out to grasp Dacia's hand as she returned her attention to Titus.

"What Lady Doncaster says," she said. "I do not need to go home. If my father still lives, I will make plans to see him when my brother is not there. I want to avoid Ansel at all costs."

Truth be told, Titus was relieved to hear it. He kissed Dacia on the cheek and pulled her hand from Katiana's.

"You are as wise as you are beautiful, Lady Doncaster," he said. "But I do not want you here. Get out so I can have my wife all to myself."

He said it in a jesting way, and Dacia grinned, sauntering her way over to the door. "Are you sure you do not need any advice?" she said.

Titus rolled his eyes. "Nay," he said flatly. "Go, you little minx."

"I did not mean you, Titus. I meant the lady."

Titus turned to her, sneering. "If I must go over to that door and push you out, I will. Do not test me."

"If you push me, I will tell Cass."

"I do not care. He does not frighten me."

"Then I'll tell your mother."

Titus immediately surrendered, throwing up his hands, as Dacia giggled in victory and quit the chamber, shutting the door behind her. Once she was gone, Katiana turned to Titus and started laughing.

"I do like her," she said, hand over her mouth to stifle the giggles. "She's absolutely delightful."

Titus' features contorted in distaste. "She's a bold wench who will get her comeuppance someday," he said, but he didn't mean a word of it. In fact, his gaze was on his wife, a light of warmth coming to his eyes. "Do you really need some advice about tonight?"

Katiana lowered her gaze coyly. "She has already given me sage advice," she said. "She is very kind."

"What did she tell you?"

"To relax and let you do the work."

Titus fought off a grin. "She was right," he said. "But if you have any questions, I am more than happy to answer them."

Katiana's expression took on a mischievous cast. "I cannot imagine that you've done this before," she said. "How would you know anything? You've never been married, so surely not."

Titus let out a guffaw, which sounded like a choke, and he coughed a couple of times as he headed over to the bed. "I should send for some food," he said. "Neither one of us has eaten. Are you hungry?"

Katiana could see that he was obviously trying to change the subject, but she wasn't so willing to let it go yet. "I am hungry," she said. "I can just as easily send for the food. Mayhap you would like to sit down in front of the fire and remove your boots? We can discuss what is to happen tonight, since I've never had a husband and you've never had a wife. Mayhap we really do need Dacia to come back in here and give us some advice."

"I do not need any advice," he said, though he was heading over to the chair next to the hearth. "Stop jesting. You are embarrassing me."

"Why?"

"Because you are trying to force me into a confession I'm not yet ready to make."

"What confession is that?"

He turned to look at her, sharply, only to see that she was verging on laughter. When their eyes met, she burst out into giggles, and he smiled weakly.

"I see," he said. "You *are* trying to embarrass me."

Katiana shook her head. "Not really," she said. "I just find it ironic that women are supposed to remain untouched and unkissed until they are married, but men... There are not the same expectations. And I certainly do not expect that you have remained untouched and unkissed."

Titus sat on the chair, a smile tugging on his lips. "Men are animals," he said simply. "They have needs that women do not, but in truth, I think it is better that men experience those things before they are wed."

"Why is that?"

"So they can perfect their skills for their wives," he said, holding out a hand to her. "I want you to think I am so very perfect, Katia."

Katiana went to him, sliding her hand into his. "You are my champion," she said, a twinkle in her eye. "Of course I think you are perfect. I always have."

He kissed her hand. "And I think that I am unworthy of you, but here we are," he said. "Do you want to eat first?"

Katiana shrugged. "I will do whatever you wish."

He glanced over at the bed. "I think you know what I wish."

She chuckled and let go of his hand, kneeling down in front of him. "Then let me help you with your boots," she said. "I will not let you into our marital bed with your shoes on."

He watched her as she fumbled with his laces. "You are not afraid of what is to come?"

She shrugged. "Afraid is a strong word," she said. "I am curious, I suppose. It must be done, so whether or not I am apprehensive is immaterial."

"A remarkable way to look at it."

With a shy smile, she began to unlace his boots. He leaned forward to help her, but she pushed his hands out of the way and took them off herself, both of them. Unfortunately, his feet smelled horrible, and she burst into laughter as he cringed in embarrassment. The basin of water was still on the table where it had been brought to Katiana earlier in the day, so she quickly brought it over, setting it down on the ground by his feet before going in search of her lavender soap.

All the while, Titus protested.

"You do not have to do that," he said, watching her bustle around. "Truly, love, I can just as easily summon a bath and do this myself. It's simply that I've been traveling for weeks and months, and bathing… I admit it, I'm much like a child who hates to bathe. I hate to take the time, and it is only me smelling my own stench, so I do not bother."

"No longer," Katiana said as she brought her soap over to the basin. "Now, I have to smell you also. Put your feet in the water, please."

"But…"

"Titus de Wolfe, put your feet in the water or you will be sleeping in the stable tonight."

His feet went into the water. As he sat there, horribly embarrassed, Katiana washed his feet with her lavender soap. Truth be told, he was only embarrassed until he realized how lovely it felt for someone to wash his feet. He watched Katiana's lowered head as she scrubbed his toes and thought himself the most fortunate man in the world that such a beautiful, accomplished woman would think enough of him to do such a thing. It was a humbling gesture, and a kind one. So very kind.

That was when he realized that he loved her.

So very much.

"There," she said softly. "All washed and rinsed. I'll see if I can find a cloth to dry them with."

"No need," he said, standing up with wet limbs from mid-shin down. "I have a feeling the rest of me is going to be just as offensive, so I think I should wash… everything."

"If you wish."

"Go sit on the bed and turn your back."

Katiana did as she was told. She could hear the water splashing as Titus went to work washing the smell away, something she thought was very sweet of him. It may have been a small gesture, but it was a considerate one in her eyes. Not that she would have cared, more than likely, because smelly bodies were part of their world, but the fact that he didn't want to offend her on the wedding night with his overwhelming odor was a thoughtful gesture. She sat there with her back turned and a smile on her lips.

"How far is Berwick from here?" she asked.

Titus was in the process of getting the entire floor wet as he washed between his legs and under his armpits.

"We're still at least five days away," he said, running wet hands over his face. "It depends on how good the roads are and how quickly we can move. And I think that we should send your aunt's servants back to London. There is really no need for them any longer."

"True," Katiana said. "And I suspect that Aunt Ethyl will be pleased that we married. She's tried to marry me off for two long years."

"Thankfully, she did not."

"Thankfully."

More splashing sounded behind her. Katiana was about to ask him again if he needed something to dry off with when the bed behind her suddenly gave way. Startled, she fell back into a very big, very wet body.

"There," he said, putting his wet arms around her and nuzzling her neck. "I am clean for you, wife. Remove your clothing and join me."

Chills ran down her spine as his hot breath caressed her ear.

Turning in his arms, she fixed her lips to his, and Titus responded fiercely. He became the aggressor, and she gave herself over to him completely. No fear, no reserve. She'd trusted the man her entire life and she would trust him now, when it meant the most. She was still wearing the dark red dress, which wasn't meant to be wet, and his dampness was causing the dye to bleed. Quickly, they separated, and Katiana was forced to turn around so he could untie the stays on the back. Once those were loose, Titus pulled the dress over her head and tossed it onto the floor.

"Titus!" she gasped. "That belongs to Lady Doncaster. It must not be on the floor!"

Titus used her distraction to pull her shift over her head, tossing that on top of the red dress. "I'll pick it up later," he whispered.

His arms went around her again, pulling her down onto the mattress. His big, damp body covered her, his weight bearing down on her, but Katiana hardly cared. Fears for Dacia's dress were erased as he kissed her firmly, pulling the coverlet over them both, hiding their nakedness from the world. At the moment, it was a privilege of discovery for just the two of them. The more he touched, the more Katiana responded.

She was eager to know all of it.

Titus didn't keep her waiting. As his lips feasted on hers, he closed a big hand gently over her breast, feeling the silken texture against his palm. The action startled Katiana, but she didn't pull away from him. She came to like it when he began tugging at her nipple, toying with it, and when his mouth left hers and he began nursing against that nipple, she gasped in surprise. But surprise turned to ecstasy. Every suckle sent bolts of excitement shooting through her body and between her legs, and something began to spark. It was something that sent her pelvis wriggling, moving against him, as if someone else was in control.

Very quickly, the situation overheated.

Titus could feel her squirming, and he knew exactly what she needed. As he worked her breasts hungrily, his fingers sought out the curls between her legs. Katiana was already wet, her body preparing itself for his entry, and he pushed a finger into her tight, wet sheath simply to introduce her to what was about to take place. He expected resistance at the very least, but when Katiana groaned and opened her legs to him, instinctively, Titus could wait no longer.

He was on fire.

Carefully, he positioned his enormous phallus at her threshold, pushing into her slick and waiting body. He was so big that Katiana's passion was somewhat doused as she felt his big body mating with hers. She tried to move away, trying to ease the sting of possession, but Titus held her firm. She wasn't going anywhere. Coiling his buttocks, he thrust into her once, twice, a third time before seating himself fully. He broke her maiden's barrier, claiming this woman for his wife as he'd never claimed anyone in his life. No one had ever meant this much to him before. Katiana became his, body and soul, and he would kill anyone who tried to separate them.

Ansel de Edington included.

She belonged to him, forever.

Carefully, Titus began to thrust, gathering her up tightly against him, her chest to his, the feel of her soft breasts against his flesh feeding his lust. Beneath him, Katiana groaned and gasped at the new sensations, splaying her legs wider for him, silently begging him to thrust deeper. It was purely instinct, her body responding to his, as her nails dug crescent-shaped wounds into his shoulders.

They were badges of honor as far as Titus was concerned. He could feel the sting, and it spurred him onward. His body pounded into hers, and she accepted all of him, moving with him, thrusting her pelvis against his. It was a magical moment as his manhood buried itself in her wet folds, and he tried to hold back his seed because he simply didn't want the moment to end too quickly. But the de Wolfe seed was waiting to take root impatiently. When Katiana's hands moved from his shoulders to his buttocks, timidly gripping him, Titus could no longer control himself.

His hot seed exploded into her womb, and Katiana felt him shudder as he released. He kept moving within her, however, his hand moving to the junction between her legs, stroking her until she, too, experienced her first release. Gasping as wave after wave of pleasure rolled over her, Katiana had little idea of what had just happened. All she knew was that Titus had put some kind of spell on her, and she had loved every moment of it.

Relax and let Titus do the work.

She had.

As the ripples of pleasure died down, Titus remained buried in his wife, kissing her gently, showing her with his actions his growing feelings for her. He wanted to say something to her, something eloquent and appropriate for the moment, but he simply couldn't find the words. For a man who was never speechless, it was a surprising reaction to the moment. It had meant more to him than he thought it would.

Feelings were running deep.

When Titus finally opened his mouth to speak, he was interrupted by gentle snoring. Shifting slightly, he could see that Katiana had fallen asleep in his arms, and he smiled faintly, laying his head down next to hers simply to watch that glorious woman sleep. The words he'd spoken to her when he'd first proposed marriage, and when she'd finally agreed, came flooding back to him.

You are the easiest decision I have ever made.

And she was.

CHAPTER FOURTEEN

Berwick Castle

BERWICK CASTLE WAS the jewel of the north, a massive fortress built from the gray granite so prevalent to the area. It had enormous towers and an enormous curtain wall, including a stretch of the wall that went all the way down to the river to protect the cogs that would come to do business with the castle. Set within the complex of walls and towers sat an equally massive keep, five stories including the vaults below.

Berwick was the stuff of legends.

That was mostly why it was so coveted by the English and the Scots. It was probably one of the most fought-over castles in all of England because there were times when it would belong to the Scots and then times that it belonged to the English. Each faction tried to hang on to the castle for an extended amount of time, but in the end, the other faction would come for it and it would change hands once again.

At this point in time, happily, it belonged to England. Technically, it was a royal outpost that had been garrisoned by the de Wolfe family. Patrick de Wolfe, the third-born son of

William de Wolfe, had been the garrison commander for more years than he cared to admit. He had been married there, and all his children were born there. Several years ago, the king acknowledged that extended service and made Patrick the Earl of Berwick. It was because Patrick had been able to hold the castle against the Scots for possibly more years than anybody else had, and he was rewarded for that vigilance.

These days, no one referred to Berwick as a royal property, but as part of the de Wolfe empire. There weren't even any royal troops in Berwick, in fact, because de Wolfe had enough men that he didn't need the reinforcements. It was staffed completely with de Wolfe soldiers, and there were almost two thousand of them. More than half of them were stationed in the castle itself, but the other half of them were housed throughout the village of Berwick because the castle didn't have enough space for them.

That kind of an arrangement made the villagers feel very safe, so it worked out well for all. There were always hundreds of soldiers throughout the village ensuring that it was safe for everyone. The castle itself, because it was so contested, was almost always locked up, and those who did come in through the massive gatehouse were heavily screened. Essentially, the entire village of Berwick was a heavily armed outpost.

And the Scots knew it.

The only thing that kept the Scots from completely and constantly laying siege to the castle was the fact that Patrick's wife was Scottish. So was Patrick's mother, in fact, and several border clans claimed some kind of an alliance with the House of de Wolfe because of it. The Scots would fight amongst each other without hesitation, but oddly enough, when it came to an English knight being married to a Scotswoman, they tended to be hesitant to ruffle that relationship. More than that, Patrick de Wolfe and his five brothers were the toughest, meanest, and fiercest knights on the Scottish borders.

That was intimidating in and of itself.

But it wasn't just the sons of William de Wolfe to be feared. Those sons had sons, and the de Wolfe cubs, as they were called, tended to be just as fierce, if not fiercer, than their fathers. Each de Wolfe son had at least four or more sons, which meant all of Northumberland and the borders were overrun with de Wolfe knights.

That made the borders relatively safe, in many cases.

On this fine, sunny day, the earl himself happened to be on the walls of Berwick, watching the sea. The castle was close to the ocean, and from the top of the castle walls, they could see the water in the distance. Many a Northman had come to Berwick, and the castle had always seen them coming and had time to prepare. Fortunately, that had not happened in decades because Patrick's wife was the daughter of the king of the Northmen. There were other Northmen princes to the north, ruling islands and causing problems with the Scots, but they tended to avoid Berwick altogether. Still, there were those that watched the sea to make sure there were no longships on the approach.

Old habits died hard.

"Still looking for Farfar to return?"

Patrick heard a voice behind him, turning to see his son, Magnus. The knight had been referring to his mother's father, the Viking king sometimes affectionately called "Farfar" by his grandchildren. Smiling weakly, Patrick returned his attention to the sea in the distance.

"Possibly," he said. "Though your grandfather does not take

to the seas any longer, he has plenty of men who would happily steer a longship into the mouth of the river and bring a horde of Northmen to overrun my village."

Magnus laughed softly. "He would, but the men would bring barrels of wine and feast with us when it was all over," he said. "I remember when I was young and Magnus would come and literally feast for days. How on earth did you ever make it through those orgies?"

Patrick snorted. "Why do you think I look so old?" he said. "Those days of too much wine and days of nonstop feasting have taken their toll."

Magnus was still chuckling as he came to stand next to his father. "You will not look so old when I tell you what I know."

"What do you know?"

"Our scouts have returned from the south, and they tell me Titus will be here very shortly."

Patrick's face lit up. "My youngest terror has come home?"

Magnus' eyes twinkled. "He has," he said. "I'm glad I happened to be here and not back at my home of Raechester. I've not seen my youngest brother in quite some time."

"Does your mother know?"

"Nay."

"Then you'd better hurry and tell her," Patrick said, already moving away from the wall and toward one of the towers with stairs that led down to the bailey. "I will go to the gatehouse and await my favorite son."

Magnus nearly doubled over laughing. "That is me, and I am already here."

Patrick winked at him, taking the stairs in front of him as they both headed down to the bailey.

With Magnus off toward the keep, preparing to tell his

mother that one of her sons was returning, Patrick hurried toward the enormous gatehouse of Berwick. There were actually two—one attached to the curtain wall and then, across the bridge that spanned the brook-fed moat, a second, smaller gatehouse that was squat and solid. As he crossed the bridge, he could see several soldiers, along with a familiar knight, clustered at the smaller gatehouse.

"Did Magnus tell you the news, my lord?" A very big knight with a crown of glorious red hair came out to meet him. "Titus is approaching. He must be in town by now, for the news is about twenty minutes old."

Patrick nodded. "He told me," he said. "Open the gate. Do not keep it closed or Titus might try to burn us to the ground if he thinks we are not welcoming him."

Sir Peter Summerlin grinned as he turned for the gatehouse and bellowed for the portcullis to be lifted. Patrick had had many knights at Berwick over the years because it was such an active outpost, but Peter was one of the better ones. He was young and idealistic and hell on the field of battle, much as his father had been. Peter's father was Alec Summerlin, a knight known as The Legend to the armies of Edward I, and Peter had followed in his father's footsteps.

He was a man to be trusted, and usually in command when Patrick was away.

Word that Titus was approaching had gotten around, and men were moving to the walls to catch sight of him. Patrick and Peter walked out to the portcullis that opened directly into the town, noting villagers passing by, smelling the salt and sea from the fish markets down by the river. As Patrick stood there, looking down the main road for a glimpse of his son, he was joined by another knight, the son of his youngest sister,

Penelope.

Penny, as the family called her, had married the hereditary king of Anglesey years ago and had a fine brood of children, including six sons. They were men of two worlds, of Welsh royalty and English nobility, and all six had trained in England as knights. However, only four of them chose to serve in England at the de Wolfe properties, while the other two sided much more with the Welsh. It was difficult for them, being warriors of two bloodlines, but Bowen de Shera had never been confused about his heredity.

He was all English.

"I hear Titus is coming, Uncle Atty?" he said with some excitement. "Do you think he's come to stay for a time?"

Patrick grinned at his eager nephew, who, coincidentally, happened to look exactly like his mother with his green eyes and nearly black hair. Bowen was young, but experienced, with his father's muscular build and a keen intellect. But he also had an immature streak in him and loved his cousin Titus, because between the two of them, mischief was a given.

"Why do you want him to stay?" Patrick asked. "So you and he can get into as much trouble as possible?"

Bowen snorted. "I have missed Titus," he said. "I hardly ever see him anymore."

"Am I going to have to order the taverns in town closed for the duration of his visit simply to keep you two out of them?"

Bowen was having a marvelous laugh at his uncle's expense. "It would not stop us," he said. "We will ride over to Norham or Coldstream, where they have taverns for our choosing."

Patrick rolled his eyes. "That I exactly what I need," he said. "The two of you roaming the countryside, raiding taverns for drink."

"We would not be so terrible."

"How am I going to explain it to your mother when you end up pickled?"

Bowen laughed, putting his arm around his uncle affectionately, but Patrick put up a big hand and pushed him away by the forehead. As Bowen and Peter congregated and discussed the taverns they should visit with Titus that very night, Patrick stepped away from them because he caught sight of a horse and rider down the road.

The road itself was on a slope, tilting in the direction of the River Tweed and the old stone bridge that spanned the water. It wasn't difficult to see people on the road because of the elevated position of the castle, and from the size and shape of the rider, Patrick was fairly convinced that it was Titus. He could feel someone standing beside him, and he turned to see Peter on one side of him and Bowen on the other.

Both of them watching and waiting.

"I do believe that Jesus is approaching," Peter finally said.

That observation had Bowen turning for the gatehouse to make sure the portcullis was lifted high enough to accommodate Titus' height on horseback. But down the road, Titus caught sight of his father and spurred Jesus into a canter, loping up the hill until he came to within close proximity of the smaller gatehouse. Patrick beamed at his son, who was also smiling broadly, and Titus suddenly came off his horse, holding the reins as he rushed his father and nearly knocked the man over in his eagerness to embrace him.

"Papa!" he said, emotion in his tone. "It is good to see you. I have missed you!"

Patrick hugged his youngest son, a man who was his height and his size. But even so, he still saw him as a little boy and probably always would.

"My son," he murmured into the side of Titus' head. "You've come home. Praise the saints."

Titus pulled back to look his father in the eye, checking him over, making sure he was healthy and whole. He looked as he always had, though his hair was a little grayer. Perhaps there were a few more lines on his face. But to Titus, he'd never looked better.

"Cass sends his love," he said. "We left him about five days ago. You should see his sons—he's got quite a brood now. They'll be swinging swords before you know it."

"I must make a trip to Doncaster soon," Patrick said. "How are Cass and Dacia?"

"Very well," Titus said. But quickly, he sobered. "I've come with news, Papa. I… I do not even know where to start, but I can tell you that Morgen sent me. There have been some developments you must be aware of. But also… I brought someone for you to meet."

"Who?"

"My wife."

Patrick's eyes widened. "Your… *wife*?"

Titus nodded, pulling the man over to Jesus, where Katiana sat on the saddle. She'd been blocked from Patrick's view by the horse's head and Titus' body. Beaming with pride, Titus indicated the beautiful woman on the back of his horse, resplendent in her dark green traveling dress.

"This is Lady de Wolfe," he said. "Well, *my* Lady de Wolfe. She was Katiana de Edington before she married me. Katia, this is my father, the Earl of Berwick."

Katiana smiled at the man who bore a striking resemblance to Titus. "My lord," she greeted him in her soft, sweet voice.

"Though we've never met, I saw you once at Roxburgh Castle. You came for a feast, and I was part of Lady Sydenham's group of wards."

She referred to Lady Asmara de Wolfe's title, as the wife of Baron Sydenham of Roxburgh Castle. But Patrick couldn't seem to conceal his surprise.

"My lady," he greeted her politely. "You… you fostered at Roxburgh Castle?"

As Katiana nodded, Titus spoke for her. "She was there when I was there," he said. "I've known her for that long. I have quite a lot to tell you, Papa. May we please go inside? We have been on the road since before dawn."

Patrick nodded, but he was already mentally gearing up to tell his wife that Titus had married and they had known nothing about it. He had no idea how Brighton was going to react, but when he saw her walking quickly across the bridge between the larger gatehouse and the smaller gatehouse, he knew he had to figure it out. And fast.

Brighton de Wolfe, Countess of Berwick, squealed when she saw her youngest son.

"Titus!" she cried, throwing her arms open to him. "My d-darling boy, you've come home!"

Brighton had a slight stutter and a faint Scots accent, all wrapped up in a honeyed tone. Titus threw his arms around his mother, a truly lovely creature, and nearly squeezed the life out of her.

"Mama," he said happily, kissing both cheeks. "How is it possible that you grow younger while Papa grows older? His hair is all white!"

Brighton put both hands on Titus' cheeks, taking a good look at him, but her expression was a wry one. "The same old

Titus," she said. "Leave it to you to remind us how wretched we have become."

Titus smiled broadly. "Not you," he said. "Never you. And Papa will outlive us all, so I am only jesting. Have you been well?"

Brighton nodded. "V-Very well, my darling," she said. She was about to say something more, but she caught sight of the lovely young woman on Titus' horse, and her attention turned in that direction. "Oh? Who have we here?"

Patrick was already trying to shoo everyone away from Titus because he suspected the moment his wife heard that their son had married, there could very well be an explosion. Peter took the hint and ordered the soldiers back inside the gatehouse, but Bowen was oblivious. He was standing next to Titus' horse, looking up at Katiana, as Titus took his mother by the hand and led her over to his steed.

"Mama," he said, his tone full of pride. "I would like you to meet Lady Katiana. My wife."

Brighton had the same reaction that Patrick had—her eyes widened and she looked at Titus as if the man had grown another head. "*Wife?*" she gasped. "T-Titus, you cannot be serious."

"I am."

"B-But… how? When? And you did not think to tell us before now?"

Titus took her hand and kissed it. "It happened rather suddenly," he said, unsure if he had his mother's support or not. "Her family is from Callerton Castle. It is not far from here. She fostered at Roxburgh, and that is how I met her, many years ago. We were reacquainted when I was in London recently, and…"

"And you *m-married* her?"

"Aye, I married her," Titus said, no longer smiling because he thought his mother was becoming irate. "I married her and I do not regret it. But I did what you and Papa did—I married her without permission. I married her because… because I loved her and I wanted her to be my wife, so please do not be angry. Marrying for love is never wrong, but now I have a problem. I need Papa's help."

Brighton stared at Titus a moment before looking to Patrick, who was standing by the horse's head. He didn't look so surprised anymore because now, he had what he thought was the gist of the story behind Titus' sudden marriage. Frankly, he had no idea how to react, but something told him that Titus had indeed come home for a reason, and it wasn't simply to visit.

Titus had a problem.

Patrick was looking at Titus, refusing to meet his wife's gaze because he wasn't sure what he could say to her. He wasn't sure what he could say at all. Brighton sensed that, so she returned her attention to the beautiful woman on horseback.

"B-Bowen," she said to her nephew standing next to her. "G-Go into the keep and tell my daughter that Titus has come home with his wife and to prepare a comfortable chamber. Tell her to have a bath and food sent to the chamber immediately. I will be there shortly."

Bowen, who sensed that all was not well between Titus and his parents, quite willingly fled to do his aunt's bidding. When he was gone, Brighton extended a hand to Katiana.

"W-Would you like to come down from there?" she said. "Y-You must be weary from traveling."

Silently, Titus lifted Katiana off the horse and put her on her feet next to his mother. Katiana smiled hesitantly at

Brighton, who grasped her hands and kissed her on each cheek.

"W-Welcome to Berwick, my lady," she said kindly. "I-I do not know what circumstances have seen you and my son married so unexpectedly, but I do know that if he loves you, so do I. Will you come with me? Let us leave Titus to speak with his father."

Katiana didn't even look at Titus. She let Brighton lead her through the smaller gatehouse and toward the keep as Titus and Patrick watched them go. Once they were out of earshot, Patrick turned to his son.

"What happened?" he asked quietly. "Why did you marry her without permission?"

Titus looked at his father. "It is a complicated situation, Papa," he said. "I wanted to seek permission. Believe me, I did. But Katiana's father is Paulus de Edington of Callerton Castle, and Katiana received word not long ago that the man is dying. That is why she is with me—I have come to you with news from Morgen de Lohr, and since I was heading north anyway, I offered to escort her home to see her father. But somewhere along the way, I fell in love with her."

"That does not tell me why you married her without permission."

"Nay, it does not," Titus said. "But I wanted to give you some information on what has transpired and why. To your point, Katiana does not have a good relationship with her father. She has an even worse relationship with her brother, who is her father's heir. Simply put, Ansel de Edington is a vile beast of a man. You can ask Uncle Blayth, for Ansel fostered at Roxburgh and was sent home because of his horrific behavior. Among other things, he used to beat his sister. With Katiana's father dying or already dead, that leaves Ansel as her guardian.

The man hates the House of de Wolfe and will undoubtedly deny my request to marry her. More than that, he will probably kill her before he would allow her to marry me. So… I married her without permission from her father or brother. And I would do it again a thousand times over."

Patrick listened to the concise, rather defensive explanation with a heavy heart. Not because Titus had done something wrong, but because the situation was so dire. It was a tragic thing all the way around, it seemed. However, he immediately recognized the de Edington name because it reminded him of the encounter with Ansel de Edington at Thornton Tower not long ago. The knight who burned the bodies of his enemy when he'd been told not to.

But they'd get into that later.

"Come inside," he said quietly, putting a hand on Titus' shoulder. "Let me digest what you've told me and we'll speak on it later. Meanwhile, you have a message from de Lohr, and I want to hear it."

Titus nodded, somewhat relieved that he wasn't going to get into a big argument with his father right away about his surprise marriage and the circumstances surrounding it. Titus adored his father and was loath to upset him in any way, and truthfully, he'd been dreading telling the man what had happened. But it couldn't be helped.

As he'd told his father, he didn't regret a thing.

Following his father through the smaller gatehouse and into the bailey of mighty Berwick Castle, Titus realized that it was very good to be home again.

He only hoped that he could keep that feeling.

CB

"So Lancaster and Warwick have run amuck and executed Gaveston. Is that the crux of the situation?"

The question came from Patrick, and Titus nodded his head. "Aye, Papa," he said. "You know there has been a great deal of activity going on here in the north. Lancaster was chasing Edward, and Pembroke was chasing Gaveston. I was in Middlesbrough with Ronan in May, keeping my ears open as to the movements. As I said, Pembroke captured Gaveston but gave his word that he would be protected. That nothing would happen to him. That wasn't good enough for Lancaster, who abducted Gaveston from Pembroke's custody. They took him to Warwick, and after some kind of farce trial, he was executed. De Lohr says to tell you that he is going to side with Edward because he cannot stomach Lancaster's betrayal. We do not want to live in a world where Lancaster is lord and master. It would be a disaster."

Patrick knew that. God help him, he knew all that and more. He turned away from his son, processing what he'd been told and the implications therein. Thomas of Lancaster had always been a greedy bastard. He held five earldoms alone, making him the richest and most powerful single lord in England. Of course, the House of de Wolfe held most of Northumbria, making them the most powerful family in the north, but Thomas was spread out throughout England. He'd always been ambitious, but this went beyond what Patrick thought he was capable of.

This went beyond everything.

Glancing up, he looked at the men around him. They were in his solar at Berwick, a mighty chamber where many important things had been decided. The walls fairly reeked with power. In addition to Bowen and Peter, Titus and Magnus were there, two of his four sons, men who were deeply entrenched in the politics of England. Magnus had been the king's personal protector for years before passing that position to Denys de Winter when he married. Magnus knew, probably better than Titus did, what Lancaster's actions meant.

Also present were Rian, Espen, and Krister, who had been called in from the patrols they'd been on. It was usual at Berwick for the knights to ride patrol because of the volatility of their location on the Scots borders. Krister had been almost to Northwood when he'd been summoned back. He'd ridden hard and now stood near the lancet windows that overlooked the bailey, listening to something quite shocking. They all were. Berwick's solar was full of powerful knights, listening to something that could quite easily change the course of England.

"How long ago did this happen?" Patrick finally asked.

"Sometime in the middle of June," Titus said. "A few weeks now, at least."

Patrick grunted. "Long enough for the news to have spread," he said. "It must be spreading everywhere by now. Where is Edward?"

Titus shook his head. "I do not know," he said. "The last I heard, he was in York."

Patrick thought hard on that. The entire situation with the king and the rebelling warlords had been put on a tilt, sliding in the king's favor as far as he was concerned. There was no world in which he would capitulate to Thomas of Lancaster, and he knew his brothers felt the same.

He looked to Bowen and Peter.

"Bowen, I want you to ride to Castle Questing and tell Scott what you have heard," he said. "Tell Scott that all commanders should be summoned to Questing for a war council, and I will bring Titus and Magnus with me. Peter, you will ride to my brother, Thomas, and inform him of what you have heard. Tell him to ride for Questing before the week is out and bring his garrison commanders with him."

"What about Uncle Troy and Uncle Blayth and Uncle Eddie?" Titus wanted to know. "Will you not tell them, too?"

Patrick nodded, looking to his remaining knights. "Rian, head for Troy's demesne," he said. "Espen, you will go to Roxburgh and Krister, to Northwood Castle. The Earl of Teviot isn't part of the de Wolfe empire, but he must be told. Tell all of them to head to Castle Questing within the week."

"And then what?" Titus asked. "Will we take a stand and side with Edward?"

Patrick's attention turned to Magnus, who had been close to the king, once. "If Edward is still in York, I will send him word to come to Berwick for safe haven," he said. "Will you go to him with this message?"

Magnus nodded. "I will."

"If he is not in York, find out where he has gone," Patrick said. "Tell him that Berwick is with him. We will support Morgen de Lohr and Lioncross Abbey."

That was a shocking declaration without support from his brothers. Magnus looked at Titus, who gazed back at his brother with some apprehension. Things were changing rapidly in the north.

Things were changing rapidly all around.

"Good knights, you have your orders," Patrick commanded quietly. "Depart swiftly and deliver the news. Return as quickly as you can."

Without hesitation, the five knights headed out. The wheels were in motion, and Patrick seemed fueled by it. The man was in his seventh decade, but he was ageless when he was in the midst of something important. He was power personified, focused and sharp. When the knights were gone, Patrick turned to Titus.

"I have no doubt that Scott and Tommy will agree with me," he said quietly. "There is no possibility that they will support Lancaster and Warwick, and, I suspect, we will not be able to remain neutral for much longer. Titus, when you return to de Lohr, I want you to stop at Norwich Castle first and inform de Winter of our situation."

Titus nodded, but hesitantly. "I was ordered to remain here, with you," he said. "I am not returning to de Lohr for quite some time, I think. He wanted me to remain in the north and observe what is happening here."

Patrick grunted. "I see," he said. "I suppose my command will not supersede his?"

"It will not, my lord."

Patrick pursed his lips wryly. "I command thousands, but my own son will not listen to me," he muttered, watching Titus grin. "Very well. Stay with me. I will send someone else to de Winter. But now that we have discussed the issue with Gaveston, we will move on to your sudden marriage. Honestly, Titus, you could have knocked me down with a feather."

Magnus lit up with a smile. "And me," he said, putting his arm around Titus' shoulders. "Well done, old man. I'm very happy for you."

Titus grinned at his brother, the brother that he was the closest to in both age and relationship. "Thank you," he said. "It was very sudden, I don't deny it, but it was right. Nothing has ever been so right."

As the brothers hugged, Patrick sat down behind his cluttered table. "Right or wrong, Titus, you have a problem," he said wearily. "Of course I cannot berate you for doing it. I did the same thing, long ago."

Titus looked at his father. "And Poppy was irate?"

Poppy was what the de Wolfe grandchildren called William de Wolfe, now gone these several years. But he was much loved, still, and they always spoke of him as if he were in the next room.

"Irate? He was," Patrick said. "Irate because your mother was a postulate and committed to the church. But those were the same bastards who were trying to kill her. I married her because I loved her, but also because I wanted to put her under de Wolfe protection. Poppy was very angry at me, and when I insulted his honor, Uncle Kieran slapped me."

Both Titus and Magnus looked at him in astonishment. "Uncle Kieran?" Titus gasped. "That giant man?"

"That giant man."

"Did he send you through the wall?"

Magnus started laughing as Patrick scowled. "He hit like a woman," he insisted. "Well, a very big and powerful woman. Nay, he did not send me through a wall, you dolt. But the message was clear. And I deserved it."

"But Poppy clearly forgave you," Titus said. "Surely he could not stay angry, since you married for love."

Patrick nodded. "Nay, he did not stay angry for long," he said. "But the circumstances were quite complicated, as your situation is. What are we going to do about the lady's father and brother?"

Titus shrugged. "Pay them," he said simply. "I am willing to pay handsomely for the marriage."

"How much?"

"Three hundred gold marks."

Magnus' eyes bulged. "Where did you get such a fortune?"

Titus jabbed a finger at him. "While you've been out playing royal knight, I've been riding the tournament circuit and making a fortune," he said. "I have that much money and more besides, but I should hope to keep some to provide amply for my wife."

Patrick held up a hand to stop any bickering from getting started. "You plan to face them, soon, to make this offer?" he said.

Titus looked at his father, and his shoulders seemed to slump. The mood of the room seemed to darken as he pondered his answer.

"Nay," he finally said. "I do not plan to face them because they do not deserve that respect. For the way they've treated Katia her entire life, for the slander and disrespect and physical abuse they've seen fit to dole out, I do not feel that they deserve my respect, Papa. Don't you understand? I saved her from those bastards and, in particular, her brother. When I was about fifteen years of age, I caught her brother beating her in the stables at Roxburgh. I fought with him, and Poppy and Uncle Blayth discovered us. That was the moment Ansel was sent away from Roxburgh, and, soon after, Katia was sent to another place to foster also. I'm the only one who has ever protected her, and, God willing, I shall do it until the day I die. But I will not face her father and brother, who have treated her so abominably. Why should I show them any measure of honor when they've shown her none?"

It was an impassioned speech, one that made Patrick instantly sympathetic because he understood Titus' position well. But his son appeared very defensive, as if he was waiting for the condemnation to come flying out at him. Patrick was sorry his son had to feel that way, but he understood why he did what he did. He understood that it was in defense of something—or someone—he loved.

He couldn't, in good conscience, batter him for it.

"That is ironic," he said after a moment. "When I met your mother, men from a rival clan were trying to kill her also. There were those who were supposed to protect her who weren't. That's part of the reason why I married her, so if anyone understands your position, I do. And I do not disagree."

Realizing that he had his father's support, Titus let out an exhale that nearly collapsed him. "Thank you, Papa," he said sincerely. "All I can say is thank you. But I will give them money to compensate them for her loss. I am not a thief. I will pay for what I have taken, no matter what I think of the House of de Edington personally. I was hoping that you might send word to them announcing the marriage. It would sound better—and give them less chance to protest—if it came from you."

Patrick nodded, thinking on the situation and what needed to be done. He had an idea.

"I shall do better than that," he said. "I will invite them to the wedding feast. I will announce, with great joy, the marriage between you and Lady Katiana and demand they come so we can reaffirm our alliance. In fact, I will invite every neighbor and ally I can think of so the hall will be full of people congratulating them. They'll not act up if they know everyone is happy about the marriage. They'll simply have to go along with it."

Titus was smiling faintly. "Brilliant," he said. "I knew you could come up with the best way to handle this. But keep in mind that the last word she had from Callerton was that her father was dying. He may not be able to attend. He may even be dead already. But her brother, who presumably received the same missive that Katiana did, is more than likely already at Callerton. We are bringing the jackal himself into our home if we invite him here."

Patrick looked at him, unconcerned. "Let him come," he said. "I will personally convey my happiness at the marriage and imply in no uncertain terms how protected Lady Katiana is and how we would deeply frown upon anyone, including her family, lifting a hand against her. And we have plenty of trained de Wolfe knights to enforce this."

Titus had to chuckle. "What I remember of Ansel de Edington is a spoiled, arrogant arse."

Patrick cocked an eyebrow. "I did not tell you this because there has not been the opportunity, but we chased off a raid from Thornton Tower not long ago," he said. "You know that Ansel de Edington is serving Edmund de Allery, do you not?"

Titus nodded. "I do," he said. "Katia told me. In fact, she told me that her father cannot stand his own son and pushed him off on de Allery, so that is evidently why he serves there. But I did not know you were in recent contact with him."

"I was." Patrick nodded. "Briefly. He seems to be the same arrogant arse you remember, for when I told him not to burn the bodies of the dead Scots following the skirmish at Thornton, he did it anyway."

"No wonder his own father cannot stand him."

"Indeed," Patrick said. "Ansel and I have already gotten off on the wrong foot. If he gets off on another wrong foot with me, he'll not like my response."

"Nor mine," Titus growled. "While I understand the brilliance of inviting her family here for a wedding feast, I'm not sure how I feel about it. I'm not sure I can keep my rage toward them at bay."

"You must," Patrick said. "Let's be honest, Titus—you are in the wrong. It may be that they were cruel to your wife, but they are her family. They have every right to do as they please with her. But you—you married her without permission. That could be very serious if they decide to take their grievance to the church. So, I would suggest you at least be polite to them. We shall offer them some money and hope that placates them. And we shall have an enormous feast in your honor."

"But when?" Magnus wanted to know. He'd been listening to the entire conversation, but it seemed to him that his father and brother had forgotten that something more imperative was going on. "Papa, we need to deal with what has happened with Gaveston and Warwick. We do not have time for a great feast right now."

"Aye, we do," Patrick said. "If we do not get his out of the way, then it will be hanging over our heads, and there is more of a chance of de Edington finding out about the marriage without hearing it from my lips. Then there really *will* be a problem."

"Then when do you intend to have it?" Magnus asked.

Patrick shrugged. "In five days," he said. "That will give us time to get invitations to the local allies. In fact, we can use the gathering to spread the news about Gaveston's execution. The allies will want to know. Magnus, catch Bowen and Peter before they depart and tell them to relay the wedding feast invitation to my brothers. Tell them to hurry. We can gather here before the feast instead of at Questing."

"Use the feast as an excuse to gather the allies?"

"It seems as convenient as any."

That seemed to settle it. Magnus headed out of the solar to

carry out his father's orders as Titus moved closer to his father as the man sat wearily at his table.

"Whom do you plan to invite?" he said. "There are a few houses within a day or two's ride from Berwick. And you should send word to Farfar, you know. He will be furious if you do not tell him I have wed."

Patrick yawned, running a hand through his graying hair. "God's Bones," he said. "I would like to have one situation where everyone will not be furious either for it, by it, or against it. Of course I will send word to your grandfather, but keep in mind he will demand naming rights on your sons. He has done it for all of your brothers. He will do it for you."

Titus shrugged at what had become a family tradition. His mother's father claimed naming rights on all of his great-grandchildren, as he had with his own male grandchildren.

Some things never changed.

"I would like to see de Vesci at the feast," Titus said thoughtfully. "De Velt, too, and Payton-Forrester of Beverly Castle. What about the Grays of Ancroft?"

Patrick nodded. "All of them shall be invited," he said. "Inviting all of Northwood Castle goes without saying. Long has the de Longley family and the de Wolfe family been associated. And I should invite Edmund de Allery and his daughter, though that may be slightly awkward."

"Why?"

"Because de Allery was trying to broker a contract between you and his daughter," Patrick said. "I suppose it was in gratitude for helping them fight off the reivers, but they were both trying very hard to coerce me into agreeing to a betrothal. Of course, this was before I knew you had already married."

Titus cocked his head. "De Allery," he muttered as he tried to place the family. Then his eyes widened. "Not Zora de

Allery?"

"The same."

"Christ," Titus hissed. "Not her!"

"Aye, *her*."

Titus rolled his eyes and turned away. "You know how horrible she was when she fostered here, Papa," he said. "She was always causing trouble and always spreading lies. She followed me around and then told everyone that we were sweet on each other. If another girl as much as looked at me, that girl would find herself with her hair cut in the middle of the night or all of her clothing shredded. Zora did that."

Patrick nodded patiently. "I know," he said. "But that was long ago. People change. Like it or not, I want to keep her father as an ally, so I will invite them both and you will simply be polite to them both. Agreed?"

"Agreed," Titus said begrudgingly.

"But keep Katiana away from Zora."

Titus nodded fervently. The last thing he needed was for a petty, jealous woman to make a brittle situation even more tense, but he understood his father's reasoning. This was a wedding celebration and a perfect time for allies to converge, and Patrick wanted to maintain an alliance with de Ellery for obvious reasons. Titus understood even if he would rather not see Edmund de Allery and his ghastly daughter at all.

"Can I help you with anything, then?" he asked. "Or may I see to my wife?"

Patrick turned to the writing kit he had on his table. "You may see to your wife," he said. "And I will see you both at sup. I am looking forward to coming to know this young lady who has stolen your heart. Truthfully, I did not know if such a thing was possible with you. You always seemed so impervious to a woman's charms."

Titus bent over and kissed his father on the head before he turned for the door.

"Not *this* woman, Papa," he said, giving the man a wink.

"I can see that, you cheeky devil."

Titus' laughter was like music to Patrick's ears. No matter what the circumstances, it was simply good to have him home. Patrick watched Titus disappear from view before returning to his writing kit and collecting a quill. Vellum was laid out before him, and he began to scratch out the first of what would be several invitations. But only to those within a day or two's ride of Berwick, because they simply couldn't wait on anything. Several things were happening here, in layers, and resolutions and plans needed to be made.

The first invitation he wrote was to Paulus de Edington and his son, Ansel:

Our children have made the decision to be joined in marriage. We are honored to have Lady Katiana as an addition to our family when she married my son, Titus. Please join us for a wedding feast in honor of our children, where we shall discuss compensation to be paid to the House of de Allery upon the occasion of this sudden event. We are certain you will find our alliance, and our offer of compensation, to your liking.

Come to Berwick Castle with all due haste.

Lord Berwick

The second missive, of course, was addressed to Edmund de Allery and his daughter, Zora.

That one was a little easier to write. And perhaps a little more satisfying.

CHAPTER FIFTEEN

Thornton Tower

"I T'S NOT POSSIBLE! How can he do this to me?"

Zora wasn't simply weeping. She was hysterical. Edmund didn't seem to have the power to calm his daughter, who was positively distraught. He'd come bearing Patrick de Wolfe's missive announcing the marriage of Titus and inviting the House of de Allery to a wedding feast, but Zora hadn't heard that part of it. As soon as Edmund read the part in the missive about Titus being married, Zora had gone into fits.

Now, Edmund stood in his daughter's bedchamber, watching her go through the throes of grief. She'd been standing in his solar when he'd told her of de Wolfe's missive, but hearing that Titus had married had sent her running to her chamber with Edmund shuffling after her. Now, he was watching her break her pretty things and tear her linens off her bed as she threw a raging tantrum.

"Zora, dearest," Edmund said in a tone tainted with desperation. "Please compose yourself. You are going to hurt yourself!"

"I don't *care!*" Zora screamed. "How could they humiliate me so? I am to be embarrassed for all to know!"

Edmund had to duck when a cup came sailing past his head. "Be reasonable," he pleaded. "We hoped for a betrothal, my dearest. We spoke to Lord Berwick, and he told us he would speak with Titus, but Titus must have already been betrothed and his father was unaware."

Zora turned to her father, hands extended like claws. "How could Berwick not know this his own son was betrothed?" she shouted. "Berwick promised that *I* would be Titus' wife! He has gone back on his word!"

Edmund shook his head. "We tried to make it so," he said. "I tried to make it so. I tried to do everything I could, but it was not enough. Titus is married, and all of the screaming in the world will not change that."

That brought a primal scream from Zora's lips and she rushed to her bed, pulling at the posters and rocking them so hard that the frame started to crack. When it didn't break, she climbed onto the bed and started jumping on it, kicking at the posts and losing her balance. Then she screamed louder when she fell off the bed.

Edmund sighed heavily and dared to move closer.

"Lord Berwick did not give us his word, Zora," he said. "I wanted you to marry into the family as much as anyone, but even I know the man did not give us his word. There was nothing written that we could hold him to. Even so, Titus is married and there is nothing we can do. We cannot break the marriage up, so have your cry and be done with it."

Zora was still sitting on the floor, her dark hair askew. She had paused momentarily in her tantrum, but it was only to catch her breath. She still had plenty of anger left to display.

"It's not fair," she said, real tears starting to form. "I knew Titus when I fostered at Roxburgh. He was sweet on me, I know it."

"Then why has he never come to Thornton Tower to see you?"

Zora looked at her father in outrage. "Do you not support me in this?" she cried. "Do you not see that I have been wronged?"

Edmund simply lifted his shoulders. "I am sorry you are disappointed, my dearest, but there are other men out there who would be happy to have you as their wife," he said. "Men who can have your dowry, who will become lord of Thornton Tower when I am gone. You must think of the others out there who would be lucky to have you. In fact, Lord Berwick has invited us to Titus' wedding feast. Think of the fine young men who will be there. They will be yours for the picking!"

Zora simply roared in response, a sound that came from what was left of her soul. That gutless thing deep inside her that was filled with selfish ambition.

"I'll go to the feast and slit the throat of Titus' wife," she declared. "Whom did he marry? Does the missive say?"

Edmund still had the announcement in his hand. He looked at it, reading through it. "He married Lady Katiana de Edington," he said. Then he looked at his daughter, shocked. "My God… He married Ansel's sister."

Zora suddenly lurched to her knees. "Katiana?" she repeated. "I know of her! I met her at several of the de Wolfe feasts back when we both fostered!"

Edmund nodded. "I do not know her," he said. "But her father must have solicited the betrothal from Berwick. He is allied with the man like we are. He must have approached Titus about it, because surely his father knew nothing. He would have said something if he had. Ansel has never mentioned it, either."

Zora grunted as she climbed to her feet. "Ansel hates de Wolfe," she muttered. "He hates the entire family."

"Why do you say that?"

"Because if he knew about a de Wolfe betrothal, he would have said something," Zora said, exhausted from her outburst. "He probably would not have allowed his father to settle the contract had he known."

Edmund nodded faintly. "Ansel tries to control everything around him," he said wearily. "Even his father. I'm sure even his sister."

Zora plopped onto her bed, despondent. "This isn't fair, Papa," she said. "Titus was meant for *me*."

Edmund didn't know what more he could say to her about it. "There is nothing we can do," he said quietly. "It is over. We must think of someone else. As much as I hate to say it, would you consider Ansel?"

Zora scowled. "Him?" she sneered. "I cannot stand him. He's rude and unhandsome, and he would make a terrible husband."

"He would bring the de Edington fortune with him."

"I have more money than he does."

"True," Edmund said, scratching his head. "He's gone home to see to his dying father, and I do not know when he will return, *if* he will return, but given Titus de Wolfe has married his sister, I am certain he has been invited to the wedding feast. We shall see him there."

Zora looked at him. "I do not care if I see him there," she said. "And who says that I am going? It should be *my* wedding feast."

"And yet it is not," Edmund said, rather firmly. "Zora, I realize you are disappointed, but I told you that all the screaming in the world will not change things. Because we wish to maintain a good alliance with de Wolfe and show there are no hard feelings, we will attend the wedding feast and use it as an opportunity to find you a young man you will want to marry."

Zora hung her head. "Katiana," she muttered. "*Katiana*. She was a little lass, plain, and without spirit. How could Titus choose her over me? I do not understand."

Edmund scratched his head. "It does not matter," he said. "We will attend the feast and you can see for yourself why he chose her. Mayhap he has a soft spot for plain lasses with no spirit. She is Ansel's sister, so it is possible she is just as ambitious and conniving as he is."

"She stole what was mine."

"I will not argue this with you any longer," Edmund said, becoming irritated. "We tried to force a betrothal, but we were simply too late. We should have started long ago because, clearly, de Edington has bested us. He, too, had a marriageable daughter, and he managed to capture Titus de Wolfe. But there are many other de Wolfe males, and that is what we shall do when we go to Berwick for the feast. We shall make a list and I will solicit young men for your review. Titus was never good enough for you, Zora. You deserve an heir, not a fourth son."

Zora didn't say anything. She was too disappointed, too angry. Edmund had nothing more to say to her, so he wandered from her bedchamber, leaving his daughter sitting there to stew.

And plot.

Perhaps Titus wasn't good enough for her, but that was whom she wanted. Ever since her father had discussed it with Lord Berwick, she had her heart set on it. Set on a man she hadn't seen in many years, but that wasn't the point. Zora always got what Zora wanted.

Except this time.

And she wasn't going to stand for it.

She wasn't exactly sure how she was going to make Titus de Wolfe pay, but somehow, she was going to figure it out. Perhaps at the wedding feast, she could ensure his wife was found in a compromising position. It would be enough to ruin any newlywed dreams. Or perhaps she would accidentally set the woman's hair on fire. She'd hardly had any contact with Katiana de Edington back in the days when they both fostered at de Wolfe properties, but that didn't matter. Now, she had a vendetta against a woman she hadn't seen in at least twenty years.

No de Edington bitch was going to usurp her place beside Titus.

They were all going to pay.

CHAPTER SIXTEEN

Callerton Castle

HE'D READ IT several times.

Our children have made the decision to be joined in marriage.

Now, those words were echoing through his brain. At first, he'd been outraged. Furious was more like it. The de Wolfe messenger who brought it had departed quickly, so he had no one to take his anger out on, but that didn't matter. He began to drink, so he was essentially taking that anger out on himself.

We are honored to have Lady Katiana as an addition to our family when she married my son, Titus.

Bloody hell. He'd read that line again and again, too. Perhaps that's what made Ansel the angriest—that his sister had escaped his clutches. He hadn't seen her in many years, and, truthfully, he had been looking forward to her returning to

Callerton. He already had her chamber prepared for her, one that couldn't open from the inside, so he could keep her like a prisoner whilst he began to hunt for the highest bidder. He already had a lord in Carlisle whom he'd written to, a man he once owed a gambling debt to, and the man had already sent him a missive in return stating that he was quite interested to inspect the lady.

But now, that wasn't going to happen.

Please join us for a wedding feast in honor of our children, where we shall discuss compensation to be paid to the House of de Allery upon the occasion of this sudden event.

That was the part of the missive that had Ansel's interest. The word "compensation" soothed his outrage quickly. The House of de Wolfe was rich, so if they were offering compensation, then perhaps it would be worth his while. Perhaps if he was congenial and agreeable, and gave his blessing to this marriage, they might feel particularly generous. He wasn't sure how they would take it if he went in there with his usual sense of entitlement. It might lessen the amount they'd be willing to part with.

But if they found him agreeable to the entire situation…

We are certain you will find our alliance, and our offer of compensation, to your liking.

Now they'd come to the meat of it. That was the sentence that meant the most to him. Not the alliance—he didn't care about that. But Ansel wasn't beyond playing the affable ally, one who was very glad his sister had married into the House of de

Wolfe. The truth was that he hated the family, and if he could burn down all of their properties and get away with it, he would. He thought that he might have hated Blayth the most, the man who exiled him from Roxburgh those years ago and then ruined his chances at Kenilworth, but now he thought he might hate the Earl of Berwick the most because the man had tried to tell him what to do. *Don't burn the bodies of the dead Scots,* he'd said.

Ansel hadn't listened to him.

He showed him who was in charge.

Now, he was going to have to head to Berwick for this farce of a wedding feast simply to obtain what was owed to him. He'd take it and then he'd probably file a grievance through the courts, anyway. Maybe he'd even pull the church into this. Titus de Wolfe had taken his sister, his only source of regaining his fortune, without permission, and he simply wasn't going to be so easily placated. Maybe he'd continue to bleed money from Berwick for years to come because of it. But for now… for now, he'd play the happy ally.

And then he'd catch them off guard.

Come to Berwick Castle with all due haste.

Ansel planned to. God help those at Berwick, he planned to. They were all going to pay for this, and he'd find a way to make them.

He'd find a way to make his sister pay most of all.

CHAPTER SEVENTEEN

Five Days Later

"MOTHER!" TITUS BELLOWED from his open chamber door. "Mother, help!"

He was standing there with a broken tie in his hand, one he'd been trying to fasten on his wife's dress, and he'd pulled too hard and broken it. Now, Katiana was in a state because the tie was broken, the feast was about to commence, and Titus felt like the biggest dolt in all of England.

"*Mother!*"

"I'm c-coming, Titus," Brighton said, coming off the stairs from the upper level where she shared a massive chamber with her husband. She heard Titus bellowing through stone and floor, just like the old days when he was the loudest child in her brood. "What on earth is the matter that you're shouting so?"

Titus held up the silken tie. "I broke it," he said, nearly in tears. "Katia is furious with me because the feast is ready to start and she is not there to greet those who are arriving. She is going to throw me out of the window if you do not help me!"

Brighton fought off a smile. "I th-think you can fight her off if she tries," she said, taking the tie from his hand as she entered the chamber. "N-Now, lass, let me see what he's done."

Katiana was standing over near the hearth, in front of a big mirror of polished bronze, resplendent in her party-going clothing. But she was trying desperately not to cry.

"I am so terribly sorry," she said. "This is your beautiful dress, and I tried to take such good care of it."

Brighton could see how crushed she was. "Th-There, there, lass," she said, patting her on the cheek before turning her around to get a look at where the tie was supposed to be. "It wasn't your fault. Accidents happen."

Katiana wiped at her eyes, and Titus felt as bad as he possibly could. "A servant came to help her dress, and I sent her away," he said with great remorse. "I thought I could help her just as well. I tried. But I pulled too hard."

Brighton could see what had happened—her big, strong son and his big, strong hands had been a little too powerful. "Th-That you did, lad," she said. "Listen to me—I want you to find Kristiana and tell her I need her sewing kit. H-Hurry, now. There is no time to waste."

Titus did. Dressed in a pair of fine leather breeches, cleaned-up boots, and a fine tunic made from blue embroidered silk, he was washed and shaved and looked absolutely magnificent. Magnus, who had delayed returning home to Raechester, had even cut his hair for him, so he looked quite princely. At least, his wife thought so.

She thought he was the most handsome creature she had ever seen.

They could hear Titus running down the hall, calling for his youngest sister, Kristiana. Meanwhile, Brighton tried to comfort Katiana, who was genuinely distressed about the garment.

Brighton had loaned her the dress, in a shade of blue to match Titus' tunic, while the youngest de Wolfe sister had styled Katiana's hair for the big event. She looked absolutely beautiful.

But she was absolutely devastated.

Finally, they could hear Titus coming back down the corridor. Feet were shuffling as people approached. The chamber door swung back on its hinges, and Titus came through, pulling his youngest sister with him.

Kristiana Jordan Mary Joseph de Wolfe had arrived.

Krissie, as the family called her, was something of an anomaly in the world of women in that she was extremely tall for her sex. All of the Patrick's children had inherited his extreme height, with the exception of Thora, who was her mother's petite size. But Kristiana was tall—very tall—for a woman. She was almost as tall as Magnus, who, at four inches over six feet, was the shortest brother. Kristiana came close. A glorious goddess of beauty with long, brilliant blonde hair, her mother's blue eyes, and a magnificent smile, she was a Valkyrie that had made her Northman grandfather proud. In fact, she looked more Northman than most Northmen. Give the lass a sword and a longship and she would look perfectly at home.

And she intimidated the hell out of her English suitors.

But she was sweet and kind and very accomplished with the things fine ladies learned, and that included sewing. She didn't take kindly to Titus yanking on her, and she gave her brother a shove when he pulled too hard. That sent Titus stumbling into the open door panel, slamming it against the wall, as Kristiana went to her mother.

"What happened?" she asked.

Brighton took the sewing kit from her. "T-Titus was helping her dress and tore one of the ties," she said. "It was an accident."

As Brighton dug a needle and thread out of the sewing kit, Katiana turned to Kristiana.

"I'm so very sorry," Katiana said with great regret. "The dress is so beautiful, and you did such lovely work on it so it would fit me."

Kristiana smiled at the woman whose name was very similar to her own. "Not to worry," she assured her. "Between my mother and I, we can fix the tie in a hurry. There is nothing to fear."

Katiana genuinely liked Kristiana. Over the past several days, they'd become fast friends. "You have been so kind," she said. "Thank you for making me look so beautiful."

"You *are* beautiful," Titus said, standing back by the door mostly to stay out of his sister's way. "Other than my mother and sisters, you will be the most beautiful woman at the feast tonight."

"She is the *most* beautiful," Kristiana insisted. "The bride is always the loveliest. This is her night."

Titus frowned. "What about me?" he said. "It is my night, too."

Kristiana frowned at him. "The bride should always be the center of attention," she said. "Have you not yet learned that?"

"How would you know? You have never been a bride."

"T-Titus," Brighton scolded. "That was thoughtless. Be kind."

It was well known in the family that Kristiana, as beautiful as she was, longed to be a bride, but she'd yet to find a man who wasn't thoroughly threatened by her height. That particular fear didn't apply to Krister, however, who was sweet on her, but Patrick had been trying to discourage the relationship. Krister was a prince of his people, but Patrick wasn't so sure he wanted his daughter to marry a Northman and live amongst the savages. Titus knew that, and he knew the heartache it had caused, so he went over to his sister and pinched her gently on the cheek.

"I did not mean it," he said. "Any man would be fortunate to have you. We just haven't found one worthy of you yet."

Kristiana was trying not to hang her head. "There is a worthy man, but Papa refuses to acknowledge him."

"I will see what I can do."

Reluctantly, Kristiana gave him a grin, and he pinched her again, only to dodge a lightning-fast slap. He laughed and went back to the door, out of his sister's long-armed reach, as Brighton finally threaded the needle and went to work on Katiana's torn tie.

"It's a pity Thora could not be here tonight," Titus said, leaning against the wall as his mother and sister worked on his wife's dress. "I've not seen her in some time."

He was speaking of his other sister, the one who married Sir Callum de Reyne years ago and went to live on a de Reyne property to the south. For a family who tended to stay together like the de Wolfes did, with generations living at the same location, the loss of one of them was sorely felt by all.

"Y-You travel enough that you should stop and visit her," Brighton said as she concentrated on the stiches. "You know your sister just had her fourth child, a daughter."

"Doesn't that make four girls?"

Brighton nodded. "F-Four little lasses that your father is enamored with," she said. "Poor Callum says that even the dog they have is female. He's surrounded by women."

Titus chuckled. "He was not firm enough with Thora," he

said. "He should have demanded she bear only male children."

Brighton cast her son a long look. "I-I'll forget you said that," she said, returning her focus to the dress. "There—that should do it. What do you think, Krissie?"

Kristiana bent over, peering at her mother's repair job and tugging at it. "Feels solid enough," she said. "There you are, my lady. All fixed."

Katiana was greatly relieved. She let Kristiana finish with the tie, having a much gentler touch than Titus had, and when the tie was secure, she spun a circle for all to see. Brighton and Kristiana beamed at her as Titus came away from the door and inspected the vision before him.

"Stunning," he said. "Magnificent. I married a goddess."

Katiana was feeling much better now that the dress was fixed. She appreciated her husband's mother and sister so very much, women who had been kind and welcoming from the start. Never in her life had she felt so comfortable in the presence of other women, discovering a camaraderie with the de Wolfe women that she'd never experienced before. First Dacia, now Titus' mother and sister. It was so very different from her lonely life with Aunt Ethyl.

Now, she had finally found friends.

Family.

"Thank you," she said sincerely, grasping Brighton's hand. "I am very grateful."

Brighton patted her cheek gently. "T-Titus is correct," she said. "He married a goddess. Now, get down to the hall. The guests will want to see you."

"Aren't you coming?" Katiana asked anxiously.

Brighton nodded. "K-Krissie and I will be right behind you," she said. Then she looked to her son. "Take her and introduce her to the family. They'll all want to meet her."

With a grin, Titus held out his hand to Katiana, who took it quickly. As Brighton and Kristiana packed up the sewing kit, Titus led his wife out of the chamber, heading for the enormous great hall of Berwick, where their wedding feast was just beginning.

Little did he know what a night it would be.

ℭ

"Is that him?"

The question came from the eldest son of the Earl of Berwick, Markus de Wolfe. He had an outpost to the south of Berwick called Cheswick Castle, and he'd received word of the wedding feast from Peter Summerlin, who had been riding south to Kyloe Castle with a message for the Earl of Northumbria, Thomas de Wolfe. Cheswick was located between Berwick and Kyloe, so Peter made the stop to inform Markus of the latest news before continuing south.

Markus made it to Berwick in a hurry, and now, Markus and Magnus were on the prowl, waiting for Ansel de Edington to make an appearance. On behalf of their brother, they felt it their duty. Perched on the lowest level of the larger gatehouse, they were watching guests arrive, monitoring the activity in the torch-lit bailey. Berwick was lit up like the halls of heaven on this night, welcoming friends and allies alike for a memorable celebration.

"Nay," Magnus said, watching a lone man on a horse enter the bailey. "That's not him."

"What are you doing?"

They turned to see Krister approach, and Magnus pointed to the crowded bailey. "Looking for Ansel de Edington," he said. "Didn't you see him when you chased those reivers away from Thornton Tower?"

Krister nodded. "I did," he said. "And a more prominent horse's arse you will never meet."

Markus and Magnus chuckled. "Then you will stay up here with us and identify him," Magnus said. "I want a word with Ansel before he goes into the great hall."

Krister looked at the pair. "Why?"

Magnus cocked an eyebrow. "Because the man is a horse's arse, and I want him to understand what happens to a horse's arse when he crosses a de Wolfe."

"Ah," Krister said in understanding. "You want to threaten him."

"We want him to understand."

"It is the same thing."

He wasn't wrong. Magnus merely shrugged and continued to look over the crowd in the bailey, pointing out the arrival of the Earl of Teviot and several cousins from Northwood Castle. Scott de Wolfe from Castle Questing also arrived on their heels, and the bailey was full of men greeting one another. Everyone was family, or close to it, and they were happy to see one another as they began to head toward the hall, which was radiating light and warmth through the open doors.

Already, it was a lovely evening.

Except for the de Wolfe welcoming committee waiting to pounce on the bride's brother. Titus knew nothing about it, nor did Patrick, but Markus and Magnus were determined to make sure Ansel knew what was expected of him. Given what Titus had told Magnus and his father about Ansel's propensity toward violence against his sister, information that had been relayed to Markus, they knew what they were potentially dealing with.

And they were ready.

"Oh… Great Bleeding Christ," Krister hissed as he watched a party emerge from the gatehouse into the bailey. "That is the de Allery party. I recognize their standards."

The second part of the evening's questionable equation had just arrived in the form of the pushy lord and his unmarried daughter who'd tried to wrangle a betrothal with Titus. Markus and Magnus were jockeying to get a better look at the twenty soldiers and heavy, iron-reinforced carriage that had just entered the bailey.

"Right there?' Magnus pointed. "The yellow and red?"

Krister nodded. "The yellow and red," he confirmed. "Christ, Magnus, you should have seen de Allery and his daughter descend on your father and try to force a betrothal down his throat. It was like watching vultures trying to pick at a live carcass."

"That's pleasant," Markus said with distaste. "Peter told me about it when he came to Cheswick. Mayhap de Allery and his daughter thought they were showing their gratitude by foisting a marriage onto Titus."

"Or mayhap Lord Allery was simply trying to get rid of her."

"God's Bones, there's that ugly woman and her big-mouthed father." Peter interrupted the conversation and joined them on their vigil, having just come up the steps from the gatehouse entry. "I saw them come in. That pasty cow winked at me as they came through the gatehouse."

Markus looked at him. "The one who wanted to marry Titus?"

Peter nodded. "That's the one, unfortunately."

Magnus leaned forward on the stone windowsill, his eyes riveted to the scene below. "I just had a horrible thought," he said. "What if she is here to make trouble? She wanted the betrothal, after all. What if she's here to burn the place over our heads?"

"Go down and talk to her," Markus said. "Try to soothe her."

Magnus balked. "Not me," he said. "When she fostered at Berwick, she used to tell people that she was in love with me. She went back and forth between Titus and me, but she was a gossip who spread rumors. I am, therefore, *not* going down there to soothe her. Peter, you go."

Peter scowled. "I will *not*."

"You said she winked at you."

"Aye, she did, and I will have to gouge my eyes out now. It was like looking at Medusa!"

Markus looked at the three of them. "Such big, strong, fearless knights afraid of one small woman," he said, shaking his head in disapproval. "I'll go find some veils and shifts that you can wear to the feast. You are shaming the very breeches you wear."

Magnus and Peter burst into soft laughter. "Trust me, brother," Magnus said. "When you see her, you will fear her also."

"Look," Krister said, stopping their chatter. "She and her father are getting out of the carriage."

The four of them watched as a tall, older man disembarked the carriage, holding out his hand to a woman who followed. She had dark hair and was wearing a fur cloak, but that was all they could make out at a distance. They were talking to Bowen, who was in the bailey coordinating the arrivals, but as they watched, a man in horseback came up behind them. The man who had gotten out of the carriage caught sight of him and turned away from Bowen, greeting the new arrival. It was apparent that they knew him. As he dismounted his steed and shouted for a servant to take the animal, Krister sighed heavily.

"That's him," he muttered. "That's de Edington."

Markus and Magnus zeroed in on the short but muscular knight who turned his fine horse over to a stable servant.

"That's him?" Markus said. "Talking to de Allery?"

Krister nodded. "He serves de Allery," he said. "Or, at least, he did. But I notice that he is alone."

Markus looked at him. "What do you mean?"

"I mean his father is not with him."

That observation struck a note with Markus and Magnus, who looked at one another in realization.

"He came alone," Markus said quietly. "He either left his father at Callerton or his father is dead."

Magnus' eyebrows lifted. "Then let us talk to the man and find out."

With that, they started to move, taking the narrow stairs down to the gatehouse passage. From there, they spilled out into the bailey crowded with soldiers and servants and guests, but their focus was on de Edington, who was still speaking with de Allery. De Allery's daughter was standing next to him, but they didn't notice. For all of the resistance they'd displayed when it came to Zora de Allery, they didn't even notice her.

They were solely fixed on Ansel.

And they intended to make their presence known.

"Ansel de Edington?" Markus said as he approached. When Ansel didn't hear him, he spoke louder. "De Edington!"

That brought Ansel's attention. He turned to see four very

big knights moving swiftly in his direction, and, seeing this also, de Allery quickly moved away, taking his daughter with him. That left Ansel standing alone.

The de Wolfe pack closed in on him.

"You are Ansel, are you not?" Markus asked.

Ansel held his ground, but he was clearly edgy. "Aye," he said. "Who are you?"

"Markus de Wolfe," Markus said. "This is my brother, Magnus. We are Titus' brothers. We've been sent to give you an escort into the feast."

It was a lie, but it put Ansel at ease right away, and that's what Markus had intended. He didn't want a fight on his hands at the onset. Ansel removed his helm, propping it under his arm.

"I see," he said, still eyeing the group. "Where is my sister?"

"Where is your father?" Markus countered.

Ansel looked at him, giving him a once-over as if deciding he was worthy to answer. "Dead," he finally said. "He died some time ago. My sister was summoned to his bedside, but she did not come. Now I find out why. Where is she?"

Markus tilted his head in the direction of the great hall. "Inside with her husband," he said. "Come with me."

With that, he and Magnus led Ansel toward the hall with Peter and Krister bringing up the rear. It was a four-man escort, with Ansel in the center of it, thinking he was in a position of privilege when the truth was that he was virtually a prisoner. Only he didn't know it. There was a main entry to the great hall, but Magnus and Markus took Ansel to the north side of the hall, where there was a secondary servants' entrance. Before they reached it, they came to a halt in the shadows and faced Ansel, who was confused that they hadn't gone in yet.

"Why did you stop?" he demanded.

Markus and Magnus were about a head taller than Ansel, and they boxed him in, pushing him back against the wall of the great hall. Like any good hunter, they had their prey cornered.

Ansel was starting to catch on.

"What is wrong with you?" he said, unhappy. "What are you doing?"

"We want to talk to you before you go in," Magnus said, his voice a growl. "I want you to listen to me and listen well—I am a knight of the highest order. I was the Lord Protector of the king for years. I've trained in places that only the elite train, places where my breeding and skill have been refined into a concise killing machine. I am wealthy, handsome, and powerful, three things you don't have in your favor. I know about you, de Edington. I know you disobeyed my father after the battle at Thornton Tower those weeks ago when he told you not to burn the dead Scots. I also know that you habitually beat your sister when you were both young. I've heard rumors about your despicable behavior, and I am here to tell you that you will display none of that here. You will behave yourself. Misbehave and things will go badly. That includes any actions toward your sister. Move against her and she has ten highly trained knights at her disposal that will defend her to the death—*yours*. This is your only warning. Do you understand what I have told you so far?"

It was difficult to see Ansel's color in the shadows, but if they could have seen it, they would have seen that he'd gone pale. He wasn't used to be ganged up on because in his world, as small as it was, he was the hunter. He was never the prey. But he could see, fairly quickly, that the dynamics had changed.

He wasn't the alpha predator anymore.

But he was a man with enormous pride. That was the tough part—he had his pride. He dominated wherever he went, and when he didn't, that enormous pride he carried was fragile and petulant. In this instance, he knew he couldn't fight back. He couldn't argue or try to bark his way out of this one. He was trapped and he knew it, but something occurred to him that he hadn't realized before—his sister now had defenders. She was married to a knight, a de Wolfe, and de Wolfe knights all had brothers and cousins and uncles and fathers. Any one of them was an elite knight, something Ansel couldn't claim, so in this instance, he was no longer at the top of the food chain.

That was the hardest pill of all to swallow.

Humiliated that he had to surrender, it was a struggle. It went against his natural character. But looking into the faces of men bigger and better armed than he was, he knew he had no choice.

He put up his hands to show he was no threat.

"Is that what you think?" he said. "That I've come here to make trouble? I assure you, I've not come to make trouble."

Markus' gaze lingered on him. "Given your past behavior that I've been made aware of, you will forgive me if I do not believe you."

Ansel shook his head. "It would be a foolish man to enter a de Wolfe demesne and try to cause trouble," he said. "A lone man at that. Nay, good knights, I am sorry to disappoint you. I've not come to cause trouble. I've come to inform my sister of our father's passing and meet her husband. And that is all."

Markus still didn't believe him. He'd seen the man when he'd come in through the gates, the way he shouted at the servants, and the general way he carried himself. Even in the past few minutes, when he thought he'd had an escort into the hall, he'd behaved like a spoiled king. Markus had been around enough of them to know.

But he backed off.

"Excellent," he said. "Then we have an understanding."

Ansel nodded. "I have no quarrel with anyone, despite the fact that my sister married without permission," he said. "I would like to see my sister and her husband, if that would not be too much trouble."

Markus' brow furrowed briefly because now, Ansel was being far too amiable. "No trouble at all," he said. "Let's go inside."

They did. All four of the knights brought Ansel inside, where the guests were finding their seats and minstrels played in the gallery above. It was warm and fragrant in the hall, smelling of fresh bread and rushes, and standing near the dais with Titus and Patrick stood Katiana, lush and beautiful in her borrowed silk dress. It wasn't difficult to see her, glowing like a beacon among the men surrounding her.

"Ah," Ansel said. "There is my sister. I must go to her."

The four knights never left his side as he headed toward Katiana, who caught sight of her brother and went as white as ash. She started to move away from Titus, trying to run away from her approaching brother, but Titus caught on quickly to what was happening and put his arm around her, stilling her. Still, she cowered as Ansel came closer. She looked as if she was ready to panic, but Titus whispered in her ear and she seemed to calm.

But it was a struggle.

"Good evening, dear sister," Ansel said as he came near. "Greet your brother. It has been years since we've seen one another."

He held out his hands to her, but Katiana refused to accept them. Or him. She kept trying to back away as Titus held her firm.

"Welcome to Berwick," Titus said, decidedly unfriendly in spite of his words. "Do you remember me?"

Ansel's gaze moved from his shockingly beautiful sister to the enormous knight standing next to her. Aye, he knew him. He'd long dreamed of running that bastard through after the humiliation he suffered at his hands those years ago in Roxburgh. He'd never forgiven Titus for having him exiled from Roxburgh.

He'd never forgiven the entire de Wolfe clan for his treatment.

"Of course I remember you," he said, forcing what might have been a smile. "It has been a long time. I hope you do not hold a grudge for the last time we met. I will admit that I am ashamed for it."

Shocking words. Titus looked rather confused at the amiable manner of a man he'd learned to hate. In fact, he was caught off guard, unable to reply as he tugged on his father's arm to get the man's attention.

"You remember my father, the Earl of Berwick," Titus said. "Papa, you have met Katia's brother."

Patrick had been speaking to a knight from Northwood and he turned his attention to find Ansel standing there. Much as his sons had felt, a wave of unfriendliness washed over him.

"De Edington," he greeted Ansel. "Where is your father? I invited both of you to feast with us."

Ansel could sense the hostility. In fact, he was sensing it from everyone around him, including his sister, who was cowering behind her husband and verging on tears. At first, his act of amenability was self-serving, but now it was self-preservation. He was a lone man among a forest of armed knights, so any hostility on his part would not be well met. Nor would it serve his purpose. For his sake, he had to back down.

Or he'd never make it out alive.

"That is something I've come to discuss with my sister in private, but now that we are family, I will tell you all personally," he said. "My father passed away several days ago. His passing was peaceful. He never knew that his daughter married into the de Wolfe family. More importantly, I am now Lord Callerton, and I am grateful for our alliance."

His information had been politely delivered, but his arrogance had reared its head when he spoke of the fact that he was the new Lord Callerton. Yet even that was tempered with supplication. It was an odd combination. Tucked into Titus' torso, Katiana listened to the news without surprise or emotion, but most of all, she was watching her brother for any signs of that bully she'd known those years ago.

He was still there.

She could see it.

"Has he been buried?" she asked.

Ansel turned his attention to her. "He has," he said. "He is buried with our mother in the church in the village. I'm sorry, but I could not wait for you to come. It was done hastily, and, to be truthful, I would like to have a more appropriate service for him, one I hope you will attend. He never stopped talking about you, Katia, right until the end. He was thinking about you at the last."

It all sounded quite polite. *Too* polite. And Katiana didn't believe a word of it. There was something in Ansel's eyes that was still edgy and dangerous. She sensed that from him. She wasn't sure what to say to him, momentarily stumped, when Patrick took pity on the fact that she seemed to be tongue-tied.

"I am sorry for his passing," he said. "What was his affliction?"

Ansel's attention returned to Patrick. "An infection of the chest, my lord."

"It is a pity you did not serve at Callerton," Patrick said. "A son should serve his father, I think, yet you serve de Allery."

That brought up a touchy situation, one that Patrick knew full well about because Titus had told him that de Edington couldn't stand to be around his son and sent him away. He wasn't usually a spiteful man, but he was curious to see how Ansel would react to the comment. Would his true nature show? Or would he maintain this façade of pleasantness? Carefully, he watched as Ansel forced a smile that didn't look natural on his angular face.

"I do, my lord," he said. "Lord Allery offers good wages, and I wanted to earn my own money, not depend on my father for my fortune. But that is all over now that my father is gone. I am Lord Callerton, and the castle, and the lands, are mine."

Another declaration of his newly inherited title. Patrick thought the man might have put it on a banner and waved it around for all to see if he thought he could get away with it. It was that pride in him, begging to be let forth in a room full of titled and privileged men. Perhaps it was Ansel's way of saying he was no longer a knight, but a proper lord now, and he wanted to be treated thusly. In any case, Patrick simply nodded to his statement.

"I am sorry for the loss of your father," he said again, neglecting to congratulate him on his new title. "You will stay here tonight in the knights' quarters, and tomorrow, we will discuss the financial compensation for your sister's marriage."

Ansel frowned. "I am not to stay in the keep?"

"You will sleep with the knights," Patrick said evenly. "The keep will be full of women and family, but even so, unmarried men do not stay in the keep. They stay in the knights' quarters."

Ansel was clearly put out by that. He was a newly titled lord, after all, and deserved all due respect. Even though he didn't argue, it made his act of pleasantness less pleasant than it had been.

"I see," he said coolly. "Then I look forward to our discussion tomorrow. Your missive said that the compensation would be worth my while, so I am anticipating an offer commensurate with the fact that your son did not seek my permission."

Now, the greedy side of him was showing. Although it was a true statement, it was clear that Ansel was going to milk it. There was something in his eyes that suggested the payment had better be a big one or there would be problems. Patrick's eyes narrowed as he prepared an answer that would beat Ansel down by a few inches, but he didn't have the chance.

Katiana spoke first.

"You have your good wage from Lord Allery and the fortune Papa left you," she said. "You do not need the entire de Wolfe treasury, Ansel. Whatever the offer is will be fair and equitable."

Ansel's features changed as he looked at his sister. With the men, they were relaxed, but when looking at Katiana, something in him hardened.

"I will determine whether it is fair and equitable," he said. "That is not for you to decide. I am not in the wrong here, Katia. *You* are. You are fortunate that I did not bring a collection of church-supported soldiers from York cathedral with me to demand your return."

That was technically true. If Ansel really wanted to make trouble for them, he could have involved the church and brought a priest and a contingent of soldiers with him to cause a ruckus, but he hadn't, and he wanted them to know that he was being merciful in this situation. But that mercy was going to cost them. Katiana was feeling some courage when she realized what he was doing.

Slowly, she shook her head.

"Still the same Ansel," she said, contempt in her expression. "I've not seen you in many years, and it seems that some things never change. You'll receive fair compensation, and then I never want to—"

She was cut off when de Allery and Zora suddenly entered their group. They must have thought it was a receiving line, because Edmund took his place next to Ansel, his round face beaming at Titus and Katiana.

"May I assume you are Titus, my lord?" he said before slapping a hand on Ansel's broad shoulder. "How thrilling that Ansel is now part of your family. Well deserved, I might say. We are going to miss him a great deal at Thornton Tower, but now he is related to the mighty House of de Wolfe, and surely will no longer have time for his poor friends from his past."

He was looking at Ansel as he said it, laughing as Ansel looked as if he wanted to throttle the man, but both Titus and Patrick were grateful for the interruption.

"You are gracious, de Allery," Patrick said. "I'm glad you have come, because I wanted to speak with you. I know that we discussed a betrothal between our children, but I was unaware that my son had already married. I wanted to invite you here to ensure there were no hard feelings."

De Allery was still smiling broadly. "Of course not, my lord," he said. "What we did was only talk. Nothing was promised. Isn't that right, my dear daughter?"

Zora had been staring down Katiana, who had been looking at her brother. But hearing her father address her snapped her out of whatever trance she found herself in.

"Nay, Father," she said, smiling thinly at Titus and Katiana. "Nothing was promised. Much congratulations to you, Titus. I hope you will be very happy."

Titus was gripping Katiana tightly, feeling her trembling now that they were confronted with the two people they'd been dreading the most. It was at the same time, which was most unfortunate, but perhaps it was also for the best. They could get it over with at once and go on to enjoy the feast.

"Thank you," he said evenly. "I do not know if you know my wife, Katiana, but she fostered at Roxburgh years ago. You may have crossed paths when our families converged from time to time."

Now, Zora was looking straight at Katiana, who was resplendent in her blue silk. Zora didn't want to admit that the plain, spiritless girl she remembered had grown into a woman of exquisite beauty. Enough to tempt Titus de Wolfe, for certain. That kind of beauty, and the realization that she couldn't come close to it, infuriated her.

"Of course I remember seeing her from time to time," she said. "Congratulations, Lady de Wolfe. I wish you many happy years."

Katiana hadn't really remembered what Zora looked like, but now that she was confronted with her, she recalled the pasty, dark-haired wench with an eyebrow that went from one side of her forehead to the other. She wasn't unattractive, simply hairy. Moreover, she didn't seem nasty or embittered. She seemed polite.

Katiana forced a smile.

"Thank you," she said. "I'm flattered that you would remember me. May I accompany you and your father to the table where the wine and bread are? We can leave the men to discuss what they wish to discuss."

"*Nay!*"

The cry came from three different people—Titus, Patrick, and de Allery. They'd all shouted it at nearly the same time. When Titus and Patrick looked at de Allery, startled, the old man smiled weakly and reached out to pull his daughter away.

"You must keep the newest Lady de Wolfe with you so that she may greet her guests," he said. "We are honored to have been invited, my lord. Thank you."

With that, he pulled a clearly resistant Zora away from the bride and the groom as Titus and Patrick exchanged relieved glances over Katiana's head. No one wanted Katiana to be left alone with Titus' spurned suitor, including the woman's own father. That spoke volumes. But Ansel was still there, still lingering, and Patrick did the only thing he could do at the moment.

He made a peace offering.

"Lord Callerton," he said, addressing Ansel by his formal title. "Would you like to stand with us to welcome the guests? You are the bride's only relative in attendance. It is your right if you wish to do so."

Ansel looked at Titus, who met his gaze steadily, and then to his sister, who refused to look at him at all. He looked at Patrick, and at Markus and Magnus, who were standing behind their father. There were the other two knights who had practically strong-armed him into the hall flanking Titus, all of them looking at Ansel as if daring him to say something or do something they didn't like. Ansel was in a no-win situation. His sister may have married into the House of de Wolfe, but he knew they would never treat him as kin or, even worse, as an equal.

Already, he was nothing in their eyes.

He could read them like a book.

"Nay, my lord," he said. "I think not. Thank you for the offer, but I will go find my seat with Lord de Allery."

"As you wish," Patrick said. "We will be meeting with the allies from the north tomorrow after the feast, since many are in attendance tonight, so join us. There is news about Warwick and Edward."

That was something new for Ansel. He wasn't usually included in warlord gatherings. Quite honestly, he didn't care who was on the throne because he wasn't involved in the power struggle, so unless it had to do with his lands or money, he really didn't care. But with his father gone, he realized that he had an obligation to participate.

"I will be there," he said, turning away from Patrick and catching Katiana's eye. She was looking at him, but the moment their eyes met, she quickly looked away. He paused in front of her. "I do wish you well in your new life, Katia. Papa would have been very happy, if that makes any difference. I do… I do hope you will let me make amends for whatever affront I have ever dealt you."

With that, he walked away, heading over to one of the enormous feasting tables that was already half-full of guests.

Titus and Katiana looked at each other in puzzlement.

"Very odd," Titus said. "He seems to want to make peace

with you, but his tone and the look in his eye tells me that he wants to fight every one of us."

Katiana shook her head. "I do not believe him for a moment," she said. "He is only being cordial because I'm surrounded by a half-dozen heavily armed knights. If I were alone, he would be completely different."

"People change, my lady," Patrick said. "Though I'm not sure that pertains to your brother, given what happened at Thornton Tower, it is possible that time has softened him when it comes to his only sister. Mayhap your father's death has changed something in him."

"Papa," Magnus spoke up, pointing to the entry. "Uncle Scott and Uncle Blayth are here."

Seeing his brothers had arrived, Patrick headed off to greet them, followed by Magnus and Markus. That left Peter and Krister standing near Titus and Katiana.

"Can you spare us, Titus?" Peter asked. "Or do you want us to remain with you and your lady wife, given that her brother is in the hall?"

Titus glanced in the direction of the feasting table where de Allery, Zora, and Ansel were sitting. "Go about your duties," he told them. "But thank you for asking. And thank you for shepherding de Edington when he arrived. We did not know what to expect with him."

Peter glanced over at the table, too. "That is not the same man we saw at Thornton Tower after the raid," he said. "That man was arrogant and confrontational."

"I know," Titus said evenly. "He's on his best behavior for some reason."

"Because we told him to be," Peter said, looking at Titus. "Magnus told him that he must behave or there would be consequences."

Titus grinned. "He said that?"

Peter chuckled. "He did," he said. "Mayhap de Edington has decided not to test us this night."

With that, he and Krister headed off to the bailey, where Rian and Espen were the only knights on duty, assisting guests as they arrived for the feast. As they moved away, Titus turned to his wife.

"And you?" he said softly. "Are you feeling well enough after your contact with your brother? I thought you handled it very well."

Katiana wouldn't look at Ansel. "I do not care what he said," she muttered. "I do not care how he is behaving. It is all an act, Titus. He is behaving because he was told to behave, but given the opportunity, he would take his fists to me and do it happily. He'd slit your throat and call it justice for marrying me without his permission. He's a viper and he is not to be trusted."

"I don't."

"Are you certain?"

He smiled at her, lifting her hands to his lips for a gentle kiss. "Trust me when I tell you that I don't trust him," he said. "We've had our encounter with him and things are out in the open now, as they should be. But I want you to forget about him because I am going to introduce you to my uncles. You haven't met Uncle Scott yet, have you?"

Katiana shook her head as Titus held her hand and began leading her toward the door. "Nay," she said. "I have seen him, but that was long ago. Where are your other uncles? Thomas and Edward and Troy?"

"They should be here shortly," Titus said. "Believe me, love, before the evening is through, this entire hall will be full of de Wolfe men."

Katiana didn't feel much like smiling, but she did because he seemed so happy that most of his family would be present on this night. She thought it must be rather wonderful to have a family one was actually excited to see.

Family that was now her family, too.

All thoughts of Ansel aside, it was a lovely realization.

CHAPTER EIGHTEEN

"How does it feel to know your sister married the man I was to marry?" Zora said through clenched teeth. "Proud of yourself, are you?"

Ansel was sitting next to a woman he didn't much like. He never had. She was petty, pushy, greedy, and selfish just like he was, so in that sense, they were very much alike. Listening to her talk was like listening to himself, only tonight, he wasn't in any mood for it. He'd never had much use for Zora de Allery.

"Shut your lips, you stupid chit," he growled. "You have no idea what you are talking about."

Zora looked at him sharply. "How dare you speak to me like that?"

Ansel grabbed at a cup of wine a servant had put in front of him. "Who are you going to tell?" he said. "Your father? Go ahead. He will not do anything about it. He's as weak as you are."

Zora was inflamed, but she didn't bite back. She'd seen what Ansel was capable of when it came to verbal sparring. They'd spent the past few years managing to remain apathetic to one another, and she had no desire to buck the trend. Ansel was one of those people with a black soul that could be dangerous when engaged.

She wasn't willing to chance it.

At least, not at the moment.

"Mayhap I am," she said. "Weak because I have been betrayed by the House of de Wolfe and my father will do nothing about it."

Ansel snorted. "Betrayed," he mumbled, watching his sister in conversation with her new husband. "You have no idea."

"I think I do," Zora said. "Lord Berwick agreed to a betrothal between me and Titus, but he has gone back on his word."

"And you have this in writing?"

Zora looked at him, lips pursed irritably. "It was a promise," she said. "He told me that I would marry Titus, and that is enough. But then he brokered a marriage with your father and betrayed me. Your sister has taken what belongs to me."

Ansel took a long drink of the rich red wine, a fine drink, brought all the way from Lyon. "There was no brokered marriage."

"What do you mean?"

He looked at her then. "Haven't you been listening?" he said. "Take the pudding from your ears and you'll learn something. There was no brokered marriage. Titus and my sister married without anyone's permission, least of all my father's. The first I heard about the marriage was when I received an invitation to the wedding feast."

Zora's eyes widened. "There was no contract?"

"None at all," Ansel said, annoyed. "My sister has been living in London because my father hoped she'd find a husband there. Instead, she marries Titus de Wolfe, the same bastard who appointed himself her protector when we were children."

Zora's brow furrowed in confusion. "He did *what*?"

Ansel waved her off irritably. "We fostered together for a time at Roxburgh Castle," he said. "Somehow, Titus appointed himself my sister's protector, and that meant against me especially. Now he's gone and married her. He's robbed me of my ability to make a decent fortune off what rightfully belongs to me."

Zora was still confused. "What belongs to you?"

Ansel looked at her in frustration. "Are you daft?" he said. "Did you not just hear me say that he married my sister without permission? Now I cannot sell the woman or broker a deal of my own with her, which would ensure a fortune. *Now* do you understand?"

Zora did. She turned to watch Titus and Katiana crossing the floor of the great hall toward a group of men who had just entered. "Damnation," she muttered. "Look at him… tall and handsome and proud. Everything that should belong to me."

"He belongs to my sister."

"But he married her without permission," Zora said. "Why do you not complain to the church? You have your rights, you know. She should belong to you to do with as you please."

"I know."

"Now who's weak?"

He didn't reply. In fact, he didn't seem willing to fight at all, which surprised Zora. The Ansel she knew was adamant about having his own way, in all things. But as she watched Katiana with a host of very tall, very big de Wolfe knights, it occurred to her why Ansel wouldn't fight for his rights. More than likely, he wouldn't survive such a thing, so perhaps being accepting of the situation was, in his case, for survival. The House of de Wolfe wasn't one to be trifled with.

It was a depressing thought.

"It is a pity you cannot steal her away and sell her to the pirates," she muttered, thinking aloud. "Or the Scots in the north who live like animals. I'm sure they'd pay a princely sum for her."

Ansel finished the wine in his cup and poured himself some more. "I could steal her away, but de Wolfe and his pack would come after me," he said. "I could not hold her. They'd burn Callerton down around my ears to get at her, and then I'd have nothing."

Zora observed Katiana as she spoke with a big blond man who faintly resembled the Earl of Berwick. Katiana was quite beautiful and clearly charming, unlike Zora. No man had ever looked at her the way Titus looked at his wife. In fact, the whole family seemed smitten with her. They all looked at Katiana as if she was the sweetest thing they'd ever seen. That realization spurred Zora's jealousy as it had never been spurred before.

A pity you cannot steal her away…

Ansel said he could. He also said he couldn't keep her. Of course Titus and his family would bring their massive army to Callerton Castle, a relatively small castle, and raze it.

But what if…?

"If you *could* take her somewhere else for safekeeping, would you?" she ventured.

Ansel was already half-finished with his second cup of wine, and the question confused him. "What are you talking about?"

"Your sister," Zora said plainly. "We are not looking at this logically, Ansel. You want your sister. I want Titus. What if you were to get your sister away from him and hide her somewhere? Hide her at Thornton Tower, for example. Hide her in the vault because my father never goes down there. He would not even know she was there. That would give you time to find a buyer for her."

Ansel was quickly becoming drunk, but Zora's words penetrated his brain. As he made sense of them, his head came up and he looked at her.

"Are you mad?" he asked, incredulous.

Zora fixed him in the eye. "You said yourself that Titus stole your fortune from you when he took your sister," she said. "What if I were to give you everything I have? I have my own fortune, you know, left to me by my mother. I will give it to you if you take your sister away from Titus. My fortune is the price I will pay to have Titus a grieving widower. Or at least thinking he is a grieving widower. What you do with your sister is your own business, but with Titus unmarried—or thinking he is unmarried—surely the only way to ease his aching heart would be with another marriage. *I* can be the salve for his broken heart."

Ansel leaned away from her. "You are mad."

"Nay," Zora said, grabbing his arm so he'd listen to her. "I'm not mad in the least. Think of it! I will give you everything I have, and you send your sister to the highest bidder. That way, you have the last word. You punish de Wolfe for marrying your sister and ruining your chance to make your fortune from her without having to go up against those knights. Don't you see? It's the perfect solution!"

Ansel nearly dismissed her again, but the more he thought about it, the more he liked the idea. Perhaps she had something. Or perhaps the wine was making him weak. In any case, she had him thinking.

And interested.

"How much money do you have?" he asked.

Zora could see that she finally had his attention. "One hundred and sixty gold marks," she said. "That is more than enough money, don't you think?"

It was a princely sum. Ansel pondered the offer, the circumstances, and the consequences, his gaze drifting over to his sister as she spoke with several very large men. It seemed that all the de Wolfe men were beasts, which was a concern to him. It was perhaps the only thing keeping him from immediately agreeing to Zora's offer. If he was caught trying to abduct his own sister, he knew his life span would be measured in minutes.

Seconds.

But the lure of punishing Titus de Wolfe, and having the final word in the situation, was too great to resist. He was a better man, wasn't he? He could bring Titus to his knees in one swift action, couldn't he?

But only if he was he brave enough to consider it.

… He was.

"If I do it, I will need your help," he said after a moment. "I would have to do it while I am at Berwick because I do not know when I would get another chance."

Zora's eyes lit up. "Then you'll do it?"

"I'll consider it."

Zora couldn't keep the smile off her lips. Ansel was conniving and sly, as she'd seen before, and now… now, she had those attributes at her fingertips. She'd seen the way his eyes glittered when she mentioned the money. She knew that was what he wanted.

She knew what *she* wanted.

"Do it and I'll add another one hundred gold marks for your trouble," she said.

He looked at her. "Where are you going to get it?"

"I'll steal it from my father."

Ansel's gaze lingered on her for a few moments, and Zora was positive she saw a hint of a smile.

To her, that was as good as an agreement.

CHAPTER NINETEEN

"A ND NOW, YOU know," Patrick said as he sat on the edge of his massive table, "Lancaster executed Gaveston, and de Lohr has said he will side with Edward now. We can no longer remain neutral in this, I'm afraid. We must choose a side."

It was a bright morning after a feast that lasted until the early-morning hours. Most of the men in the room, including Patrick and Titus, were bleary-eyed from lack of sleep, but they were mostly alert.

The subject matter called for nothing less.

Warmed, watered cider and warmed wine was being passed around. Bread basted in butter and honey was also being passed around in the hope that the honey would revive them a little. The solar was full of de Wolfe family and allies, all of them having just listened to Titus and Patrick speak on the current situation between the king and Thomas of Lancaster and the execution of Piers Gaveston. It was what they'd all feared with Lancaster, because the man wasn't shy about flaunting his power or his ambition. Now, the situation was dire, indeed.

The Earl of Berwick was correct.

They would have to choose a side.

The men in the chamber were glancing at each other, expressions of concern and resignation passing between them. Along with Titus and Patrick were Markus, Magnus, Krister, Peter, Bowen, and Rian. At this early hour, Espen was on the wall and in command. The Earl of Warenton and the head of the de Wolfe empire, Scott de Wolfe, was seated at the table with Patrick while his twin, Troy, was standing in front of the hearth and warming his "old bones," as he called them. Blayth de Wolfe, Baron Sydenham, was near Troy, and the final de Wolfe brother, Thomas, Earl of Northumbria, was sitting in a cushioned leather chair with his big feet propped up on a stool. They were missing Edward de Wolfe because he was in London with his family, or so the servants at his Northumberland home told the messenger from Berwick. Edward was the diplomat of the family, working foreign affairs for the king, and not usually involved in battle planning.

That rounded out the sons of William de Wolfe.

But there were more. In the north, the linking of the de Wolfe-de Norville-Hage families was legendary. Three great knights who fostered together more than eighty years ago and then served together at Northwood Castle—William de Wolfe, Kieran Hage, and Paris de Norville—had married three Scots cousins. Those three couples had spawned at least two dozen children between them, and those children spawned dozens as well. One couldn't go to any major town or village in Northumberland and not run into a de Wolfe or a de Norville or a Hage, and the three families were still tightly bound, still manning most of the major castles in the north.

The families had become part of Northumberland's fabric.

But the short notice of Titus' wedding feast meant not all

could be in attendance. Only those within a few days' ride had been able to come. Nathaniel Hage, son of William de Wolfe's closest friend, Kieran Hage, had come from Castle Questing with Scott, leaving his brother, Alec, in command. From Northwood Castle, the Earl of Teviot, John de Longley, had come with his de Norville commander, Hector, and Hector's eldest son, Atreus.

From Pelinom Castle, Atlas de Velt was in attendance, a close ally of de Wolfe and de Lohr alike. A few of the greater warlords hadn't been able to make the feast, like Yves de Vesci of Alnwick Castle and War Herringthorpe of Bamburgh Castle, but there were four or five lesser warlords who had been able to attend at short notice, including de Allery and Ansel. They were both in the chamber as well, but Ansel was staying to the shadows.

He hadn't said a word all morning.

Not that Patrick cared, but he was keeping an eye on him. So were his brothers, who had all been informed of the situation between Titus' wife and her brother. Mostly, Troy and Blayth were watching him like a hawk, because out of William de Wolfe's sons, they were perhaps the two that would happily keep an eye on a man that no one seemed to like and take great pleasure if he happened to step out of line. Atreus de Norville, a man notoriously quick to temper, was prepared to pounce if given the word. He'd pound the man's brains in and ask questions later, but so far, Ansel hadn't given them any reason to act. He had remained quiet, which was a good thing considering the volatility of the subject matter.

There wasn't anyone in that chamber who didn't understand that.

"What of de Lohr, Atty?" Scott asked, rubbing his forehead

to stave off the aching head from too much drink the previous night. "If the man is siding with Edward, his neighbors will not be happy about it. He's a day's ride from Warwick Castle."

"I know," Patrick said. "I will tell you now that I have already decided to support de Lohr, and that means I will support Edward. Mayhap the man is an ineffective ruler and he has problems, but he is better than the alternative."

"Lancaster," Scott muttered.

"Exactly," Patrick said. "Thomas of Lancaster is unpredictable, untrustworthy, and greedy. More than that, he is not the rightful king. The simple fact is that I cannot put my support behind such a man, and unless all of you would like to pay homage to Lancaster, I would suggest you think very hard about the support you give and whom you give it to."

Scott looked at Troy, a man very astute when it came to political matters, especially with the Scots. His properties were in Scotland, so he'd spent a lifetime dealing with the brittle relations of it. But Troy simply shook his head, sighing heavily as he did so.

"There *is* no choice," he said. "If we side with Lancaster, chances are the man will be on the throne of England within a year, and he is not the true king. Edward has issues, that is true. We've never agreed with Gaveston or Despenser or his Savoyard contingent. He seems too content to give the country away to his French relatives. But even so, he is our king. Atty is right—I would rather pay homage to him than to Lancaster."

His opinion was the same as the rest of the de Wolfe brothers. They thought as one, spoke as one. Sitting near Patrick's table, with Hector de Norville by his side, the Earl of Teviot spoke up.

"I was hoping we could remain out of this, tucked up in the

north," he said softly. Named for his grandfather, John de Longley was much as his father had been, with dreamy blue eyes, golden-red hair, and a sharp mind. "We have our own troubles up here that seem removed from the rest of England, but this… Unfortunately, I believe Lancaster has pushed us into taking a stand. And I would wager to say we will not be the last to side with Edward."

"Nay, we will not," Scott said. "There is an entire group of us who always, inevitably, side with each other—de Lohr, de Lara, du Reims, de Russe, and so forth. De Winter is the only one who sides with the king regardless of what the rest of us do, but in this case, I am glad to be on his side. But I am concerned about de Lohr siding with Edward whilst surrounded by those who are allied with Lancaster. That means Warwick and Gloucester."

"It also means Wellesbourne," Patrick said. "Do not forget that Aaron Wellesbourne is just south of Warwick. Those two are usually allies, but not always. When they've gone to war against each other in the past, historically, it is an ugly thing. All Wellesbourne does is train warriors, but Warwick is larger. We cannot abandon Aaron if he sides with Edward and Warwick declares war on him."

"We would never abandon him," Thomas said quietly but firmly. "Aaron and I have served together in the past. He reinforced my ranks last year when we had a skirmish outside of Nottingham."

"When was that?"

"When Gaveston tried to take something that didn't belong to him."

Patrick snorted ironically. "I'd forgotten," he said. "I became angry at you for involving yourself."

"I'd been asked to chase the man off. I could not resist."

No one personally liked Gaveston, despite his unjust ending, and that was clear. Patrick looked at his youngest brother, grinning as he shook his head at the man, and for a moment the tension in the room lifted. The mood warmed.

But not for long.

"Are we in agreement, then?" Scott said. As the head of the family, he made the final decisions involving the empire. "We support Edward against Lancaster."

Everyone nodded, including the lesser warlords listening in. Scott looked around the chamber, making sure there were no doubters. No questions. But everyone seemed clearly in agreement.

"Good," he said. "That means we must all be in support, because if Lancaster or Warwick or their allies decide to attack Teviot, for example, that means we all go to war. Let there be no doubt. We stand united or we will fall divided."

"Understood, my lord," de Allery spoke up, daring to lend his voice to what was largely a de Wolfe discussion because they had the most to lose. "Do we know what Lancaster and Warwick are doing now? Or is the information on Gaveston's death too old?"

It was a good question. Everyone looked to Titus, who had been the original bearer of the bad news.

"It is at least a month old, if not more," Titus said. "We can send someone to the marches, to Morgen de Lohr, and find out if there are any new developments. We can also tell him that the Northerners are with Edward."

"The Northerners" were what most in England called the warlords far to the north in Northumberland and even Cumbria. They weren't usually involved in the battles in the south, mostly because they, on most occasions, were preoccupied with Scots. The Northerners held the border between England and Scotland, a difficult task in itself.

"That should be you, Titus," Patrick said quietly. When Titus looked at him, surprised, Patrick shrugged his shoulders. "Obviously, you have the relationship with de Lohr. You are the one who has the most contact with him, and the one he trusts, so it should be you."

Patrick didn't want to elaborate on what most of them didn't know—that Titus was an Executioner Knight and, as such, was always involved in the politics, especially as they were now. Of course, the uncles knew—Scott, Troy, Blayth, Edward, and Thomas—as did John Longley and Hector, but the others didn't. Not even Magnus or Markus, because Titus was afraid it might cause them to treat him differently because of the Executioner Knights' cutthroat and dark reputation. Therefore, Patrick didn't cross that line. But it was clear to him that Titus should be the one to go.

Titus, however, wasn't as convinced as his father was.

"I think I should remain here, Papa," he said. "I do not wish to leave my wife so soon after marrying her, but more than that, you may need me here. You can send anyone to de Lohr bearing news."

But Patrick shook his head. "It must be you," he said. "Things may be happening very quickly, and you can make decisions on our behalf."

"Meaning what?"

"Meaning that if de Lohr is preparing to go to battle against Lancaster, you can make the decision that the House of de Wolfe will send troops and then send word to us on what needs to be done," Patrick said in a way that left no room for argument. "Titus, you are our eyes and ears to England and her politics. This is your duty."

There wasn't anything Titus could say after that. He looked to his uncles, his cousins, realizing they were all expecting it of him. Patrick had been right about one thing—it *was* Titus' duty, because he most certainly was the eyes and ears of the de Wolfe empire as the king went head to head with opposing warlords. This was what Titus was trained to do. That's what he was expected to do.

But he was going to have to leave his wife in order to do it.

Damn...

"Very well," he said, though he was clearly unhappy. "I will leave on the morrow. The sooner I depart, the sooner I return."

"Excellent," Patrick said, secretly relieved that Titus didn't try to publicly fight him on it. "Meanwhile, to the rest of us, return and fortify your homes. I am not entirely sure how Lancaster will take the fact that we have declared for Edward, but I imagine he will not be happy about it. By siding with the king, we have just tipped the scales heavily in Edward's favor... and Lancaster will know it."

"He would not move against us," Scott said. "He is not that foolish."

Troy looked over him. "He just executed the king's favorite without including his so-called allies in the decision," he said. "I think he *is* that foolish."

There was no argument for that, but the situation was clear—it was time for de Wolfe and their allies to take a stand.

And they had.

God help England for what they were about to face.

CB

KATIANA WASN'T USED to lying around.

Living with Aunt Ethyl, she'd taken over the old woman's duties as chatelaine, which meant she was up and moving when the sun rose. Ethyl lay in bed and ate sweets while Katiana worked diligently. However, since her arrival to Berwick, there was nothing for her to do. Lady Berwick had everything under control, including a daughter who was efficient and knowledgeable, which left Katiana feeling rather useless.

It was a feeling she couldn't stomach.

Therefore, the morning after the wedding feast, she rose when Titus rose, but he had a conclave to attend and tried to convince her to go back to sleep. She wouldn't, of course, and rose from their bed, tidying their room and continuing on a project she'd created for herself since they arrived at Berwick— the inspection of her husband's well-worn clothing.

Titus knew she was trying to keep busy, and he thought it spoke well of her. He also thought it was rather sweet that she should take an interest in his wardrobe, until she started finding things wrong with his clothing—holes here, worn spots there— and it seemed that everything he had was worthy of the rubbish pile. When he came back from meeting with his father and uncles and allies, he found his wife sitting on the bed with a sewing kit beside her as she worked on a garment in her hands, with other garments strewn about her.

"What's this?" he said as he stood in the doorway. "Did you open your own seamstress business while I was away?"

Katiana looked up at him, smiling from ear to ear. "You would think so by the look of things," she said. "But I'm simply trying to salvage some of these tunics you own. Honestly, Titus, it's a wonder these didn't fall from your body when you wore them."

"Why?"

She held up the one she was working on. "Because they're unraveling at the seams," she said, displaying several holes in the seam of the tunic. "You look like a beggar."

He sneered. "How do you think I became so rich?"

"You told me you earned it in tournaments."

"What if I lied? What if I really *am* a beggar?"

"Are you?"

He broke down into a fat grin. "Nay," he said. "Of course I didn't. Someday I will prove to you what an astonishingly skilled man you married."

She giggled as he bent over and kissed her, watching her go back to the tunic as he casually went on the hunt for his saddlebags. He wasn't ready to tell her yet that he was leaving. He wanted a few minutes of lovely conversation before he had to see her unhappy face because he knew, for certain, that she wasn't going to be happy to hear it. He wasn't happy to tell her.

But he had no choice.

"I saw my mother downstairs when I came into the keep," he said. "I told her that you were eager do something around here and not lie around like a queen. I am happy to tell you that my mother requests that you take charge of the great hall."

That brought a reaction from Katiana, who quickly set the sewing aside. "She did?" she said, excited. "How lovely! But what does taking charge of the hall entail?"

He shrugged. "I am not certain," he said. "You will have to ask her, but I believe it means making sure that the floors are swept and the tables are in good repair. Making sure the hearth is cleaned out and kept fueled. Things of that nature."

Katiana nodded eagerly as he found his saddlebags under the bed where she had put them. "I can do that," she said. "I will find your mother right away and ask her what she expects. It will feel wonderful to have a purpose while we are here. By the way… what are you doing?"

Titus had just swung his saddlebags onto the bed. When she asked the question, he stopped and faced her.

"I must pack," he said. "Sit down, love. I want to talk to you."

Katiana did. She planted herself on the bed, next to his saddlebags, as he stood over her. But he was too tall to effectively communicate that way, so he sat down next to her and put his arms around her. For a moment, he simply held her, inhaling the scent of her hair, experiencing everything about her with all of his senses. The smell, the touch, the taste… all of them. He was learning to lose himself in her because it fortified everything about him. The Titus before Katiana was a boy, in a sense, because he'd never really known the love of a good woman. The Titus he was now felt more rounded and more satisfied than he ever had in his life.

He was settled.

He was whole.

"Everything between us has happened so quickly that I'm not sure you realized there is something else going on right now in England that is quite serious," he said. "You are aware that our king has warlords against him, are you not?"

Katiana's head was against Titus' chest, hearing his heartbeat strong and steady in her ear. "I have heard things," she said. "I will admit I do not pay much attention to the politics or the winds of war. Why? Is it important?"

Titus wasn't sure how to answer that question without scaring her. "You do realize that the House of de Wolfe is a warring house… right?"

"I do."

"We have one of the largest armies in England."

"I would expect so."

"Good," he said. "That will make this easier, then, because you understand that your husband is a man of war. I've fought many battles in my lifetime."

She pulled away from him, gazing up at him with her big hazel eyes. "Are you going to fight?" she asked. "Is that what you're trying to tell me?"

He shook his head. "Not at the moment," he said. "But what I am about to tell you must never leave your lips. Only a few people know it, and if it were to get around, my life would be in danger. Do you understand me so far?"

She nodded, looking both serious and a little fearful. "Of course, Titus," she said. "I would never repeat anything you tell me in confidence. But what's it all about?"

"Have you ever heard of a group called the Executioner Knights?"

Her brow furrowed as she thought on that. "I do not think so," she said. "Why? Should I have?"

He shook his head. "Nay," he said. "It is good that you haven't. The group was started by William Marshal about a hundred years ago. He took the best knights in England and used them as spies and assassins, among other things. It was a covert group that worked together in order to keep England safe. It is difficult to explain, but Executioner Knights can be guards for the king. Or they can spy on adversaries. Or they can assassinate someone who is putting someone very important in danger. They do things that are secretive and sometimes distasteful, but they do it for the good of all. Yet no one knows who they are. That is the most important thing. There are those who would like nothing better than to destroy an Executioner Knight and all they stand for. Their enemies are vast."

She was watching him closely. Then she tilted her head back as if something had just occurred to her.

"You're one of them," she said softly.

Titus nodded. "I am," he murmured. "Not even my mother knows. I never told her because I did not want to worry her. Also, the fewer people who know, the better."

"But you are telling me."

"Because you are my wife," he said. "It is important that you know who and what I am, and whom I truly serve. Surprisingly, it is not my father. The past few years, I have been serving the Earl of Pembroke."

"Does he know who you are?"

"He does, but only because he helps Morgen de Lohr from time to time by placing knights with men that need watching," he said. "William Marshal was the Earl of Pembroke many years ago. Now, it is Aymer de Valence because he married Marshal's granddaughter, though the command of the Executioner Knights has passed to the de Lohr family. But Lord Pembroke is still involved. I've been serving him because he is directly involved in the struggle against the king and the king's foreign courtiers."

"Then what you do is very important," she said. "But why are you telling me all of this?"

He rubbed her arms gently. "Because I must leave on the morrow," he said softly. "There is a great deal happening with the king and his warlords, and I must go to the Welsh marches."

"To Pembroke?"

"Nay," he said, shaking his head. "To Lioncross Abbey

Castle, seat of Morgen de Lohr. I bear a message from my father, and there are other things I must tend to, but I do not know when I will return. All I can tell you is that I will return as soon as I can, and you will live here with my family for now. But knowing I have you to return to… it will keep me going, Katia. You will occupy my thoughts day and night until we are together again."

She smiled at him, putting her arms around his neck and pulling her down to him. "I suppose it would do no good to ask if someone else can complete this task for you," she whispered.

"Nay, love," he murmured. "It must be me. I am the de Wolfe born to do this. It is my duty and my destiny."

He heard her sigh, giving up an argument she knew that she had no possibility of winning. "Then I will not ask you to be less than what you are," she said. "I would never ask you to shirk your duties. But know this—you will be all I think about until I see your smiling face once more. Just know… know how proud I am to be your wife, Titus. And how very much I love you."

He hugged her fiercely, feeling tears sting his eyes that this glorious creature should be so devoted to him. He worshipped her, of course, but to know that he was so loved in return was something he never thought he'd experience. He was greatly relieved with how well she had taken the news, but he suspected it was because she really didn't know the danger he was in every moment of every day when carrying out his duties. Perhaps it was better that way. He didn't want to frighten her.

But he did want her.

In the worst way.

Titus kissed Katiana fiercely, suckling her lips, tasting this woman he couldn't get enough of, but very quickly his kisses turned heated. His hands began to roam. That lush, beautiful body was beneath his palms, and he explored it openly. He began unfastening the ties of her simple garment, better with ties this time around and not too rough, loosening them enough to pull her bodice down and expose her right breast.

Katiana cried out softly as his mouth clamped over a tender nipple. She began to pull at his tunic, trying to undress him, and Titus helped her. He wanted her as badly as she wanted him. They were insatiable for one another as it was, taking any opportunity to be intimate, and this was a perfect moment. As Titus' tunic came off, he yanked her bodice down further to expose both luscious breasts.

Mouth on her succulent nipples, he pushed her back on the bed and flipped up her skirts. Katiana was fumbling with the ties of his breeches, and he had her skirts up about the time she pulled loose his ties. His breeches slipped down to his mid-thigh as he wedged himself between her slender legs.

His big arousal pushed at her, and Katiana's eager hands moved to his big erection as she guided him into her. When he felt her slick, wet heat, he thrust firmly into her, listening to her yelp with pleasure. She was exquisitely tight and hot, and he thrust again, feeling her legs wrap around him and draw him in deeper. His arms went around her, holding her tightly against him as he began to move.

Titus' mouth was on hers, kissing her deeply, as he made love to her on the bed that creaked and groaned under his weight. Touching her, tasting her, meant more to him with every encounter, as if it was feeding his very soul. He felt things for Katiana that he had never felt in his life, for anyone, feelings of attraction that he couldn't control. It was more than the act of sex itself. It was a demonstration of emotions that had completely overtaken him.

It was an expression of love that was timeless and honest.

Katiana was incoherent in her passion, feeling every thrust with the greatest of pleasure. He was so big, and plunging into her body so deeply, that his movements were driving her toward a swift release. Titus had spectacular form, and she was learning to crave him. Her body, when she was near him, would cry out for him. They couldn't even sleep in the same bed without making love two or three times a night.

They couldn't get enough of each other.

Titus' thrusts grew harder, firmer, and he ground his pelvis against her every time he plunged deep. He suckled her nipples as he thrust, listening to her groan with pleasure. It was a beautiful and powerful joining, and after one particularly deep thrust, he felt her release around him as gasps of rapture escaped her lips. Still, he continued to make love to her, feeling another climax a few moments later. With that, he could no longer stop his own release.

Titus spilled himself into her sweet body. He found himself wishing his seed would find its mark and that Katiana would bear him a son. A son with his size and strength and his mother's kindness and intelligence. He knew she would make a remarkable mother, and he considered himself fortunate to have married such a magnificent woman, one he loved with all his heart.

One he was loath to leave.

God, he missed her already.

"Titus?" she asked breathlessly.

"Hmm?" he muttered, eyes closed as he lay on top of her.

"Do you suppose we should be packing your bags instead of doing *this*?"

He started to chuckle, his body shaking with mirth. "Nay,"

he said flatly. "I can pack my bags in just a few minutes. We have plenty of time to do *this.*"

"For the rest of the day?"

"For the rest of the day. Or at least until my mother comes looking for us."

With a giggle, Katiana wrapped herself around him, arms around his neck, holding him tightly even though his weight was bearing down on her, smashing her into the mattress. But she didn't mind. She'd waited her whole life to feel the man in her arms, and she wasn't going to let him go so easily. But as she shifted, she caught sight of something on the back of his left bicep. She'd seen it before, but she'd never asked him about it. From her angle, she could just see the edges of it.

Her fingers traced it.

"What is that?" she asked. "I've noticed it before, but I've never asked you about it. It looks like someone drew on your arm."

Titus glanced over his shoulder even though he knew what she was talking about. "That is the de Wolfe mark," he said. "In ancient times, something like this was called a *stigmata.* It is an image that is made with needles upon the skin. Then ink is put in the needle wounds that make the mark permanent. It is the de Wolfe's head, the mark of the grandsons of William de Wolfe of Castle Questing. We all have it."

"Will our sons have it?"

He shook his head, shifting so he was nuzzling her neck. "Nay," he murmured. "Only the grandsons of William de Wolfe. It is the thing I am the proudest of, next to you."

Those sweet words were enough for Katiana to latch on to his lips again, overwhelmed with emotion. Titus brought it out in her, and she in him. They continued to make love until

Kristiana knocked on the door around the nooning hour, looking for her sewing kit. After that, they were forced to separate.

But it had been the best morning of their lives.

CHAPTER TWENTY

"Y OU SENT FOR me?" Zora asked. "What do you want?"

She met Ansel in the bailey of Berwick, a massive place that was busy with soldiers and servants and people coming to do business with the castle. The trades were going full swing, two smithy stalls sending acrid smoke into the midday air, and on the wall walk above, soldiers went about their rounds.

Ansel had sent Zora a message about an hour earlier, using a servant from the knights' quarters who gave the message to a house servant. All it said was to meet him in the bailey, and Zora had taken her sweet time doing so. She was dressed in a blue brocade gown on this day, hoping she might see Titus at some point.

Instead, she was faced with Ansel.

"Has your father returned to you yet?" Ansel asked.

Zora shook her head. "He attended a gathering with Berwick this morning," she said. "He's not come back. Why do you ask?"

Ansel motioned for her to walk with him. "Because I was at that meeting, too," he said. "I learned a great deal this morning about what, precisely, is happening with our king and the warlords who oppose them. It has given me an idea."

"What idea?"

"About what to do with my sister."

Up until that point, Zora had been ambivalent to the conversation, but now, he had her interest. "Oh?" she said. "What is your idea?"

They were heading for the western wall, which was attached to another wall that ran all the way down to the river. It was a little treacherous, but it was private.

And Ansel wanted to make sure they had complete privacy.

Putting his fingers to his lips in a silencing gesture, he led Zora to the wall walk that went down to the river. It was too steep for her, however, so she balked a few steps into it, but Ansel didn't push her. They had enough privacy where they were.

"It seems that the House of de Wolfe and her allies intend to side with the king against Lancaster and Warwick," he said. "That has given me the idea."

"You still haven't told me your idea."

Ansel leaned against the wall, his gaze moving out over the river and watching the birds fly overhead. "The House of de Wolfe has an enormous army," he said. "All of the armies from all of their properties will make one giant army, something not even Lancaster can match. He'll try, but the de Wolfe family has allies all over England. They can bring ten or fifteen thousand men to a field of battle with hardly an effort. Up until now, they'd been neutral when it came to Lancaster and Edward, but because Lancaster is taking matters into his own hands, they've decided to give their loyalty to Edward."

"And?"

"And what do you think Thomas of Lancaster would pay if he had the wife of a de Wolfe son?" Ansel said. "Lancaster is the richest man in England. Everyone knows that. I can imagine he would pay extremely well to have a de Wolfe wife as a hostage."

Zora was intrigued. "For what purpose?"

Ansel looked at her as if she were a completely stupid creature. "*Think,*" he said. "If he has my sister as a hostage, he can threaten to kill her if de Wolfe marches against him. Don't you see? He could neutralize their entire army. They wouldn't dare go to war against him if he holds one of their women. I think he would pay extremely well for such a privilege."

Now, Zora was catching on, and her eyes widened. "You could take her away, and I would show great concern to Titus and help him search for her when he realizes she has disappeared," she said. "It would endear me to him greatly if I help him search for his wife."

"Who will end up a hostage of Lancaster."

Zora was in support of the plan. "She would be," she said. "But Titus... It is quite possible he would fall in love with me instead. I would be so good and kind and helpful to him, concerned for his loss. How could he help but fall in love with me?"

She was dreaming at that point. Even Ansel knew that. But he needed her help, so he went along with her.

"His wife would still be alive, I suppose," he said. "It is possible that Lancaster would not kill her."

"Why not?" Zora said. "Do you really think the entire de Wolfe army will stay away because of one lone woman?"

Ansel shrugged. "I have no way of knowing," he said. "Mayhap he would kill her, mayhap not. In either case, she would be his prisoner, and Titus would be alone and grieving."

Zora lit up with glee. "It is a brilliant idea," she said. "Titus will not grieve alone—he'll have me."

"And I have the money Lancaster has paid me for Katia."

"We shall both come out on top."

Ansel nodded. "Indeed," he said. "But we must move quickly. I cannot remain at Berwick much longer, and I have no way of knowing when I will see my sister again. It is not as if she will ever come to Callerton to visit me, so I must take advantage of the situation now, and I require your assistance."

"What do you want me to do?"

"Bring my sister to me."

"She will not come if you send her a message like the one you just sent me?"

Ansel shook his head. "Nay," he said. "Titus has her well protected, and you surely realize there is no love lost between my sister and me. She will not come if I summon her. But she will if you do."

"What shall I do?"

Ansel's attention turned toward the castle, his gaze moving to the enormous keep with its many rooms. "Send her a missive," he said. "Have a servant deliver it to her. Are you housed in the keep?"

Zora nodded. "My father and I are."

"Then use one of the servants to send her a note," he said. "Ask her to join you. Tell her you want to thank her for the invitation and whatever else you need to tell her that will have her thinking that you want to be friends. I do not care what it is. Tell her to meet you in the kitchen yard."

Zora had thought his suggestions were good ones until he mentioned the kitchen yard. She frowned. "Why would I want her to meet me in the kitchen yard?"

"Because I will be there," he said. "More importantly, there is a postern gate. I saw it yesterday because the kitchen yard is next to the great hall. I can take her from that gate, but you must bring me my horse. I cannot get him through the postern gate, so you must walk him from the gatehouse and bring him around to the side. I will take it from there."

Zora looked at him as if he'd gone completely daft. "You do not think anyone will think it strange that I am leading your horse out of Berwick?"

Ansel thought on that. "You may be right," he said, quickly re-planning his strategy. "I will take the horse out and leave him in the trees to the north. But I cannot bring my baggage or my weapon—it will look as if I am leaving, so anyone who may see me later in the kitchen yard might think the whole thing odd. I do not want to attract any attention."

"Then what will you do?"

He looked at her. "I will put you in charge of my possessions," he said. "You will bring them all to me."

"Why can you not take them when you take your sister through the postern gate?"

He cocked an eyebrow. "Because I will more than likely have a fight on my hands with her," he said. "I cannot carry my bags and wrestle her at the same time."

Zora wasn't so certain. "Then leave them outside of the postern gate and collect them when you can."

"Bring the damnable bags to me, Zora. Do you want Titus or not?"

Zora sighed heavily. "Very well," she said. "But I am doing enough simply by getting your sister to the kitchen yard."

"And you will reap the benefits when Katia disappears and Titus needs consoling."

He was right. With a shrug, Zora agreed, and Ansel knew he had to act quickly. Time was of the essence.

"Good," he said. "Now, go back to the keep and send my sister a note of gratitude and ask her to meet you. Even if it is not in the kitchen yard, have her show you the place and end up in the kitchen yard, but give me about an hour. I'll be there, waiting."

"Where?"

"In the back, by the postern gate," he said. "But my sister cannot see me. I'll be hiding. You simply need to get her there."

Zora nodded. "And you're sure this will work?"

"It will work if you do what I've told you to do," Ansel said. "Fail and we shall both end up in a good deal of trouble, because if de Wolfe doesn't punish you, I will."

The last few words were most definitely a threat. Zora had known Ansel long enough to know that. The man meant every word of it.

She fled the wall.

Titus had disappeared.

Katiana wasn't sure where he'd gone, but he left her shortly after Kristiana came looking for her sewing kit. She and Kristiana had sat and talked for a while, looking over Titus' hole-filled tunics and deciding that it would be better to make him some new ones rather than try to salvage the old. Kristiana had some fabric that would work, but her mother called her away to attend to something more pressing, leaving Katiana alone.

Not that it mattered.

She wanted to see the great hall.

In truth, Katiana was very excited about being put in charge of the center of activity at Berwick. It was also a way to get her mind off Titus' leaving. The more she thought about his departure, the more concerned she became, but she'd already set the tone by telling him she would not worry. They'd made love all morning, content in each other's arms, until Kristiana banged on the door and Titus had been so startled that he'd fallen out of bed. They'd laughed uproariously about that as they quickly found their clothing, and Kristiana, realizing she had broken up a tryst, had been embarrassed.

They'd laughed about that, too.

Then he'd gone off, presumably to prepare for his journey, while Katiana and Kristiana spoke of sewing kits and haggard tunics. As Katiana left her chamber and emerged from the keep into the bailey, with the great hall straight ahead, she realized that she was happy. Happy for the first time in her life, and she had been since the day her horse had run wild in London. The day she saw Titus again for the first time in many years.

That's when this otherworldly joy she was experiencing commenced.

She felt as if she was walking on clouds.

Already, she was feeling comfortable at Berwick. It was the largest castle she'd ever seen, enormous in scale and population, but it had a good feeling to it. Patrick was an excellent lord, and he governed fairly, so his subjects seemed to be content. Twice, she'd ventured out into the village of Berwick with Titus, who had taken her to the shores where the fishermen brought in their catches. There was a woman down there who cooked the fish over an open fire, and for a pence, Katiana had enjoyed the most succulent fish she'd ever tasted. Then they'd brought some home for the family, but Patrick hated fish, so he'd had beef instead while the entire great hall smelled of roasted fish.

It was a good thing she was feeling comfortable at Berwick, considering she was going to be living there while Titus went about his duties. It was a world away from Aunt Ethyl and her London manse, or the spice merchant that everyone was so mad about, but Katiana didn't care. She was thrilled for it.

Thrilled for her new life to begin.

The great hall was open, and she went inside to see that servants were sweeping up from the previous night, while a couple of them were attempting to clean a blockage out of the chimney. Katiana found herself standing behind them, watching them clear the blockage, offering a couple of suggestions because she'd supervised the same thing at Ethyl's manse. She knew how the kitchen worked, how to clear chimneys, how to repair tables and floors or, at the very least, how to supervise the workmen. She wasn't a stranger to that kind of thing. But deep down, she wondered if she'd ever have a home of her own to manage.

She'd always hoped for such a thing.

It seemed that the de Wolfe family liked to live in the same place, although Titus' three older brothers all had their own homes. Markus, whom she'd talked to at length last night, had Trastamara Castle, Cassius had Edenthorpe, and Magnus had Raechester. Titus seemed to be the wanderer of the group from what she could gather, but she heard Markus and Titus speaking of an outpost called Lamberton, situated right on the border to the north. It was small as far as castles went, but it guarded an important road in and out of Scotland, or so she had heard. Markus seemed to think that Patrick was going to grant it to Titus.

Perhaps she'd spend her life in a border castle after all.

But it seemed like a dream, all of it. Meanwhile, she was very happy to remain at Berwick and make herself useful. Now, that seemed to consist of watching the servants as they finally cleared the blockage and a big pile of soot was purged from the chimney, landing smack on the stones and spraying out all over the servants. Katiana had the sense to jump back and stay clear of the black dust, but the servants were covered in it. When they turned to look at her, all she could see were eyes and teeth as they laughed at their misfortune.

It *was* rather funny.

"My lady?"

She was being addressed. Katiana turned to see a maid standing behind her, and the woman silently handed her a small, folded piece of vellum. Katiana accepted it, but she looked at the woman curiously, who simply bobbed a curtsy and nothing more. Puzzled, Katiana opened the folded vellum to find a note written to her.

Lady de Wolfe, wife of Titus –

I would like to extend my gratitude for your invitation to celebrate the event of your wedding.

Before I depart for home, I should like to thank you personally. I should like to ensure that we shall be friends someday. As a petty child, I did not realize the value of kindness or friendship. If I was ever cruel to you in the times we met, I humbly ask forgiveness. I should like to make a new friend of you, since our families are allies. I hope it will be a new beginning for us all.

I am waiting in the kitchen yard for you at this moment, should you have the time to come to me.

I remain respectfully yours,

Zora de Allery

Katiana read the note twice. Then she looked at the maid again.

"Did Lady Zora truly give you this?" she asked, just to make sure.

The servant nodded. "Aye, my lady," she said. "She asked me to find you and give it to you."

Katiana looked at the note again, noting the location of the requested meeting. "And she is in the kitchen yard now?" she asked.

"I believe so, my lady."

Katiana shrugged and lowered the note. "Right," she said. "Well, I can think of better places to meet than a kitchen yard. I will find her and bring her into the great hall. Will you send for refreshments and have them put on one of the tables?"

The maid nodded and fled. Leaving the servants at the hearth to shake off the soot and clean the mess on the floor, Katiana headed out of the hall. The kitchen yard was right next to it, to the east, along with the kitchens, the buttery, and a few other things. As she headed for the gate that led into the yard, built into a wall that was about seven feet tall and several feet thick, she noticed Markus and Magnus on the wall in the distance. It took her a moment to see that Titus was with them. With a smile at finally having located her husband, she opened the gate to the kitchen yard and stepped through.

The yard was divided into two specific areas—one for livestock, and the other, near a postern gate that dumped out into a steep gully behind the castle, cluttered with old barrels and implements used in cooking, including massive iron spits. A tree grew up in this corner of the yard, surprisingly, an almond tree that had been stripped and stripped again of both leaves and nuts. Katiana was about to go into the area where they kept the livestock, but she caught sight of Zora over near the walled postern gate area. The woman was in a pale blue garment, waving to Katiana when she caught her eye.

Katiana headed right for her.

"I received your note," she said to Zora. "It was very kind of you to write it."

Zora smiled, but it was an odd, pasted-on sort of smile. "It was no trouble," she said. "I'm glad you came."

Katiana came to within a few feet of her. "I've had refreshments sent to the hall," she said. "That is a much better place to speak than a kitchen yard."

Zora seemed resistant. "I think I would like to stay here," she said. "You saw how everyone was yesterday when you suggested escorting my father and me to the table laden with food. The knights make me nervous, and if we go to the hall, we will surely be interrupted. I'm not sure we could even have a conversation."

Katiana didn't think there was anything strange about that request, because given the incident she was referring to, Zora was more than likely right.

"As you wish," she said. "But it was very nice of you to send the note. I'm glad you were able to come to the feast. I think we should have crossed paths back when we were much younger, since we both fostered for de Wolfe, and I do remember seeing you, but I do not think we ever spoke. How long did you foster at Berwick?"

"Just a few years," Zora said. "Then I went to Alnwick."

"Did you like it there?"

"A little," Zora said, moving over toward the almond tree.

"But I have happier memories at Berwick. I made friends here. I knew Magnus and Titus. We enjoyed our time together."

That wasn't what Titus had told Katiana, but she didn't comment on it. If Zora remembered her time at Berwick with fondness, then good for her. But Titus told a completely different story.

Ironic how memories could be so subjective.

"It is good that you enjoyed your time here," Katiana said. "What have you been doing since you returned home from Alnwick?"

Zora was at the old almond tree, which was next to the shed that held the cooking implements. Reaching up, she picked at one of the leafless branches.

"My father keeps me busy," Zora said. "I am chatelaine at Thornton Tower. That is our home. We keep bees there, which make lots of honey that we sell in market towns. It has been a good crop."

Katiana warmed to the conversation, moving deeper into the smaller area because Zora had moved over by the tree. "I never thought of bees as a crop," she said. "How clever. Are… are you sure you would not like to go into the hall? It is quite vacant in there. No one will bother us."

Zora shook her head. "Nay," she said. Then she looked up at the almond tree, running her finger along a branch. "Look how barren this is. Do you know anything about trees, Lady de Wolfe?"

By this time, Katiana was over by the tree because Zora seemed interested in it. "Nay," she said, looking up at it. "But you must, given that you keep bees. I know that the almond trees flower in the spring. They are quite lovely."

"I like almonds."

"So do I."

"Have you ever had almond pudding with rose petals? It is delicious the way our cook makes it."

Katiana opened her mouth to answer, but she caught movement out of the corner of her eye. She didn't have time to turn around or even react before something heavy was slammed against the back of her skull.

She dropped like a stone.

Ansel had made his appearance.

"God's Bones!" Zora hissed, slapping her hand over her mouth in shock. "You killed her!"

Ansel dropped the rock he'd been holding, the one that had been his companion as he'd lain in wait for his sister. Now it had his sister's blood on it. Bending over her, he lifted an eyelid.

"Nay," he said. "She is alive. But hopefully, she'll stay unconscious until I can get her on the horse and get her away from here. Grab my bags and come with me."

As he scooped up Katiana, Zora let out another hiss. "I do not have your bags," she said. "I thought you brought them!"

Ansel looked at her in exasperation. "I told you to do it!"

"How could I do it when you told me to bring your sister to you!"

Ansel was furious. "Christ," he muttered. "You stupid cow."

"Insulting me won't help!"

Ansel was seriously struggling with his temper. "Then go now to the knights' quarters and get them," he said through clenched teeth. "My chamber is the second one on the left. Get my bags, and my weapon, and bring them. Quickly or all is lost!"

Zora bolted. With a limp woman in his arms, Ansel kicked open the postern gate with his foot and headed out to the trails that led behind the castle, down into the gully where his horse was tethered at the bottom. The animal was shielded by a few trees from the walls of the castle, but the slope wasn't. It was clear of trees or growth because of its proximity to the castle. Until Ansel could get down the slope and into the trees, he would be visible to any sharp eyes on the wall.

But it was a chance he had to take.

With all due speed, he fled down the trail, praying he wasn't seen, praying he could make it. He had what he'd come for, and it would be cruel, indeed, were he to be thwarted before he could carry out his plans. Off to Thornton Tower he would go, as Zora had suggested, and the vault would be Katiana's home until he could get her to Lancaster.

Ansel could feel that coinage lining his pockets already.

He was going to be a *very* rich man.

CHAPTER TWENTY-ONE

Z ORA WAS RUNNING.

Titus saw her running through the bailey like a madwoman, which was a curious sight. He'd been on the wall with his brothers, near the gatehouse, discussing his coming journey to the Welsh marches, when he caught sight of Zora in a pale dress. He found it rather odd, so he watched her rush all the way through the bailey before entering the knights' quarters.

That brought even more curiosity.

"Titus?" Markus said. "Did you hear me?"

Titus shook his head. "Nay," he said. Then he pointed toward the knights' quarters. "Did you see that?"

Markus and Magnus came over to his side of the wall. "See what?" Markus asked.

"De Allery's daughter," Titus said. "Zora. She just ran like a madwoman across the bailey and went into the knights' quarters."

Markus looked at him. "Why on earth did she go into the knights' quarters?"

Titus shook his head. "I cannot tell you," he said. "But she almost looked… frantic."

"Do you think she is looking for a knight?" Markus said.

Titus came away from the wall. "It is possible," he said. "Mayhap she needs assistance and is looking for one of us."

"Should we find out?"

Titus shrugged. "Possibly," he said. Then he sighed. "Probably. She looked as if she was in a panic."

"Then let us see what she is panicked about," Markus said.

It was enough of a sight, and enough of a curiosity, to move them off the wall. If Zora was indeed looking for a knight, or help, eventually the duty would fall to one of them, because the servants would send word to the gatehouse and the gatehouse would come to them. Therefore, the three of them simply took the initiative and headed toward the tower that contained the staircase that would take them off the wall and into the bailey, but before they could reach it, Magnus grasped Titus by the arm.

"Wait," he said, pointing. "*Look.*"

They all turned to see Zora emerging from the knights' quarters with saddlebags and a broadsword. Titus scratched his head.

"She's *stealing* from someone?" he said, incredulous. "Whose possessions are those?"

No one had any answers, but her behavior was increasingly puzzling. The three brothers took the stairs down to the bailey, emerging from the tower in time to see Zora rushing toward the kitchen yard lugging the heavy bags and the broadsword. The knights began to follow her, quickening their pace. They came around the side of the great hall just as Zora reached the gate that led into the kitchen yard.

Titus called out to her.

"Lady Zora?" he shouted. "Is something amiss?"

Startled by the sound of her name, Zora turned to see Titus, Magnus, and Markus about thirty feet away from her. Instead of pausing to answer the question, she screamed and bolted through the gate.

That brought the knights on the run.

They burst into the kitchen yard in time to catch a glimpse of Zora's dress as she went through the postern gate. Incredibly confused and the slightest bit concerned, they ran after her, plowing through the postern gate to see her halfway down the trail that led to the bottom of the gully. They started to run after her, though the trail was steep and slippery in spots. They hadn't taken five steps when Zora suddenly lost her footing midway down and rolled the rest of the way, tumbling all the way to the bottom and scattering the possessions in the bags. Everything went flying.

Dazed, Zora had no hope of recovering before Titus and his brothers descended on her. Titus was the first one, grabbing hold of her as she writhed around on the ground. He opened his mouth to question her when he heard something off to his left. Looking up, he saw a man on horseback with something, or someone, draped in front of him. Baffled, he shielded his eyes from the sun, realizing that he was looking at Ansel astride the horse he'd seen the man ride in on the night before. A horse bearing red and yellow on the saddle. And the "something" across the saddle wasn't an inanimate object as much as it was a body.

It took Titus a moment to realize that he recognized the hair.

It was Katiana.

Seized with terror, he began to run toward Ansel, as fast as he had run in his entire life. Seeing Titus heading in his direction, Ansel yanked the reins off the branch he had them tethered to, which created snapping noises as the branches broke. That startled his horse, who nearly dumped Katiana on the ground. But Ansel held on to the reins, and his sister, and he spun the horse around and took off toward the north, where there was a smaller road leading into Scotland. The big warhorse kicked up clods of earth as it tore off, faster than Titus could run.

And he knew it.

God help him, he knew it.

"Titus!" Markus shouted, running toward him. "Who was that?"

Titus was nearly in tears. "Ansel," he gasped, breathing heavily. "He has Katia!"

That was all Markus needed to hear. He turned on his heel and began to run back toward the castle with Titus on his tail, leaving Magnus to bring up the rear with a hysterical Zora as his prisoner. By the time Titus and Markus ran back up the hill and reached the castle, the alarms were already sounding. Patrick, Scott, Troy, Blayth, Thomas, Nathaniel Hage, and Atreus de Norville were already congregating, having emerged from the keep when they heard the alarm.

All hell was breaking loose, and Titus was at the head of it.

"Titus!" Patrick shouted as his sons came barreling through the kitchen yard gate. "Titus! Markus! What's happening?"

Titus was running for the stable, so it was Markus who went to his father and uncles. "Katiana's brother has captured her and is making a break for it," he said breathlessly, pointing off toward the north. "We must go after them."

Atreus, Nathaniel, and Thomas were already in motion, rushing to the stables after Titus. Scott, Troy, Patrick, and

Blayth were a little slower, but not by much. All of them rushed for their mounts as Patrick bellowed orders to the nearest soldiers, demanding they secure Berwick, lock it down, and make sure each guest from the previous night was accounted for. Truthfully, no one was quite sure what was happening, but if their liege and the others were moving that swiftly, it couldn't be good.

While Rian and Espen were making sure Patrick's orders were carried out, Peter and Krister rushed to Patrick's side to help. Bowen, who had been in the bailey, had rushed into the stables to make sure the horses were being rapidly saddled. As everyone was commandeering horses and saddles, Magnus came through the kitchen yard, dragging Zora with him. She was dirty, sobbing hysterically, and had a bloodied arm from her fall. Titus happened to catch a glimpse of Magnus with Zora, and as a groom hurriedly saddled his animal, he ran over to where his brother was holding on to the weeping woman.

"Where is he taking her?" Titus demanded, grabbing Zora by the arm and giving her a shake. "Tell me where he's taking her. And what were you doing, running to him like that? Were those his possessions in your hands?"

Zora was cornered and terrified. "I… I… I do not know where he is taking her!"

Titus gave her a good shake again. "Don't lie to me," he snarled. "Where is he taking her?"

"I don't know!" Zora screamed. "He is going to sell her to Lancaster!"

Titus froze, his eyes wide. "He… he's *what*?"

Zora had tears and mucus and dirt all over her face, her bushy hair askew. One look at Titus' pale features and she wasn't so fearful any longer. She was enraged to see such concern for Katiana on Titus' face.

Why couldn't he be that concerned for her?

"You heard me," she said, spittle flying from her lips. "You married that little bitch without permission, and it was not your right! Ansel is going to sell her to Lancaster to use her as a hostage against de Wolfe siding with Edward! And Lancaster will pay him a fortune for a de Wolfe wife, so she'll be out of your reach forever. Of course you're never going to get her back! She was never meant to be yours to begin with!"

Titus couldn't believe what he was hearing. "And you did this?" he asked, aghast. "You are *helping* him?"

Zora had one hand free. With a roar of anguish, she lashed out and tried to slap Titus, but he was too quick for her. He backed away just in time, catching the hand that tried to strike him.

"Your father promised that I would marry you!" she screamed. "*We* were to be betrothed. You were mine!"

Now, the situation was starting to make some sense. It was the same old Zora, the same girl he'd fostered with, the same troublemaker. Only now, her trouble could be deadly. Horrified, Titus turned to see his father and his Uncle Scott standing behind him, listening to everything. As Titus ran for Jesus, now saddled and waiting, Patrick ordered Zora put under arrest and locked up. Magnus turned her over to Krister, who sent Peter and several soldiers to find Edmund de Allery.

The man had to know what his daughter had done.

As the entire bailey of Berwick descended into chaos, Titus, his father, his uncles, and his brothers charged out of the gatehouses, taking the road north in pursuit of Ansel and Katiana. Titus was at the head of it, pushing Jesus faster than he'd ever pushed the animal in its life. Fortunately, Jesus was a swift horse and was up to the challenge. Even so, Titus couldn't keep the tears of genuine fear from his eyes. The same words kept rolling over and over in his mind…

Please, God. Please keep Katia safe.

CHAPTER TWENTY-TWO

S HE WAS UNCOMFORTABLE.

She was nauseated and her head hurt. Katiana was gradually aware that everything on her body was hurting and her face felt strange. Hot and swollen. As she opened her eyes, she realized that she was looking at a horse's legs and a road. Somehow, she was hanging downward, watching the road go by.

She had no idea how she got there.

Feeling sick, she started to stir, only to feel a firm hand on her back.

"Hold still. If you value your life, you will hold still and keep silent."

It was Ansel. Terror filled Katiana. She was on a horse, a running horse, and somehow her brother had her, but she had no idea what had happened. Thinking hard, she remembered the great hall and the soot. No… *wait*… Something happened after that. A servant with a note.

From Zora!

Now, things were coming back to her muddled mind. She'd gone to the kitchen yard to speak to Zora, who was too afraid to go into the great hall because she wanted to speak with Katiana uninterrupted. They were talking about trees and bees. And then… then she remembered nothing. Everything had gone black, and here she was, waking up on the back of a horse. With her brother.

God's Bones, what is happening?

"Ansel," she said, squirming. "What has happened? Let me down!"

Ansel hit her on the back, and Katiana yelped. "I told you to stop moving if you value your life," he said. "I meant it. Be still."

That told Katiana quite a bit, in truth. Her brother was in control. She wasn't allowed to move or talk. She was hanging off a horse that was running… somewhere. When Ansel smacked her on the back, that told her that this situation was something dark and terrible. She was in danger. Ansel was taking her somewhere, and she had no idea what was at the end of this road. She didn't want to find out. Something told her that she had to fight for her life now or she would have no life left to fight for.

As a child, she would cower when Ansel beat her. She'd been no match for him. She wasn't much more of a match as an adult, but she had something now she hadn't possessed back then—courage. Courage to help herself, to stop her brother from harming her.

It was time for Katiana to fight back.

She had to save herself.

But she had no weapons, nothing to use. The only thing within arm's reach was Ansel's right leg and foot. The edge of the saddle and the cinch were below her. But she turned her head slightly and could see the horse's reins to her left, about at her shoulder's level. If she stuck her left arm out, she could grab the reins about mid-neck.

Fight back!

Carefully, she reached down and grabbed the cinch to steady herself. With the other hand, she suddenly reached out and grasped the reins, yanking as hard as she could and using her grip on the cinch as leverage. Her abrupt action pulled the horse's head around to the right, and the animal screamed as it was twisted up by the yanking rein. That caused the beast to stiffen up and trip, and suddenly, the horse was going down. Ansel tried to grab on to the mane, or the saddle, but he was sent flying as the horse went down at speed.

Everything went crashing to the road.

Since the horse fell onto its left side, Katiana was able to keep her grip on the cinch, and it kept her from flying off. She ended up splayed across its belly. Feeling her feet against the rocky road, Katiana was able to stand up rather quickly. A quick glance over her shoulder saw her brother on his side, several feet away, but stirring.

Katiana took off running.

They were in the farming area of the border, so the land was mostly farming fields surrounded by wooded areas. Katiana knew she had to make it to a wooded area if she had any chance of hiding from her brother. She couldn't count on the fact that anyone knew she was gone from Berwick, much less assume help was coming. For all she knew, she was on her own and in the fight for her life.

Literally.

She didn't know the area, so she didn't know which direction to run. Head aching and stomach lurching, she ran for a heavily wooded area at the edge of a field, hearing her brother shouting her name behind her. She couldn't even look back to see if he was running after her or if he was just shouting. All she knew was that she had to make it to that wooded area.

She ran like the wind.

The safety of the trees welcomed her. She plunged into the foliage and dared to stop, just for a moment, to see if her brother was behind her. He was indeed trailing after her, running in her direction, but he was holding his left arm against his chest. That told Katiana that he'd hurt himself in the fall, which was a good thing. It would work in her favor. Beyond her brother, back by the road, she could see that the horse was up, grazing on the grass that lined the road.

If she could only make it back to the horse, she could escape her brother.

That had to be her goal.

But first, she had to survive Ansel's pursuit.

The wooded area was heavy with foliage on the ground as well a thick canopy in the trees, making it dense and dark. Katiana hunted down a big stick, something for defense, before hiding in some of the heavy bushes that were near the edge of the wooded area. She hoped that Ansel would come into the area and think she'd run deep into the forest. As he went in pursuit, she would slip back out and make a run for the horse.

Silently, she waited.

Ansel stopped running when he entered the trees. Katiana could see him from her hiding place, and he was panting heavily with exertion, looking around as if trying to decide which direction to go in. But the forest was quiet except for the birds overhead, meaning he didn't hear any running or gasps from a panicked lady in the distance. Katiana hadn't thought about that.

Ansel just stood there, listening.

Waiting.

"It would be better if you showed yourself to me," he said loudly. "If I find you, I will take it out on your hide. That was a very foolish thing to do, Katia. You could have killed us both."

He was met with tweeting birds and the wind through the branches. Then he began to walk, his gaze moving over his surroundings.

"I suppose you're wondering where we are," he said. "You're also wondering why you're with me. Your friend, Zora, helped me. She truly wasn't your friend, Katia. She only said that to get you alone. You see, she wants your husband. She has a right to him. Her father was negotiating a betrothal between Titus and Zora. You didn't even have that. You just married the man, though I suspect it was because he *had* to marry you. I'm sure you did what many women do—spread your legs to catch a husband. How very cunning of you, little sister, but not cunning enough. I had plans for you before you married de Wolfe, and I have plans for you now."

He continued walking, slowly, as he spoke. He came within about twelve feet of Katiana as he passed by the clump of underbrush she was hiding in, but he continued on into the forest. Katiana watched him, her heart in her throat and a stick in her hand. Every moment she hid from him was like torture because she was terrified that he was going to spot her.

Praying to God that he wouldn't.

"You are wondering what plans," Ansel called out. "It is simple, really. You see, our father left us nothing. Whatever de Edington wealth there was is gone. All I inherited was the castle and the lands and little else. I wish I'd known that before I suffocated our ailing father in order to get what I wanted, but I suppose that cannot be helped now. You are the only thing of value I have, and it was my intention to sell you to the highest bidder. But your marriage to Titus thwarted my plans."

He was wandering further away, but Katiana was still coiled, still terrified. She understood that he had murdered their father to gain his inheritance, which didn't surprise her in the least. She hadn't expected anything less. But the whole part about selling her was very strange. Ansel came to a halt about thirty feet away, standing in a small clearing with sunlight streaming down through the canopy. He turned in her direction, and she froze, remaining as still as possible, so he wouldn't see any movement in the bramble. She was wearing a garment that her mother-in-law had loaned her, lightweight wool the color of wine and a linen shift to match. The wine-colored wool blended in with the shadows, but it was the shift that concerned her. If he saw white moving amongst the leaves, he would surely find her.

"You cheated me out of a fortune, Katia," he said, lifting his voice to the trees. "You were mine to do with as I pleased, and you cheated me by marrying de Wolfe. Berwick says that they will offer compensation, but I doubt it will be what I want. Titus has already married you, so they do not have to pay me much. But Zora had a wonderful idea, and I must say that I am ashamed I did not think of it first. She is giving me money to remove you from Titus' side. I am, therefore, taking you to Thomas of Lancaster, and I am certain he will pay me a fortune for you. So, you will still serve my purpose. I will still have my money in the end. And you… you will be the captive of a man who has killed the lover of the king. I doubt he'll have any reservation in killing the wife of an enemy."

He was starting to move back in her direction, and Katiana was afraid that he might see her if he came any closer, but then he suddenly turned around again and started heading deeper into the forest, calling her name. Katiana was able to lift her head a little, watching him move further and further into the bramble. With a glance over her shoulder that showed the horse to still be on the side of the road, grazing, she knew this was her chance.

She had to run.

And run she did.

Bolting from her hiding place, Katiana took off toward the grazing horse. Ansel didn't catch on at first because he was deep in the trees, but he heard a distant noise and turned to see Katiana sprinting across the field, back to the road. He took off running, faster than his sister was running by sheer power. The pair of them raced across the field, with Katiana closing in on the grazing horse. But the animal saw her coming and, startled by the swift moments, scampered across the road to the meadow on the other side. Katiana was within about ten feet of the road itself when something grabbed her skirt. With a scream, she swung her stick around and caught Ansel in the eye.

Howling, he went down.

Enveloped in hysteria, Katiana began to beat him about the head with her stick. She whacked him and whacked him, leaving bloody scratches as he tried to protect himself, but he finally grabbed the stick and the wrestling began. It didn't last long, however, because he was much stronger than she was. When he finally yanked the stick away from her, she began to scream and run, but it was only momentary. Ansel caught up to her, grabbing her by the hair and the arm as she screamed at the top of her lungs.

"Stop it," Ansel commanded. "Stop it or this will go badly

for you!"

Katiana was kicking and scratching and screaming. "It is already going badly for me," she bellowed. "Let me *go*!"

Ansel yanked on her hair, and she screamed again, this time from pain. He managed to get a good grip on her shoulder, entangled his hand in her hair, and threw her to the ground. Pouncing, his hands went over her mouth and onto her neck to silence her.

He began to squeeze.

"Shut your lips," he said, squeezing as she struggled. "Shut your lips or I will shut them permanently."

Katiana managed to open her mouth, biting his fingers as hard as she could. Ansel roared in pain, slapping her across the face so hard that he momentarily dazed her. But his hands went back to her neck, squeezing hard.

This time, he was going to kill her.

To hell with Lancaster and his fortune.

Unfortunately, Katiana was in a bad way. She was already starting to see stars. But she screamed and fought, scratching him with her nails, fighting as hard as she could because she knew if she didn't, this was the end of her. It was the end of her life with Titus, the end of the children they would never have and the life they would never know. It was the end of every dream she'd ever had, a future she had hoped for. All of it, ending.

Dying like she was.

Dying...

The world was growing dim.

Suddenly, there was a commotion around them. The thunder of hooves. Something hit Ansel from the side, because the man grunted with the force of the blow. He toppled off Katiana as several bodies jumped on him, and, half-conscious, Katiana could hear her brother crying out in pain. But someone was kneeling beside her, gently slapping her cheek and telling her to breathe.

"Breathe, lass, breathe!"

She wasn't sure if she could. She was in limbo, hearing sounds of fighting, as someone lifted her up and someone else rubbed her arms briskly, her cheeks. Someone even rubbed at her neck, and then she was coughing and gagging as air filled her lungs. Sweet, clean air. Katiana's eyes flew open, and she found herself looking at Patrick and Scott and Troy. They were all rubbing at her wrists and arms and even her torso, trying to get her to breathe.

She sucked a long, ragged breath.

"He tried to kill me!" she cried, coughing and sputtering. "I was dead! I was almost *dead*!"

Patrick held her tightly. "You're all right, Katia," he said softly. "You're safe now, I swear it."

It took Katiana a moment to process what he was saying. Only a few moments ago, she had been in the fight for her life, and now... now, she was surrounded by Titus' father and uncles. Was she really safe?

Realization struck, and she burst into tears.

"My God," she sobbed as Patrick sat her up and steadied her. "He... he said that he was going to sell me to Lancaster as a hostage. He was going to make Lancaster pay!"

"A hostage?" Scott repeated, trying to soothe the frightened woman. "But why?"

Katiana was holding on tightly to Patrick as she answered him. "He said that you would not fight if Lancaster held me as a hostage," she said. "He said that Lancaster would pay handsomely for a de Wolfe wife to use against the House of de Wolfe.”

Patrick and Scott looked at each other in astonishment. “Then your brother sides with Lancaster?” Patrick asked her.

Katiana shook her head, or tried to. She wiped at her nose with the back of her hand. “Nay,” she said, her voice trembling. “He said I cheated him out of a fortune by marrying Titus. He couldn’t marry me off to the highest bidder. He just wanted the money. It was all about the money.”

A great deal became clear in those sobbing words. She was weeping heavily again, traumatized by the entire event, as Patrick and Scott and Troy looked at each other in shock. They were old men and understood the nature of men in general, especially the greedy ones. As Katiana wept in Patrick’s arms, the three of them looked over to see Ansel being beaten to a pulp by Titus, his brothers, and his cousins. Even Blayth and Thomas landed a good blow now and again. But Titus was a madman, breaking bones in Ansel’s face and knocking out his front teeth. There was blood and teeth everywhere, spraying back on Titus and Magnus and Markus until Ansel was nothing but an unconscious heap on the ground. Then, and only then, did Titus stagger over to Katiana and throw his arms around her.

“She’ll be fine, Titus,” Patrick said, watching his son break down in relief and grief. “She’s got a few bruises, but she’ll be well, I promise.”

Titus couldn’t even answer his father. All he could hear were Katiana’s sobs as he held her against him, squeezing the life from her. When they’d charged up the road and caught sight of the battle between Ansel and Katiana at the edge of the road, he didn’t even remember jumping off his horse and throwing himself at Ansel. One moment, he was on his horse, and in the next, he was on top of Ansel, breaking the man's face. Titus had been a knight for almost twenty years, and he'd never had a fight like that in his life. A fight fueled with blind, unadulterated rage.

As he sat on the ground with Katiana in his arms, he could feel hands on his shoulders, knowing it was his father and his uncles. They knew how frightened he'd been and were trying to comfort him, but the only thing giving him comfort at the moment was the woman in his embrace. Finally, he relaxed his grip enough to look her in the eye.

"Thank God you're whole," he said, his lower lip trembling and his eyes swimming with tears. "I thought he'd killed you."

Katiana had her hands on Titus' face, touching him, convincing herself that she was, indeed, safe. "Nay," she whispered. "He tried, but I did something I've never done before—I fought back. I think that confused him."

Titus sighed heavily. "Thank God you did," he said "What happened? How did he get to you?"

Katiana shook her head. "I do not really know," she said. "I was in the kitchen yard with Zora and—"

He cut her off. "So she *was* part of this," he said. "I knew she was, but I wasn't sure how she fit into the situation."

Katiana shrugged. "I do not know, either," she said. "She sent me a note telling me that she wanted us to be friends and to meet her in the kitchen yard, so I did. We were talking, and then suddenly, I woke up on Ansel's horse. He must have knocked me unconscious."

Titus began running his hands over her scalp, finding a bump and some dried blood on the back of her head. "He hit you there," he said as she lifted her hand to finger the bump.

"And he took you out from the postern gate. That's where we saw Zora. Thank God we saw her at all."

"Where *is* Zora?"

"Back at Berwick," Titus said. "She has been arrested. I will deal with her later, but for now… now, I must deal with your brother, who has earned my eternal hatred."

Katiana was feeling a little stronger, so she looked over at Ansel, a heap on the ground as a few men stood around him. Taking hold of Titus, Katiana managed to get to her feet with help from her husband and his father. Scott, who was an experienced healer, took a look at the bump on the back of her head and told Titus to get her home and into bed.

And that was exactly where Titus planned to go.

"Papa," he said, his gaze lingering on Ansel. "I must tend to my wife, for she is my priority now. I will leave Ansel to your good justice. Whatever you decide for him and for Zora, I trust you. All I ask is that the punishment fit the crime. He tried to kill my wife. Zora tried to help him. Keep that in mind when passing judgment."

With that, Titus lifted Katiana into his arms and, with the help of Scott, carried her back to Jesus, leaving Patrick, Troy, Blayth, and Thomas standing in a group watching Markus, Magnus, Nathaniel, and Atreus as they huddled around Ansel. There was an occasional kick to the kidneys when they thought the older knights weren't watching.

But they were.

"I would say attempted murder on a de Wolfe wife is a serious offense," Patrick said. "But I fear I am too emotionally involved to be fair. Troy, you and Scott and Blayth and Tommy can pass judgment. Do what you will with him, but I want him away from Berwick. I do not want to see him, or Zora de Allery, for the rest of my life."

The brothers understood.

Leaving the de Wolfe men to deal with Ansel, Titus mounted with Katiana in his arms and tried to leave everything behind him. He didn't want to waste any more time on his wife's brother. As they headed back to Berwick, the only thing on his mind was the woman in his arms, the woman he came close to losing this day. A woman who, a scant month ago, had crashed into him on a London street on a runaway horse. Little did Titus know that a skittish horse and a frightened rider would be the moment his life changed forever. Little did he know that the goddess of a woman he saved from injury or death would become his all for living. It was true that he was an Executioner Knight and he had a duty to his country as well as to his family. But the woman in his arms, at this moment, was his most important duty of all.

He'd never forget it.

Funny how love could change everything.

Gazing down into Katiana's pale but smiling face, Titus understood what it meant to love and be loved. For the youngest of four brothers who had always been the wanderer, the impulsive and unruly one, he found his greatest strength— and his greatest source of contentment—in a woman who had never known the blessing of a family.

Now, she did.

And so did he.

EPILOGUE

Year of Our Lord 1312
The Month of December
Castle Questing

"AND THAT'S WHAT Morgen says," Titus said. "Pembroke has made the offer of peace between Lancaster, Warwick, and those siding with Edward. They've already tentatively agreed because they know they cannot fight against Edward any longer with de Lohr and de Wolfe backing him. Pembroke will have them sign the treaty soon, but meanwhile, it seems that we may know some peace. At least for now."

He was giving the report to his uncles and father in the solar of Castle Questing, the seat of the de Wolfe empire. This had been William de Wolfe's solar for fifty years, and it still reeked of the man in every corner, every table, and every chair. It was where the sons of William de Wolfe felt him the most. Every shelf had something to remember him by, and the big chair behind the table still had the shape of his body imprinted on the leather cushions. No one would sit in that chair, in fact. The day his father died, Scott had pushed it back against the wall and used another chair for himself.

William's spirit was still in that chair, still watching over the room.

"Praise the saints," Scott said, running a hand through his graying blond hair. "When we sent you off those months ago, we did not imagine this would be the result. Pembroke is a forgiving man."

Titus nodded, but it was clear that he was distracted now that his report had been given. He kept looking toward the lancet windows that overlooked the bailey, and they knew it was because he was expecting his wife to appear. Not that anyone blamed him, because he'd been gone for months, but he was most anxious to see her.

Still, there was business at hand.

"He is forgiving and wise," Titus said. "He is the one who has largely orchestrated this peace treaty between both sides. He and de Lohr have put a lot of effort into it."

"Then let's hope that Lancaster and Warwick agree to it and sign it," Troy said as he stood up, heading for the table near the wall that held the pewter pitcher of wine. Paris de Norville had thrown it years ago, and it had a big dent as a result. "But given how Lancaster has behaved over the past few years, I'm not holding out hope that the peace will be lasting."

"At least they didn't go after de Lohr," Patrick pointed out. "Both Lancaster and Warwick have left him alone, and that is good news."

"It's because they are afraid we'll bring our army to defend him," Blayth said, looking around at his brothers. "You know I am correct. The last thing they want is having the de Wolfe army all along the Welsh marches. God forbid we bring de Velt with us. That would put the fear of God into them."

There were a few grins around the chamber at that remark. The House of de Velt had a longstanding tradition of being the most terrifying army in England, through deeds as well as sheer determination. But it seemed that big armies were to have a measure of peace, which was something of a foreign concept these days.

It would take time to get used to it.

"Now what?" Thomas wanted to know. "Do we simply go on with life as usual?"

"I would say so," the sixth de Wolfe brother, Edward, chimed in. He had been in London until recently, but news of Gaveston's execution had him coming north to confer with his brothers. The diplomat of the family, he looked at the men around him. "Edward, of course, is devastated at the loss of Gaveston, as we knew he would be, but he is focused on France now. I am going with him to Paris in a few months to help negotiate with the French king for lands that were part of Edward's dowry when he married Isabella. It promises to be a grand spectacle through the streets of Paris, with two kings and God knows how many knights and nobles. But getting Edward out of the country right now is the best thing for us. The situation can settle down and Lancaster can understand his place. He has more warlords than he can count willing to deal him a punishment should he misbehave."

That seemed to settle it. For the moment, England, and the de Wolfe empire, was at peace, largely in part due to men like Edward and Titus, who were always at the heart of things, making sure the country was safe and secure for their families and future generations. As Troy poured a couple of cups of wine, handing one to Edward, Titus suddenly let out a cry.

"She's here," he said from his position by the lancet windows. "My God, I haven't seen my wife in five months. Five damn months. Thank you, Papa, for bringing her to Questing so I wouldn't have to wait to see her."

"If I didn't bring her here, you would go mad," Patrick said, watching his son practically run to the solar door. "You would be on your horse at this very moment now, riding all night to get to her. It seemed the kindest thing to do, bringing her to you."

Titus paused at the door, grinning brightly. "And I love you for it."

"Wait, Titus," Scott said, coming from around his table. "There's something more I want to talk to you about before you greet Katia."

Titus was practically twitching with excitement, but also reluctance. He didn't want to stay and listen to his uncle. He wanted to run out to the bailey where his wife's carriage was just pulling in.

"Now?" he said, sounding as if he was whining. "Can it wait?"

Scott shrugged. "It can, I suppose," he said. "You can find out later that I want you to take command of Jedburgh Castle. It's not as if it is important or anything."

Titus was nearly through the door, but his uncle's words had him skidding to a halt. Wide-eyed, he looked at Scott.

"Jedburgh?" he repeated in shock. "You want me to have it?"

Scott fought off a grin, glancing at Patrick, who was smirking. "I think you have earned it," he said. "You know that we just regained it from the Scots not long ago. It needs an experienced, firm commander, and I think that is you. It's an enormous bastion, Titus. Very important and strategic. Do you think you can handle it?"

Titus burst into an enormous smile, rushing to his uncle and grabbing the man's face, kissing his cheek. Then he ran to his father, who was seated, and grabbed the man around the neck as he kissed his head. He tried to run at Troy, who pushed him away by the face, and as the room broke into laughter, Titus shook his fists in victory and raced from the room to meet his wife. But as soon as he left, Patrick bolted up from his chair and beckoned to the group.

"Come along," he said quickly. "You will not want to miss this."

Together, the six of them followed Titus out into the enormous bailey of Castle Questing, hanging back by the entry door as Titus rushed toward the fortified carriage bearing the colors of Berwick. The conveyance had come to a halt by that point, away from the mud puddles that peppered the bailey after the heavy rains the night before, and Titus rushed forward to the open window where his wife was sitting. She squealed at the sight of him, and he ran at her, reaching through the window to cup her face and kiss her deeply. They hugged one another through the window as Brighton opened the cab door.

Grinning, she started to climb out, until Titus realized his mother needed some assistance. He helped his mother from the cab, followed by Kristiana, who punched him when he tried to help her. He kissed her anyway before reaching in to pull his wife out.

But Titus was in for a surprise.

He had Katiana around the waist as he pulled her out and set her down, but something felt different about her. He saw what it was once she was on her feet—she was wearing layers of winter clothing against the cool temperatures, but she tossed the cloak back, revealing a blossoming belly straining against the red woolen dress that she wore.

A baby.

Titus' jaw dropped.

"My sweet God," he breathed as he realized what he was seeing. He pointed. "You… you're *pregnant!*"

Katiana laughed at his shock. "Your son is growing bigger and stronger by the day," she said. "Are you happy, my love?"

Titus was so astonished that he couldn't answer. He actually felt a little woozy, listing to one side and catching himself as he heard the laughter coming from behind him. He turned to see his father and uncles chuckling at his reaction.

"You knew!" he said to them all, still pointing to his wife's belly. "You knew all along!"

Patrick had Brighton by the hand. "We did," he said. "But Katia wanted to surprise you. We were sworn to secrecy."

Titus looked back at his wife, his jaw hanging slack. "Why didn't you tell me?" he said. "In all of the missives we exchanged, you never said a word about it. Why not?"

She was still grinning. "Because you were off doing something very important," she said. "I knew that if I told you, you would be thinking of coming home and nothing else. You needed your focus, so I did not tell you. Your son will be born in the spring. But you haven't answered me."

"Answered what?"

"Are you happy?"

Titus just looked at her. For a moment, all he could do was stare at her. Then his eyes grew moist and he reached out, putting his hands on her swollen belly for the very first time. Closing his eyes, tears popped out on his cheeks, and Katiana reached up with both hands, wiping them away as he became accustomed to their very joyous and overwhelming news.

"Happy?" he said after a moment, his voice tight. "There has not yet been a word invented that conveys how I feel, Katia. It's joy and love, all melding together. It's a feeling of something eternal and bright. When I look at you, there aren't any words big enough or deep enough. I told you once that you were the easiest decision I have ever made. And loving you… it has been the easiest thing I have ever done."

Katiana smiled up at him, her hands on his cheeks as he bent over to kiss her, a lingering kiss of the joy and love he spoke of. Of something eternal and bright. As Titus put his arm around her shoulders and led her inside Castle Questing, along with his mother and sister, his uncles followed, but Scott held Patrick back. They waited until everyone went back inside before Scott turned to Patrick.

"You asked me something when you first arrived, and I've not had the chance to answer you because Titus came shortly after you did," he said. "I know he doesn't want to know anything, but you do. I can show you if you wish."

Patrick glanced over toward the entry door before nodding to his brother. "Quickly," he said. "I never asked what you did with them."

"Let me show you."

"Let's be swift about it."

They headed off to the gatehouse, a massive thing that also contained the vault in the sub-levels. It was a bright winter's day, but the cold wind was whistling off the moors, blustery. It blew against them as they reached the gatehouse and headed down into the vault below.

The narrow stairwell was lit by torches every few feet. The stone was slick and icy, and they moved slowly so they wouldn't slip. Down at the bottom was a locked door. Scott used a key that was hanging nearby to open it, revealing four cells beyond. There were torches lit in this chamber, too, but it was dark and freezing, smelling of hay and urine and mold.

It was everything a collection of prison cells should be.

Taking the torch off the wall next to the door, Scott held it up so Patrick could see the content of the cells. Two of them were occupied, but he couldn't see the occupants of one cell. Only the other, which happened to be a man he recognized.

A man missing several teeth and one eye.

Ansel de Edington gazed back at them with a baleful expression.

"Well?" Ansel said. "So the mighty Lord Berwick has come to see the sights? Am I everything you had hoped for, my lord?"

Patrick could hear the arrogance, the disdain in the man's voice. Ansel limped over to the cell grate, leaning against it because when he'd received the terrible beating those months ago, his left arm and left leg had been broken and they hadn't healed correctly. He could hardly use his arm, and his leg was twisted. But he'd lost none of that fearsome and misplaced pride.

"What about me?"

The figure in the cell next to him suddenly came to life, leaning against the grate. Patrick found himself looking at Zora, dressed in woolens, wrapped up like an old woman. She tried to shake the iron grate.

"What about me, my lord?" she demanded. "When do I go home?"

Patrick lifted an eyebrow. "Your father says you are to remain here until I decide otherwise," he said. "You and your friend can sit here and think about what you did and decide if it was worth spending the rest of your lives in this vault."

Zora didn't like that answer. "I've done nothing wrong!" she declared. "I was forced into it by Ansel. He coerced me!"

Patrick didn't believe her for a moment. He could still see that troublemaker who had fostered at Berwick those years ago, the lass who had forced his patient wife to send her away simply for the good of all. Zora would never change, and this time, her distressing ways would cost her.

His focus turned to Ansel.

"As for you, I'll answer your question," he said. "Are you everything I hoped for? You are exactly where you belong, and for that, I am satisfied. For the murder of your sickly father and the abduction of your sister, you will pay the price. Aye, I hoped for that."

As Ansel thought of something insulting to say, Zora growled and beat on her bars. "It's not *fair*!" she shouted. "He's far more evil that I am! I do not belong here at all!"

"Shut up, you stupid cow," Ansel rumbled. "We all know that your greed for Titus brought you here."

"And your hatred for your sister caused all of this!"

"Shut your lips."

"I'll say what I like!"

Patrick listened to the two of them bicker. That was enough for him. After a moment, he silently turned for the exit. Scott followed him, depositing the torch back into the old iron sconce, listening to Zora plead and threaten and growl as he shut the door and locked it. He didn't hang the key up again, but rather brought it with him, following Patrick up the stairs to the door that led outside. He told the sergeant on guard that if anyone wanted to get into the cells, including for feeding the prisoners, that they would have to come to him first for the key. He wasn't taking any chances that it might somehow end up in the wrong hands.

And with that, Scott and Patrick headed back toward the keep.

"Well?" Scott finally said. "What do you want me to do with them?"

Patrick pondered the question. "I think keeping them there, the way they are, is adequate," he said. "Now, the two of them can fight and argue for as long as we decide to keep them there, and longer still. I'll bury them side by side outside of the churchyard so they can spend eternity together, miserable in each other's company. I think that is a fitting end for that pair."

Scott smiled, shaking his head at the thought. "They deserve one another," he said. "Like two cats in a bag, they can kill each other for all I care. But they're never coming out of there alive, Atty. I promise you that."

Patrick nodded, more than satisfied. As they approached the keep, the entry door opened up and Titus was there, shouting something about a harpsichord that Scott's wife had bought as a gift for Katiana so she could play for the baby. Both Patrick and Scott watched Titus, the unbridled joy in his movements, and knew they'd made the right decision where it pertained to Titus and Katiana's enemies.

The de Wolfe pack protected their own.

For Titus and Katiana, the threats had been removed and the joy of their new life was on the horizon. There was no beginning or end in their world, only love.

And that's all there would ever be.

You are the easiest decision I have ever made, Titus had once said.

He meant it.

෮ THE END ෨

De Wolfe Pack Generations:

WolfeHeart

WolfeStrike

WolfeSword

WolfeBlade

WolfeLord

WolfeShield

Nevermore

WolfeAx

WolfeBorn

Children of Titus and Katiana

Thaddeus

Atticus

Genevieve

Madeleine

Catherine

Patrick

Evelina

Rhett

William

THE PARENTS, CHILDREN, AND GRANDCHILDREN OF DE WOLFE

(Note: Don't be intimidated by these family trees—refer to them if you need clarification on a relationship)

<u>**William (deceased 1296 A.D.) and Jordan Scott de Wolfe**</u>
Total children: 10
Total grandchildren: 75+ (including 4 deceased, 7 adopted, 3 step grandchildren)

Scott (Troy's twin)—(Wife #1 Lady Athena de Norville, has issue. Wife #2 Lady Avrielle Huntley du Rennic, has issue)

With Athena

- William "Will"
- Thomas "Tor"
- Andrew (deceased)
- Beatrice (deceased)

With Avrielle

- Sophia (with Nathaniel du Rennic)
- Stephen (with Nathaniel du Rennic)
- Sorcha (with Nathaniel du Rennic)
- Jeremy
- Nathaniel
- Alexander

- Seraphina
- Jordan

Troy (Scott's twin)—(Wife #1 Lady Helene de Norville, has issue. Wife #2 Lady Rhoswyn Kerr, has issue)

With Helene
- Andreas
- Acacia (deceased)
- Arista (deceased)

With Rhoswyn
- Gareth
- Corey
- Reed
- Tavin
- Tristan
- Elsbeth
- Madeleine

Patrick—(Married to Lady Brighton de Favereux, has issue)
- Markus
- Cassius
- Magnus
- Titus
- Thora
- Kristiana

James—(Wife #1 Lady Rose Hage, has issue. Wife #2 Asmara ferch Cader, has issue)

With Rose

- Ronan
- Isabella

With Asmara (as Blayth)

- Maddoc
- Bowen
- Caius
- Garreth (known as Garr)

Katheryn (James' twin)—(Married to Sir Alec Hage, has issue)

- Edward
- Axel
- Christoph
- Kieran
- Christian

Evelyn—(Married to Sir Hector de Norville, has issue)

- Atreus
- Hermes
- Lisbet
- Adele
- Aline
- Lesander (goes by Zander)

Baby de Wolfe—(Died same day. Christened Madeleine)

Edward—(Married to Lady Cassiopeia de Norville, has issue)

- Helene

- Phoebe
- Hestia
- Asteria
- Leonidas
- Dorian
- Dayne
- Stephan
- Pallas

Thomas—(Married to Lady Maitland "Mae" de Ryes Bowlin, has issue)

- Artus (adopted)
- Nora (adopted)
- Phin (adopted)
- Marybelle (adopted)
- Renard & Roland (adopted)
- Dyana (adopted)
- Alexander
- Cabot
- Matthew
- Wade
- Tacey
- Morgan

Penelope—(Married to Bhrodi de Shera, Earl of Coventry, hereditary King of Anglesey, has issue)

- William
- Perri

- Bowen
- Dai
- Catrin
- Morgana
- Maddock
- Anthea
- Talan

Kieran and Jemma Scott Hage

- Mary Alys (adopted)—(married, has issue)
- Baby Hage, died same day. Christened Bridget
- Alec (married to Lady Katheryn de Wolfe, has issue)
- Christian (died in the Holy Land 1269 A.D., no issue)
- Moira (married to Sir Apollo de Norville, has issue)
- Kevin (married to Lady Annavieve de Ferrers, has issue)
- Rose (widow of Sir James de Wolfe, has issue)
- Nathaniel

Paris and Caladora Scott de Norville

- Hector (married to Lady Evelyn de Wolfe, has issue)
- Apollo (married to Lady Moira Hage, has issue)
- Helene (married to Sir Troy de Wolfe, has issue)
- Athena (married to Sir Scott de Wolfe, has issue)
- Adonis
- Cassiopeia (married to Sir Edward de Wolfe, has issue)

HOLDINGS AND TITLES OF THE HOUSE OF DE WOLFE AND CLOSE ALLIES AS OF 1293 A.D.

Scott de Wolfe—Baron Kilham, heir to the Earldom of Warenton (Heir: William "Will" de Wolfe)

Troy de Wolfe—Lord Braemoor (Heir: Andreas de Wolfe)

Patrick de Wolfe—Earl of Berwick (Heir: Markus de Wolfe, Lord Ravensdowne.)

Blayth (James) de Wolfe—Baron Sydenham (Heir: Ronan de Wolfe)

Edward de Wolfe—Baron Kentmere (Heir: Leonidas de Wolfe)

Thomas de Wolfe—Earl of Northumbria (Heir: Alexander de Wolfe, Lord Easington)

Wark Castle (Wolfe's Eye):

Larger outpost for the Earl of Warenton. Literally sits on the border between England and Scotland.

- Titus de Wolfe (son of Patrick de Wolfe), commander (moved to Jedburgh as of 1312)

Berwick Castle (Wolfe's Teeth):

Massive border castle, strategically important, de Wolfe holding and seat of the Earl of Berwick, Patrick de Wolfe.

- Alec Hage, commander
- Edward "Eddie" Hage, commander

Castle Questing (Wolfe's Heart):
Massive fortress, seat of the Earl of Warenton, Scott de Wolfe.
- Apollo de Norville, second
- Nathaniel Hage
- Owen le Mon

Rule Water Castle (Wolfe's Lair):
The largest outpost in the de Wolfe empire, known as The Lair. At this time, commanded by Thomas "Tor" de Wolfe.
- Magnus de Wolfe, second
- Adonis de Norville, second
- Perri de Shera, son of the Earl of Coventry and Penelope de Wolfe de Shera (squire)

Monteviot Tower (Wolfe's Shield):
Smaller outpost in Scotland, strategic. Holding of Troy de Wolfe.
- Brodie de Reyne, commander

Kale Water Castle (Wolfe's Den):
Larger outpost on the England side of the border, strategic.
- Troy de Wolfe, Lord Braemoor, commander
- Troy also commands Sibbald's Hold, former home of Red Keith Kerr (his wife's father). A minor property commanded by son, Gareth de Wolfe.

Kyloe Castle (Wolfe's Howl):
Seat of the Earl of Northumbria, Thomas de Wolfe.
- Christoph Hage, second

Roxburgh Castle (Wolfe's Claw—unofficially) *
Large royal-held castle near Kelso, formerly manned by knights

from Northwood, but awarded to the House of de Wolfe by royal decree for meritorious service to the crown. Volatile location, often attacked by Scots, and is manned by both royal and de Wolfe troops.

- Blayth (James) de Wolfe, Lord Sydenham, commander
- Axel Hage, second

*Note: Because of the extreme volatile location and nature of this garrison, Blayth (James) de Wolfe was given the title Lord Sydenham and the Sydenham Barony, a small but strategic barony between Wark Castle and the town of Kelso.

Carlisle Castle (Wolfe's Fangs):

Massive and large royal-held castle, perhaps one of the largest castles in the north. Awarded to the House of de Wolfe by royal decree. Very volatile location, often attacked by Scots, and has changed hands many times in its history. The castle is manned by both royal and de Wolfe troops.

- Will de Wolfe, Lord Irthington, commander
- Hermes de Norville

Northwood Castle:

Massive border castle, very important and strategic. Belonging to the Earls of Teviot. Not part of the de Wolfe empire, but strongly allied to de Wolfe by marriage and blood. The Earl of Teviot is John Adrian de Longley, Adam de Longley's eldest son. John's mother is Cayetana Fernanda Teresita Silva y Fausto de Longley, Princess of Aragon.

- Hector de Norville, captain of the guard (also Lord Bowmont)
- Atreus de Norville, second

- Tobias de Bocage, second

Castle Canaan (Wolfe's Bite):
The Earl of Warenton's southernmost holding in Kendal, not directly related to the Scottish border but a source of additional troops if needed. Inherited the property when he married the widow of Castle Canaan.

- Stephan du Rennic, commander

Seven Gates Castle:
Seat of Edward de Wolfe's Barony—Kentmere in Kendal that adjoins brother Scott's lands at Castle Canaan.

- Isleworth House, Surrey

Hell's Guardhouse (The Hermitage):
- Andreas de Wolfe, commander
- Theodis de Velt, second

Ravenscar (fortified manse near Scarborough):
- Ronan de Wolfe
- Christian Hage

Jedburgh Castle (1312)
- Titus de Wolfe, Commander
- Peter Summerlin
- Reynard and Roland de Wolfe

KATHRYN LE VEQUE NOVELS

Medieval Romance:

De Wolfe Pack Series:
Warwolfe
The Wolfe
Nighthawk
ShadowWolfe
DarkWolfe
A Joyous de Wolfe Christmas
BlackWolfe
Serpent
A Wolfe Among Dragons
Scorpion
StormWolfe
Dark Destroyer
The Lion of the North
Walls of Babylon
The Best Is Yet To Be
BattleWolfe
Castle of Bones

De Wolfe Pack Generations:
WolfeHeart
WolfeStrike
WolfeSword
WolfeBlade
WolfeLord
WolfeShield
Nevermore
WolfeAx
WolfeBorn

The Executioner Knights:
By the Unholy Hand
The Mountain Dark
Starless
A Time of End
Winter of Solace
Lord of the Sky
The Splendid Hour
The Whispering Night
Netherworld
Lord of the Shadows
Of Mortal Fury
'Twas the Executioner Knight
Before Christmas
Crimson Shield

The de Russe Legacy:
The Falls of Erith
Lord of War: Black Angel
The Iron Knight
Beast
The Dark One: Dark Knight
The White Lord of Wellesbourne
Dark Moon
Dark Steel
A de Russe Christmas Miracle
Dark Warrior

The de Lohr Dynasty:
While Angels Slept
Rise of the Defender
Steelheart
Shadowmoor
Silversword
Spectre of the Sword

Unending Love
Archangel
A Blessed de Lohr Christmas
Lion of Twilight

The Brothers de Lohr:
The Earl in Winter

Lords of East Anglia:
While Angels Slept
Godspeed
Age of Gods and Mortals

Great Lords of le Bec:
Great Protector

House of de Royans:
Lord of Winter
To the Lady Born
The Centurion

Lords of Eire:
Echoes of Ancient Dreams
Blacksword
The Darkland

Ancient Kings of Anglecynn:
The Whispering Night
Netherworld

Battle Lords of de Velt:
The Dark Lord
Devil's Dominion
Bay of Fear
The Dark Lord's First Christmas
The Dark Spawn
The Dark Conqueror
The Dark Angel

Reign of the House of de Winter:
Lespada

Swords and Shields

De Reyne Domination:
Guardian of Darkness
The Black Storm
A Cold Wynter's Knight
With Dreams
Master of the Dawn

House of d'Vant:
Tender is the Knight (House of d'Vant)
The Red Fury (House of d'Vant)

The Dragonblade Series:
Fragments of Grace
Dragonblade
Island of Glass
The Savage Curtain
The Fallen One
The Phantom Bride

Great Marcher Lords of de Lara
Dragonblade

House of St. Hever
Fragments of Grace
Island of Glass
Queen of Lost Stars

Lords of Pembury:
The Savage Curtain

Lords of Thunder: The de Shera Brotherhood Trilogy
The Thunder Lord
The Thunder Warrior
The Thunder Knight

The Great Knights of de Moray:
Shield of Kronos

The Gorgon

The House of De Nerra:
The Promise
The Falls of Erith
Vestiges of Valor
Realm of Angels

Highland Warriors of Munro:
The Red Lion
Deep Into Darkness

The House of de Garr:
Lord of Light
Realm of Angels

Saxon Lords of Hage:
The Crusader
Kingdom Come

High Warriors of Rohan:
High Warrior
High King

The House of Ashbourne:
Upon a Midnight Dream

The House of D'Aurilliac:
Valiant Chaos

The House of De Dere:
Of Love and Legend

St. John and de Gare Clans:
The Warrior Poet

The House of de Bretagne:
The Questing

The House of Summerlin:
The Legend

The Kingdom of Hendocia:
Kingdom by the Sea

The BlackChurch Guild: Shadow Knights:
The Leviathan

Regency Historical Romance:
Sin Like Flynn: A Regency
Historical Romance Duet
The Sin Commandments
Georgina and the Red Charger

Gothic Regency Romance:
Emma

Contemporary Romance:

Kathlyn Trent/Marcus Burton Series:
Valley of the Shadow
The Eden Factor
Canyon of the Sphinx

The American Heroes Anthology Series:
The Lucius Robe
Fires of Autumn
Evenshade
Sea of Dreams
Purgatory

Other non-connected Contemporary Romance:
Lady of Heaven
Darkling, I Listen
In the Dreaming Hour
River's End
The Fountain

Sons of Poseidon:

The Immortal Sea

Pirates of Britannia Series (with Eliza Knight):
Savage of the Sea by Eliza Knight

Leader of Titans by Kathryn Le Veque
The Sea Devil by Eliza Knight
Sea Wolfe by Kathryn Le Veque

<u>Note:</u> All Kathryn's novels are designed to be read as stand-alones, although many have cross-over characters or cross-over family groups. Novels that are grouped together have related characters or family groups. You will notice that some series have the same books; that is because they are cross-overs. A hero in one book may be the secondary character in another.

There is NO reading order except by chronology, but even in that case, you can still read the books as stand-alones. No novel is connected to another by a cliff hanger, and every book has an HEA.

Series are clearly marked. All series contain the same characters or family groups except the American Heroes Series, which is an anthology with unrelated characters.

For more information, find it in **A Reader's Guide to the Medieval World of Le Veque**.

ABOUT KATHRYN LE VEQUE

Bringing the Medieval to Romance

KATHRYN LE VEQUE is a critically acclaimed, multiple USA TODAY Bestselling author, an Indie Reader bestseller, a charter Amazon All-Star author, and a #1 bestselling, award-winning, multi-published author in Medieval Historical Romance with over 100 published novels.

Kathryn is a multiple award nominee and winner, including the winner of Uncaged Book Reviews Magazine 2017 and 2018 "Raven Award" for Favorite Medieval Romance. Kathryn is also a multiple RONE nominee (InD'Tale Magazine), holding a record for the number of nominations. In 2018, her novel WARWOLFE was the winner in the Romance category of the Book Excellence Award and in 2019, her novel A WOLFE AMONG DRAGONS won the prestigious RONE award for best pre-16th century romance.

Kathryn is considered one of the top Indie authors in the world with over 2M copies in circulation, and her novels have been translated into several languages. Kathryn recently signed with Sourcebooks Casablanca for a Medieval Fight Club series, first published in 2020.

In addition to her own published works, Kathryn is also the President/CEO of Dragonblade Publishing, a boutique publishing house specializing in Historical Romance. Dragonblade's success has seen it rise in the ranks to become Amazon's #1 e-book publisher of Historical Romance (K-Lytics report July 2020).

Kathryn loves to hear from her readers. Please find Kathryn on Facebook at Kathryn Le Veque, Author, or join her on Twitter @kathrynleveque. Sign up for Kathryn's blog at www.kathrynleveque.com for the latest news and sales.

www.ingramcontent.com/pod-product-compliance
Lightning Source LLC
Chambersburg PA
CBHW072005190726

48293CB00001B/163